Femmes de Siècle

Femmes de Siècle

❧

STORIES FROM THE '90S: WOMEN WRITING AT THE END OF TWO CENTURIES

Edited and introduced by
JOAN SMITH

Chatto & Windus

LONDON

Published in 1992 by
Chatto & Windus Ltd
20 Vauxhall Bridge Road
London SW1V 2SA

A CIP catalogue record for this book is available from
the British Library

ISBN 0 7011 3984 6

Designed by Humphrey Stone
Printed and bound in Great Britain by
Mackays of Chatham PLC, Chatham, Kent

CONTENTS

INTRODUCTION

The end of a century concentrates the mind. A heightened consciousness of the passage of time, of the years slipping away, lends an urgency to contemporary problems; it highlights the old century's mistakes and dilemmas. Yet who is to differentiate between ends and beginnings, between the very audible last gasp of a dying culture and the birth pangs of the new? Between what is tried, trusted and worth keeping, and a sentimental attachment to outmoded ways of thinking and behaving?

Nowhere is this more true than in the arena of gender. The early years of the 1990s have already seen the battle lines redrawn over feminism, whose enemies cannot decide whether it is stone dead or alarmingly alive. A small but vocal men's movement has sprung up, principally in the United States but with offshoots in Britain, whose spokesmen make forays into genetics and Norse myth in a desperate attempt to re-establish separate roles for men and women. The parallels with the 1890s are striking, for that decade saw much anguished debate about the New Woman and her outlandish demands for the vote, for university degrees, for economic independence. *Punch* satirised her, in its traditionally humourless way, in issue after issue; moralists claimed she was already having a feminising effect on men, and this fear almost certainly influenced the savage punishment meted out to Oscar Wilde after his conviction for homosexuality in 1895.

The public humiliation of Wilde, and the outrage generated by Aubrey Beardsley's 'obscene' drawings in the decade's most celebrated literary quarterly, *The Yellow Book*, suggest that both the cultural icons of the period and its victims – often the same individuals – were men. Certainly there was no shortage of men willing to pronounce on the Woman Question, frequently in terms which revealed deep seams of scorn and misogyny, yet the detractors of the Victorian woman could not agree on what they wanted from her; it must have seemed, then as now, that women couldn't win. In one corner was Alfred Marshall, a Cambridge professor implacably opposed to university degrees for women on the ground that 'woman was a subordinate being' whose chief attraction would be lost if she succeeded in improving her mind or her status; in the other was the novelist George Gissing, fulminating against those Victorian women who obediently accepted Marshall's prescription of housewifely virtue: 'More than half the misery of life is due to the ignorance and childishness of women . . . I am driven frantic by the crass imbecility of the typical woman'. His story 'The Foolish Virgin', which appeared in *The Yellow Book*, is a cruel portrait of just such a woman – Rosamund Jewell, an unmarried woman of perhaps thirty, who is unable to find a husband but reluctant to throw herself into the hard, menial work which Gissing implies is all she is fit for.

Many of the star contributors to *The Yellow Book* were men: Gissing, Henry James, W. B. Yeats, Max Beerbohm, Edmund Gosse. Yet its assistant literary editor was a woman, Ella D'Arcy, and her short stories appeared in many of its thirteen volumes. So did the work of other women writers, from the poet Olive Custance to the feminist novelist George Egerton. *The Yellow Book* was not quite as male-dominated nor as misogynist as it is sometimes said to be, and the novelist Ada Leverson was able to use its pages to mock the fashionable young aesthetes who modelled themselves on her great friend, Oscar Wilde – and who, no doubt, experienced a *frisson* of excitement each time they bought the scandalous quarterly.

Leverson's elegant parody, 'The Quest of Sorrow', is unusual among the stories from the 1890s reprinted in *Femmes de Siècle* in both tone and subject. Most of the authors featured here focus, in one way or another, on the Woman Question – on the foolishness of upper- and middle-class women denied all but the most trivial occupations, on the inevitable distortion of male-female relations when women enjoy neither power nor independence, on the grinding poverty of female servants and middle-class women who have fallen on hard times. Around half the stories come from *The Yellow Book*; they include Charlotte Mew's astonishing debut, 'Passed', in which a bored, wealthy woman, confronted with starvation in a London tenement, suffers a catastrophic failure of human sympathy. Mew's dense, poetic language, and her protagonist's dreamlike account of her first encounter with death, still have the power to chill.

The stories divide, broadly, into those which take a sympathetic view of the Victorian woman's predicament and those which blame her for it. Of the former, perhaps the most accomplished is Edith Wharton's 'Souls Belated', in which a New York socialite who has eloped to Europe with her lover recognises that she has merely exchanged one form of dependency for another. This long story, first published in 1899, predates the breakdown of Wharton's own marriage by more than a decade and shows she was already sharply conscious of the stark choices facing the divorced woman. Evelyn

Sharp, whose support of the suffragist cause was to lead to her imprisonment in Holloway in 1911, takes a much tougher line in 'A New Poster', borrowing from farce in her portrait of a widow with social pretensions who fears the revelation that her late husband's fortune was derived from trade. Even more scathing is Ella D'Arcy's 'At Twickenham', a savage commentary on two frivolous suburban women who once 'took first-class tickets to Waterloo, returning by the next train, merely to pass the time'.

Two stories stand out for their optimism, their conviction that the new century would bring momentous change. In 'A Nocturne' by George Egerton, a penniless, hungry woman is saved from throwing herself into the Thames by a bookish bachelor who persuades her to spend the night in his rooms overlooking the river; the echo of Mary Wollstonecraft's real suicide attempt a century earlier, when she was fished out of the Thames after throwing herself off Putney Bridge, may or may not have been deliberate. For an even more Utopian vision of the future I have turned to Olive Schreiner, South African author of *The Story of an African Farm*, whose ambitious allegory, 'Three Dreams in a Desert', seeks to encompass the whole of human history in a few pages. Using uncompromising, mystical language, Schreiner looks forward to a new world peopled by 'brave women and brave men' who 'looked into each other's eyes, and [. . .] were not afraid'.

From the standpoint of 1992, Schreiner's vision appears sadly over-optimistic. Popular culture is as misogynist as ever, and glaring inequalities continue to exist between men and women. Yet the balance of power has shifted, and this is reflected in the twentieth-century contributions to *Femmes de Siècle*. Helen Simpson's reptilian seducer in 'Sugar and Spice' miscalculates when he assumes his victim will be tractable because her speech is commonplace and her origins working-class; the heroine of Shena Mackay's elegiac 'Glass' is torn between her family and her lover, but her dilemma arises from competing ties of affection and not financial or social obligation.

The material improvement in the lives of most women is reflected in another way in *Femmes de Siècle*: our own Woman Question, though fiercely debated in contemporary non-fiction, is touched on only obliquely by the modern contributors, if at all. It is perhaps an index of their confidence that only one author, Alice Thomas Ellis, writes under a pseudonym, compared with four in the book's Victorian section. The range of subjects they have chosen – and most of the stories were written specially for the book – is diverse; what links them is a tone, an absence of futurist fantasies or any attempt to look forward to a better, brighter future. Perhaps this is because a century of rapid change, not to mention two world wars, has engendered a sense of caution, even of pessimism, in its writers. '"I know you're from the Sixties and you believed in love, am I right? 'Love is all you need', Beatles, the whole number,"' says a character in Emily Prager's 'Moon Walk', vividly conjuring up the optimism of that long-gone decade.

The Sixties mean little to Candia McWilliam's unnamed narrator in 'Pass the Parcel', an elderly woman whose memories extend the length of the century. McWilliam, along with Claire Harman, takes an unsparing look at the institutional horrors facing an ageing population as the extended family of the Victorian period all but disappears. Harman's dreary urban landscape in 'An Act of Kindness' finds an unexpected echo in Elizabeth Jolley's 'Motel Marriage', in which a comically ill-matched couple spend a night in a cheap Australian hotel where the furniture is fixed to the floor. Isolation and lack of communication are also the themes of 'The Actress' by Alice Thomas Ellis, although she allows the possibility that an imaginative sympathy can bridge the gap between different generations. Moy McCrory, by contrast, presents us with a child's inner life in a story which is funny, touching and highly original.

Lynne Truss's subject in '*Possunt Quia Posse Videntur*' – animal rights and our changing attitude to non-human species – would have mystified most Victorians who, with honourable exceptions like Thomas Hardy, tended to look at lions and tigers only through the sights of a gun. The same subject has fascinated Brigid Brophy ever since the publication of her first novel, *Hackenfeller's Ape*, in 1953; because she was too ill to write for this collection, I have included her unsentimental story about deer-hunting, 'The Woodcutter's Upright Son', which first appeared in 1973.

Femmes de Siècle was never an attempt to be representative, and it is certainly not definitive. Some potential contributors ruled themselves out: Margaret Forster and Diane Johnson do not write short stories; Anita Desai and the young Scottish poet Jackie Kay were too busy with other projects. My selection, in the end, is largely personal, and an attempt to represent the abundance of talent and imaginative range of women writing today. I hope the reader will approach the book as a series of snapshots, the Victorian pictures formal in subject and composition, the twentieth-century ones in Kodak colours and fast focus. Here are the aspirations and anxieties, the thoughts and feelings, of two groups of women a century apart; the contrasts and surprises a similar book would contain a hundred years from now, in 2092, is a piece of speculation I am happy to leave to the reader.

JOAN SMITH
Kidlington, Oxford
April 1992

❧ *At Twickenham*

ELLA D'ARCY

When John Corbett married Minnie Wray, her sister Lœtitia, their parents being dead, came to live under his roof also, which seemed to Corbett the most natural arrangement in the world, for he was an Irishman, and the Irish never count the cost of an extra mouth. 'Where there's enough for two, there's enough for three,' is a favourite saying of theirs, and even in the most impecunious Irish household no one ever dreams of grudging you your bite of bread or your sup o' th' crathur.

But Corbett was not impecunious. On the contrary, he was fairly well off, being partner in and traveller for an Irish whiskey house, and earning thus between eight and nine hundred a year. In the income tax returns he put the figure down as five hundred, but in conversation he referred to it casually as over a thousand; for he had some of the vices of his nationality as well as most of its virtues, and to impress Twickenham with a dull sense of the worth of John Corbett was perhaps his chief preoccupation out of business hours.

He lived in an imitation high art villa on the road to Strawberry Hill; a villa that rejoiced in the name of 'Braemar', gilded in gothic letters upon the wooden gate; a villa that flared up into pinnacles, blushed with red brick, and mourned behind sad-tinted glass. The Elizabethan casements let in piercing draughts, the Brummagem brass door-handles came off in the confiding hand that sought to turn them, the tiled hearths successfully conducted all the heat up the chimneys to disperse it generously over an inclement sky. But Corbett found consolation in the knowledge that the hall was paved with grey and white mosaic, that the 'Salve' bristled at you from the doormat, that the dining-room boasted of a dado, and that the drawing-room rose to the dignity of a frieze.

Minnie Corbett, whose full name was Margaret, but preferred to be called Rita, although she could not teach her family to remember to call her so, and Lœtitia, who had recently changed the 'Tish' of her childhood to the more poetical 'Letty', dressed the windows of 'Braemar' with frilled Madras muslin, draped the mantelpieces with plush, hung the walls with coloured photographs, Chinese crockery, and Japanese fans. They made expeditions into town in search of pampas grass and bulrushes, with which in summertime they decorated the fireplaces, and in winter the painted drainpipes which stood in the corners of the drawing-room.

Beyond which labours of love, and Minnie's perfunctory ordering of the dinner every morning, neither she nor Lœtitia found anything to do, for Corbett kept a cook, a house-parlourmaid, and two nurses to look after Minnie's three children, in whom her interest seemed to have ceased when she had bestowed on them the high-sounding names of Lancelot, Hugo, and Guinevere. Lœtitia had never pretended to feel any interest in the children at all.

The sisters suffered terribly from dulness, and one memorable Sunday evening, Corbett being away travelling, they took first-class tickets to Waterloo, returning by the next train, merely to pass the time.

When Corbett was not travelling, his going to and fro between Twickenham and the City lent a spice of variety to the day. He left every morning by the 9.15 train, and came home in the evening in time for a seven o'clock dinner. On Saturdays he got back by two, when he either mowed the lawn in his shirt-sleeves, or played a set of tennis with Lœtitia, or went with both girls for a row on the river. Or, if Minnie made a special point of it, he escorted them back into town, where he treated them to a restaurant *table d'hôte* and a theatre afterwards. On Sundays he rose late, renewed his weekly acquaintance with the baby, read through the *Referee* from first line to last, and, accompanied by his two little boys dressed in correct Jack Tar costume, went for a walk along the towing-path, whence they could watch the boating.

Humanly speaking, he would have liked to have followed the example of those flannel-shirted publicans and sinners who pushed off every moment in gay twos and threes from Shore's landing-stage, but consideration for the susceptibilities of Providence and of Twickenham held him in check.

It is true he did not go to church, although often disquieted by the thought of the bad effect this omission must produce on the mind of his next-door neighbour; but he salved his conscience with the plea that he was a busy man, and that Sunday was his only day of home life. Besides, the family was well represented by Minnie and Lœtitia, who when the weather was fine never missed morning service. When it was wet they stayed away on account of their frocks.

Sunday afternoons were spent by them sitting in the drawing-room awaiting the visitors who did not come. The number of persons in Twickenham with whom they were on calling terms was limited, nor can it be maintained that 'Braemar' was an amusing house at which to call. For though Corbett was one of the most cordial, one of the most hospitable of young men, his womenfolk shone rather by their silences than by their conversational gifts.

Minnie Corbett was particularly silent. She had won her husband by lifting to his a pair of blankly beautiful eyes, and it did not seem to her requisite to give greater exertion to the winning of minor successes.

Lœtitia could talk to men providing they were unrelated to her, but she found nothing to say to members of her own sex. Even with her sister she was mostly silent, unless there was a new fashion in hats, the cut of a sleeve, or the set of a skirt to discuss. There was, however, one topic which invariably aroused her to a transitory animation. This was the passing by the windows, in his well-appointed dog-cart, of a man whom, because of his upright bearing, moustache, and close-cut hair, she and Minnie had agreed to call 'the Captain'.

He was tall, evidently, and had a straight nose. Lœtitia also was straight-nosed and tall. She saw in this physical resemblance a reason for fostering a sentimental interest in him.

'Quick, Minnie, here's the Captain!' she would cry, and Minnie would awake from the somnolency of Sunday with a start, and skip over to the window to watch a flying vision of a brown horse, a black and red painted cart, and a drab-coated figure holding the reins, while a very small groom in white cords and top-boots maintained his seat behind by means of tightly folded arms and a portentous frown.

'He's got such a pretty horse,' observed Minnie on one occasion, before relapsing back into silence, the folding of hands, and a rocking-chair.

'Yes,' Lœtitia agreed pensively, 'it has such a nice tail.'

Although she knew nothing concerning the Captain, although it did not seem probable that she ever would know anything, although it was at least a tenable supposition that he was married already and the father of a family, she saw herself, in fancy, the wife of the wearer of the drab coat, driving by his side along the roads of Twickenham, up the High Street of Richmond. She wore, in fancy, a sealskin as handsome as Minnie's and six inches longer, and she ordered lavishly from Gosling and the other tradesmen, giving the address of Captain Devereux of Deepdene, or Captain Mortimer of the Shrubberies. The names were either purely imaginary, or reminiscent of the novels she constantly carried about with her and fitfully read.

She sat nearly always with an open book upon her knee, but neither Hall Caine nor Miss Marie Corelli even in their most inspired moments could woo her to complete self-forgetfulness. She did not wish to forget herself in a novel. She wished to find in it straw for her own brick-making, bricks for her own castle-building. And if a shadow fell across the window, if a step was heard along the hall, she could break off in the most poignant passage to lift a slim hand to the better arrangement of her curls, to thrust a slim foot in lace stocking and pointed shoe to a position of greater conspicuousness.

On Sunday evenings at 'Braemar' there was cold supper at eight, consisting of the early dinner joint, eaten with a salad scientifically mixed by Corbett, the remains of the apple or gooseberry pie, cheese, and an excellent Burgundy obtained by him at trade price. When the cloth was removed he did not return to the drawing-room. He never felt at ease in that over-furnished, over-ornate room, so darkened by shaded lamps and pink petticoated candles that it was impossible to read. The white, untempered flames of three gas-burners in the dining-room suited him better, and here he would sit on one side of the hearth in an armchair grown comfortable from continual use, and read over again the already well-read paper, while Minnie, on the other side of the hearth, stared silently before her, and Lœtitia fingered her book at the table.

Sometimes Corbett, untaught by past experience, would make a hopeful appeal to one or the other, for an expression of opinion concerning some topic of the day; the last play, the newest book. But Minnie seldom took the trouble to hear him at all, and Lœtitia would answer with such superficial politeness, with so wide an irrelevance to the subject, that, discouraged, he would draw back again into his shell. At the end of every Sunday evening he was glad to remember that the next day was Monday, when he would return to his occupations and his acquaintances in the City. In the City men were ready to talk to him, to listen to what he said, and even to affect some show of interest in his views and pursuits.

The chief breaks in his home life, its principal excitements, were the various ailments the children developed, the multifarious and unexpected means they found of putting their lives in jeopardy and adding items to Dr Payne's half-yearly accounts. Corbett would come home in the happiest mood, to have his serenity roughly shattered by the news that Lancelot had forced a boot-button down his ear, and was rolling on the floor in agony; that Hugo had bolted seventeen cherry-stones in succession and obstinately refused an emetic; that the baby had been seized with convulsions; that the whole family were in for chicken-pox, whooping-cough, or mumps.

On such occasions Minnie, recovering something of her ante-nuptial vivacity, seemed to take a positive pleasure in unfolding the harrowing details, in dwelling on the still more harrowing consequences which would probably ensue.

When, on turning into Wetherly Gardens on his way from the station, Corbett perceived his wife's blonde head above the garden gate, he knew at once that it betokened a domestic catastrophe. It had only been in the very early days of their married life that Minnie had hurried to greet his return for the mere pleasure it gave her.

The past winter had brought rather more than the usual crop of casualties among the children, so that it had seemed to Corbett that the parental cup of bitterness was already filled to overflowing, that Fate might well grant him a respite, when, returning from town one warm May Saturday, his thoughts veering riverwards, and his intention being to invite the girls to scull up and have tea at Tagg's, his ears were martyrised by the vociferous howls of Hugo, who had just managed to pull down over himself the kettle of water boiling on the nursery fire.

While the women of the household disputed among themselves as to the remedial values of oil, treacle, or magnesia, Corbett rushed round to Payne's to find him away, and to be referred to Dr Matheson of Holly Cottage, who was taking Payne's cases. At the moment he never noticed what Matheson was like, he received no conscious impression of the other's personality. But when that evening, comparative peace having again fallen upon the villa, Lœtitia remarked for the twentieth time, 'How funny that Dr Matheson should be the Captain, isn't it?', he found in his memory the picture of a tall fair man, with regular features and a quiet manner, he caught the echoes of a pleasantly modulated voice.

The young women did not go to service next morning, but Lœtitia put on her best gown nevertheless. She displayed also a good deal of unexpected solicitude for her little nephew, and when Matheson looked in, at about 11 am, she saw fit to accompany him and Corbett upstairs to the night-nursery, where Minnie, in a white wrapper trimmed with ribbons as blue as her eyes and as meaningless, sat gazing into futurity by her son's bedside.

Hugo had given up the attempt to obtain illuminating answers to the intricate social and ethical problems with which he whiled away the pain-filled time. For when by repeated interrogatives of 'Mother?' 'Eh, mother?' 'Well, mother?' he had induced Minnie at least to listen to him, all he extracted from her was some unsatisfying vagueness, which added its quota to the waters of contempt already welling up in his young soul for the intelligence of women.

He rejoiced at the appearance of his father and the doctor, despite some natural heart-sinkings as to what the latter might not purpose doing to him. He knew doctors to be perfectly irresponsible autocrats, who walked into your bedroom, felt your pulse, turned you over and over just as though you were a puppy or a kitten, and then with an impassive countenance ordered you a poultice or a powder, and walked off. He knew that if they condemned you to lose an arm or a leg they would be just as despotic and impassible, and you would have to submit just as quietly. None of the grown-ups about you would ever dream of interfering in your behalf.

So he fixed Matheson with an alert, an inquiring, a profoundly distrusting eye, and with a hand in his father's, awaited developments. Lœtitia he ignored altogether. He supposed that the existence of aunts was necessary to the general scheme of things, but personally he hadn't any use for them. His predominate impression of Auntie Tish was that she spent her day heating curling-irons over the gas-bracket in her bedroom, and curling her hair, and although he saw great possibilities in curling-irons heated red-hot and applied to reasonable uses, he was convinced that no one besides herself ever knew whether her hair was curled or straight. But women were such ninnies.

The examination over, the scalds re-dressed and covered up again, Matheson on his way downstairs stopped at the staircase window to admire the green and charming piece of garden, which ending in an inconspicuous wooden paling, enjoyed an illusory proprietorship in the belt of fine old elm trees belonging to the demesne beyond.

Corbett invited him to come and take a turn round it, and the two young men stepped out upon the lawn.

It was a delicious blue and white morning, with that Sunday feeling in the air which is produced by the cessation of all workaday noises, and heightened just now by the last melodious bell-cadences floating out from the church on the distant green. The garden was full of flowers and bees, scent and sunshine. Roses, clematis, and canariensis tapestried the brick unsightlinesses of the back of the house. Serried ranks of blue-green lavender, wild companies of undisciplined sweet pea, sturdy clumps of red-hot poker shooting up in fiery contrast to the wide-spreading luxuriance of the cool white daisy bushes, justled side by side in the border territories which were separated from the grass by narrow gravel paths.

While Corbett and his guest walked up and down the centre of the lawn, Minnie and Lœtitia watched them from behind the curtains of the night-nursery window.

'He's got such nice hands,' said Lœtitia, 'so white and well kept. Did you notice, Minnie?' Lœtitia always noticed hands, because she gave a great deal of attention to her own.

But Minnie, whose hands were not her strong point, was more impressed by Matheson's boots. 'I wish Jack would get brown boots, they look so much smarter with light clothes,' she remarked, but without any intensity of desire. Before the short phrase was finished, her voice had dropped into apathy, her gaze had wandered away from Matheson's boots, from the garden, from the hour. She seemed not to hear her sister's dubious: 'Yes, but I wonder he wears a tweed suit on Sundays?'

Lœtitia heard herself calling him Algernon or Edgar, and remonstrating with him on the subject. Then she went into her bedroom, recurled a peccant lock on her temple, and joined the men just as the dinner gong sounded.

Matheson was pressed to stay and share the early dinner. 'Unless,' said Corbett, seeing that he hesitated, 'Mrs Matheson . . . perhaps . . . is waiting for you?'

'There is no Mrs Matheson, as yet,' he answered smiling, 'although Payne is always telling me it's my professional duty to get married as soon as possible.'

Lœtitia coloured and smiled.

From that day Matheson was often at 'Braemar'. At first he came ostensibly to attend to Hugo, but before that small pickle was on his feet again and in fresh mischief, he was sufficiently friendly with the family to drop in without any excuse at all.

He would come of an evening and ask for Corbett, and the maid would show him into the little study behind the dining-room, where Corbett enjoyed his after-dinner smoke. He enjoyed it doubly in Matheson's society, and discovered he had been thirsting for some such companionship for years. The girls were awfully nice, of course, but . . . and then, the fellows in the City . . . he compared them with Matheson, much to their disadvantage. For Matheson struck him as being amazingly clever – a pillar of originality – and his fine indifference to the most cherished opinions of Twickenham made Corbett catch his breath. But the time spent with his friend was only too short. Minnie and Lœtitia always found some pretext to join them, and they would reproach Matheson in so cordial a manner for never coming into the drawing-room that presently, somewhat to Corbett's chagrin, he began to pay his visits to them instead.

Then as the summer advanced, the fine weather suggested river picnics, and the young women arranged one every week. They even ventured under Matheson's influence to go out on a Sunday, starting in the forenoon, getting up as far as Chertsey, and not returning till late at night. Corbett, half delighted with the abandoned devilry of the proceedings, half terrified lest Wetherly Gardens should come to hear of it, or Providence deal swift retribution, was always wholly surprised and relieved when they found themselves again ashore, as safe and comfortable as though the day had been a mere Monday or Wednesday. And if this immunity from consequence slightly shook Corbett's respect for Providence, it sensibly increased his respect for his friend.

Corbett would have enjoyed this summer extremely, but for the curious jealousy Minnie began to exhibit of his affection for Matheson. It seemed to him it could only be jealousy which made her intrude so needlessly on their *tête-à-têtes*, interrupt their conversation so pointedly, and so frequently reproach Corbett, in the privacy of the nuptial chamber, for monopolising all the attention of their guest.

'You're always so selfish,' Minnie would complain.

Yet, reviewing the incidents of the evening – Matheson had been dining perhaps at 'Braemar' – it seemed to Corbett that he had hardly had a chance to exchange a word with him at all. It seemed to Corbett that Lœtitia had done all the talking; and her light volubility with Matheson, so different from the tongue-tiedness of her ordinary hours, her incessant and slightly meaningless laugh, echoed in his ears at the back of Minnie's scoldings, until both were lost in sleep.

But when the problem of Minnie's vexation recurred to him next morning, he decided that the key to it would only be jealousy, and he was annoyed with himself that he could find no excuses for a failing at once so ridiculous and so petty. The true nature of the case never once crossed his mind, until Minnie unfolded it for him one day, abruptly and triumphantly.

'Well, it's all right. He's proposed at last.'

'What do you mean? Who?' asked Corbett, bewildered.

'Why Jim Matheson, of course! Who else do you suppose? He proposed to Tish last night in the garden. You remember how long they were out there, after we came in? That was why.'

Corbett was immensely surprised, even incredulous, although when he saw that his incredulity made his wife angry, he stifled it in his bosom.

After all, as she said with some asperity, why shouldn't Matheson be in love with Lœtitia? Lœtitia was a pretty girl . . . a good girl . . . yet somehow Corbett felt disappointed and depressed.

'You're such a selfish pig,' Minnie told him. 'You never think of anybody but yourself. You want to keep Tish here always.'

Corbett feared he must be selfish, though scarcely in respect of Lœtitia. In his heart he would have been very glad to see her married. But he didn't want Matheson to marry her.

'Jim's awfully in love,' said Minnie, and it sounded odd to Corbett to hear his wife call Matheson 'Jim'. 'He fell in love with her the very first moment he saw her. That's why he's been here so often. You thought he came here to see you, I suppose?'

Her husband's blank expression made her laugh.

'You *are* a pig!' she repeated. 'You never do think of anyone but yourself. Now hurry up and get dressed, and we'll go into town and dine at the Exhibition, and after dinner we'll go up in the Big Wheel.'

'Is Letty coming too?' Corbett asked.

'Don't be so silly! Of course not. She's expecting Jim. That's why I'm taking you out. You don't imagine they want your society, do you? Or mine?' she added as an afterthought, and with an unusual concession to civility.

Henceforward Corbett saw even less of Matheson than before. He was as fond of him as ever, but the friendship fell into abeyance.

It seemed too that Matheson tried to avoid him, and when he offered his congratulations on the engagement, the lover showed himself singularly reticent and cold. Corbett concluded he was nervous. He remembered being horribly nervous himself in the early days of his betrothal to Minnie Wray, when her mother had persisted in introducing him to a large circle at Highbury as 'My daughter Margaret's *engagé*'.

On the other hand, Corbett could not enough rejoice at the genial warmth which the event shed over the atmosphere of 'Braemar'. Both young women brightened up surprisingly, nor was there any lack of conversation between them now. Corbett thankfully gathered up such crumbs of talk as fell to his share, and first learned that the wedding was to take place in October when Minnie informed him she must have a new frock. She rewarded him for his immediate consent by treating him to a different description of how she would have it made, three nights in the week.

Lœtitia thought of nothing but new frocks, and set about making some. A headless and armless idol, covered in scarlet linen, was produced from a cupboard, and reverentially enshrined in the dining-room. Both sisters were generally found on their knees before it, while a constant chattering went on in its praise. Innumerable yards of silk and velvet were snipped up in sacrifice, and the sofas and chairs were sown with needles and pins, perhaps to extract involuntary homage from those who would not otherwise bow the head. The tables were littered with books of ritual having woodcuts in the text and illuminated pictures slipped between the leaves.

There were constant visits to Richmond and Regent Street, much correspondence with milliners and dressmakers, a long succession of drapers' carts standing in the road, of porters laden with brown-paper parcels passing up and down the path. Lœtitia talked of Brighton for her wedding tour, and of having a conservatory added to the drawing-room of Holly Cottage. Friends and acquaintances called to felicitate her, and left to ask themselves what in the world Dr Matheson could have seen in Letty Wray. Presents began to arrive, and a transitory gloom fell upon 'Braemar' when Lœtitia received two butter dishes of identical pattern from two different quarters, neither of which, on examination by the local clockmaker, proved to be silver.

In this endless discussion of details, it did occasionally cross Corbett's mind that that which might perhaps be considered an essential point, namely, Matheson's comfort and happiness, was somewhat lost sight of. But as he made no complaint, and maintained an equable demeanour, Corbett supposed it was all right. Every woman considered the acquisition of fallals an indispensable preliminary to marriage, and it was extravagant to look for an exception in Lœtitia.

Matters stood thus when, turning into Wetherly Gardens one evening at the end of August, Corbett perceived, with a sudden heart-sinking, Minnie awaiting him at the gate. He recited the litany of all probable calamities, prayed for patience, and prepared his soul to endure the worst.

'What *do* you think, Jack,' Minnie began, with immense blue eyes, and a voice that thrilled with intensity. 'The most dreadful thing has happened – '

'Well, let me get in and sit down at least,' said Corbett, dispiritedly. He was tired with the day's work, weary at the renewal of domestic worry. But the news which Minnie gave him was stimulating in its unexpectedness.

'Jim Matheson's been here to break off the engagement! He actually came to see Tish this afternoon and told her so himself. Isn't it monstrous? Isn't it disgraceful? And the presents come and everything. She's in a dreadful state. She's been crying on the bed ever since.'

But Lœtitia, hearing her brother-in-law's step in the hall, came downstairs, her fringe, ominous sign, out of curl, her eyes red, her face disfigured from weeping.

And when she began, brokenly, 'He's thrown me over, Jack! He's jilted me, he's told me so to my face! Oh, it's too hard. How shall I ever hold up my head again?', then Corbett's sympathy went out to her completely. But he wanted particulars. How had it come about? There had been some quarrel surely, some misunderstanding?

Lœtitia declared there had been none. Why should she quarrel with Jim when she had been so happy, and everything had seemed so nice? No, he was tired of her, that was all. He had seen someone else perhaps, whom he fancied better, someone with more money. She wept anew, and stamped her foot upon the floor. 'I wish you'd kill him, Jack. I wish you'd kill him!' she cried. 'His conduct is infamous!'

Matheson's conduct as depicted by the young women did seem infamous to Corbett, and after the first chaotic confusion of his mind had fallen into order again, his temper rose. His Irish pride was stung to the quick. No one had a right to treat a woman belonging to him with contumely. He would go up to Matheson, at once, this very evening, and ask him what he meant by it. He would exact ample satisfaction.

He swallowed a hurried and innutritious meal, with Lœtitia's tears salting every dish, and Minnie's reiterations ringing dirges in his ears. She and Lœtitia wanted him to 'do something' to Matheson; to kill him if possible, to horsewhip him certainly. Corbett was in a mood to fall in with their wishes, and the justice of their cause must have seemed unimpeachable to them all, since neither he nor they reflected for a moment that he could not have the smallest chance in a tussle with the transgressor, who overlooked him by a head and shoulders, and was nearly twice his size.

This confidence in righteousness is derived from the storybooks, which teach us that in personal combat the evil-doer invariably succumbs, no matter what the disparity of physical conditions may be; although it must be added that in every properly written storybook it is always the hero who boasts the breadth of muscle and length of inches, while the villain's black little soul is clothed in an appropriately small and unlovely body.

Corbett, however, set off without any misgivings.

He found Matheson still at table, reading from a book propped up against the claret-jug. He refused the hand and the chair Matheson offered him, and came to the point at once.

'Is this true what I hear at home? That you came up this afternoon to break off your engagement with Lœtitia?'

Matheson, who had flushed a little at the rejection of his hand-shake, admitted with evident embarrassment that it was true.

'And you've the – the cheek to tell me that, to my face?' said Corbett, turning red.

'I can't deny it, to your face.'

'But what's your meaning, what's your motive, what has Letty done? What has happened since yesterday? You seemed all right yesterday,' Corbett insisted.

'It's not Letty's – it's not Miss Wray's fault at all. It's my mistake. I've made the discovery we're not a bit suited to each other, that's all. And you ought to be thankful, as I am, that I've discovered it in time.'

'Damn it!' exclaimed Corbett, and a V-shaped vein rose in the centre of his forehead, and his blue eyes darkened. 'You come to my house, I make a friend of you, my wife and sister receive you into their intimacy, you ask the girl to be your wife . . . I suppose you admit doing that?' he interpolated in withering accents; 'and now you throw her away like an old glove, break her heart, and expect me to be thankful? Damn it all, that's a bit steep.'

'I shouldn't think I've broken her heart,' said Matheson, embarrassed again. 'I should hope not.' There was interrogation in his tone.

'She feels it acutely,' said Corbett. 'Any woman would. She's very – ' He stopped, but Matheson had caught the unspoken word.

'Angry with me? Yes. But anger's a healthy sign. Anger doesn't break hearts.'

'Upon my soul,' cried Corbett, amazed at such coldness. 'I call your conduct craven! I call it infamous!' he added, remembering Lœtitia's own words.

'Look here, Jack,' appealed the other, 'can't you sit down? I want to talk the matter over with you, but it gets on my nerves to see you walking up and down the room like that.'

Corbett, all unconscious of his restlessness, now stood still, but determined that he would never sit down in Matheson's house again. Then he weakly subsided into the chair which his friend pushed over to him.

'You call my conduct craven? I assure you I never had to make so large a demand upon my courage as when I called upon Lœtitia today. But I said to myself, a little pluck now, a bad quarter of an hour to live through, and in all probability you save two lives from ruin. For we should have made each other miserable.'

'Then why have engaged yourself?' asked Corbett with renewed heat.

'Yes . . . why? Do you know, Jack, that the very morning of our engagement, five minutes even before the fateful moment, I'd no more idea . . . but you know how such things can come about. The garden, the moonlight, a foolish word taken seriously . . . and then the apparent impossibility of drawing back, the reckless plunging deeper into the mire . . . I don't deny I was attracted by Letty, interested in her. She is a pretty girl, an unusually pretty girl. But like most other girls she's a victim to her upbringing. Until you are all in all to an English girl you are nothing at all. She never reveals herself to you for a moment; speaks from the lips only; says the things she has been taught to say, that other women say. You've got to get engaged to a woman in England, it seems, if you're ever to know anything about her. And I engaged myself, as I told you, in a moment of emotion, and then hopefully set to work to make the best of it. But I didn't succeed. I didn't find in Letty the qualities I consider necessary for domestic happiness.'

'But Letty is a very good – '

Matheson interrupted with 'In a way she's too good, too normal, too well regulated. I could almost prefer a woman who had the capacity, at least, for being bad! It would denote some warmth, some passion, some soul. Now, I never was able to convince myself that Lœtitia was fond of me. Oh, she liked me well enough. She was satisfied with my position, modest as it is, with my prospects. My profession pleased her, principally, as she confessed to me, that it necessitates my keeping a carriage. But *fond* . . . do you think she is capable of a very passionate affection, Jack?

'Of course. I know this is going to do me a lot of harm. Twickenham, no doubt, will echo your verdict, and describe my conduct as infamous. I daresay I shall have to pull up stakes and go elsewhere. But for me, it has been the only conduct possible. I discovered I didn't love her. Wouldn't it be a crime to marry a woman you don't love? I saw we could never make each other happy. Wouldn't it be a folly to rush open-eyed into such misery as that?'

Which was, practically, the end of the matter, although the

friends sat long over their whisky and cigarettes, discussing all sublunary things. Corbett enjoyed a most delightful evening, and it had struck twelve before he set off homewards, glowing outside and in with the warmth which good spirit and good fellowship impart. He reaffirmed to his soul the old decision that Matheson was undoubtedly the cleverest, the most entertaining, the most lovable of men – and suddenly he remembered the mission on which he had been sent nearly four hours ago; simultaneously he realised its preposterous failure. All his happy self-complacency radiated off into the night. Chilled and sobered and pricked by conscience, he stood for a moment with his hand upon the gate of 'Braemar', looking up at the lighted windows of Minnie's room.

What was he going to say to her and to Lœtitia? And, more perturbing question still, what, when they should hear the truth, were his womenfolk going to say to him?

⁊ *Sugar and Spice*

HELEN SIMPSON

'Sometimes I can't stop,' she said, and threw a fistful of Japanese rice crackers into her maw with precise and startling violence. 'I can't control myself. Take them away from me!' She was giggling and crunching at the kitchen table, her back to the window, the last of the light turning her hair into a bonfire. Redheads have less hair to the scalp than the rest of us, but frequently they make up for this in coarseness.

'Is there anything you dislike?' I asked, knife poised, and she confessed to not being very keen on foreign muck. I almost yawned in her face at this bêtise, but she was exceptionally pretty so I controlled myself. Have you ever salivated wolfishly over some delicate noisette of milk-fed lamb? That was the variety of lip-smacking she provoked in me. She prattled on about her mum and her journey on the underground and how much dogs' mess there was on London's pavements while I watched her hotly from under my lizard lids.

Bending over her to pour a glass of wine I was relieved to find that she smelled only of herself and soap and water. Taste is very largely smell, and many a promising meal has been ruined by Diorissimo.

'I'm sure you've heard of the seven deadly sins, Rosemary,' I said at random, 'but can you list the primary odours?'

Her eyes swivelled and frowned, and she swung them up sideways in ruminant pretence to the ceiling corner. They had the same soft gleam as the buttocks of babies squatting in the sun.

'Floral, putrid, pepperminty,' I rattled off, 'musky, pungent, ethereal, camphoraceous.'

The herb rosemary has a strong flavour of camphor, and I toyed with the idea of describing to her how spiritedly her namesake grows on the hillsides of the Lubéron, or even, how a needle from its dried branches can be sharp enough to pierce the intestinal wall. But she was off again, telling me some story of mayhem in a pizza parlour, so I did not bother.

I placed a Venetian dish of *risi e bisi* in front of her, the Arborio rice fattened with peapod stock, the young peas sweet and fresh and infantine. She tucked in with an appetite.

Rice and peas?

Why not?

Let me explain now that the more traditional foods of seduction have always struck me as vulgar and unsuited to their purpose. What could be less aphrodisiac than to watch each other lipping the limp tips of flaccid though empurpled asparagus branches. I would always try to spare the blushes of a young person from such snigger-provoking simulacra as *cotechino*, *knackwurst*, *saucisses de Toulouse*, or God help us, ripe figs. As for the rehearsal for rape involved in serving oysters, it is something I find frankly embarrassing: the insertion and quick twist of the blade down at the clamped shell's hinge; slicing the bivalve's muscle from its bed; watching it flinch naked at the lemon juice; and at the last tossing it live down one's throat after a cursory gnashing to release flavour.

No, I restrict myself to verbal rather than visual puns, amusing myself without, I hope, alarming my guests.

'What's this?' asked Rosemary as I produced a platter of sizzled hammered veal slices overlaid with air-dried ham, each coupling fastened with a sage leaf and a toothpick.

'*Saltimbocca*,' I replied, baring my yellow teeth. 'Which, roughly translated, means, jump-into-the-mouth.'

'Yummy!' she chortled, and set to with a will. It did my old heart good to watch her, eyes bright, lips and teeth flashing with butter, deep in the act of mastication.

She was unused to talking during a meal, it seemed.

'We don't really eat together at home,' she remarked. 'We just help ourselves from the fridge when we get the munchies.'

I choose to cook for my young friends rather than take them to restaurants, not only to honour their youth and beauty but also to obviate the very real ravages of boredom. That stultifying chatter about personal fulfilment, the identikit aims and indignations, are ignorable as chaff if I can meanwhile be diverting myself in weaving a cage of hot caramel athwart the bowl of a ladle.

I gave her another plateful of *saltimbocca*, and she tucked in gratefully. Making the effort at last, I commenced the real business of self-inveiglement, questioning her respectfully about her future career, listening with an appropriately impressed expression to her worries on behalf of the third world, and eventually posing gentle queries about her boyfriend situation. At this she started to sigh and wrinkle her forehead and even to sniff a little. I could hardly have been more tender towards her than she was towards herself. We nursed her little hurts, coddled the smarting, spoonfed her self-esteem. I passed her a fresh damask napkin and she grinned and dabbed her eyes.

'That was *brilliant*!' she said as I cleared the plates. 'What was it again?'

Absently I listed the ingredients of *saltimbocca*, and it was at this point that she fell silent. To tell the truth I was not at all sorry at the cessation of her rather ugly suburban voice with its corncrake edge, stuffed to the gills with thanks-a-lots and ever-so-nices.

The kitchen was now in that strange domestic gloaming where steel and copper implements send out sharply unexpected gleams. I set assorted branches of candelabra in front of Rosemary and gave her a box of matches. In my experience, children like to play with fire, and she made the candles bloom like crocuses. Meanwhile I rolled little bundles of lollo rosso and peppery nasturtium leaves, then sliced them into a generous *chiffonade*.

I like to pay compliments to the individual beauties of my young guests in my choice of menu by introducing some subliminally referential food at a certain point in the meal. So it was that I had prepared sole *bonne femme* for stand-offish little Hannah and had baked *piroshki* for Natasha, wasted on her, of course, since she came from Tooting, but satisfying even so. For a certain toothsome Charlotte I had once assembled the eponymous Malakoff, equal parts of sugar, *beurre d'Isigny*, cream and ground almonds in a bucket-shaped mould with *boudoir* fingers. Now, for rufous Rosemary, I composed a salad punctuated with vivid orange nasturtium flowers to stand alongside the eccentric but indubitably orange cheese tray, upon whose plaited straw glowered a sunset wedge of Leicester, the same of Mimolette, a block of *gjetost*, ochreously fudge-like, and a very fair specimen of crumbling cadmium Cheshire. To complete this flush of rubicundity I opened a bottle of Chinon, softly purple.

'Do you like the wines of the Loire, Rosemary?' I asked.

Now that she had piped down, it was possible to concentrate on the neatness of her cat-like muzzle and the mournful set of her eyes, from which I could imagine creeping a pellucid tear or two. Despite my reassurances, she avoided nibbling the flowers, which denied me the *frisson* of marigold on vermeil. Never mind! She would have a greedy adolescent tooth for sweetness, I was sure, and so I prepared myself for the necromancy involved in concocting my chosen set piece, *Îles Flottantes*.

I scoured the copper bowl with a salted cut lemon until it winked pinkly, and while I did this I began to think less idly about the various conjunctions to be managed next door in the very near future. Bringing egg whites up to eight times their own volume with a balloon whisk is quite a little performance. The expressionless face, slight breathlessness and controlled energy of the rhythmically moving arm is nothing short of an erotic spectacle. I placed a folded towel beneath the bowl and commenced my exertions.

Rosemary stared. In her short life of boxed and tinned meals she had probably never even seen an egg before, let alone witnessed what it can do.

A little later on in the proceedings, the poached drift of bubbled albumen floating in a shallow vanilla lake, myself crooning Purcell's *Fairest Isle* beneath my breath, I decided to crown all with a veil of malleable brittleness, and cast loose nets of spun sugar over the whiteness. While teasing out the thousand molten strands mid-air, I had been touched to catch my innocent imagination wandering off to a wedding breakfast in some wood, crimson *fraises de bois* heaped in an ice bowl set with wood anemones, all goatishness translated to the sound of Pan pipes in a glade of greening larch. An unwound scroll was pinned to the bark of a tree.

'Doubtless it reads, "The world must be peopled",' I scoffed to the Bard (off-stage).

Rosemary looked wise. I loved her silence. I led her to a low sofa, her docile little hand in my hairy paw, and she sank with the slight gasp they all make at its unexpected softness and lack of upright support. Then I made coffee and produced the illustrated matter which is my equivalent of after-dinner mints.

In most cases they are so softened at being shown by my culinary efforts how much I *care* for them, so socially unsure of what's what, so intimidated by the whole process, that they automatically restrain any slight terror produced by the pictured suggestions. And during those faltering moments, of course, curiosity has time to sink its teeth in.

Not so with Rosemary.

'Oh yuk,' she said, and not merely her lip but the entire left side of her face appeared to curl.

I recoiled.

'It figures,' she sneered. 'I might have guessed. You're nothing but a dirty old man. I had a creepy feeling about you ever since you told me what was in that recipe. Pervert! Fancy tricking me into eating slices off some poor calf that's been hanging upside down with a slit neck, bleeding to death. It's made me sick to my stomach ever since.'

She carried on in this vein for some minutes while I wondered dismally how long it would take her to leave.

'I thought you were my *friend*,' she said. 'You were just *pretending*. I thought you really *liked* me.' She lapsed into trite wimperings of outrage. Then we had some more stuff about friends, and straight up, and on the level.

I considered informing her that she had been taken in by a trendy fib; that women and men are different and not *made* to be friends; that there is the consumer and the consumed; and so on. Her nastiness was escalating, however, and noise filled the room.

Some men prolong the moments before orgasm by remembering

school dinners; similarly it is possible to divert tiresome and unproductive emotions by the cold production of disgust. I watched her closely as she ranted, noting the flecks of saliva flying into the candlelight, the half-concealed eructation halfway through the diatribe, and even, when I concentrated, the newly gathered fleece of plaque at the junction of her teeth and gums.

'Where's the toilet?' she demanded at last. Wordlessly I pointed, then listened for what seemed a very long while to a urination of equine copiousness and vigour. When she returned her nose was red and moist, her mouth as shapeless as a jellyfish. She couldn't leave fast enough for either of us.

I stood looking round me at the broken funeral baked meats. I had been deceived by the appearance of the fleshly envelope into believing its enclosure would be equally graceful. It wasn't her crudeness that had so disconcerted me, nor her easy sentimentality, nor yet the blinkered commonplaceness of her outlook. It was more that she now appeared to me in her true colours, as a camp follower to the Goths and Vandals, squatting down on her hunkers in the ruined courtyard of some library gnawing on a bone, belching out her contempt for civilisation and *douceur de vivre*.

I felt saddened, and considered ringing the agency. But that dirty-minded girl had spoiled the impulse, she had muddied the crystal spring.

I twiddled a nasturtium flower. I drained a final atrabilious glass of Chinon. Then I carried what was left of my Floating Islands off to the refrigerator.

A Nocturne

GEORGE EGERTON

I have rather nice diggings. I got them last year, just after you went on that Egyptian racket. They are on the embankment, within sight of Cleopatra's Needle. I like that anachronism of a monument; it has a certain fascination for me. I can see it at night, if I lean out of my window, outlined above the light-flecked river sacred to our sewer goddess that runs so sullenly under its canopy of foggy blue.

To me the embankment has beauties unsurpassed in any city in Europe. I never tire of it at night. The opaque blotches of the plane-trees' foliage, the glistening water, the dotted lines of golden light, the great blocks of buildings rearing to the clouds like shadow monuments, the benches laden with human flotsam and jetsam.

I was leaning out of my window one night in November, in a lull in the rainfall; Big Ben had just boomed out one, when I noticed a woman rise from a seat below. She had been sitting there an hour, for I had seen the light shine on her hair, yellow hair like a child's, when I went down to the pillarbox at midnight.

Her carriage was that of a gentlewoman. Curious how gait tells. She walked a little way, stumbled, stood with her hand pressed to her heart, – a drunken woman would have lurched again. Then she went to the parapet, and leant against it, staring into the water.

A good many women I have known could not gaze steadily into running water, or look down from a height without feeling more than an impulse to throw themselves over – something impelled them to it, so they have assured me. I don't know the reason for it any more than I know why a man always buttons from left to right; a woman from right to left. It's a fact, though. The buttonholes on a woman's garments are always made on the right side, never on the left; and it is just as awkward for her to button our way, as for us to try hers. – Hang it, man, I know it's so. I got a poor woman to make me some pyjamas, and she put the darned buttonholes wrong side. I had to get the beastly things changed. – Well, to come back to the story, I didn't like the way that lady looked into the river; it had rained all day, the streets glistened with water, and a northeast wind scooped round the corners. I went down to have a look at her. Just as I crossed over she dropped her head in an odd sort of way, took a step out, then fell back against the wall. The measured beat of a policeman's step struck the pavement a little farther down. I steadied her, and asked, 'Are you ill, madam; can I help you?'

She lifted the strangest face I ever saw to mine. It was like some curious mask – more than a flesh and blood phiz. Her eyes were beautifully set and burned sombrely; they looked as live eyes might through the sockets of a mask. Her yellow hair seemed like a wig against her forehead and temples. She started and shrank as I touched her; her teeth chattered.

'Yes, I *am* ill; I feel faint, strangely faint . . .'

She evidently suffered from some heart trouble. There was a bluish tinge around her mouth. She rocked on her feet, her lids drooped. I put my arm through hers; the steps came nearer; she roused and moaned mutteringly, 'Yes, I'm only resting; I'll move on in a few minutes.'

'Come with me,' I said, 'you can't stay here; try and walk.'

She came all right, in a dazed sort of way, though. All the under floors of the building in which I have my rooms are offices, so we met no one. She panted a bit as she mounted the stairs. I kept close behind, in case of a fall. Her boots must have been broken, for she left little wet splotches on each step. I showed her into the room. The electric light roused her; she hesitated and coloured up, – it was the most curious thing I ever saw, the way her face thawed and quickened. She turned round, and looked straight at me; I braced myself to meet her eyes, miserable, honest eyes they were too, that probed me like steel; she would have detected the least sign of bad faith, like a shot.

I pushed an armchair nearer the fire; she sat down, leant back her head against the cushion, and before she could say whatever she intended to, fainted dead away. Faith, it gave me an uncomfortable sensation. I forced some brandy between her teeth and tried to pull her round. I like doing things for women, – any kind of woman almost, – they all interest me tremendously. I don't think I do them. Women seem at fault some way in their choice of men, they so often give themselves to brutes or sneaks – it may be these types don't scruple to seize the opportune moment with them.

I took off her hat, a quiet, little black felt affair, positively soaked with rain. She had lovely hair, glossy yellow, not 'brown at the roots' kind, you know; it had a crinkle in it, and the line down the middle of her head was white as an almond. I hate the type of blonde that has a pink skin to her scalp. I concluded she couldn't have been long in the streets, for the bit of white at her neck and the handkerchief in her lap were clean, – a day's soil at most. She wore woollen gloves; I pulled them off; she opened her eyes, closed them again. She wore an old-fashioned thin wedding-ring on her right hand, perhaps her mother's; she had pretty, long hands; but hands don't attract me like feet or ears. I belong to the race of men to whom temptation comes in the guise of little feet. An instep or ankle appeals irresistibly to my senses; I acknowledge it frankly; it's damned odd, but I can't help it – the appeal, I mean. My friend Foote says delicately perfumed *lingerie* is his weak spot; his fall is sure at a flutter of lace and ribbon. To be virtuous, he would have to live in a land where the drying of women's frillikins on a clothesline would be prohibited by law. Her feet were not pretty, although her boots were decently cut. What an odd face she had; I can see it in white relief on the red of the leather. A bit like Christine Nilsson about the forehead, big clever nose, tremendous jaw, – a devil or a saint, or I'm no judge. She opened her eyes at last. I held out the glass; she shuddered, pushed it away almost roughly, and said, 'No, please not that, I am afraid of it; I daren't touch it, it would be so easy to get to want it – when one is miserable.'

'Quite right; suppose you have some tea instead.'

She flushed and smiled; the saint was certainly uppermost just then.

'You are *very* good; yes, I should like some.'

I am rather a dab at making tea. Lloyd gets me the best in the market; never get good tea in a woman's house, – afraid of the price or something.

'You had better take off that wet jacket.'

Odd woman that; she stood up at once – she was still shaking – and took it off, hanging it over an oak stool. She was a well set up woman, of the thoroughbred flat, spare English type; getting on for the age the lady novelists find interesting, – thirty, perhaps. They may say what they like though, there is nothing like milk-fresh youth. By the Lord Harry, it's a beauty in itself! The plainest fresh-skinned wench with the dew of life in her eyes is worth ten of any beauty of thirty-five. Her dress was literally soaked, it hung heavily about her ankles; there were two wet patches too, where her feet had rested.

I dug the poker into the fire, and said, without looking round, 'You'll be laid up tomorrow if you keep that skirt on; go into the other room and take it off; don't mind me, I've seen petticoats before now. Hang it to dry before the fire and put your boots in the fender. You'll see a collection of Eastern footwear – it's rather a fad of mine – on the wall, find a pair to fit and slip them on . . .'

Didn't see her face, busy with the kettle. A moment's silence, then I heard the door shut softly. Admirable woman that! When I come to think of it, the only woman I ever met who could do a thing without arguing about it; never wanted a reason, never gave any. It's curious, the inclination women have to gab about everything; they spoil a caress by asking you if you liked it. The weather had not improved; I felt quite glad I had kept on my diggings. The adventure was one after my own heart. I would honour my unknown lady with my best china. I took down an old Worcester cup and saucer, tipped the sugar into my prettiest lacquer bowl, put out some sandwiches and biscuits, and was surveying my arrangements when the door behind me opened. By Jove, how rarely that woman changed when she smiled! It reminded me of the first spray of almond bloom one sees in spring in some dingy, sordid London street. It youthened her, melted the stark, hungry grip about her mouth. I suppose the petticoat was too short or something – women are so devilishly illogical. I have seen halfway down a woman's back and bosom, and she didn't mind in the least; yet she'd have fainted at the idea of showing the calf of her decently stockinged leg.

She had taken down an old Jap kimono, once a gorgeous affair, but time had faded the flowery broidery on the plum-blue ground to mellow half-tones.

Her embarrassment was pretty to see; what a fetching thing a woman is when she is perfectly natural. I pointed to the chair, and uncovered the teapot.

She sat down and poured out the tea rather awkwardly; I don't fancy it lay much in her line. She drank it eagerly, but paled a bit when I offered her a sandwich. I know that sensation, I had it during the last days of the Siege of Paris; ask me to tell you about that some other time – the poor thing was faint with hunger, the very sight of food made her feel sick, she put her handkerchief to her mouth; I took the sandwiches away and got out some dry biscuits.

'Have some more tea?' I said, 'and try these dry biscuits by and by, when you feel better.'

She leant back; she had the prettiest line of throat I ever saw, quite white and soft, under that jaw, too. I poured out some more tea for her.

'You have been fasting too long; when did you eat last . . .?'

'Not since yesterday morning!'

Good God! She forgot that the hour made it over two days.

She put the tea down and said simply, 'May I ask you for a cigarette? I think I should feel better if I were to smoke one or two. I don't feel as if I could eat just now.'

'Of course,' I said; 'how jolly that you smoke! You must have some of my special baccy.' She was smoking tranquilly when a gust of wind howled and shook the window-sash viciously, and the rain rattled like gravel thrown against the panes. She started and looked at the clock, the hands pointed to 1.45; the colour rushed to her face; I took the bull by the horns.

'My dear lady, don't bother about the hour, time is an entirely artificial arrangement. You can't go out in that rain, it's not to be thought of. You wouldn't be out on that seat, if you had any shelter to go to. I don't want to know anything you don't volunteer to tell me. You do me proud in accepting my hospitality, such as it is; indeed you do, it's a charity; I hate going to bed. When you have had a good rest you'll think of some way out of the snarl, whatever it is. Good baccy, ain't it?'

She held out her hand and gave mine an honest grip, as a nice lad might have done. Those big, grey eyes of hers got black when the tears filled them.

She was a vexatious sort of contradictory person; there was a tantalising lack of finality about her – just as you had made up your mind that she was really deuced ugly, she flushed and bloomed and sparkled into downright charm, and before you had time to drink it in she was plain again. Her voice too was twin to her face. It was deep, and at times harsh with sudden soft rushing inflections and tender lilts in it.

'You have Irish blood in you?' I ventured.

'Yes, on the distaff side; how did you know?'

'Oh, voice, and I suppose it's the kin feeling of race.'

We talked of a good many things during the next hour. I noticed that her eyes wandered wistfully to my books. I rather pride myself on some of my specimens of rare binding – two little shelves represent a good many years' income.

'Do you like books?' I asked. She caught what I meant at once, and her face lit up. I gave her my only heirloom, an, from me at least, unpurchasable, Aldine classic. She positively handled it lovingly. The more I think of that woman the more I am persuaded of her rarity; one is almost afraid to give one of one's book pets into most women's hands. She knew it at once – didn't say anything banal or gushing, only, 'I love the peculiar olive colour of the leather.'

'Have you ever seen any of Le Gaston's work? Look how well the lines of gold dot-work tell upon the scarlet of the morocco. How it has kept its colour. Machinery and cloth have played the deuce with the art of it.'

'If I were a rich woman I'd have any book I cared to keep especially bound for myself.'

Funny situation! Well, I suppose it was, rather. But if you come to think of it, the rummiest situations and most unlikely incidents in life are just those that don't get treated in fiction. Most poor devils have to write with one eye fixed on the mental limitations of their publisher or the *index expurgatorius* of the booksellers; that is, if they want to pay income tax.

She dropped off to sleep with a book in her lap. I covered her knees with a rug, turned out the light; the glow of the fire surrounded her with a magic circle. I went and lay down; I can sleep or wake at will. I decided to sleep till five. She had never stirred. I made up the fire; it was jolly to think of her there in the warmth instead of being out in that awful night, perhaps bobbing under a barge or knocking against the arches in the swirl of that filthy water.

I went back and slept till seven, tubbed, and took a peep at her. Her face looked good as a child's in her sleep, but a child that had suffered under bad treatment and grown prematurely old. It was dreadfully haggard; that woman had been slowly starving to death.

It was one of those beastly mornings, fine under protest, with a sun that looked as if he had been making a night of it. I hate the mornings, except out in wild nature; someway in civilisation they are always a sort of ill-natured comment on the night before. Like some excellent women, there is a brutal lack of semitone about them. I slipped the bolt on the door; Bates never came up unless I rang for him, but sometimes fellows drop in for a pick-me-up or a devil, – by the way, a red herring done in whisky isn't half bad.

She woke in a fright with a fearsome sort of half cry. I expect she thought she had been asleep on that seat. I knew the beastly morning would unsettle her; she was right as a trivet the night before. She flushed horribly when she realised where she was, and the time, and stammered, 'I'm so sorry, oh, I *am* so sorry! I was so tired, I really couldn't help myself. I haven't slept for many nights, you know, and one gets so stupid – '

'That's all right. I've been asleep, slept like a top; always do. Suppose you freshen up a bit in my dressing-room; your frock is dry. You will find hot water and things if you look about, – help yourself. I am going to lock you in if you don't mind: I want my man to fix things up a bit . . .'

She flushed again. I'll stake my oath that kind of blush hurts a woman.

My usual hour is eleven, but Bates cleared up and laid breakfast without an atom of expression in his face or voice. Odd man, Bates! He brought enough for two; makes a good living, that fellow, by an expedient regulation of the organs of sight and hearing. He finished at last, never knew him take so long; he asked, 'Shall you want me again, sir?'

'No, I'll shove the tray outside; I am going out later on, not in to any one.'

'All right, sir.'

I knocked at the door as I unlocked it. She came out, self-possessed, straight and somewhat stiffly slim in her black frock. I bet she could ride.

'You look better already,' I cried; 'would you like tea better than coffee? No! Come, then.'

She took her seat, outwardly unembarrassed, anyhow. I opened the papers and glanced at the headings. The *Globe* was lying on a chair, I don't know why I got it; she asked me might she see it. She glanced at the first page, and whatever she saw pleased her. I dawdled through my meal, for I did not know how to get any further with her. She was not the sort, you see, one could give a kiss and a quid and say, 'Now, run along, Polly, and don't get into any more trouble than you can help.' However, she gave me a lead herself, for when we had finished she came over, put out her hand and – well, what she said don't matter; anyway, it made me feel a bally idiot.

I put her into the armchair without any ceremony and pushed over the cigarettes, saying, 'Can't talk unless I smoke. Now, my dear lady, granted you consider you owe me something, suppose you take it out in as much confidence as you care to give away. How did you come to be without a bed last night?'

'Simply enough; to explain, I must go back a bit. Some years ago a younger brother and I were left almost penniless. Neither of us had been brought up to do anything except to get rid of money in the most happy-go-lucky way. That makes it difficult to get a living when even the trained people are crowded out. We got it as best we could. I've played the piano at bean feasts, "devilled" at sixpence an hour, done whatever offered itself, don't you know,' she had a trick of ending her statement that way. 'We kept together, were saving to emigrate. Then he was ill for months; he died at Christmas. That broke me up, don't you know; I was very fond of him; and left me without a penny. I went as nurse companion to a Christian gentlewoman in Bath at twelve pounds a year; pay for my own washing. I broke down under it in six months. Came to town ill, and went into the fever hospital three days after, stayed there six weeks; had to go to a convalescent home for a month. It was very cheap, but it took all I had left. I couldn't get anything to do. I tried for a place as domestic; I didn't look it, so they said. Things have been going steadily from bad to worse, don't you know? I used to work at the British Museum. A fortnight ago my landlady gave me notice; she wasn't a bad sort, but she had the brokers in herself, and there was a sale. I had to leave; she let me take my box to her sister's for a few days. I sat in St James's Park the night before last, and sent a description of it to a paper – ' She hesitated. 'I have been trying journalism, paragraphs, and articles,' and with the most abject tone of apology, 'verse, rubbish, you know; but sometimes it gets taken. Only one has to wait such a time before one knows. I have had a turnover in the *Globe*; it's a guinea, and there was another last night . . .'

(I had skimmed it, not half a bad one on 'Adder lore in the Fens' . . .) 'I'll get along all right now; it was rather bad last night; I was overtired or . . .'

I interrupted her.

'My dear woman, you can't go far on a guinea with arrears of rent, however small, to pay out of it.'

To cut it all short, I proposed to give her a note to an editress I know, a jolly, good little woman, who would stretch more than a point to serve me. I hinted as delicately as I could that she had better not let her feelings rush her ever, and give away the genesis of our acquaintance; sort of thing, you know, might be annotated badly. She gave me her word of honour that she would let me know the result, and see me next day if nothing came of the interview. She took my pasteboard. I got Bates out of the way with an empty Gladstone bag and a note to Paddy Foote to take it in and say nothing. She put on her things whilst I wrote the note. I watched her put on her hat; she looked better without it.

'I am going to speak of you as "bearer",' I said. 'I won't ask your name now; I'd like to learn it just when you like – or leave it to chance – I've an idea you'd rather . . .'

She nodded gravely; we shook hands – she has lovely eyes, as I said before – and went, leaving one the poorer by herself.

I haven't a thing belonging to her except the ashes of her cigarette. I tipped it into my matchbox; I suppose I am a damned fool; most Irishmen are, in one way or another.

It's curious how things have a knack of running in twos; I had never met her before that night, and yet, that same evening, as I came out of the Charing Cross post office, I felt a touch on my arm, turned round, and, by Jove, there she was. The little woman had fixed her up all right, and things were going to hum, so she said.

Sometimes, when the rain beats, and that beastly old river yawns like a grave, I stand up at the window and look down. I never felt a want in my old digs before. It was jolly to have a woman – a woman of that kind, you know – taking an interest in one's first editions.

❧ *'Possunt Quia Posse Videntur'*

They can because they seem to be able to

LYNNE TRUSS

I knew there was something wrong immediately I spotted Aunt Miriam queueing up with a jar of sun-dried tomatoes in Fortnum's food hall. Not like Aunt Miriam, I thought, as I peered from behind a sea-green column and studied her reflection in a fancy floor-length mirror. She normally slips such items into the pocket of her coat, and heads nonchalantly towards the door, giving little waves like the Queen Mum. She took a whole box of crystallised fruit once, I swear to God. Always gets away with it, too; and only afterwards asks herself what you are supposed to do with blackcurrant teabags or peppercorns (green). Resplendent in the old fox-fur that she's been promising me for years, she has always seemed pretty conspicuous to me, swanning around the food halls of our finest department stores, her pockets bulging, yet somehow she contrives to be invisible at the same time. A glorious woman, Miriam, like a – like a kind of ship. But something was definitely up, if she had started paying for things. And why wasn't she wearing the fur coat? It was late October, after all.

'Miriam?'

It was an innocent remark, but she leapt a couple of inches from the floor, and thumped a leather-gloved fist against her ribcage so hard that it might have jolted her teeth out.

'Oh, I didn't mean – '

'Susan!' she gasped.

'Auntie, whatever is the matter?'

I had never seen her look so pale – or so confused and gaga, for that matter. She looked more like a rubber dinghy than a mighty ship. A deflated one, if I'm honest. Possibly with a hole in it.

She took a moment to catch her breath, and went all clammy with panic and sweat. Honestly, it was ghastly: I could smell the *steam*. I put my arm around her shoulder, and she clutched the sleeve of my leather jacket.

'Susan, you wouldn't care for a cream tea, or something? I think I need to sit down.'

'Look, it was nothing I said, was it?' I joked.

'What? No, of course not. I just want to sit down.'

'Right-o,' I said readily, laughing a bit. It would be like old times, I thought, having the mad old shoplifter treat me to some buns. She picked up the Fortnum's bag, which had fallen to the floor when I first accosted her, but she didn't seem to remember anything about it. Oh well, I thought; bring out the toasted teacakes, and the jars of strawberry jam! I cheerfully led the way.

The reason I am telling you all this is that it then turned into a rather extraordinary afternoon – a bit spooky, if you know what I mean. Perhaps it was the geeky old-fashioned clergyman at the next table reading his little book of ghost stories that first gave me the creeps. But the main thing was the change in Aunt Miriam. She looked like someone who had been assaulted, and was expecting any moment to be assaulted again. The third cup of Earl Grey perked her up a bit, but I noticed when she reached out to pour it that there was a bandage on her hand, under her glove, and that she was sloshing the tea unsteadily. Just below her ear, too, there seemed to be a graze of some sort, visible when she craned her neck to check the customers at the other tables. Oh goodness, I thought, the poor woman really *has* been mugged, and she thinks her attacker lurks in tearooms. I put my hand on her shoulder again, and followed her gaze to a corner where a woman, in a squirrel jacket, was tucking into a nut cutlet and putting bits of it into her handbag. I could feel Aunt Miriam quiver at the sight. Perhaps her attacker had been a vegetarian.

'So all right, Miriam,' I said, thinking it time to break the ice. 'What have you done with it?'

'With what?'

'With my fur.'

I had meant to be light-hearted, but the horrible haunted look was back again, so I had evidently boobed.

My aunt took a deep breath, and said without punctuation, 'Well to be honest Susan I took it to a fur-coat amnesty in Trafalgar Square and threw it in a skip and they said they were going to burn it which I said was all right with me.'

I was rather taken aback. She knocked some icing sugar off her glove, on to her plate, and looked at the napkin across her knees.

'You didn't,' I said.

'I did.'

'You couldn't.'

'I did.'

'Oh, Miriam.'

She took a long look around the tearoom, narrowing her eyes at the squirrel lady, and then returned her gaze to our plate of cakes.

'Good Lord,' she said, airily. 'That vicar is reading M. R. James. Not something you often see, is it?'

'Miriam. Why?'

'Because he's not that fashionable, I suppose.'

'No, why did you throw away the coat?'

'Well, my dear, I'm not sure you would understand.'

'You haven't gone over to the animal-rights mob, surely?'

'Oh no.'

'So what, then?'

'Look, if I tell you – promise me you won't think I've gone mad.'

'Why ever should I think that?' I said (slightly evading the promise really, because I thought she was mad already).

'All right, then. But I warn you it is a long story, and one that troubles me. It is enough, I think, to freeze the blood and unseat the reason.'

Wow. She was suddenly talking like a book. 'Throw another log on the fire,' I felt like saying, but I thought she might consider me flippant. After all, the poor old thing was looking pretty flaky. So instead I said, 'Why don't we order another lovely pot of Earl Grey?' In the following pages I shall try to give you the story, as my nice Aunt Miriam told it to me.

A month before our chance encounter in Fortnum's, my aunt had been attending a gymnasium in North London, on her customary Tuesday afternoon, and had unexpectedly bumped into an old acquaintance.

'Miriam! Geraldine! What – ? Ha-ha. Gosh, did you – ?' (Their conversation went something like this, I imagine, but I wasn't there.)

Miriam – a spry figure, by the by, in her mid-fifties – was lying on a sort of padded table at the time, with a small dumb-bell in each hand, her arms extended above her head. Geraldine had just completed her workout and was about to leave, but she stopped to chat to my recumbent aunt, rather in the manner of a royal personage visiting a disaster victim in a hospital. Miriam said she felt a powerful urge to say something like 'Just grateful to be alive, Ma'am', but managed to suppress it. She had never liked the lordliness of Geraldine, and at her present horizontal disadvantage she remembered why. However, both women pretended to be overjoyed by the chance reunion, and agreed to meet the following week and pop across the road for coffee.

The following Tuesday, therefore, they left the gymnasium together – my aunt short and dynamic in her magnificent fox, Geraldine tall and broad-shouldered, bony and arrogant. Naturally she commented on Aunt Miriam's coat (you know: *my* coat) and equally naturally their talk turned to the frightful prejudice decent women had started to encounter in public places, simply for wearing their own, bought-and-paid-for foxes and leopard skins. Miriam had been upset to discover a note in the pocket of the fur, evidently placed there while she was exercising. It said 'SCUM' and it was unsigned. She said it made her blood run cold to think of someone writing it (in lipstick, it looked like), while she had been just a few yards away, diligently wrestling with her dumb-bells.

'What I always say,' said Geraldine, matter-of-factly over their first cappuccinos, 'whenever anybody starts on *me*, is that my coat is twelve years old, and that their darling ickle flopsy cottontails' – she was sneering a bit, here – 'would have been bloody well dead by now anyway.'

'Good point,' said Miriam, though a bit dubiously.

'You should try it. It soon shuts them up. They forget how bloody vicious and destructive some of those sodding little fur-bearing beasts are, too. Racoons, beavers, minks, stoats – they'd all tear your eyes out as soon as look at you. Red in tooth and claw, the lot of them. I mean, even a *hamster* will turn on you for no reason, you know.'

Miriam thought about it.

'Rabbits don't,' she said, after a bit.

'Oh well, if you're going to split hairs – ' said Geraldine, and then must have noticed the unfortunate pun, because she changed the subject. 'I tell you the fur I've always fancied. The old possum. It's got a darling little kink in it. My mother used to have one, but I think the moth got it. They were quite cheap, I think, in the old days.'

'I suppose the possum would tear your eyes out, too?' asked Miriam, unconsciously stroking the rust-red pelt that rested on her leg.

'No, but it's got a nasty grip. They play dead, you know, the little devils. But then, presumably, they could go for your throat.'

Miriam didn't like to mention it, but she remembered during this conversation that her own mother (my Great-Aunt Sylvie) had likewise possessed a possum coat. Quite possibly it was still packed away in one of the wardrobes on the top floor of the big family house in Kensington. Great-Aunt Sylvie had died twenty years before, in a rather bizarre and ghastly accident – falling from a balcony in her evening clothes and breaking her back on the railings beneath – and Miriam had rarely ventured into the old suite of rooms. Nobody knew what made Great-Aunt Sylvie fall, by the way; although a gardener working in the square said he heard her scream 'Get off! Get off!' in the moments before the fatal plunge. A few scratch marks on her face had puzzled the coroner, but in the end he had shrugged them off. Great-Aunt Sylvie had grown her nails rather long and sharp in the last few weeks of her life, so presumably she had caused the scratches herself.

By this stage in Miriam's story, I confess, my blood had not begun to freeze. My reason, far from unseated, was actually jolly comfy. But I noticed with some amusement that our clergyman was taking an avid interest – despite his pretence of studying the contents of a smoked-salmon sandwich. He had put down his book, and was dabbing his face with a large white handkerchief. Had I missed something? I saw that Miriam was watching the squirrel woman in the corner again, who was now making a meal out of a large meringue, nibbling all round it, and holding it with both hands.

'Did you find the possum?' I asked.

Yes she had, she said, returning to her story. Having left Geraldine, she had gone straight home, pausing only at a butcher's to buy some nice fresh chickens (more than she could eat, actually), and had decided to search for Sylvie's old coat. Perhaps the garment was valuable; perhaps she could sell it to Geraldine. It was uncharacteristic of Miriam to think in such terms, but she was suddenly feeling rather bold and crafty – just like she did when she was shoplifting in the fox-fur coat. What about giving the possum to Geraldine, and then claiming it as 'lost' on the contents insurance? With the price of furs going down, she had heard that the insurance money might be double the cost in the shops. Was the possum insured? She would have to ask the solicitor. But if it was, perhaps she could buy two new coats with the money. What a cunning old thing she was turning into!

So upstairs she went at about 8.30, straight to her mother's dressing-room, unvisited for twenty years. Of course, the light switch didn't work, but she found that she could see perfectly well by the moonlight shining through the uncurtained balcony window. Things had hardly been touched since the day of Great-Aunt Sylvie's spectacular defenestration on to the pikes. She had been dressing for a gala, if Miriam's memory served – and the room was honestly rather like Miss Havisham's in *Great Expectations*. No cake or mice, alas – but bits of furbelow scattered about, all covered in dust and cobwebs. When Miriam touched the door handle, she heard a rustling, scuttling noise, but in the room everything was still. And on the back of a chair, looking as perfect as the day it was bought, was Great-Aunt Sylvie's possum, its sheen reflecting the late-September moonlight so that it seemed to glow in the dark.

The following week, she packed the possum into a nice big Harrods bag, and took it to the gym, with the intention of showing it to Geraldine. The idea of the insurance scam had started to lose its appeal, but perhaps Geraldine would buy the coat from her; she had said she was sick of her usual leopard. And thus it came about that Geraldine – amazed by the condition of the old coat – took the possum home, wore it to the theatre the same night, and found in the pocket the note that had been waiting there for twenty years. It alarmed her so considerably that she stood stock-still in the bar at the National; in fact she told Aunt Miriam that she was sure her heart stopped beating. ('She played possum,' I said, and laughed.) In shaky handwriting, on a slip of faintly lined paper, were the words, 'It is not dead.' While on the back, when she turned it over: 'I think it's hungry.'

Knowing nothing of Great-Aunt Sylvie's death (or Great-Aunt Sylvie's life, for that matter), Geraldine was nevertheless spooked by this message from the grave. She phoned Aunt Miriam late the same evening, holding the receiver so tightly that the forensic experts later said she had actually bent it. She told my aunt she had found something in the coat which had frightened her, and asked her if she would please come over at once. Miriam was surprised; but on the other hand she had recently started a new regime of staying up half the night anyway, so said she would oblige. She took the fox from its hanger and put it on, but somehow caught the side of her neck with it, because she felt a sharp nick under her ear, which made her yelp.

It was at this point, unfortunately, that the vicar at the next table fell off his chair in a dead faint.

'Leave him,' I said. 'Carry on.'

But Aunt Miriam was on her knees, flapping his face with a napkin, and calling for iced water.

'Oh, the poor man,' she said. 'The poor man. I feel terrible.'

'Why should *you* feel terrible?' I said impatiently. 'Come on, Auntie, you didn't invite him to listen. Serves him right.' I swiped a couple of sandwiches from his plate, and laughed.

She gave me a funny look, and helped the newly-revived vicar back into his chair.

'I'm most frightfully sorry,' he said. 'I couldn't help overhearing your story – ' And he looked around with a pained expression, catching the eye of the woman from the corner. She had done a quick little run into the middle of the tearoom (to see what was up), and now she did another quick little run back again. She fixed her eyes on us, and froze in her seat, looking so frightened that you could almost hear her heart beat.

Miriam found a taxi quite quickly, and she was soon speeding along the north side of Regent's Park, near enough to the zoo to hear the wolves moaning at the night sky. She huddled down into her coat, and shivered.

'What a night,' she shouted to the taxi driver.

'What?' he shouted back.

'Doesn't matter.'

She looked north to the houses on Primrose Hill, and tried to remember which was Geraldine's. It wasn't so bad being out late at night. She passed a pub called The Fox and Grapes and noticed that its lights were still on, but as she sped past she told herself that she didn't really want a drink anyway.

But then she heard the breathing, and she stopped thinking about anything at all. *Breathing?* That's right: there was audible breathing in the cab; a warm, panting breath was actually steaming up the windows. Oh my God, she thought, and put out her hand for the light-switch. But then something wet and leathery touched her face, and a terrible pungent smell – a sort of smoky animal *tang* – rose all around her in the cab. 'Oh God, oh Jesus,' she said. She lunged forwards to beat on the glass partition, but no sooner had she moved, of course, than it bit her. The fur coat bit her very hard on the back of the hand, just as the taxi was pulling up at Geraldine's door.

She did not scream. The cab light came on, and she saw that her hand was bleeding, so she wrapped a hanky around it, and paid the driver, telling him to keep the substantial change from a ten-pound note (because she knew she would only drop the coins he gave her). She was in shock, probably. The coat seemed to heave slightly on her shoulders, and she said she felt enormous tears roll down her face, although she could have sworn she wasn't crying. Sinking to the pavement, she put her fingers in her mouth, and tried to imagine that none of this was happening. But it was then that she heard a horrible, unearthly scream, followed by a crash of glass. In an instant the body of her old pal Geraldine came hurtling from an upstairs window, and shattered on the pavement beside her. Dead. Miriam howled, wet herself, and passed out. In that order.

Of course Aunt Miriam had no proof that the coat had anything to do with Geraldine's death. But the coroner again recorded scratches, as well as mysterious bruising on the windpipe. The police allowed Miriam to retrieve the possum coat, which was draped innocently across a chair in Geraldine's bedroom; and this was how she came to read Great-Aunt Sylvie's message. She also took away Geraldine's old leopard, which she found in the garden in a tree, which it had presumably climbed. She took all three furs to the amnesty in Trafalgar Square, making the Lynx people promise that the coats would be burned, and not distributed to the London homeless ('They've got enough problems,' she said). She felt the loss of her fox very deeply; it had always given her a lot of nerve. But she would simply have to find some nerve without it. At least she now understood why she had bought all those chickens.

As a kind of postscript to the story, she mentioned that scouring through the local London papers to see whether there were any reports of Geraldine's death, she came across an interesting news item relating to the same night as her trip to Primrose Hill. Evidently the largest fur-trading warehouse in London had been burgled that night, and the thieves had made a completely silent getaway. Police were puzzled, the article said, by the strange fact that the only evidence of breaking and entering was a broken window, and *it appeared to have been broken from the inside*.

I put my hand on hers. Poor old Miriam. She clearly was mad, after all. Mad and stupid, to be exact.

'So, dear,' I said, 'that's the only reason you got rid of my coat?'

'Well, yes.' She seemed disappointed.

'You do know how much I wanted it?'

'Of course, but – ' She shrugged, sort of helplessly, and I made a face in return. She lowered her voice.

'Look, it's not just me,' she whispered, and she jerked her head in the direction of the woman with the squirrel jacket, who was now halfway up a pillar, and looking down on us with her head cocked to one side.

'Oh good grief, Miriam. You and your imagination.'

And I threw down my napkin and walked off. I left her to comfort the quivering clergyman, and slunk off home.

I suppose I have to resign myself to losing the fox-fur coat. Still, when I think of poor old Miriam standing there at midnight, with wee-wee running down her leg, I suppose I have to see the funny side. Luckily there are still a few more years in the old leather jacket, so I shan't freeze. But goodness knows it's dog-eat-dog these days, and you take what you can get. There is a chance, I suppose, that Miriam might die from all this accumulated shock – in which case I shall doubtless get a share of the house, and can buy all the fox-furs I want. In the meantime, perhaps I might try to cadge a ticket to North Africa again, to get another one of these amazing bargain jackets. I remember when I bought this one and they told me in the shop that it was made of hyaena. It still makes me laugh, just to think of it.

The Quest of Sorrow

ADA LEVERSON

It is rather strange, in a man of my temperament, that I did not discover the void in my life until I was eighteen years old. And then I found out that I had missed a beautiful and wonderful experience.

I had never known grief. Sadness had shunned me, pain had left me untouched; I could hardly imagine the sensation of being unhappy. And the desire arose in me to have this experience; without which it seemed to me that I was not complete. I wanted to be miserable, despairing: a Pessimist! I craved to feel that gnawing fox, Anxiety, at my heart; I wanted my friends (most of whom had been, at some time or other, more or less heartbroken) to press my hand with sympathetic looks, to avoid the subject of my trouble, from delicacy; or, better still, to have long, hopeless talks with me about it, at midnight. I thirsted for salt tears; I longed to clasp Sorrow in my arms and press her pale lips to mine.

Now this wish was not so easily fulfilled as might be supposed, for I was born with those natural and accidental advantages that militate most against failure and depression. There was my appearance. I have a face that rarely passes unnoticed (I suppose a man may admit, without conceit, that he is not repulsive), and the exclamation, 'What a beautiful boy!' is one that I have been accustomed to hear from my earliest childhood to the present time.

I might, indeed, have known the sordid and wearing cares connected with financial matters, for my father was morbidly economical with regard to me. But, when I was only seventeen, my uncle died, leaving me all his property, when I instantly left my father's house (I am bound to say, in justice to him, that he made not the smallest objection) and took the rooms I now occupy, which I was able to arrange in harmony with my temperament. In their resolute effort to be neither uninterestingly commonplace nor conventionally bizarre (I detest – do not you? – the ready-made exotic), but at once simple and elaborate, severe and florid, they are an interesting result of my complex aspirations, and the astonishing patience of a bewildered decorator. (I think everything in a room should not be entirely correct; and I had some trouble to get a marble mantelpiece of a sufficiently debased design.) Here I was able to lead that life of leisure and contemplation for which I was formed and had those successes – social and artistic – that now began to pall upon me.

The religious doubts, from which I am told the youth of the middle classes often suffers, were, again, denied me. I might have had some mental conflicts, have revelled in the sense of rebellion, have shed bitter tears when my faiths crumbled to ashes. But I can never be insensible to incense; and there must, I feel, be something organically wrong about the man who is not impressed by the organ. I love religious rites and ceremonies, and on the other hand, I was an agnostic at five years old. Also, I don't think it matters. So here there is no chance for me.

To be miserable one must desire the unattainable. And of the fair women who, from time to time, have appealed to my heart, my imagination, etc, every one, *without a single exception*, has been kindness itself to me. Many others, indeed, for whom I have no time, or perhaps no inclination, write me those letters which are so difficult to answer. How can one sit down and write, 'My dear lady – I am so sorry, but I am really too busy'?

And with, perhaps, two appointments in one day – a light comedy one, say, in the park, and serious sentiment coming to see one at one's rooms – to say nothing of the thread of a flirtation to be taken up at dinner and having perhaps to make a jealous scene of reproaches to some one of whom one has grown tired, in the evening – you must admit I had a sufficiently occupied life.

I had heard much of the pangs of disappointed ambition, and I now turned my thoughts in that direction. A failure in literature would be excellent. I had no time to write a play bad enough to be refused by every manager in London, or to be hissed off the stage; but I sometimes wrote verses. If I arranged to have a poem rejected I might get a glimpse of the feelings of the unsuccessful. So I wrote a poem. It was beautiful, but that I couldn't help, and I carefully refrained from sending it to any of the more literary reviews or magazines, for there it would have stood no chance of rejection. I therefore sent it to a commonplace, barbarous periodical, that appealed only to the masses; feeling sure it would not be understood, and that I should taste the bitterness of Philistine scorn.

Here is the little poem – if you care to look at it. I called it:

FOAM-FLOWERS

Among the blue of Hyacinth's golden bells
(Sad is the Spring, more sad the new-mown hay),
Thou art most surely less than least divine,
Like a white Poppy, or a Sea-shell grey.
I dream in joy that thou art nearly mine;

Love's gift and grace, pale as this golden day,
Outlasting Hollyhocks, and Heliotrope
(Sad is the Spring, bitter the new-mown hay).
The wandering wild west wind, in salt-sweet hope,
With glad red roses, gems the woodland way.

Envoi

A bird sings, twittering in the dim air's shine,
Amid the mad Mimosa's scented spray,
Among the Asphodel, and Eglantine,
'Sad is the Spring, but sweet the new-mown hay.'

I had not heard from the editor, and was anticipating the return
of my poem, accompanied by some expressions of ignorant contempt
that would harrow my feelings, when it happened that I took up the
frivolous periodical. Fancy my surprise when there, on the front
page, was my poem – signed, as my things are always signed, '*Lys
de la Vallée*'. Of course I could not repress the immediate exhilaration
produced by seeing oneself in print; and when I went home I found
a letter, thanking me for the 'amusing parody on a certain modern
school of verse' – and enclosing ten-and-six!

A parody! And I had written it in all seriousness!

Evidently literary failure was not for me. After all, what I wanted
most was an affair of the heart, a disappointment in love, an
unrequited affection. And these, for some reason or other, never
seemed to come my way.

One morning I was engaged with Collins, my servant, in putting
some slight final touches to my toilette, when my two friends,
Freddy Thompson and Claude de Verney, walked into my room.

They were at school with me, and I am fond of them both, for
different reasons. Freddy is in the army; he is two-and-twenty,

brusque, slangy, tender-hearted, and devoted to me. De Verney has nothing to do with this story at all, but I may mention that he was noted for his rosy cheeks, his collection of jewels, his reputation for having formerly taken morphia, his epicurism, his passion for private theatricals, and his extraordinary touchiness. One never knew what he would take offence at. He was always being hurt, and writing letters beginning: 'Dear Mr Carington' or 'Dear Sir' – (he usually called me Cecil), 'I believe it is customary when a gentleman dines at your table,' etc.

I never took the slightest notice, and then he would apologise. He was always begging my pardon and always thanking me, though I never did anything at all to deserve either his anger or gratitude.

'Hallo, old chap,' Freddy exclaimed, 'you look rather down in the mouth. What's the row?'

'I am enamoured of Sorrow,' I said, with a sigh.

'Got the hump – eh? Poor old boy. Well, I can't help being cheery, all the same. I've got some ripping news to tell you.'

'Collins,' I said, 'take away this eau de Cologne. It's corked. Now, Freddy,' as the servant left the room, 'your news.'

'I'm engaged to Miss Sinclair. Her governor has given in at last. What price that? . . . I'm tremendously pleased, don't you know, because it's been going on for some time, and I'm awfully mashed, and all that.'

Miss Sinclair! I remembered her – a romantic, fluffy blonde, improbably pretty, with dreamy eyes and golden hair, all poetry and idealism.

Such a contrast to Freddy! One associated her with pink chiffon, Chopin's nocturnes, and photographs by Mendelssohn.

'I congratulate you, my dear child,' I was just saying, when an idea occurred to me. Why shouldn't I fall in love with Miss Sinclair? What could be more tragic than a hopeless attachment to the woman who was engaged to my dearest friend? It seemed the very thing I had been waiting for.

'I have met her. You must take me to see her, to offer my congratulations,' I said.

Freddy accepted with enthusiam.

A day or two after, we called. Alice Sinclair was looking perfectly charming, and it seemed no difficult task that I had set myself. She was sweet to me as Freddy's great friend – and we spoke of him while Freddy talked to her mother.

'How fortunate some men are!' I said, with a deep sigh.

'Why do you say that?'

'Because you're so beautiful,' I answered, in a low voice, and in my *earlier manner* – that is to say, as though the exclamation had broken from me involuntarily.

She laughed, blushed, I think, and turned to Freddy. The rest of the visit I sat silent and as though abstracted, gazing at her. Her mother tried, with well-meaning platitudes, to rouse me from what she supposed to be my boyish shyness . . .

What happened in the next few weeks is rather difficult to describe. I saw Miss Sinclair again and again, and lost no opportunity of expressing my admiration; for I have a theory that if you make love to a woman long enough, and ardently enough, you are sure to get rather fond of her at last. I was progressing splendidly; I often felt almost sad, and very nearly succeeded at times in being a little jealous of Freddy.

On one occasion – it was a warm day at the end of the season, I remember – we had gone to skate at that absurd modern place where the ice is as artificial as the people, and much more polished. Freddy, who was an excellent skater, had undertaken to teach

Alice's little sister, and I was guiding her own graceful movements. She had just remarked that I seemed very fond of skating, and I had answered that I was – on thin ice – when she stumbled and fell . . . She hurt her ankle a little – a very little, she said.

'Oh, Miss Sinclair – "Alice" – I am sure you are hurt!' I cried, with tears of anxiety in my voice. 'You ought to rest – I am sure you ought to go home and rest.'

Freddy came up, there was some discussion, some demur, and finally it was decided that, as the injury was indeed very slight, Freddy should remain and finish his lesson. And I was allowed to take her home.

We were in a little brougham; delightfully near together. She leaned her pretty head, I thought, a little on one side – *my* side. I was wearing violets in my buttonhole. Perhaps she was tired, or faint.

'How are you feeling now, dear Miss Sinclair?'

'Much better – thanks!'

'I am afraid you are suffering . . . I shall never forgot what I felt when you fell! – My heart ceased beating!'

'It's very sweet of you. But, it's really nothing.'

'How precious these few moments with you are! I should like to drive with you for ever! Through life – to eternity!'

'Really! What a funny boy you are!' she said softly.

'Ah, if only you knew, Miss Sinclair, how – how I envy Freddy.'

'Oh, Mr Carington!'

'Don't call me Mr Carington. It's so cold – so ceremonious. Call me Cecil. Won't you?'

'Very well, Cecil.'

'Do you think it treacherous to Freddy for me to envy him – to tell you so?'

'Yes, I am afraid it is; a little.'

'Oh no. I don't think it is – How are you feeling now, Alice?'

'Much better, thanks very much . . .'

Suddenly, to my own surprise and entirely without premedita-
tion, I kissed her – as it were, accidentally. It seemed so shocking,
that we both pretended I hadn't, and entirely ignored the fact:
continuing to argue as to whether or not it was treacherous to say I
envied Freddy . . . I insisted on treating her as an invalid, and lifted
her out of the carriage, while she laughed nervously. It struck me
that I was not unhappy yet. But that would come.

The next evening we met at a dance. She was wearing flowers that
Freddy had sent her; but among them she had fastened one or two
of the violets I had worn in my buttonhole. I smiled, amused at the
coquetry. No doubt she would laugh at me when she thought she
had completely turned my head. She fancied me a child! Perhaps,
on her wedding-day, I should be miserable at last.

'. . . How tragic, how terrible it is to long for the impossible!'

We were sitting out, on the balcony. Freddy was in the ballroom,
dancing. He was an excellent dancer.

'*Impossible!*' she said; and I thought she looked at me rather
strangely. 'But you don't really, really – '

'Love you?' I exclaimed, lyrically. 'But with all my soul! My life
is blighted for ever, but don't think of me. It doesn't matter in the
least. It may kill me, of course; but never mind. Sometimes, I
believe, people *do* live on with a broken heart, and – '

'My dance, I think,' and a tiresome partner claimed her.

Even that night, I couldn't believe, try as I would, that life held for
me no further possibilities of joy . . .

*

About half past one the next day, just as I was getting up, I received a thunderbolt in the form of a letter from Alice.

Would it be believed that this absurd, romantic, literal, beautiful person wrote to say she had actually broken off her engagement with Freddy? She could not bear to blight my young life; she returned my affection; she was waiting to hear from me.

Much agitated, I hid my face in my hands. What! was I never to get away from success – never to know the luxury of an unrequited attachment? Of course, I realised, now, that I had been deceiving myself; that I had only liked her enough to wish to make her care for me; that I had striven, unconsciously, to that end. The instant I knew she loved me all my interest was gone. My passion had been entirely imaginary. I cared nothing, absolutely nothing, for her. It was impossible to exceed my indifference. And Freddy! Because *I* yearned for sorrow, was that a reason that I should plunge others into it? Because I wished to weep, were my friends not to rejoice? How terrible to have wrecked Freddy's life, by taking away from him something that I didn't want myself!

The only course was to tell her the whole truth, and implore her to make it up with poor Freddy. It was extremely complicated. How was I to make her see that I had been *trying* for a broken heart; that I *wanted* my life blighted?

I wrote, endeavouring to explain, and be frank. It was a most touching letter, but the inevitable, uncontrollable desire for the *beau rôle* crept, I fear, into it and I fancy I represented myself, in my firm resolve not to marry her whatever happened – as rather generous and self-denying. It was a heartbreaking letter, and moved me to tears when I read it.

This is how it ended:

. . . You have my fervent prayers for your happiness, and it may be that some day you and Freddy, walking in the daisied fields together, under God's beautiful sunlight, may speak not unkindly of the lonely exile.

Yes, exile. For tomorrow I leave England. Tomorrow I go to bury myself in some remote spot – perhaps to Trouville – where I can hide my heart and pray unceasingly for your welfare and that of the dear, dear friend of my youth and manhood.

Yours and his, devotedly, till death and after,

Cecil Carington

It was not a bit like my style. But how difficult it is not to fall into the tone that accords best with the temperament of the person to whom one is writing!

I was rather dreading an interview with poor Freddy. To be misunderstood by him would have been really rather tragic. But even here, good fortune pursued me. Alice's letter breaking off the engagement had been written in such mysterious terms, that it was quite impossible for the simple Freddy to make head or tail of it. So that when he appeared, just after my letter (which had infuriated her) – Alice threw herself into his arms, begging him to forgive her; pretending – women have these subtleties – that it had been a *boutade* about some trifle.

But I think Freddy had a suspicion that I had been 'mashed', as he would say, on his *fiancée*, and thought vaguely that I had done something rather splendid in going away.

If he had only stopped to think, he would have realised that there was nothing very extraordinary in 'leaving England' in the beginning of August; and he knew I had arranged to spend the summer holidays in France with De Verney. Still, he fancies I acted nobly. Alice doesn't.

And so I resigned myself, seeing, indeed, that Grief was the one thing life meant to deny me. And on the golden sands, with the gay striped bathers of Trouville, I was content to linger with laughter on my lips, seeking for Sorrow no more.

❧ *An Act of Kindness*

CLAIRE HARMAN

An unpleasant thing happened to Ray Purvis in the spring of 1965, when he was eleven years old. He had been visiting his mother in hospital, when he was waylaid – tricked, as he thought later – by another of the patients. It happened when he loped off for five minutes by himself, bored with being told off for fidgeting. Propped up in the hospital bed, his mother had looked large and clumsy, and turned her eyes mournfully on the boys without moving her head. 'What about their socks? Are you keeping up with their socks?'

It was at no point like an adventure. Ray had responded to the familiar, impatient click of authority in the voice as meekly as a little dog. *Come here, boy. Do this, do that.* And as soon as he had taken the first obedient steps towards the bed, he was committed, compromised, and hurried to fetch the clothes, hurried to tie the old man's laces, hurried to steal a wheelchair and get him out of the building, if only to shorten the period of his humiliation. The back of the old chap's head looked pink and vulnerable in the cool spring sunlight, the soft hair dancing up and down foolishly; he seemed irritable, and cursed when Ray dropped him down the curb by the back wheels, the way he'd seen his mum do with the pushchair. If there hadn't been a bus already in – they had to run for it – Ray would certainly have left him at the bus stop, but as it turned out, it was the wheelchair they left behind.

It was only when they had got out of town, beyond anywhere that Ray recognised, that he began to wonder what the old man intended to do. He stole a glance at him: he was hugging the leather bag the clothes had come out of and swayed exaggeratedly with the motion of the bus. It dawned on Ray that the old man might not know what he was doing; it had sounded as if he did, in the hospital, but now he seemed to have lost impetus, and could only stare out of the window and wobble. As they neared the end of the route, and the bus emptied, it seemed clear that they had no real destination, and by the time the driver nagged them to get off, cranking his head round and addressing them like an inevitable pair, Ray had somehow become responsible for what happened next. His face burned with indignation and embarrassment. He didn't even know this man's name, for goodness' sake. An act of weakness, of automatic obedience, had been hijacked into something like an act of charity.

It had been a mild day, and almost pleasant to stagger up towards the woods beyond the church, which Ray had sort of chosen, on an impulse, from the steps of the bus. But the ground under the trees was damp and cold, and there was nothing to sit on but the leather bag. It was called E. J. Bullen and had hard projecting metal corners, but the old chap fell on to it gratefully, crushing dozens of emerging bluebells. Ray stood feeling useless, waiting for the wheezing to stop. None of this was right; it wasn't being properly managed. He should have sent Ray back to his house – he must have a house – for supplies: sandwiches, miraculously packed up ready in the kitchen, a board game, a torch, Wellington boots. The old chap could have given him the key to the back door, the sound of which would have set off a little dog barking. It would be an old person's sort of dog, a Westie, perhaps, or a spaniel. And while Ray was fiddling with the key, the dog would have slipped out unnoticed and followed him, faithful to the scent of his master's tartan blanket, and come out of the undergrowth, noiselessly and suddenly, to the old man's muted but dignified rapture.

E. J. Bullen lay breathing heavily for a few minutes. Now the sun had gone off his face it was clear that he hadn't been squinting, but in pain. He opened his eyes slightly and muttered something towards Ray.

'Gerway.'

Ray took a step forwards, thinking he must have done something wrong.

'Gerway. Scar pa.'

'I'm sorry?'

'Pissoff,' he said, closing his eyes again.

Ray walked quickly back through the wood, fingering a ten-pound note he had taken as a precaution while helping the old chap to dress in the hospital. They would never take it on the bus, if there was a bus. It was Sunday. Not only would they never take it, but the conductor would lean down menacingly and inquire where he'd got that amount of money from, and then there would be silence, followed by thin excuses, followed by trouble. If he walked home, there'd be trouble. They'd never believe him, whatever he said. His pride smarted under the blow of being told to piss off, and the thought struck him that he should go to the police, get E. J. Bullen arrested.

The sun was setting, and people started to arrive, mostly on foot, at the little church opposite. The lights were on inside; it looked to

Ray vaguely like their local pub, and he began to wonder whether or not there was an off licence in this village, where the sight of £10 might not be as shocking as to a bus conductor, and where, by the expedient of buying, say, twenty bottles of Tizer, 'Tizer the Appetizer', he could get some change.

'No more buses, tonight, son,' said a man waiting to cross the road.

Brainwave. The collection at church. Loose change. And he'd seen a wheelbarrow in the churchyard. He'd dump the old chap and phone for a taxi. It couldn't be all that difficult.

Coming down the slope, the barrow lurched and tilted, and at every stone or projecting root, the impact jarred Ray's body. The old man's legs and arms seemed everywhere, flopping about like india rubber, and he was moaning and complaining and shivering violently from having been woken in the cold. Serves him right, Ray thought with satisfaction, keeping his eyes on the darkening ground ahead. Patrons are warned to keep all their limbs in the carriage while the ride is in motion.

When he tipped up the wheelbarrow in the porch, E. J. Bullen slid out so unceremoniously that Ray laughed out loud.

The congregation was not very large, and they were rotten singers. The organ came in with an encouraging 'WAARGH!' at the beginning of every verse, but no one seemed keen to plunge in after it, and the hymns were pitched too high anyway – they simply faded out at the highest points. Ray became restless. He read the spines of the hymn-books, he read the brasses glinting in the aisle, he read the windows, and when his head went down in imitation of everyone else, he read the hassocks: 'St Mary's Mothers' Union', 'In His Service', and one called, simply, '1957'. He wondered if they had missed the collection already. The service seemed to go on and on, as if waiting for a signal which no one was impolite enough to give. The old chap kept falling off his seat, in a silly way, as if he was just being naughty, and he was getting noisy again, muttering and burping. Ray had to prop him up at the end of the pew, and sit right next to him to stop him moving. Even then, his head rolled round; now down on his chest, now right back, with his mouth open, like an exercise Ray had seen the PE teacher do. He could see straight up E. J. Bullen's nose, two huge hairy tunnels with a delicate tracery of veins at the edges, and a mole the colour of a wine gum. He smelled of the woods, and crushed sappy stalks, and something else, reasserting itself now that they were drying off slightly: hospital pong.

There had been a reading, and now everyone was standing and singing a psalm, the stupidest tune in the world, Ray thought: 'toot toot toot, la la la di da – '

> They came round about me daily like water: and compassed me together on every side.
> My lovers and friends has thou put away from me: and hid mine acquaintance out of my sight.

There weren't any money boxes on show, or plates full of change. Nothing. A mean-eyed man, obviously some sort of church official, was looking at them with suspicion and distaste. E. J. Bullen gave a lurch and Ray began to pray: Please God, don't let him be sick all over me.

It was unbelievable. There was no collection. The congregation had begun slowly seeping towards the door of the church, like a basin being emptied, and Ray suddenly felt painfully conspicuous. He stooped forward as if to pray: too late. A middle-aged woman, with an appalled and already reproachful look, was bearing down on them, and through the chinks of his fingers, Ray could see the same look of disapproval and alarm spreading on the faces beyond her. He felt relieved, and suddenly hungry.

Years later, in the summer of 1991, Ray sat staring out of his front window, listening to his wife Marnie tell this story for the umpteenth time. It was one of her favourites, and she had a special voice for it, rather insistent at first, as if she were trying to prove a point, modulating down to a confident, cosy contralto. It excited her to tell it, it almost seemed to shock her. It was fluid, slightly variable, but with a few fixed poles of phrases which would always be exactly the same, which she seemed to aim at, grasp, and use to swing into the next section.

Marnie's version was pretty much what Ray had told her when they were courting, swinging their legs on the sea wall. At that time, he still felt vaguely guilty about the whole incident, felt, on reflection, that something more had been required of him. Telling Marnie was both a confession and an absolution, for he gave her, of course, a much neater, shorter and more tellable account than was strictly true. He didn't realise then that she would latch on to it, in the way he now knows is typical, or that she would be so impressed by his part in it – the affable child, the Holy Dove, the Comforter. And now she was telling it to Mr Duncan, whom they had met the week before at The Towers nursing home twenty miles away, where his mother and Marnie's aunt were co-patients. She was telling him the ending, the bit that Ray had entirely made up. Ray had sensed that without an ending Marnie would have been somehow reproachful, insincerely troubled: and he had been right. Whatever she missed out, it was never the end. For her, the end was the whole point.

'Well, they stuck it out for half a night and then the old chap started to make rasping noises in his throat, like this – and Ray thought, bloody hell, and ran down to the road and got a motorist to come and help. I expect the poor woman was terrified, going into those woods at night. I wouldn't have.

'They had to be very careful with him, got him down to the road in a *wheelbarrow*, and got him settled in the back. He was very upset, didn't want to go. They had to promise to take him home, and the poor old chap was jabbering away. Ray reckons the woman *was* going back to the hospital, or the police, because she didn't get on the bypass. At any rate, she was a bad driver, he said – nervy – and anyway, next thing you know – bang. Going thirty miles an hour in the middle of the night down a quiet road and they have an accident! Someone reversing out of a drive.

'And the poor old chap in the back had a heart attack, and died.'

Mr Duncan was leaning forward, nodding his agreement that it just goes to show, doesn't it, and that there was no point worrying too much. He also agreed that it wouldn't happen the same way nowadays – kids couldn't wander off like that. There was no such thing as a poor old chap any more: he'd have matured into a pervert. Mr Duncan was wearing pale-blue shoes in a soft leather, like a baby's, and a gold watch glinted importantly up his sleeve. He played the piano with a group called the Harry Daley Four. Ray felt a sudden rush of affection for Marnie, thinking how loyal she was, loyal to the story, loyal to him, for she had only told all this to Mr Duncan in retaliation for his odd, glum swanking, and it had worked. All through lunch he had been going on about how close to death his mother was, as if seventy-six and a tumour is such a big deal.

The following Sunday afternoon, Ray and Marnie drove out to see Aunt Lily at The Towers. Marnie had brought some photographs with her, and another box of chocolates. Ray always remarked on them, because Aunt Lily was not allowed to eat chocolates, but as Marnie pointed out, you have to keep the staff sweet – they'll be dealing with the nitty gritty when the time comes, after all.

The Towers was a former hospital built in red sandstone with Gothic windows and decorative wrought-ironwork along the peak of the roof. The dual carriageway swooped round on stilts within fifty yards of its front border and rather spoiled the view, as everyone always remarked, as did the roundabout, and the twenty-four-hour garage and the carpet warehouse. The tall dark clock-tower was visible from the road. 'Oh good,' said Marnie, 'we're rather late.'

They went straight in, through the waiting-room where they had first met Mr Duncan, sitting looking mournful under a sign which said, 'Join the Urinary Conduit Association'. Aunt Lily was in the day-room, fingering the edges of her cardigan. She smiled unre-proachfully as she saw Ray and Marnie come through the door. She was a dear old lady, meek to her illness, quite subdued by it, and Ray had grown very fond of her. The troublesome old woman who usually sat flicking her medicine at other people and who constantly made a noise like a wet bough scraping against a window had been moved, Ray noticed with relief. Mr Duncan's mother, disappointed by the demands of the Harry Daley Four, had decided to stay in bed.

Aunt Lily did not seem particularly interested in the photos, which were of a great-niece in uniform at Sandhurst. Lily had been a WAAF herself during the war, and in the WRVS later, but smiled at the pictures of Janet's passing-out as blandly as at a knitting pattern. Ray looked round the day-room, and thought of all the things that these old men and women had been, lying around them like dust, like the invisible silt they seemed to shuffle through. They are almost lucky, he thought: they have this inviolable, automatic pathos, whether they are aware of it or not, and people who are not there yet, people like himself and Marnie, people who might die suddenly, stupidly, falling off ladders or stepping into the road too soon, have to defer to it.

Marnie's story came back to mind, and he remembered the ending that should have gone with it. There had been no accident, no nervy woman driver. The reproachful woman from church had stopped her Morris Oxford at the lights by The Three Feathers, and Ray had waited till the opposing lights turned red, then jumped out of the car and ran away. He looked back briefly from the corner, and the car was moving off. The woman had shouted as he dashed away, but hadn't bothered to give chase. The old man in the back was too ill; Ray had been counting on that.

He had almost wiped the incident out of his mind by the next Sunday, when the boys were taken to visit their mother again. The flowers by her bed had changed from freesias to daffodils, and the staff nurse from a Liverpudlian to a Scot, but otherwise there was no change, and Ray began to feel uneasy, as if just being in the building again might suddenly expose his secret. And then something awful almost happened as Ray was going down the corridor, clutching a sixpence for the vending machine. A nurse came out of a room holding up a container like a miniature watering can, Ray moved to avoid her, and glancing into the open doorway caught sight of the leather bag on the floor under a chair. It must have been the one with the label E. J. Bullen on it. There couldn't be two like that. He hadn't even considered that the old man might still be alive – and he didn't know if he thought it was a good thing or not. He didn't want to think about it at all. On the way back, Ray was praying that the door would be closed, and it was.

In the day-room two flies were buzzing round sleepily; one tenor and one bass. A metal wastebin began to tick in the sun. It was time for tea, and Aunt Lily sat up obligingly, grateful in advance. With their tea, Ray and Marnie were offered some remains of cake from the day before, when George, the oldest resident, had celebrated his ninety-eighth birthday. Those were his balloons, she pointed out, and that his birthday card from the staff – a picture of a little boy playing football, 'You're 9 today!', with an '8' written in in gold pen. He'd be along in a minute. There wasn't any point bringing him in for the whole of visiting, as he hadn't got any family. Marnie ate the cake in small, critical bites. It had been made from a packet, and was filled with a synthetic yellow cream.

The nurse parked George, an unsmiling bundle, underneath the balloons, and in a huge voice assured Ray and Marnie that he wouldn't mind at all about the cake. They all called him George, as if he had lost the use of his surname along with all the other things he had lost. George seemed to stare at Ray. He reminded Ray of an old teabag, and the nurses with all their bobbing about and smirking were like a parody of the servants he might just be old enough to have had, or been. Ray watched the clock bouncing softly from one minute to another, with a slight backward reaction. It was always pretty accurate, probably for the visitors' sake, and told him that they were on the downward slope towards home, and that he could if necessary fill up the remaining time by going out to inspect the shrubs, of which The Towers had a great many, all labelled. But George was still staring at him, and this was unnerving. And there was something else about George, that Ray couldn't place. Not his eyes, which were whited over like addled frogspawn – his nose. He had a mole on his nose, huger, redder and hairier than that of E. J. Bullen, but in the same place, and surely, the same nose?

It couldn't be. But even as he thought this, Ray realised that, technically, it could. He squeezed a picture out of his memory: it was the old man slumped in the back of the Morris Oxford. He was, on inspection, considerably younger than Ray had understood before – possibly only seventy – comparatively youthful, vigorous in his illness, sane in his desire to escape. Ray looked again at the old teabag in the wheelchair and felt a sudden panic. With an effort he checked himself, turned his gaze with instant fake interest on the plaster coving and thought of the word 'paranoid', a sure-fire measure, as it was one of his words of last resort when arguing with Marnie. All her anecdotes were like this: man marries estranged twin sister, lost fortune found in carpet slippers. It was part of the compact between them: she sniffed out natural ironies and coincidences, and he refused to be amazed by them.

Dying man survives for quarter of a century.

Without looking again at George, Ray wondered fleetingly if there was anything he ought to do. Even if – no, he meant even *though* it wasn't the same old man, they could perhaps slip him a bottle of aspirin next time. Except he was too old to know what to do with aspirin: he was past it. How come decaying people could always wrong-foot you, either with their dependency or with their cackling know-it-all or forget-it-all derisiveness? It was useless to consider anything other than their immediate needs – which is what the nurses knew – they were beyond being social. With most of their senses disconnected, sight, touch, mind going; lights off, roof damaged, draughts from all the windows – you didn't move in next door to such people while you still had the choice. Perhaps E. J. Bullen had realised something like that as he stared at the bland magnolia walls of his hospital room.

Ray was glad when the road turned southward and the clock tower finally disappeared from his rear-view mirror. Marnie was relating how the medicine-flicking woman at The Towers had started telling Lily that her husband, dead of course, was waiting for her outside in the car, and that Lily had called her a pathetic old creature.

'I thought you weren't listening,' she said. 'It's not really very funny though, is it? It could happen to Lily herself any time now. She'll be wearing that same cardigan, and the same shoes, but one of these days she'll have quite gone.' Marnie pushed her hair away from her face and said what she usually said at this point on the way back – 'Just make sure you put a shot through my head before I get like that, won't you, love?'

And Ray as usual said, 'Will do.'

✌ *Passed*

CHARLOTTE MEW

Like souls that meeting pass,
And passing never meet again

Let those who have missed a romantic view of
London in its poorest quarters – and there will romance be found –
wait for a sunset in early winter. They may turn north or south,
towards Islington or Westminster, and encounter some fine pictures
and more than one aspect of unique beauty. This hour of pink
twilight has its monopoly of effects. Some of them may never be
reached again.

On such an evening in mid-December, I put down my sewing
and left tame glories of firelight (discoverers of false charm) to
welcome, as youth may, the contrast of keen air outdoors to the
glow within.

My aim was the perfection of a latent appetite, for I had no mind
to content myself with an apology for hunger, consequent on a
warmly passive afternoon.

The splendid cold of fierce frost set my spirit dancing. The road
rung hard underfoot, and through the lonely squares woke sharp
echoes from behind. This stinging air assailed my cheeks with
vigorous severity. It stirred my blood grandly, and brought thought

back to me from the warm embers just forsaken, with an immeasurable sense of gain.

But after the first delirium of enchanting motion, destination became a question. The dim trees behind the dingy enclosures were beginning to be succeeded by rows of flaring gas jets, displaying shops of new aspect and evil smell. Then the heavy walls of a partially demolished prison reared themselves darkly against the pale sky.

By this landmark I recalled – alas that it should be possible – a church in the district, newly built by an infallible architect, which I had been directed to seek at leisure. I did so now. A row of cramped houses, with the unpardonable bow window, projecting squalor into prominence, came into view. Robbing these even of light, the portentous walls stood a silent curse before them. I think they were blasting the hopes of the sad dwellers beneath them – if hope they had – to despair. Through spattered panes faces of diseased and dirty children leered into the street. One room, as I passed, seemed full of them. The window was open; their wails and maddening requirements sent out the mother's cry. It was thrown back to her, mingled with her children's screams, from the pitiless prison walls.

These shelters struck my thoughts as travesties – perhaps they were not – of the grand place called home.

Leaving them I sought the essential of which they were bereft. What withheld from them, as poverty and sin could not, a title to the sacred name?

An answer came, but interpretation was delayed. Theirs was not the desolation of something lost, but of something that had never been. I thrust off speculation gladly here, and fronted Nature free.

Suddenly I emerged from the intolerable shadow of the brickwork, breathing easily once more. Before me lay a roomy space, nearly square, bounded by three-storey dwellings, and transformed, as if by quick mechanism, with colours of sunset. Red and golden spots wavered in the panes of the low scattered houses round the bewildering expanse. Overhead a faint crimson sky was hung with violet clouds, obscured by the smoke and nearing dusk.

In the centre, but towards the left, stood an old stone pump, and some few feet above it irregular lamps looked down. They were planted on a square of paving railed in by broken iron fences, whose paint, now discoloured, had once been white. Narrow streets cut in five directions from the open roadway. Their lines of light sank dimly into distance, mocking the stars' entrance into the fading sky. Everything was transfigured in the illuminated twilight. As I stood, the dying sun caught the rough edges of a girl's uncovered hair, and hung a faint nimbus round her poor desecrated face. The soft circle, as she glanced toward me, lent it the semblance of one of those mystically pictured faces of some medieval saint.

A stillness stole on, and about the square dim figures hurried along, leaving me stationary in existence (I was thinking fancifully), when my medieval saint demanded 'who I was a-shoving of?' and dismissed me, not unkindly, on my way. Hawkers in a neighbouring alley were calling, and the monotonous 'ting-ting' of the muffin-bell made an audible background to the picture. I left it, and then the glamour was already passing. In a little while, darkness possessing it, the place would reassume its aspect of sordid gloom.

There is a street not far from there, bearing a name that quickens life within one, by the vision it summons of a most peaceful country, where the broad roads are but pathways through green meadows, and your footstep keeps the time to a gentle music of pure streams. There the scent of roses, and the first pushing buds of spring, mark the seasons, and the birds call out faithfully the time and manner of the day. Here Easter is heralded by the advent in some squalid mart of air-balls on Good Friday; early summer and late may be known by observation of that unromantic yet authentic calendar in which alley-tors, tip-cat, whip- and peg-tops, hoops and suckers, in their courses mark the flight of time.

Perhaps attracted by the incongruity, I took this way. In such a thoroughfare it is remarkable that satisfied as are its public with transient substitutes for literature, they require permanent types (the term is so far misused it may hardly be further outraged) of Art. Pictures, so-called, are the sole departure from necessity and popular finery which the prominent wares display. The window exhibiting these aspirations was scarcely more inviting than the fishmonger's next door, but less odoriferous, and I stopped to see what the ill-reflecting lights would show. There was a typical selection. Prominently, a large chromo of a girl at prayer. Her eyes turned upwards, presumably to heaven, left the gazer in no state to dwell on the elaborately bared breasts below. These might rival, does waxwork attempt such beauties, any similar attraction of Marylebone's extensive show. This personification of pseudo-purity was sensually diverting, and consequently marketable.

My mind seized the ideal of such a picture, and turned from this prostitution of it sickly away. Hurriedly I proceeded, and did not stop again until I had passed the low gateway of the place I sought.

Its forbidding exterior was hidden in the deep twilight and invited no consideration. I entered and swung back the inner door. It was papered with memorial cards, recommending to mercy the unprotesting spirits of the dead. My prayers were requested for the 'repose of the soul of the Architect of that church, who passed away in the True Faith – December – 1887.' Accepting the assertion, I counted him beyond them, and mentally entrusted mine to the priest for those who were still groping for it in the gloom.

Within the building, darkness again forbade examination. A few lamps hanging before the altar struggled with obscurity.

I tried to identify some ugly details with the great man's complacent eccentricity, and failing, turned toward the street again. Nearly an hour's walk lay between me and my home. This fact and the atmosphere of stuffy sanctity about the place, set me longing for space again, and woke a fine scorn for aught but air and sky. My appetite, too, was now an hour ahead of opportunity. I sent back a final glance into the darkness as my hand prepared to strike the door. There was no motion at the moment, and it was silent; but the magnetism of human presence reached me where I stood. I hesitated, and in a few moments found what sought me on a chair in the far corner, flung face downwards across the seat. The attitude arrested me. I went forward. The lines of the figure spoke unquestionable despair.

Does speech convey intensity of anguish? Its supreme expression is in form. Here was human agony set forth in meagre lines, voiceless, but articulate to the soul. At first the forcible portrayal of it assailed me with the importunate strength of beauty. Then the Thing stretched there in the obdurate darkness grew personal and banished delight. Neither sympathy nor its vulgar substitute, curiosity, induced my action as I drew near. I was eager indeed to be gone. I wanted to ignore the almost indistinguishable being. My will cried: Forsake it! – but I found myself powerless to obey. Perhaps it would have conquered had not the girl swiftly raised herself in quest of me. I stood still. Her eyes met mine. A wildly tossed spirit looked from those ill-lighted windows, beckoning me on. Mine pressed towards it, but whether my limbs actually moved I do not know, for the imperious summons robbed me of any consciousness save that of necessity to comply.

Did she reach me, or was our advance mutual? It cannot be told. I suppose we neither know. But we met, and her hand, grasping mine, imperatively dragged me into the cold and noisy street.

We went rapidly in and out of the flaring booths, hustling little staggering children in our unpitying speed, I listening dreamily to the concert of hoarse yells and haggling whines which struck against the silence of our flight. On and on she took me, breathless and without explanation. We said nothing. I had no care or impulse to ask our goal. The fierce pressure of my hand was not relaxed a breathing space; it would have borne me against resistance could I have offered any, but I was capable of none. The streets seemed to rush past us, peopled with despair.

Weirdly lighted faces sent blank negations to a spirit of question which finally began to stir in me. Here, I thought once vaguely, was the everlasting No!

We must have journeyed thus for more than half an hour and walked far. I did not detect it. In the eternity of supreme moments time is not. Thought, too, fears to be obtrusive and stands aside.

We gained a door at last, down some blind alley out of the deafening thoroughfare. She threw herself against it and pulled me up the unlighted stairs. They shook now and then with the violence of our ascent; with my free hand I tried to help myself up by the broad and greasy balustrade. There was little sound in the house. A light shone under the first door we passed, but all was quietness within.

At the very top, from the dense blackness of the passage, my guide thrust me suddenly into a dazzling room. My eyes rejected its array of brilliant light. On a small chest of drawers three candles were guttering, two more stood flaring in the high window ledge, and a lamp upon a table by the bed rendered these minor illuminations unnecessary by its diffusive glare. There were even some small Christmas candles dropping coloured grease down the wooden mantelpiece, and I noticed a fire had been made, built entirely of wood. There were bits of an inlaid workbox or desk, and a chair-rung, lying half burnt in the grate. Some peremptory demand for light had been, these signs denoted, unscrupulously met. A woman lay upon the bed, half clothed, asleep. As the door slammed behind me the flames wavered and my companion released my hand. She stood beside me, shuddering violently, but without utterance.

I looked around. Everywhere proofs of recent energy were visible. The bright panes reflecting back the low burnt candles, the wretched but shining furniture, and some odd bits of painted china, set before the sputtering lights upon the drawers, bore witness to a provincial intolerance of grime. The boards were bare, and marks of extreme poverty distinguished the whole room. The destitution of her surroundings accorded ill with the girl's spotless person and well-tended hands, which were hanging tremulously down.

Subsequently I realised that these deserted beings must have first fronted the world from a sumptuous stage. The details in proof of it I need not cite. It must have been so.

My previous apathy gave place to an exaggerated observation. Even some pieces of a torn letter, dropped off the quilt, I noticed, were of fine texture, and inscribed by a man's hand. One fragment bore an elaborate device in colours. It may have been a club crest or coat-of-arms. I was trying to decide which, when the girl at length gave a cry of exhaustion or relief, at the same time falling into a similar attitude to that she had taken in the dim church. Her entire frame became shaken with tearless agony or terror. It was sickening to watch. She began partly to call or moan, begging me, since I was beside her, wildly, and then with heartbreaking weariness, 'to stop, to stay'. She half rose and claimed me with distracted grace. All her movements were noticeably fine.

I pass no judgement on her features; suffering for the time assumed them, and they made no insistence of individual claim.

I tried to raise her, and kneeling, pulled her reluctantly towards me. The proximity was distasteful. An alien presence has ever repelled me. I should have pitied the girl keenly perhaps a few more feet away. She clung to me with ebbing force. Her heart throbbed painfully close to mine, and when I meet now in the dark streets others who have been robbed, as she had been, of their great possession, I have to remember that.

The magnetism of our meeting was already passing; and, reason asserting itself, I reviewed the incident dispassionately, as she lay like a broken piece of mechanism in my arms. Her dark hair had come unfastened and fell about my shoulder. A faint white streak of it stole through the brown. A gleam of moonlight strays thus through a dusky room. I remember noticing, as it was swept with her involuntary motions across my face, a faint fragrance which kept recurring like a subtle and seductive sprite, hiding itself with fairy cunning in the tangled maze.

The poor girl's mind was clearly travelling a devious way. Broken and incoherent exclamations told of a recently wrung promise, made to whom, or of what nature, it was not my business to conjecture or inquire.

I record the passage of a few minutes. At the first opportunity I sought the slumberer on the bed. She slept well: hers was a long rest; there might be no awakening from it, for she was dead. Schooled in one short hour to all surprises, the knowledge made me simply richer by a fact. Nothing about the sternly set face invited horror. It had been, and was yet, a strong and, if beauty be not confined to youth and colour, a beautiful face.

Perhaps this quiet sharer of the convulsively broken silence was thirty years old. Death had set a firmness about the finely controlled features that might have shown her younger. The actual years are of little matter; existence, as we reckon time, must have lasted long. It was not death, but life that had planted the look of disillusion there. And romance being over, all goodbyes to youth are said. By the bedside, on a roughly constructed table, was a dearly bought bunch of violets. They were set in a blue bordered teacup, and hung over in wistful challenge of their own diviner hue. They were foreign, and their scent probably unnatural, but it stole very sweetly round the room. A book lay face downwards beside them – alas for parochial energies, not of a religious type – and the torn fragments of the destroyed letter had fallen on the black binding.

A passionate movement of the girl's breast against mine directed my glance elsewhere. She was shivering, and her arms about my neck were stiffly cold. The possibility that she was starving missed my mind. It would have found my heart. I wondered if she slept, and dared not stir, though I was by this time cramped and chilled. The vehemence of her agitation ended, she breathed gently, and slipped finally to the floor.

I began to face the need of action and recalled the chances of the night. When and how I might get home was a necessary question, and I listened vainly for a friendly step outside. None since we left it had climbed the last flight of stairs. I could hear a momentary vibration of men's voices in the room below. Was it possible to leave these suddenly discovered children of peace and tumult? Was it possible to stay?

This was Saturday, and two days later I was bound for Scotland; a practical recollection of empty trunks was not lost in my survey of the situation. Then how, if I decided not to forsake the poor child, now certainly sleeping in my arms, were my anxious friends to learn my whereabouts, and understand the eccentricity of the scheme? Indisputably, I determined, something must be done for the half-frantic wanderer who was pressing a tiring weight against me. And there should be some kind hand to cover the cold limbs and close the wide eyes of the breathless sleeper, waiting a comrade's sanction to fitting rest.

Conclusion was hastening to impatient thought, when my eyes let fall a fatal glance upon the dead girl's face. I do not think it had changed its first aspect of dignified repose, and yet now it woke in me a sensation of cold dread. The dark eyes unwillingly open reached mine in an insistent stare. One hand lying out upon the coverlid, I could never again mistake for that of temporarily suspended life. My watch ticked loudly, but I dared not examine it, nor could I wrench my sight from the figure on the bed. For the first time the empty shell of being assailed my senses. I watched feverishly, knowing well the madness of the action, for a hint of breathing, almost stopping my own.

Today, as memory summons it, I cannot dwell without reluctance on this hour of my realisation of the thing called Death.

A hundred fancies, clothed in mad intolerable terrors, possessed me, and had not my lips refused it outlet, I should have set free a cry, as the spent child beside me had doubtless longed to do, and failed, ere, desperate, she fled.

My gaze was chained; it could not get free. As the shapes of monsters of ever-varying and increasing dreadfulness flit through one's dreams, the images of those I loved crept round me, with stark yet well-known features, their limbs borrowing death's rigid outline, as they mocked my recognition of them with soundless semblances of mirth. They began to wind their arms about me in fierce embraces of burning and supernatural life. Gradually the contact froze. They bound me in an icy prison. Their hold relaxed. These creatures of my heart were restless. The horribly familiar company began to dance at intervals in and out of a ring of white gigantic bedsteads, set on end like tombstones, each of which framed a huge and fearful travesty of the sad set face that was all the while seeking vainly a pitiless stranger's care. They vanished. My heart went home. The dear place was desolate. No echo of its many voices on the threshold or stair. My footsteps made no sound as I went rapidly up to a well-known room. Here I besought the mirror for the reassurance of my own reflection. It denied me human portraiture and threw back cold glare. As I opened mechanically a treasured book, I noticed the leaves were blank, not even blurred by spot or line; and then I shivered – it was deadly cold. The fire that but an hour or two ago it seemed I had forsaken for the winter twilight, glowed with slow derision at my efforts to rekindle heat. My hands plunged savagely into its red embers, but I drew them out quickly, unscathed and clean. The things by which I had touched life were nothing. Here, as I called the dearest names, their echoes came back again with the sound of an unlearned language. I did not recognise, and yet I framed them. What was had never been!

My spirit summoned the being who claimed mine. He came, stretching out arms of deathless welcome. As he reached me my heart took flight. I called aloud to it, but my cries were lost in awful laughter that broke to my bewildered fancy from the hideously familiar shapes which had returned and now encircled the grand form of him I loved. But I had never known him. I beat my breast to wake there the wonted pain of tingling joy. I called past experience with unavailing importunity to bear witness the man was wildly dear to me. He was not. He left me with bent head a stranger, whom I would not if I could recall.

For one brief second, reason found me. I struggled to shake off the phantoms of despair. I tried to grasp while it yet lingered the teaching of this never-to-be-forgotten front of death. The homeless house with its indefensible bow window stood out from beneath the prison walls again. What had this to do with it? I questioned. And the answer it had evoked replied, 'Not the desolation of something lost, but of something that had never been.'

The half-clad girl of the wretched picture-shop came into view with waxen hands and senseless symbolism. I had grown calmer, but her doll-like lips hissed out the same half-meaningless but pregnant words. Then the nights of a short life when I could pray, years back in magical childhood, sought me. They found me past them – without the power.

Truly the body had been for me the manifestation of the thing called soul. Here was my embodiment bereft. My face was stiff with drying tears. Sickly I longed to beg of an unknown God a miracle. Would He but touch the passive body and breathe into it the breath even of transitory life.

I craved but a fleeting proof of its ever possible existence. For to me it was not, would never be, and had never been.

The partially relinquished horror was renewing dominance. Speech of any incoherence or futility would have brought mental power of resistance. My mind was fast losing landmarks amid the continued quiet of the living and the awful stillness of the dead. There was no sound, even of savage guidance, I should not then have welcomed with glad response.

'The realm of Silence,' says one of the world's great teachers, 'is large enough beyond the grave.'

I seemed to have passed life's portal, and my soul's small strength was beating back the noiseless gate. In my extremity, I cried, 'Oh God! for man's most bloody war shout, or Thy whisper!' It was useless. Not one dweller in the crowded tenements broke his slumber or relaxed his labour in answer to the involuntary prayer.

And may the 'Day of Account of Words' take note of this! Then, says the old fable, shall the soul of the departed be weighed against an image of Truth. I tried to construct in imagination the form of the dumb deity who should bear down the balances for me. Soundlessness was turning fear to madness. I could neither quit nor longer bear company the grim Presence in that room. But the supreme moment was very near.

Long since, the four low candles had burned out, and now the lamp was struggling fitfully to keep alight. The flame could last but a few moments. I saw it, and did not face the possibility of darkness. The sleeping girl, I concluded rapidly, had used all available weapons of defiant light.

As yet, since my entrance, I had hardly stirred, steadily supporting the burden on my breast. Now, without remembrance of it, I started up to escape. The violent suddenness of the action woke my companion. She staggered blindly to her feet and confronted me as I gained the door.

Scarcely able to stand, and dashing the dimness from her eyes, she clutched a corner of the drawers behind her for support. Her head thrown back, and her dark hair hanging round it, crowned a grandly tragic form. This was no poor pleader, and I was unarmed for fight. She seized my throbbing arm and cried in a whisper, low and hoarse, but strongly audible: 'For God's sake, stay here with me.'

My lips moved vainly. I shook my head.

'For God in heaven's sake' – she repeated, swaying, and turning her burning, reddened eyes on mine – 'don't leave me now.'

I stood irresolute, half stunned. Stepping back, she stooped and began piecing together the dismembered letter on the bed. A mute protest arrested her from a cold sister's face. She swept the action from her, crying, 'No!' and bending forward suddenly, gripped me with fierce force.

'Here! Here!' she prayed, dragging me passionately back into the room.

The piteous need and wild entreaty – no, the vision of dire anguish – was breaking my purpose of flight. A fragrance that was to haunt me stole between us. The poor little violets put in their plea. I moved to stay. Then a smile – the splendour of it may never be reached again – touched her pale lips and broke through them, transforming, with divine radiance, her young and blurred and never-to-be-forgotten face. It wavered, or was it the last uncertain flicker of the lamp that made me fancy it? The exquisite moment was barely over when darkness came. Then light indeed forsook me. Almost ignorant of my own intention, I resisted the now trembling figure, indistinguishable in the gloom, but it still clung. I thrust it off me with unnatural vigour.

She fell heavily to the ground. Without a pause of thought I stumbled down the horrible unlighted stairs. A few steps before I reached the bottom my foot struck a splint off the thin edge of one of the rotten treads. I slipped, and heard a door above open and then shut. No other sound. At length I was at the door. It was ajar. I opened it and looked out. Since I passed through it first the place had become quite deserted. The inhabitants were, I suppose, all occupied elsewhere at such an hour on their holiday night. The lamps, if there were any, had not been lit. The outlook was dense blackness. Here too the hideous dark pursued me and silence held its sway. Even the children were screaming in more enticing haunts of gaudy squalor. Some, whose good angels perhaps had not forgotten them, had put themselves to sleep. Not many hours ago their shrieks were deafening. Were these too in conspiracy against me? I remembered vaguely hustling some of them with unmeant harshness in my hurried progress from the church. Dumb the whole place seemed; and it was, but for the dim stars aloft, quite dark. I dared not venture across the threshold, bound by pitiable cowardice to the spot. Alas for the unconscious girl upstairs. A murmur from within the house might have sent me back to her. Certainly it would have sent me, rather than forth into the empty street. The faintest indication of humanity had recalled me. I waited the summons of a sound. It came.

But from the deserted, yet not so shamefully deserted, street. A man staggering home by aid of friendly railings set up a drunken song. At the first note I rushed towards him, pushing past him in wild departure, and on till I reached the noisome and flaring thoroughfare, a haven where sweet safety smiled. Here I breathed joy, and sped away without memory of the two lifeless beings lying alone in that shrouded chamber of desolation, and with no instinct to return.

My sole impulse was flight; and the way, unmarked in the earlier evening, was unknown. It took me some minutes to find a cab; but the incongruous vehicle, rudely dispersing the haggling traders in the roadway, came at last, and carried me from the distorted crowd of faces and the claims of pity to peace.

I lay back shivering, and the wind crept through the rattling glass in front of me. I did not note the incalculable turnings that took me home.

My account of the night's adventure was abridged and unsensational. I was pressed neither for detail nor comment, but accorded a somewhat humorous welcome which bade me say farewell to dying horror, and even let me mount boldly to the once death-haunted room.

Upon its threshold I stood and looked in, half believing possible the greeting pictured there under the dead girl's influence, and I could not enter. Again I fled, this time to kindly light, and heard my brothers laughing noisily with a friend in the bright hall.

A waltz struck up in the room above as I reached them. I joined the impromptu dance, and whirled the remainder of that evening gladly away.

Physically wearied, I slept. My slumber had no break in it. I woke only to the exquisite joys of morning, and lay watching the early shadows creep into the room. Presently the sun rose. His first smile greeted me from the glass before my bed. I sprang up disdainful of that majestic reflection, and flung the window wide to meet him face to face. His splendour fell too on one who had trusted me, but I forgot it. Not many days later the same sunlight that turned my life to laughter shone on the saddest scene of mortal ending, and, for one I had forsaken, lit the ways of death. I never dreamed it might. For the next morning the tragedy of the past night was a distant one, no longer intolerable.

At twelve o'clock, conscience suggested a search. I acquiesced, but did not move. At half past, it insisted on one, and I obeyed. I set forth with a determination of success and no clue to promise it. At four o'clock, I admitted the task hopeless and abandoned it. Duty could ask no more of me, I decided, not wholly dissatisfied that failure forbade more difficult demands. As I passed it on my way home, some dramatic instinct impelled me to re-enter the unsightly church.

I must almost have expected to see the same prostrate figure, for my eyes instantly sought the corner it had occupied. The winter twilight showed it empty. A service was about to begin. One little lad in violet skirt and goffered linen was struggling to light the benediction tapers, and a troop of school children pushed past me as I stood facing the altar and blocking their way. A grey-clad sister of mercy was arresting each tiny figure, bidding it pause beside me, and with two firm hands on either shoulder, compelling a ludicrous curtsey, and at the same time whispering the injunction to each hurried little personage – 'always make a reverence to the altar.'

'Ada, come back!' and behold another unwilling bob! Perhaps the good woman saw her Master's face behind the tinsel trappings and flaring lights. But she forgot His words. The saying to these little ones that has rung through centuries commanded liberty and not allegiance. I stood aside till they had shuffled into seats, and finally kneeling stayed till the brief spectacle of the afternoon was over.

Towards its close I looked away from the mumbling priest, whose attention, divided between inconvenient millinery and the holiest mysteries, was distracting mine.

Two girls holding each other's hands came in and stood in deep shadow behind the farthest rows of high-backed chairs by the door. The younger rolled her head from side to side; her shifting eyes and ceaseless imbecile grimaces chilled my blood. The other, who stood praying, turned suddenly (the place but for the flaring altar lights was dark) and kissed the dreadful creature by her side. I shuddered, and yet her face wore no look of loathing nor of pity. The expression was a divine one of habitual love.

She wiped the idiot's lips and stroked the shaking hand in hers, to quiet the sad hysterical caresses she would not check. It was a page of gospel which the old man with his back to it might never read. A sublime and ghastly scene.

Up in the little gallery the grey-habited nuns were singing a long Latin hymn of many verses, with the refrain 'Oh! Sacred Heart!' I buried my face till the last vibrating chord of the accompaniment was struck. The organist ventured a plagal cadence. It evoked no 'Amen'. I whispered one, and an accidentally touched note shrieked disapproval. I repeated it. Then I spit upon the bloodless cheek of duty, and renewed my quest. This time it was for the satisfaction of my own tingling soul.

I retook my unknown way. The streets were almost empty and thinly strewn with snow. It was still falling. I shrank from marring the spotless page that seemed outspread to challenge and exhibit the defiling print of man. The quiet of the muffled streets soothed me. The neighbourhood seemed lulled into unwonted rest.

Black little figures lurched out of the white alleys in twos and threes. But their childish utterances sounded less shrill than usual, and sooner died away.

Now in desperate earnest I spared neither myself nor the incredulous and dishevelled people whose aid I sought.

Fate deals honestly with all. She will not compromise though she may delay. Hunger and weariness at length sent me home, with an assortment of embellished negatives ringing in my failing ears.

I had almost forgotten my strange experience, when, some months afterwards, in late spring, the wraith of that winter meeting appeared to me. It was past six o'clock, and I had reached, ignorant of the ill-chosen hour, a notorious thoroughfare in the western part of this glorious and guilty city. The place presented to my unfamiliar eyes a remarkable sight. Brilliantly lit windows, exhibiting dazzling wares, threw into prominence the human mart.

This was thronged. I pressed into the crowd. Its steady and opposite progress neither repelled nor sanctioned my admittance. However, I had determined on a purchase, and was not to be baulked by the unforeseen. I made it, and stood for a moment at the shop door preparing to break again through the rapidly thickening throng.

Up and down, decked in frigid allurement, paced the insatiate daughters of an everlasting king. What fair messengers, with streaming eyes and impotently craving arms, did they send afar off ere they thus 'increased their perfumes and debased themselves even unto hell'? This was my question. I asked not who forsook them, speaking in farewell the 'hideous English of their fate'.

I watched coldly, yet not inapprehensive of a certain grandeur in the scene. It was Virtue's very splendid Dance of Death.

A sickening confusion of odours assailed my senses; each essence a vile enticement, outraging Nature by a perversion of her own pure spell.

A timidly protesting fragrance stole strangely by. I started at its approach. It summoned a stinging memory. I stepped forward to escape it, but stopped, confronted by the being who had shared, by the flickering lamplight and in the presence of that silent witness, the poor little violet's prayer.

The man beside her was decorated with a bunch of sister flowers to those which had taken part against him, months ago, in vain. He could have borne no better badge of victory. He was looking at some extravagant trifle in the window next the entry I had just crossed. They spoke, comparing it with a silver case he turned over in his hand. In the centre I noticed a tiny enamelled shield. The detail seemed familiar, but beyond identity. They entered the shop. I stood motionless, challenging memory, till it produced from some dim corner of my brain a hoarded 'No'.

The device now headed a poor strip of paper on a dead girl's bed. I saw a figure set by death, facing starvation, and with ruin in torn fragments in her hand. But what place in the scene had I? A brief discussion next me made swift answer.

They were once more beside me. The man was speaking: his companion raised her face; I recognised its outline, its true aspect I shall not know. Four months since it wore the mask of sorrow; it was now but one of the pages of man's immortal book. I was conscious of the matchless motions which in the dim church had first attracted me.

She was clothed, save for a large scarf of vehemently brilliant crimson, entirely in dull vermilion. The two shades might serve as symbols of divine and earthly passion. Yet does one ask the martyr's colour, you name it 'Red' (and briefly thus her garment): no distinctive hue. The murderer and the prelate too may wear such robes of office. Both are empowered to bless and ban.

My mood was reckless. I held my hands out, craving mercy. It was my bitter lot to beg. My warring nature became unanimously suppliant, heedless of the debt this soul might owe me – of the throes to which I left it, and of the discreditable marks of mine it bore. Failure to exact regard I did not entertain. I waited, with exhaustless fortitude, the response to my appeal. Whence it came I know not. The man and woman met my gaze with a void incorporate stare. The two faces were merged into one avenging visage – so it seemed. I was excited. As they turned towards the carriage waiting them, I heard a laugh, mounting to a cry. It rang me to an outraged Temple. Sabbath bells peal sweeter calls, as once this might have done.

I knew my part then in the despoiled body, with its soul's tapers long blown out.

Wheels hastened to assail that sound, but it clanged on. Did it proceed from some defeated angel? or the woman's mouth? or mine? God knows!

☙ *The Coming of Sound*

MOY MCCRORY

Would the job applicants please line up?

The thing to remember is that none of you will make any real difference. Your role, if you are chosen, is one of activating. You will simply set into motion that which has already been determined. Any one of you might do equally well for the job.

Bearing that in mind, those interested parties will shortly be asked to race each other and the top performers will be considered on a first come, first served basis.

Considered. I choose my words carefully. Remember there is no guarantee. It may be the second, or the third who will achieve a result.

Gentlemen, it is a competitive business. If you find it distasteful you shouldn't have applied.

Now, without further ado, it just remains for me to wish you good luck and may the best one . . .

STARTS QUIETLY. Starts in the 1950s. This is the memory forming, starting here. This spot. Without this spot nothing follows. A sperm just this size, here. By accident.

*

What do you call this then?
Voice.
Which is?
Built of many parts.
And?
Expresses a chain of thoughts.
How?
Through sounds: noises/ squeals/ grunts/ taking shape into . . .
Word?
Sound is meaningless until it takes shape and becomes . . .
Word?

Please stop interrupting. If you would listen for a moment you might learn something. Being eager is no guarantee of success. Gentlemen, I would ask you to remember where you are. There is no need to push.

STARTS NOISILY. Starts with the wail of life; unformed the dark cry tumbles into day. Light gives it reason. Out of that pure noise, words are tongued into being. Given meaning, shaped into a sentence.

Hold on a minute. You're going too fast. I wonder if you could explain . . .
What?
Where we are? Because you've lost me.
Where did I lose you?
Before the word. Before the second start. You lost me in the silent section. I'm afraid I was quite confused. And then there was all that shouting.
Memory? Did I lose you there?
I've forgotten.

*

Are you really sure you want to continue in this? There are plenty of others, only too glad to take up a cause, to be given the chance, without your difficulties. There are others who wouldn't even need to ask, wouldn't care, and they might do the job just as well as . . .

No. I really want to learn.
Then stop interrupting and listen.

STARTS DIFFERENTLY. He thinks it begins with the essence, the drop, the spurt, his death to produce that handful. She thinks it begins with that seed, that fleck, that time.

And new life takes shape before they are even aware of it.

So they count time, what they understand as time, which is only its progression, as a sort of ageing. They mark it from the first minute of birth.

They recognise some uncounted time spent growing in silence in this dark ship, but they can't understand back time, forward time and no time, all happening together. That's your advantage. That's how you know it began long before. The impression was in the seed, in the sperm long before.

She will be conceived in a great bed, made heavy with her mother's fear. And although she can't know that, it won't be any less true. Later when she sees the bed – in the middle of that damp room – she comes upon it like an old friend, no, not a friend, because it is unwelcoming, but she knows it already and won't remember a time when it had not stood just as it did then.

And there was the spot, the start, the essence, in that spurt, his death to produce that handful. Which was too many. But from that handful would be only one. One which rushes up fastest, races, charges, screams, and meets this half. Your contribution to this thought.

*

It started like this: in the 1950s along the west coast of America, babies were conceived in the backs of cars. It was Kienholz who created the image, after the phrase, the Buick convertible, said to be THE ONE. Dusty now in a museum of modern art.

She definitely sees the image. She will be a collector of postcards. Have this pinned up. It grips her, she won't know why.

Definitely a she then?

'Fraid so. Does that bother you?

No. I can live with it.

If her origins had been there, along that coast in the steaming teenage rows, things would be different. If she had been conceived in such a way this would be a different story and she would be a cheerleader not a handmaid of the Blessed Sacrament.

But she isn't to be?

Her father was a notoriously bad sea-traveller who got off the first time the boat docked.

Lucky they weren't all Manx. What could she make of that?

Indeed.

Her father kissed English soil because it didn't move. So her conception takes place in a northern town, smelling of mildew, in a solid upright bed bought from the Salvation Army.

Listen. Occasionally you can hear a brass band. That sound will always get her in the guts, she's no idea why. She imagines she must like it.

Her mother shut her eyes and, being unable to think of England in any favourable light, switched to duty.

So it's all by accident? Are you sure? It's not how I imagined it at all. I thought there was some design, some great controlling plan. There must be?

Sorry.

*

Are you sure you are still interested? Do you want to be considered? I must say you have gone quite pale. Quite.

No. Please continue.

They meet, embed, sink down and as one, wait for the germination to shake something into being. They fuse, heat, split and fuse endlessly.

Do you think you could manage that?

Please. I'd like to hear the rest, before I make up my . . .

Haphazard. Rapid. And along the outline little indentations of memory, pressed along the edge long before there is any sound, the fuzzy edges of memory are shaping inside to allow the first cry, the shout at the end of a long incubation spent in silence, while outside the waiting words are lapping like waves.

What chance do I get to, you know, put my mark on to . . .

Her? Sure you're not disappointed with that?

No. Really . . .

Because, if you're not happy with that you can always move out of the way, let another come through.

No really. I'm happy, I just want to make sure . . .

What?

That I can achieve something, leave my mark.

Well you can't.

Didn't you read the job description? Didn't you study it? Set into motion, that's what's required of you. Now do you think you could achieve this?

*

Yes. But I'd like to study all the options.

There aren't any. By the time she emerges, rushing and screaming into life she is writ in full. Some decide it's not worth the bother, stay put. But you have to face up to the fact that this is your only chance. Think. You can make the best of, make the most of, make the worst of, that's the choice. That's the challenge. Listen to the heartbeat of the great carrying mother. It surrounds. Wraps. Protects. Loves.

You have to go out there to know about any of that. But if you won't there are plenty more who will. You see, she will still be born, despite you. I carry the impression of her history, embedded in a thumbprint, in the sworl of a hair. I know her already.

When there is too much to fit inside she will push down hard and be pulled out along a slippery wall of muscle and hair (shaved, remember it is the 1950s) in a prickly rush and it is cold inside her chest, right down inside her centre as the cord darkens and lets her go.

There is a name already selected. This crashes against her unworn skin. A dead name pulling a memory behind it, a dead weight. Already it worms into her new skull, like a maggot on a corpse.

The father, a tall one, appears at a window. You can see him, can't you. He has wet eyes.

She will be held up in strong hands, displayed.

The tall one watches behind a glass wall. His mouth is moving, noiselessly, like a stupid fish. The poor mother is angry with him. After what she's been through. All he had to do was send that spot, this spot now, tumbling towards her. If you listen you can hear her: 'Jesus, men don't know the half of it.'

And the nurse will nod, 'Certainly don't.'

Warm, touched, nursed, held, loved, wanted, wept for.

*

Can I ask a question? Is that all we do it for?

Hate to upset you. That's the perfect moment. Downhill all the way after.

Go on. I want to know.

They shout.

Is that all? Loud noise is nothing.

Fear.

What's that?

A cold something absorbed during those months of incubation.

He shouts. Is silent. Her mother's mind is fevered. But that is not her concern. For a time anyhow, she will be content while people hold things out towards her. They say her name, her name and they hold things. She repeats. A game.

Jay-ay-sus.

Relief is letting breath out.

They will watch his back each morning as he leaves for work.

And she will continue to grow. Her memory is longer than it ought to be.

The thing she remembers is seeing a man in a long mac creeping towards their home.

Every Friday he comes to write in tiny, but spectacular copperplate the weekly contributions responsible fathers make towards burial policies and artificial teeth.

He is soundless. Turns up like a shadow. Is kept standing outside front doors, occasionally allowed inside on wettest days when he leaves dark puddles behind.

Two shillings and sixpence. As a child she will watch the impeccable writing appear from his pen with a flourish, like magic letters.

No one talks. A sober business, this weekly account of mortality and he is a reminder of decay, the journey back to dust, with teeth alone remaining in the earth to grin obscenely from the soil and have the last laugh. She can't remember if the club man laughed.

After he'd gone they would open the windows, shift the curtains to let more light in. 'At least we'll all be in the same grave, along with your grandmother.' A dread of letting the policy lapse. The disgrace of the pauper's funeral.

She listens to tales of drunken fathers.

Whose fathers? Who will tell her?

Memory and morality tales: the man who cashed in the lot and went on a bender. Found dead within a fortnight. She hears of burials without marker or headstone, tales of collective graves where the dead rub shoulders. A voice says, 'Imagine, with all class of person'; and her mother pays her weekly two-and-six to keep five bodies in a tight family group.

She will listen hardest to those stories about the collective dead, those where the dead broke out of the family bond and went to lie among strangers and she will hear corpses whispering, telling their histories.

It is the chattering dead who will continue to fill this child with tales. While the living call her morbid, say it is an unhealthy trend. But she ignores them or simply listens to their teeth clacking, as if in there she will hear secrets.

When she is older she will remember how most adults she knew had false teeth. They were a status symbol, a rite of passage. Sensible fathers saved so their daughters could be presented with a brilliant set as a wedding present.

Women embarked on married life with false smiles, smiles which were too perfect, smiles which the corpse-dresser set in their mouths for their funerals.

She will become adept. Know how to recognise a cheap set when she sees them, understands what this means: burial without a headstone.

In her world teeth are useless. They break down, grow lacey with holes, let wind whistle against nerves.

Sweet-eating is serious. Started in childhood and continued through to hard-gummed dotage sucking like a newborn thing.

'All the pleasure I ever got,' a friend's mother tells her. All the pleasure contained in that sweet burst of sugar on the tongue, red, blue, yellow, green lozenges of pure colour, cubes of crystal, pear drops, and everyone's breath was perfumed. All the pleasure, bursting on the tongue.

Anything else is an event, dressed for a day trip. One Saturday she will be taken to see a pineapple.

It turns up in the greengrocer's like an alien life form. Her father sees it on his way back from work.

'Comb your hair and wash your face,' he says.

By the time they arrrive there is a queue filing silently past the grocer's window with as much reverence as the relatives of the waked.

And the pineapple? She sees it, yellow, lumpy. She remembers how it sat there all day. No one dared ask how much it was. No one had a clue how you ate it.

Finally it was bought by the priest's housekeeper who wheeled it back to the presbytery in her shopper, followed by a straggle of children.

For a while after, this pineapple is called Holy Fruit. Only those who were there know what this means. When she talks about it years later her mother will laugh, say, 'You're making it up,' and 'Stop acting the cod.'

And because her father went to the theatre only once she remembers a play the priest recommended because it was about the Irish arriving.

Her father thought it would be an education for them all and so they sat in the dark.

She hears him eating boiled sweets throughout, rustling the cellophane wrappers and crunching with his false teeth. Her mother was an exceptional woman because she had all her own and preferred savouries. While he ate through the first act, heads turned in their direction, people shushed and glared at the girl and her brothers.

She has brothers now?

Always did.

You never said.

She doesn't think about them, until they become necessary to the story. And will you stop interrupting.

People shushed and glared at the girl and her brothers.

'Snobs,' their father remarked in the interval, 'Bloody English.'

Every time an actor cursed on stage her father would stare round wildly and tut. 'God knows,' he said later, 'suppose there was someone who knew him.'

What was the play about?

Well, you'd have her there. All she will remember is that there was a row on the bus going home, and her mother had a coughing fit.

*

Years later, she is an adult and she takes her mother, widowed now, to the theatre. Attempts it several times. But her mother can't get past the first act. A terrific attack always seizes her. She starts choking, has to claw her way to the exit.

She will always find her mother in the interval, being thumped on the back by an usher. When she re-enters the theatre she remains by the exit for safety.

The curtain rising, the hush of expectancy. Something always defeats her mother. She thinks it is the ghostly rustling of his boiled sweets behind their shoulders.

I told you she was morbid. There's plenty of dead here. And previous memories. They're not hers, but they slip in.

That's a habit she has, like pinning up postcards. The Statue of Liberty, the Empire State Building. It's a legacy. They should have gone, things would have been different. Instead they remained and the playgrounds were awash with American comics.

As a small girl she swapped superheroes. Believed in huge men who soared over mountainous columns of window, in a strange country. Her mother said, 'That's where we ought to be.'

She grows up in a house where outside each bedroom there is an empty suitcase. Ready to fly. Any day, any moment.

And all the time her mother was putting things into boxes. They said she should have been an undertaker.

She sorted fabric remnants into neat squares, threaded odd buttons on to snaking rows, secured with a determined knot. She saved brown paper and newsprint.

'What do you want with all that?'

'Come in handy for packing.'

She untied string carefully, rolled it into balls. 'You never know.'

She stacked things away, wrote labels for everything so nothing would get lost. The boxes were stacked, their contents described and stuck down like the brass plates on coffins.

Same as in the larder. She hoarded: corned beef, powdered milk. Wanted to know they'd be all right.

'If rationing's ever re-introduced, we'd do all right,' she used to say. 'We'd survive three months.' Scarcity terrified her, the last slice of bread, the solitary egg.

And a memory of hunger was passed on. Of real hunger, of the living giving birth to the dead, starved in the womb, the mother fails and lets die the random kick-start that in another place would have meant life. And the terrible open cry swallows her. The womb bellows as the baby is brought out, not kicking, but still.

Instead she told her child about the movies. The silents. Talked about the shock of Al Jolson in *Mammy* when he opened his mouth and sound came out.

In the beginning was the word.

Uproar in the cinema. A woman at the front fainted. When she went to the ladies, her ears were ringing.

And the word was sacred. And it was profane. And it could not be voiced.

The silents were the ones. Those ridiculous cards which came up with a sentence were never equal to the words in her head.

She remembered a silent werewolf. On screen he was stalking a victim when a woman in the balcony lost her fox-fur over the edge. She started yelling.

It happened in seconds, the stole falling through the dark, the woman yelling instructions. 'Stop it! Catch it!'

She can see it. The fox-fur plummets through tense audience air, lands on a man's shoulder, slides down to his chest. Glassy eyes reflect light from the screen.

She remembers he was in the row behind her.

The film was stopped. As the houselights went up, the man was escorted out by his shamefaced wife.

The pianist plays 'Land of Hope and Glory'.

The local paper ran a story. 'AUDIENCE PANIC. THE MOST REALISTIC HORROR FILM YET.'

The cinema played it for a month to packed houses.

But the child grows into Sensurround and Panoramascope. Multi-screen complexes come into being. Parents lose children and the elderly will be found wandering in foyers.

Bit like this? The all-envelopingness. Delights and disturbs.

There is nothing more disturbing than the coming of sound. As soon as they talk they will argue. Her mother becomes angry with her, all the time, for anything. Her father loses . . .

What? A child, an old relative?

His teeth.

I can't take much more of this.

His false teeth.

Is that an improvement?

During *Ben Hur*.

What will her mother do?

Tell him to stop fussing.

Yes. I can imagine them now.

The woman is whispering. 'They'll probably turn up when we get to the end of the popcorn.'

He says he can't eat any more. She accuses him of sulking.

'That's the last time I go anywhere with him,' she says. 'He makes us wait till everyone's gone and then he's crawling on his hands and knees. Ruined his good trousers. Any other man would have left his name and address at the kiosk, but not him. Oh no. He has to be a hero.'

The teeth will be handed in after a week.
A week?
Encrusted in popcorn.
They spend each noisy evening at the Gaumont, grinning in the dark as the chariot race is won.
How does he know they are his?
By the crack in the plate. He will claim to recognise them by that.
And will he?
He says that they feel different. He will never be sure.
What do they do?
They smile disarmingly.
But they're not happy.
Neither are brass bands.
They grin from his coffin and the child hears music start up some streets away. The Salvation Army. She cries and thinks it is for her father.

Do I have to give you a decision right away. Can't I just think it over?
I'm afraid not. There are thousands out there, behind you. If not you, then one of those.
I'd prefer to be in the back of the car then, I mean if I had a choice.
You don't get a choice.
But I'd really prefer America. Like her mother. I'd prefer to wait.

For what?

Well, I'd like to be sure.

Of what?

The conditions. And no one's mentioned pay yet. I mean, that has to be a consideration?

I really think we ought to move on. We don't want to lose the heat, the right moment. I do hope, gentlemen, that those of you remaining are serious. No more time-wasters, please. Could the second applicant come forward. Now if you have any questions, could you make them short?

Thy Heart's Desire

NETTA SYRETT

I

The tents were pitched in a little plain surrounded by hills. Right and left there were stretches of tender vivid green where the young corn was springing; further still, on either hand, the plain was yellow with mustard-flower; but in the immediate foreground it was bare and stony. A few thorny bushes pushed their straggling way through the dry soil, ineffectively as far as the grace of the landscape was concerned, for they merely served to emphasise the barren aridness of the land that stretched before the tents, sloping gradually to the distant hills.

The hills were uninteresting enough in themselves; they had no grandeur of outline, no picturesqueness even, though at morning and evening the sun, like a great magician, clothed them with beauty at a touch.

They had begun to change, to soften, to blush rose-red in the evening light, when a woman came to the entrance of the largest of the tents and looked towards them. She leant against the support on one side of the canvas flap, and putting back her head, rested that too against it, while her eyes wandered over the plain and over the distant hills.

She was bareheaded, for the covering of the tent projected a few feet to form an awning overhead. The gentle breeze which had risen with sundown stirred the soft brown tendrils of hair on her temples, and fluttered her pink cotton gown a little. She stood very still, with her arms hanging and her hands clasped loosely in front of her. There was about her whole attitude an air of studied quiet which in some vague fashion the slight clasp of her hands accentuated. Her face, with its tightly, almost rigidly closed lips, would have been quite in keeping with the impression of conscious calm which her entire presence suggested, had it not been that when she raised her eyes a strange contradiction to this idea was afforded. They were large grey eyes, unusually bright and rather startling in effect, for they seemed the only live thing about her. Gleaming from her still set face, there was something almost alarming in their brilliancy. They softened with a sudden glow of pleasure as they rested on the translucent green of the wheat-fields under the broad generous sunlight, and then wandered to where the pure vivid yellow of the mustard flower spread in waves to the base of the hills, now mystically veiled in radiance. She stood motionless watching their melting elusive changes from palpitating rose to the transparent purple of amethyst. The stillness of evening was broken by the monotonous, not unmusical creaking of a Persian wheel at some little distance to the left of the tent. The well stood in a little grove of trees: between their branches she could see, when she turned her head, the coloured saris of the village women, where they stood in groups chattering as they drew the water, and the little naked brown babies that toddled beside them or sprawled on the hard ground beneath the trees. From the village of flat-roofed mud houses under the low hill at the back of the tents, other women were crossing the plain towards the well, their terracotta water jars poised easily on their heads, casting long shadows on the sun-baked ground as they came.

Presently, in the distance, from the direction of the sunlit hills opposite, a little group of men came into sight. Far off, the mustard-coloured jackets and the red turbans of the orderlies made vivid splashes of colour on the dull plain. As they came nearer, the guns slung across their shoulders, the cases of mathematical instruments, the hammers and other heavy baggage they carried for the Sahib became visible. A little in front, at walking pace, rode the Sahib himself, making notes as he came in a book he held before him. The girl at the tent entrance watched the advance of the little company indifferently it seemed; except for a slight tightening of the muscles about her mouth, her face remained unchanged. While he was still some little distance away, the man with the notebook raised his head and smiled awkwardly as he saw her standing there. Awkwardness, perhaps, best describes the whole man. He was badly put together, loose-jointed, ungainly. The fact that he was tall profited him nothing, for it merely emphasised the extreme ungracefulness of his figure. His long pale face was made paler by a shock of coarse, tow-coloured hair; his eyes even looked colourless, though they were certainly the least uninteresting feature of his face, for they were not devoid of expression. He had a way of slouching when he moved that singularly intensified the general uncouthness of his appearance. 'Are you very tired?' asked his wife gently when he had dismounted close to the tent. The question would have been an unnecessary one had it been put to her instead of to her husband, for her voice had that peculiar flat toneless sound for which extreme weariness is answerable.

'Well, no, my dear, not very,' he replied, drawling out the words with an exasperating air of delivering a final verdict, after deep reflection on the subject.

The girl glanced once more at the fading colours on the hills. 'Come in and rest,' she said, moving aside a little to let him pass.

She stood lingering a moment after he had entered the tent, as though unwilling to leave the outer air; and before she turned to follow him she drew a deep breath, and her hand went for one swift second to her throat as though she felt stifled.

Later on that evening she sat in her tent sewing by the light of the lamp that stood on her little table.

Opposite her, her husband stretched his ungainly length in a deckchair, and turned over a pile of official notes. Every now and then her eyes wandered from the gay silks of the table cover she was embroidering to the canvas walls which bounded the narrow space into which their few household goods were crowded. Outside there was a deep hush. The silence of the vast empty plain seemed to work its way slowly, steadily in, towards the little patch of light set in its midst. The girl felt it in every nerve; it was as though some soft-footed, noiseless, shapeless creature, whose presence she only dimly divined, was approaching nearer – *nearer*. The heavy outer stillness was in some way made more terrifying by the rustle of the papers her husband was reading, by the creaking of his chair as he moved, and by the little fidgeting grunts and half exclamations which from time to time broke from him. His wife's hand shook at every unintelligible mutter from him, and the slight habitual con-traction between her eyes deepened.

All at once she threw her work down on to the table. 'For Heaven's sake – *please*, John, *talk*!' she cried. Her eyes, for the moment's space in which they met the startled ones of her husband, had a wild hunted look, but it was gone almost before his slow brain had time to note that it had been there – and was vaguely disturbing. She laughed a little, unsteadily.

'Did I startle you? I'm sorry. I – ' she laughed again. 'I believe I'm a little nervous. When one is all day alone – ' She paused without finishing the sentence. The man's face changed suddenly. A wave of tenderness swept over it, and at the same time an expression of half-incredulous delight shone in his pale eyes.

'Poor little girl, are you really lonely?' he said. Even the real feeling in his tone failed to rob his voice of its peculiarly irritating grating quality. He rose awkwardly and moved to his wife's side.

Involuntarily she shrank a little, and the hand which he had stretched out to touch her hair sank to his side. She recovered herself immediately and turned her face up to his, though she did not raise her eyes; but he did not kiss her. Instead, he stood in an embarrassed fashion a moment by her side, and then went back to his seat.

There was silence again for some time. The man lay back in his chair, gazing at his big clumsy shoes, as though he hoped for some inspiration from that quarter, while his wife worked with nervous haste.

'Don't let me keep you from reading, John,' she said, and her voice had regained its usual gentle tone.

'No, my dear; I'm just thinking of something to say to you, but I don't seem – '

She smiled a little. In spite of herself, her lip curled faintly. 'Don't worry about it – it was stupid of me to expect it. I mean – ' she added hastily, immediately repenting the sarcasm. She glanced furtively at him, but his face was quite unmoved. Evidently he had not noticed it, and she smiled faintly again.

'Oh, Kathie, I knew there was *something* I'd forgotten to tell you, my dear; there's a man coming down here. I don't know whether – '

She looked up sharply. 'A man coming *here*? What for?' she interrupted breathlessly.

'Sent to help me about this oil-boring business, my dear.'

He had lighted his pipe, and was smoking placidly, taking long whiffs between his words.

'Well?' impatiently questioned his wife, fixing her bright eyes on his face.

'Well – that's all, my dear.'

She checked an exclamation. 'But don't you know anything about him – his name? where he comes from? what he is like?' She was leaning forward against the table, her needle, with a long end of yellow silk drawn halfway through her work, held in her upraised hand, her whole attitude one of quivering excitement and expectancy.

The man took his pipe from his mouth deliberately, with a look of slow wonder.

'Why Kathie, you seem quite anxious. I didn't know you'd be so interested, my dear. Well,' – another long pull at his pipe – 'his name's Brook – *Brookfield*, I think.' He paused again. 'This pipe don't draw well a bit; there's something wrong with it, I shouldn't wonder,' he added, taking it out and examining the bowl as though struck with the brilliance of the idea.

The woman opposite put down her work and clenched her hands under the table.

'Go on, John,' she said presently in a tense vibrating voice – 'his name is Brookfield. Well, where does he come from?'

'Straight from home, my dear, I believe.' He fumbled in his pocket, and after some time extricated a pencil with which he began to poke the tobacco in the bowl in an ineffectual aimless fashion, becoming completely engrossed in the occupation apparently. There was another long pause. The woman went on working, or feigning to work, for her hands were trembling a good deal.

After some moments she raised her head again. 'John, will you mind attending to me one moment, and answering these questions as quickly as you can?' The emphasis on the last word was so faint as to be almost as imperceptible as the touch of exasperated contempt which she could not absolutely banish from her tone. Her husband, looking up, met her clear bright gaze and reddened like a schoolboy.

'Whereabouts "*from home*" does he come?' she asked in a studiedly gentle fashion.

'Well, from London, I think,' he replied, almost briskly for him, though he stammered and tripped over the words. 'He's a university chap; I used to hear he was clever – I don't know about that, I'm sure; he used to chaff me, I remember, but – '

'Chaff *you*? You have met him then?'

'Yes, my dear' – he was fast relapsing into his slow drawl again – 'that is, I went to school with him, but it's a long time ago. Brookfield – yes, that must be his name.'

She waited a moment, then 'When is he coming?' she inquired abruptly.

'Let me see – today's – '

'*Monday*,' the word came swiftly between her set teeth.

'Ah, yes, – Monday – well,' reflectively, '*next* Monday, my dear.'

Mrs Drayton rose, and began to pace softly the narrow passage between the table and the tent wall, her hands clasped loosely behind her.

'How long have you known this?' she said, stopping abruptly. 'Oh, John you *needn't* consider; it's quite a simple question. Today? Yesterday?'

Her foot moved restlessly on the ground as she waited.

'I think it was the day before yesterday,' he replied.

'Then why in Heaven's name didn't you tell me before?' she broke out fiercely.

'My dear, it slipped my memory. If I'd thought you would be interested – '

'Interested!' She laughed shortly. 'It *is* rather interesting to hear that after six months of this' – she made a quick comprehensive gesture with her hand – 'one will have someone to speak to – someone. It is the hand of Providence; it comes just in time to save me from – ' She checked herself abruptly.

He sat staring up at her stupidly, without a word.

'It's all right, John,' she said, with a quick change of tone, gathering up her work quietly as she spoke. 'I'm not mad – yet. You – you must get used to these little outbreaks,' she added after a moment, smiling faintly, 'and to do me justice, I don't *often* trouble you with them, do I? I'm just a little tired, or it's the heat or – something. No – don't touch me,' she cried, shrinking back, for he had risen slowly and was coming towards her.

She had lost command over her voice, and the shrill note of horror in it was unmistakable. The man heard it, and shrank in his turn.

'I'm so sorry, John,' she murmured, raising her great bright eyes to his face. They had not lost their goaded expression, though they were full of tears. 'I'm awfully sorry, but I'm just nervous and stupid, and I can't bear *anyone* to touch me when I'm nervous.'

II

'Here's Broomhurst, my dear! I made a mistake in his name after all, I find. I told you *Brookfield*, I believe, didn't I? Well, it isn't Brookfield, he says; it's Broomhurst.'

Mrs Drayton had walked some little distance across the plain to meet and welcome the expected guest. She stood quietly waiting while her husband stammered over his incoherent sentences, and then put out her hand.

'We are very glad to see you,' she said with a quick glance at the newcomer's face as she spoke.

As they walked together towards the tent after the first greetings, she felt his keen eyes upon her before he turned to her husband.

'I'm afraid Mrs Drayton finds the climate trying?' he asked. 'Perhaps she ought not to have come so far in this heat?'

'Kathie is often pale. You *do* look white today, my dear,' he observed, turning anxiously towards his wife.

'Do I?' she replied. The unsteadiness of her tone was hardly appreciable, but it was not lost on Broomhurst's quick ears. 'Oh, I don't think so. I *feel* very well.'

'I'll come and see if they've fixed you up all right,' said Drayton, following his companion towards the new tent that had been pitched at some little distance from the large one.

'We shall see you at dinner then?' Mrs Drayton observed in reply to Broomhurst's smile as they parted.

She entered the tent slowly, and moving up to the table, already laid for dinner, began to rearrange the things upon it in a purposeless mechanical fashion. After a moment she sank down upon a seat opposite the open entrance, and put her hand to her head.

'What is the matter with me?' she thought wearily. 'All the week I've been looking forward to seeing this man – *any* man, *anyone* to take off the edge of this.' She shuddered. Even in thought she hesitated to analyse the feeling that possessed her. 'Well, he's here, and I think I feel *worse*.' Her eyes travelled towards the hills she had been used to watch at this hour, and rested on them with a vague unseeing gaze.

'Tired, Kathie? A penny for your thoughts, my dear,' said her husband, coming in presently to find her still sitting there.

'I'm thinking what a curious world this is, and what an ironical vein of humour the gods who look after it must possess,' she replied with a mirthless laugh, rising as she spoke.

John looked puzzled.

'Funny my having known Broomhurst before, you mean?' he said doubtfully.

'I was fishing down at Lynmouth this time last year,' Broomhurst said at dinner. 'You know Lynmouth, Mrs Drayton? Do you never imagine you hear the gurgling of the stream? I am tantalised already by the sound of it rushing through the beautiful green gloom of those woods – *aren't* they lovely? And *I* haven't been in this burnt-up spot as many hours as you've had months of it.'

She smiled a little. 'You must learn to possess your soul in patience,' she said, and glanced inconsequently from Broomhurst to her husband, and then dropped her eyes and was silent a moment.

John was obviously, and a little audibly, enjoying his dinner. He sat with his chair pushed close to the table, and his elbows awkwardly raised, swallowing his soup in gulps. He grasped his spoon tightly in his bony hand so that its swollen joints stood out larger and uglier than ever, his wife thought.

Her eyes wandered to Broomhurst's hands. They were well shaped, and though not small, there was a look of refinement about them; he had a way of touching things delicately, a little lingeringly, she noticed. There was an air of distinction about his clear-cut, clean-shaven face, possibly intensified by contrast with Drayton's blurred features; and it was, perhaps, also by contrast with the grey cuffs that showed beneath John's ill-cut drab suit that the linen Broomhurst wore seemed to her particularly spotless.

Broomhurst's thoughts, for his part, were a good deal occupied with his hostess. She was pretty, he thought, or perhaps it was that, with the wide dry lonely plain as a setting, her fragile delicacy of appearance was invested with a certain flower-like charm.

'The silence here seems rather strange, rather appalling at first, when one is fresh from a town,' he pursued, after a moment's pause, 'but I suppose you're used to it; eh, Drayton? How do *you* find life here, Mrs Drayton?' he asked a little curiously, turning to her as he spoke.

She hesitated a second. 'Oh, much the same as I should find it anywhere else, I expect,' she replied; 'after all, one carries the possibilities of a happy life about with one – don't you think so? The garden of Eden wouldn't necessarily make my life any happier, or less happy, than a howling wilderness like this. It depends on oneself entirely.'

'Given the right Adam and Eve, the desert blossoms like the rose, in fact,' Broomhurst answered lightly, with a smiling glance inclusive of husband and wife; 'you two don't feel as though you'd been driven out of Paradise evidently.'

Drayton raised his eyes from his plate with a smile of total incomprehension.

'Great Heavens! What an Adam to select!' thought Broomhurst involuntarily, as Mrs Drayton rose rather suddenly from the table.

'I'll come and help with that packing case,' John said, rising, in his turn, lumberingly from his place; 'then we can have a smoke – eh? Kathie don't mind, if we sit near the entrance.'

The two men went out together, Broomhurst holding the lantern, for the moon had not yet risen. Mrs Drayton followed them to the doorway, and, pushing the looped-up hanging further aside, stepped out into the cool darkness. Her heart was beating quickly, and there was a great lump in her throat that frightened her as though she were choking.

'And I am his *wife* – I *belong* to him!' she cried, almost aloud.

She pressed both her hands tightly against her breast, and set her teeth, fighting to keep down the rising flood that threatened to sweep away her composure. 'Oh, what a fool I am! What an hysterical fool of a woman I am!' she whispered below her breath.

She began to walk slowly up and down outside the tent, in the space illumined by the lamplight, as though striving to make her outwardly quiet movements react upon the inward tumult. In a little while she had conquered; she quietly entered the tent, drew a low chair to the entrance, and took up a book, just as footsteps became audible. A moment afterwards Broomhurst emerged from the darkness into the circle of light outside, and Mrs Drayton raised her eyes from the pages she was turning to greet him with a smile.

'Are your things all right?'

'Oh yes, more or less, thank you. I was a little concerned about a case of books, but it isn't much damaged fortunately. Perhaps I've some you would care to look at?'

'The books will be a godsend,' she returned with a sudden brightening of the eyes; 'I was getting *desperate* – for books.'

'What are you reading now?' he asked, glancing at the volume that lay in her lap.

'It's a Browning. I carry it about a good deal. I think I like to have it with me, but I don't seem to read it much.'

'Are you waiting for a suitable optimistic moment?' Broomhurst inquired smiling.

'Yes, now you mention it, I think that must be why I am waiting,' she replied slowly.

'And it doesn't come – even in the garden of Eden? Surely the serpent, pessimism, hasn't been insolent enough to draw you into conversation with him?' he said lightly.

'There has been no one to converse with at all – when John is away, I mean. I think I should have liked a little chat with the serpent immensely by way of a change,' she replied in the same tone.

'Ah, yes,' Broomhurst said with sudden seriousness, 'it must be unbearably dull for you alone here, with Drayton away all day.'

Mrs Drayton's hand shook a little as she fluttered a page of her open book.

'I should think it quite natural you would be irritated beyond endurance to hear that all's right with the world, for instance, when you were sighing for the long day to pass,' he continued.

'I don't mind the day so much – it's the evenings.' She abruptly checked the swift words and flushed painfully. 'I mean – I've grown stupidly nervous, I think – even when John is here. Oh, you have no idea of the awful *silence* of this place at night,' she added, rising hurriedly from her low seat, and moving closer to the doorway. 'It is so close, isn't it?' she said almost apologetically. There was silence for quite a minute.

Broomhurst's quick eyes noted the silent momentary clenching of the hands that hung at her side as she stood leaning against the support at the entrance.

'But how stupid of me to give you such a bad impression of the camp – the first evening too,' Mrs Drayton exclaimed presently, and her companion mentally commended the admirable composure of her voice.

'Probably you will never notice that it *is* lonely at all,' she continued, 'John likes it here. He is immensely interested in his work, you know. I hope *you* are too. If you are interested it is quite all right. I think the climate tries me a little. I never used to be stupid – and nervous. Ah, here's John; he's been round to the kitchen tent, I suppose.'

'Been looking after that fellow cleanin' my gun, my dear,' John explained, shambling towards the deckchair.

Later, Broomhurst stood at his own tent door. He looked up at the star-sown sky, and the heavy silence seemed to press upon him like an actual, physical burden.

He took his cigar from between his lips presently and looked at the glowing end reflectively before throwing it away.

'Considering that she has been alone with him here for six months, she has herself very well in hand – *very* well in hand,' he repeated.

III

It was Sunday morning. John Drayton sat just inside the tent, presumably enjoying his pipe before the heat of the day. His eyes furtively followed his wife as she moved about near him, sometimes passing close to his chair in search of something she had mislaid. There was colour in her cheeks; her eyes, though preoccupied, were bright; there was a lightness and buoyancy in her step which she set to a little dancing air she was humming under her breath.

After a moment or two the song ceased, she began to move slowly, sedately; and as if chilled by a raw breath of air, the light faded from her eyes, which she presently turned towards her husband.

'Why do you look at me?' she began suddenly.

'I don't know, my dear,' he began, slowly and laboriously as was his wont. 'I was thinkin' how nice you looked – jest now – much better you know – but somehow' – he was taking long whiffs at his pipe, as usual, between each word, while she stood patiently waiting for him to finish – 'somehow, you alter so, my dear – you're quite pale again all of a minute.'

She stood listening to him, noticing against her will the more than suspicion of a cockney accent and the thick drawl with which the words were uttered. His eyes sought her face piteously. She noticed that too, and stood before him torn by conflicting emotions, pity and disgust struggling in a hand-to-hand fight within her.

'Mr Broomhurst and I are going down by the well to sit; it's cooler there. Won't you come?' she said at last gently.

He did not reply for a moment, then he turned his head aside, sharply for him.

'No, my dear, thank you; I'm comfortable enough here,' he returned huskily.

She stood over him, hesitating a second, then moved abruptly to the table, from which she took a book.

He had risen from his seat by the time she turned to go out, and he intercepted her timorously.

'Kathie, give me a kiss before you go,' he whispered hoarsely. 'I – I don't often bother you.'

She drew her breath in deeply as he put his arms clumsily about her, but she stood still, and he kissed her on the forehead, and touched the little wavy curls that strayed across it gently with his big trembling fingers.

When he released her she moved at once impetuously to the open doorway. On the threshold she hesitated, paused a moment irresolutely, and then turned back.

'Shall I – Does your pipe want filling, John?' she asked softly.

'No, thank you, my dear.'

'Would you like me to stay, read to you, or anything?'

He looked up at her wistfully. 'N-no, thank you, I'm not much of a reader, you know, my dear – somehow.'

She hated herself for knowing that there would be a 'my dear', probably a 'somehow' in his reply, and despised herself for the sense of irritated impatience she felt by anticipation, even before the words were uttered. There was a moment's hesitating silence, broken by the sound of quick firm footsteps without. Broomhurst paused at the entrance, and looked into the tent.

'Aren't you coming, Drayton?' he asked, looking first at Drayton's wife and then swiftly putting in his name with a scarcely perceptible pause. 'Too lazy? But you, Mrs Drayton?'

'Yes, I'm coming,' she said.

They left the tent together, and walked some few steps in silence. Brookhurst shot a quick glance at his companion's face. 'Anything wrong?' he asked presently.

Though the words were ordinary enough, the voice in which they were spoken was in some subtle fashion a different voice from that in which he had talked to her nearly two months ago, though it would have required a keen sense of nice shades in sound to have detected the change. Mrs Drayton's sense of niceties in sound was particularly keen, but she answered quietly, 'Nothing, thank you.'

They did not speak again till the trees round the stone well were reached. Broomhurst arranged their seats comfortably beside it. 'Are we going to read or talk?' he asked, looking up at her from his lower place.

'Well, we generally talk most when we arrange to read, so shall we agree to talk today for a change, by way of getting some reading done?' she rejoined, smiling. '*You* begin.'

Broomhurst seemed in no hurry to avail himself of the permission, he was apparently engrossed in watching the flecks of sunshine on Mrs Drayton's white dress. The whirring of insects and the creaking of a Persian wheel somewhere in the neighbourhood filtered through the hot silence.

Mrs Drayton laughed after a few minutes; there was a touch of embarrassment in the sound. 'The new plan doesn't answer. Suppose you read as usual, and let me interrupt, also as usual, after the first two lines.'

He opened the book obediently, but turned the pages at random. She watched him for a moment, and then bent a little forward towards him.

'It is my turn now,' she said suddenly. 'Is anything wrong?'

He raised his head, and their eyes met. There was a pause. 'I will be more honest than you,' he returned. 'Yes, there is.'

'What?'

'I've had orders to move on.'

She drew back, and her lips whitened, though she kept them steady. 'When do you go?'

'On Wednesday.'

There was silence again; the man still kept his eyes on her face. The whirring of the insects and the creaking of the wheel had suddenly grown so strangely loud and insistent, that it was in a half-dazed fashion she at length heard her name – '*Kathleen*!'

'Kathleen!' he whispered again hoarsely.

She looked him full in the face, and once more their eyes met in a long grave gaze. The man's face flushed, and he half rose from his seat with an impetuous movement, but Kathleen stopped him with a glance.

'Will you go and fetch my work? I left it in the tent,' she said, speaking very clearly and distinctly; 'and then will you go on reading? I will find the place while you are gone.'

She took the book from his hand, and he rose and stood before her. There was a mute appeal in his silence, and she raised her head slowly. Her face was white to the lips, but she looked at him unflinchingly; and without a word he turned and left her.

IV

Mrs Drayton was resting in the tent on Tuesday afternoon. With the help of cushions and some low chairs she had improvised a couch, on which she lay quietly with her eyes closed. There was a tenseness, however, in her attitude which indicated that sleep was far from her. Her features seemed to have sharpened during the last few days, and there were hollows in her cheeks. She had been very still for a long time, but all at once with a sudden movement she turned her head and buried her face in the cushions with a groan. Slipping from her place she fell on her knees beside the couch, and put both hands before her mouth to force back the cry that she felt struggling to her lips.

For some moments the wild effort she was making for outward calm, which even when she was alone was her first instinct, strained every nerve and blotted out sight and hearing, and it was not till the sound was very near that she was conscious of the ring of horse's hoofs on the plain. She raised her head sharply with a thrill of fear, still kneeling, and listened.

There was no mistake. The horseman was riding in hot haste, for the thud of the hoofs followed one another swiftly.

As Mrs Drayton listened her white face grew whiter, and she began to tremble. Putting out shaking hands, she raised herself by the arms of the folding chair and stood upright. Nearer and nearer came the thunder of the approaching sound, mingled with startled exclamations and the noise of trampling feet from the direction of the kitchen tent.

Slowly, mechanically almost, she dragged herself to the entrance, and stood clinging to the canvas there. By the time she had reached it, Broomhurst had flung himself from the saddle, and had thrown the reins to one of the men.

Mrs Drayton stared at him with wide bright eyes as he hastened towards her.

'I thought you – you are not – ' she began, and then her teeth began to chatter. 'I am so cold!' she said, in a little weak voice.

Broomhurst took her hand, and led her over the threshold back into the tent.

'Don't be so frightened,' he implored; 'I came to tell you first. I thought it wouldn't frighten you so much as – Your – Drayton is – very ill. They are bringing him. I – '

He paused. She gazed at him a moment with parted lips, then she broke into a horrible discordant laugh, and stood clinging to the back of a chair.

Broomhurst started back.

'Do you understand what I mean?' he whispered. 'Kathleen, for God's sake – *don't* – he is *dead*.'

He looked over his shoulder as he spoke, her shrill laughter ringing in his ears. The white glare and dazzle of the plain stretched before him, framed by the entrance to the tent; far off, against the horizon, there were moving black specks, which he knew to be the returning servants with their still burden.

They were bringing John Drayton home.

V

One afternoon, some months later, Broomhurst climbed the steep lane leading to the cliffs of a little English village by the sea. He had already been to the inn, and had been shown by the proprietress the house where Mrs Drayton lodged.

'The lady was out, but the gentleman would likely find her if he went to the cliffs – down by the bay, or thereabouts,' her landlady explained, and, obeying her directions, Broomhurst presently emerged from the shady woodland path on to the hillside overhanging the sea.

He glanced eagerly round him, and then with a sudden quickening of the heart, walked on over the springy heather to where she sat. She turned when the rustling his footsteps made through the bracken was near enough to arrest her attention, and looked up at him as he came. Then she rose slowly, and stood waiting for him.

He came up to her without a word, and seized both her hands, devouring her face with his eyes. Something he saw there repelled him. Slowly he let her hands fall, still looking at her silently. 'You are not glad to see me, and I have counted the hours,' he said at last in a dull toneless voice.

Her lips quivered. 'Don't be angry with me – I can't help it – I'm not glad or sorry for anything now,' she answered, and her voice matched his for greyness.

They sat down together on a long flat stone half embedded in a wiry clump of whortleberries. Behind them the lonely hillsides rose, brilliant with yellow bracken and the purple of heather. Before them stretched the wide sea. It was a soft grey day. Streaks of pale sunlight trembled at moments far out on the water. The tide was rising in the little bay above which they sat, and Broomhurst watched the lazy foam-edged waves slipping over the uncovered rocks towards the shore, then sliding back as though for very weariness they despaired of reaching it. The muffled pulsing sound of the sea filled the silence. Broomhurst thought suddenly of hot eastern sunshine, of the whirr of insect wings on the still air, and the creaking of a wheel in the distance. He turned and looked at his companion.

'I have come thousands of miles to see you,' he said; 'aren't you going to speak to me now I am here?'

'Why did you come? I told you not to come,' she answered, falteringly. 'I – ' she paused.

'And I replied that I should follow you – if you remember,' he answered, still quietly. 'I came because I would not listen to what you said then, at that awful time. You didn't know *yourself* what you said. No wonder! I have given you some months, and now I have come.'

There was silence between them. Broomhurst saw that she was

crying; her tears fell fast on to her hands, that were clasped in her lap. Her face, he noticed, was thin and drawn.

Very gently he put his arm round her shoulder and drew her nearer to him. She made no resistance – it seemed that she did not notice the movement; and his arm dropped at his side.

'You asked me why I had come? You think it possible that three months can change one, very thoroughly, then?' he said in a cold voice.

'I not only think it possible, I have proved it,' she replied wearily.

He turned round and faced her.

'You *did* love me, Kathleen!' he asserted. 'You never said so in words, but I know it,' he added fiercely.

'Yes I did.'

'And – You mean that you don't now?'

Her voice was very tired. 'Yes – I can't help it,' she answered, 'it has gone – utterly.'

The grey sea slowly lapped the rocks. Overhead the sharp scream of a gull cut through the stillness. It was broken again, a moment afterwards, by a short hard laugh from the man.

'Don't!' she whispered, and laid a hand swiftly on his arm. 'Do you think it isn't worse for me? I wish to God I *did* love you,' she cried passionately. 'Perhaps it would make me forget that to all intents and purposes I am a murderess.'

Broomhurst met her wide despairing eyes with an amazement which yielded to sudden pitying comprehension.

'So that is it, my darling? You are worrying about *that*? You who were as loyal, as – '

She stopped him with a frantic gesture.

'Don't! *don't*!' she wailed. 'If you only knew; let me try to tell you – will you?' she urged pitifully. 'It may be better if I tell someone – if I don't keep it all to myself, and think, and *think*.'

She clasped her hands tight, with the old gesture he remembered when she was struggling for self-control, and waited a moment. Presently she began to speak in a low hurried tone: 'It began before you came. I know now what the feeling was that I was afraid to acknowledge to myself. I used to try and smother it, I used to repeat things to myself all day – poems, stupid rhymes – *anything* to keep my thoughts quite underneath – but I – *hated* John before you came! We had been married nearly a year then. I never loved him. Of course you are going to say: "Why did you marry him?"' She looked drearily over the placid sea. 'Why *did* I marry him? I don't know; for the reason that hundreds of ignorant inexperienced girls marry, I suppose. My home wasn't a happy one. I was miserable, and oh, – *restless*. I wonder if men know what it feels like to be restless? Sometimes I think they can't even guess. John wanted me very badly – nobody wanted me at home particularly. There didn't seem to be any point in my life. Do you understand? . . . Of course being alone with him in that little camp in that silent plain' – she shuddered – 'made things worse. My nerves went all to pieces. Everything he said – his voice – his accent – his walk – the way he ate – irritated me so that I longed to rush out sometimes and shriek – and go *mad*. Does it sound ridiculous to you to be driven mad by such trifles? I only know I used to get up from the table sometimes and walk up and down outside, with both hands over my mouth to keep myself quiet. And all the time I *hated* myself – how I hated myself! I never had a word from him that wasn't gentle and tender. I believe he loved the ground I walked on. Oh, it is *awful* to be loved like that, when you –' She drew in her breath with a sob. 'I – I – it made me sick for him to come near me – to touch me.' She stopped a moment.

Broomhurst gently laid his hand on her quivering one. 'Poor little girl!' he murmured.

'Then *you* came,' she said, 'and before long I had another feeling

to fight against. At first I thought it couldn't be true that I loved you
– it would die down. I think I was *frightened* at the feeling; I didn't
know it hurt so to love anyone.'

Broomhurst stirred a little. 'Go on,' he said tersely.

'But it didn't die,' she continued in a trembling whisper, 'and the
other *awful* feeling grew stronger and stronger – hatred; no, that is
not the word – *loathing* for – for – John. I fought against it. Yes,' she
cried feverishly, clasping and unclasping her hands, 'Heaven knows
I fought it with all my strength, and reasoned with myself, and –
oh, I did *everything*, but – ' Her quick-falling tears made speech
difficult.

'Kathleen!' Broomhurst urged desperately, 'you couldn't help it,
you poor child. You say yourself you struggled against your feelings
– you were always gentle. Perhaps he didn't know.'

'But he did – he *did*,' she wailed, 'it is just that. I hurt him a
hundred times a day; he never said so, but I knew it; and yet I
couldn't be kind to him – except in words – and he understood. And
after you came it was worse in one way, for he knew. I *felt* he knew
that I loved you. His eyes used to follow me like a dog's, and I was
stabbed with remorse, and I tried to be good to him, but I couldn't.'

'But – he didn't suspect – he trusted you,' began Broomhurst. 'He
had every reason. No woman was ever so loyal, so – '

'Hush,' she almost screamed. 'Loyal! it was the least I could do –
to stop you, I mean – when you – After all, I knew it without your
telling me. I had deliberately married him without loving him. It
was my own fault. I felt it. Even if I couldn't prevent his knowing
that I hated him, I could prevent *that*. It was my punishment. I
deserved it for *daring* to marry without love. But I didn't spare John
one pang after all,' she added bitterly. 'He knew what I felt towards
him – I don't think he cared about anything else. You say I mustn't
reproach myself? When I went back to the tent that morning –

when you – when I stopped you from saying you loved me, he was sitting at the table with his head buried in his hands; he was crying – bitterly. I saw him – it is terrible to see a man cry – and I stole away gently, but he saw me. I was torn to pieces, but I *couldn't* go to him. I knew he would kiss me, and I shuddered to think of it. It seemed more than ever not to be borne that he should do that – when I knew *you* loved me.'

'Kathleen,' cried her lover again, 'don't dwell on it all so terribly – don't –'

'How can I forget?' she answered despairingly, 'and then' – she lowered her voice – 'oh, I can't tell you – all the time, at the back of my mind somewhere, there was a burning wish that he might *die*. I used to lie awake at night, and, do what I would to stifle it, that thought used to *scorch* me, I wished it so intensely. Do you believe that by willing one can bring such things to pass?' she asked, looking at Broomhurst with feverishly bright eyes. 'No? – Well, I don't know – I tried to smother it. I *really* tried, but it was there, whatever other thoughts I heaped on the top. Then, when I heard the horse galloping across the plain that morning, I had a sick fear that it was *you*. I knew something had happened, and my first thought when I saw you alive and well, and knew that it was *John*, was *that it was too good to be true*. I believe I laughed like a maniac, didn't I? . . . Not to blame? Why, if it hadn't been for me he wouldn't have died. The men say they saw him sitting with his head uncovered in the burning sun, his face buried in his hands – just as I had seen him the day before. He didn't trouble to be careful – he was too wretched.'

She paused, and Broomhurst rose and began to pace the little hillside path at the edge of which they were seated.

Presently he came back to her.

'Kathleen, let me take care of you,' he implored, stooping towards her. 'We have only ourselves to consider in this matter. Will you come to me at once?'

She shook her head sadly.

Broomhurst set his teeth, and the lines round his mouth deepened. He threw himself down beside her on the heather.

'Dear,' he urged still gently, though his voice showed he was controlling himself with an effort. 'You are morbid about this. You have been alone too much – you are ill. Let me take care of you: I *can*, Kathleen – and I love you. Nothing but morbid fancy makes you imagine you are in any way responsible for – Drayton's death. You can't bring him back to life, and – '

'No,' she sighed drearily, 'and if I could, nothing would be altered. Though I am mad with self-reproach, I feel *that* – it was all so inevitable. If he were alive and well before me this instant my feeling towards him wouldn't have changed. If he spoke to me, he would say "My dear" – and I should *loathe* him. Oh, I know! It is *that* that makes it so awful.'

'But if you acknowledge it,' Broomhurst struck in eagerly, 'will you wreck both of our lives for the sake of vain regrets? Kathleen, you never will.'

He waited breathlessly for her answer.

'I won't wreck both our lives by marrying again without love on my side,' she replied firmly.

'I will take the risk,' he said. 'You *have* loved me – you will love me again. You are crushed and dazed now with brooding over this – this trouble, but – '

'But I will not allow you to take the risk,' Kathleen answered. 'What sort of woman should I be to be willing again to live with a man I don't love? I have come to know that there are things one owes to *oneself*. Self-respect is one of them. I don't know how it has come to be so, but all my old feeling for you has *gone*. It is as though it had burnt itself out. I will not offer grey ashes to any man.'

Broomhurst, looking up at her pale, set face, knew that her words were final, and turned his own aside with a groan.

'Ah!' cried Kathleen with a little break in her voice, '*don't*. Go away and be happy and strong, and all that I loved in you. I am so sorry – so sorry to hurt you. I – ' her voice faltered miserably. 'I – I only bring trouble to people.'

There was a long pause.

'Did you never think that there is a terrible vein of irony running through the ordering of this world?' she said presently. 'It is a mistake to think our prayers are not answered – they are. In due time we get our heart's desire – when we have ceased to care for it.'

'I haven't yet got mine,' Broomhurst answered doggedly, 'and I shall never cease to care for it.'

She smiled a little with infinite sadness.

'Listen, Kathleen,' he said. They had both risen and he stood before her, looking down at her. 'I will go now, but in a year's time I shall come back. I will not give you up. You shall love me yet.'

'Perhaps – I don't think so,' she answered wearily.

Broomhurst looked at her trembling lips a moment in silence, then he stooped and kissed both her hands instead.

'I will wait till you tell me you love me,' he said.

She stood watching him out of sight. He did not look back, and she turned with swimming eyes to the grey sea and the transient gleams of sunlight that swept like tender smiles across its face.

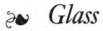 # *Glass*

SHENA MACKAY

The bus shelter was a skeleton. Her feet crunched its smashed glass, like coarse soda crystals, under her shoes as she walked to the cash machine, and a glittering pyramid of uncut diamonds had been swept into the call box where an eviscerated telephone dangled. Someone had passed in the night who loved the sound of breaking glass. She had been thinking about the possibilities of working in glass herself lately. She was an artist. Her cashpoint card bore the name Jessamy Jones; its number was a mnemonic of her children's birthdays. All grown up now, with children of their own. Jessamy had sketched their baby heads in tender pastels that stroked the curves of cheek and eye and ear and feathered hair; and a painting of them as children was sold as a postcard in the Tate. There was a wistful look about it, reminiscent of the nursery rhyme:

> Hark, hark, the dogs do bark,
> Beggars are coming to town.
> Some in rags and some in jags
> And one in a velvet gown.

Two people were waiting behind the man using the machine. Judging from the time he was taking, he was negotiating a mortgage, buying a pension plan, and making his will. The woman on his heels shifted her shopping bags and sighed; the boy lit a cigarette and looked murderous.

The autumn sunshine, gilding brick and berried trees, was beneficent, like a matriarch bestowing gold and jewels on her heirs, all their sins forgiven; the plane trees were dappled benign giraffes. Jess stood a foot or so away to wait her turn, and looked down, on to cubes of viscous glass. She hadn't noticed them for years, but they must have been there all the time, those skylights set into pavements, the little squares of thick opaque glass letting out light from the cellars of shops, swimmy subaqueous light from the dank green cottages and gloomy caves of public conveniences. There was something she should have been thinking about, a decision to be made, but she stooped to study the tiles, seeing them with a child's eye, as if for the first time, pinkish, yellowish, greyish, dirtily opalescent, the colours of fish. Children are closer to the pavement, she was thinking, they know that the striped awning that encloses the greengrocer's emerald slope can suddenly snap in the wind and slap them in the face, that wooden cellar doors could fold back like heavy wings and plummet them into the underworld, that glass squares might hold more than bears.

Crouching there at a child's level, she heard a mother's voice: 'Will you shut up, or I'll give you something to cry for!' A howling infant was dragged past her. Something to cry for. That seemed doubly cruel, and unnecessary, as the child was already smeared and incoherent with an abundance of grief.

'You have no heart,' Jess had been told last night. 'You haven't got a heart.' Not true, not true. 'All you care about is your work.' There was a pretty iron grille in the wall above the skylight. 'You've got to decide. Come with me to America, or it's over.' Victorian, undoubtedly, the elaborate ironwork lattice. 'Crunch time,' said the broken glass under people's feet. 'Make or break.' Jessamy realised that she was squatting in the street and that she would be thought mad or drunk, if anyone noticed her at all; not that that bothered her, it was just that her knees were aching. She straightened up and looked into the shop window. From the back, in her huge sweater and jeans stiff with paint, she might have been a man, a girl, a woman or a boy; she was all of them, and none of them in particular when she worked. As she gazed, she realised the truth of the saying that 'Charity begins at home'; everything in this jumbled display had once been in somebody's home. An earlier proprietor's name was engraved in an ornamental strip across the top of the window: *Adèle. Coiffeuse and Wigmaker.* She must have been very sure of herself, to have her name incised in silvery Deco letters in the frosty glass. Where was Adèle now? The shop was closed and its interior dim; Jess saw her reflection doubled for an instant in the slightly distorted glass, as if another self had stepped sideways from her body and was looking at her. Beyond her selves, on a shelf, stood a light fitting comprising three frilly-bottomed bells of *crème brûlée*, as brittle as the caramelised topping that you crackle with your spoon. Was it camp, covetable kitsch, or that brass-stemmed cluster, BHS circa 1990? It was hard to tell. Jessamy knew that she had only to flick a switch, pull a string, and her life would be bathed in sweet toffee-coloured light. What to do? But look! The twin of the lustrous pearly globe, flecked blue and orange like a party balloon, that had been suspended on three chains from her childhood ceiling. Every so often Mother had stood on a chair to unhook it and empty it of its prey; daddy-long-legs, flies, moths, all silhouetted against the glass, and once, most horribly, a red admiral.

Decide. Make a decision. Decide whether or not to pick up the phone when you get home. Decide whether to sit beside someone in a Virgin aircraft, holding hands over the Atlantic. She remembered holding up their entwined fingers, that seemed to float in the dusk above the bed, and saying 'our fingers make a candelabrum'. There, in the window, was a three-tiered cake stand, bordered in nasturtiums, with a tarnished fork, dating from the days when waitresses in white caps and aprons served cakes on decorous doilies, when the disseminated department store Bon Marché, down the road, had been the Harrods of south-east London. She wondered if perhaps Adèle, looking down, ever paused in the marcel-waving of an angel's wing and remembered. Over the noise of the traffic Jess could hear the boom and echoing crash of bottles being cast into the bottle bank, three council tumuli colour-coded Brown, White and Green.

Misbegotten garments, acrylic, fluorescent, trimmed with gilt and plastic, rubbed shoulders with the shrunken and drab in a brave, hopeless, queue. Then a mildewed leather jacket brought a memory she would have preferred to forget, of a circle of Hell's Angels peeing on the brand-new leather jacket she had saved for months to buy, and on which she still owed money. That had been the initiation ceremony in which Jess was to be made the official Old Lady of the leader of the pack. She had made her excuses and left. Well, fled in fact, pursued by burning brands and beer bottles. Her conversion to vegetarianism had come soon after, outside a butcher's shop. Tearing off the jacket, still smelly after repeated hosings and a trip to the dry cleaner's, she had thrust it on a youth idling on a parked motorbike at the kerb.

'Here, take this jacket!' she had ordered, adding graciously, 'you can pee on it if you like.' He had vanished, vroom vroom, in a terrified trail of exhaust. She had gone home and applied to go to art school. The past, the past. What about the future? Was there a future in glass? Nobody was buying paintings; her last exhibition had been well received but not a single painting had sold. Out of embarrassment she had stuck red dots on a few frames herself. Now she imagined herself in a booth at the end of a pier, twirling glass like spun sugar in the flame of a blow-torch, spinning the rigging of fragile ships, the legs of glass animals, fish with fissile fins, bambis with glaucoma; seaside souvenirs. How did one go about getting such a job? Surely the position would be occupied by a gentle bearded young man? Off the edge of the pier with him! – a faint hiss as a wave quenched and then closed over his Bunsen burner.

'You've never loved anyone.' Not true. People from the past stepped forward to prove it. Then she saw that they were reflections in the shop window; perhaps she had always been looking in a mirror, watching others loving her? Damn. She had lost her place in the queue. The light would be quite gone by the time she got home. Two jacket potatoes would be splitting their sides in the oven waiting for her; Jess took as her example Soutine, who had kept a bucket of boiled eggs beside him as he painted, so that he need not break off work to eat. As she was leaving the window, a flash of sapphire caught her eye, a shimmer of turquoise and flamingo pink. A powder compact with a lid of butterflies' wings under glass. There had been a shop window, long ago, filled with those vibrant wings made into pictures of silky tropical seas and black palm trees against savage sunsets; and set in silver jewellery, vivid on black velvet. If you looked closely you could see the veins in the wings.

Jessamy turned away angrily. Was this really what it was all about? Are we so imprinted in childhood, like orphaned ducklings who bond with Wellington boots, or cartoon chicks squawking 'Mommy! That's my mommy!' at exasperated wolves, that we spend the rest of our lives in pursuit of long-dead butterflies, chasing babyhood bunnies in an endless circle round and round the rim of a nursery bowl before sliding into the flames on a sledge painted with a blistering rosebud? Look at the Harlequins. What colours, she wondered, would activate her children's nervous systems; some dress she herself had worn, a necklace of glass beads? What English *madeleine* rolled in coconut and topped with a *glacé* cherry would dissolve into memory in her lover's mouth? Then she speculated on whether we should love one another if we were made of glass, with all the workings visible, like transparent factories. We should have to; after all, we found beauty in eyes, ears and noses which were nothing but utilitarian. There was a boy going past, whose mouth was a more blatant organ than most, with his big fragile upper teeth puckering his lower lip like the skin of a deflating balloon. No heart? She could feel it heavy in her chest. She was all heart, had been from the start. Had she not been inconsolable when that pearly, flecked balloon had burst? It had had a pair of cardboard feet, and she had been left with the disembodied feet in her hand. She had kept them for weeks. Did not spring evening skies of Indian ink drizzled over daffodil, or autumn sunsets like this one of apricot and sapphire, suffuse her with *tendresse*? She felt her eyes fill, the aqueous humour, the vitreous humour, glazed with tears. Decide if you want me in your life – a dear face fallen asleep over a book, spectacles slipping down a familiar nose, discs of glass magnifying closed eyelids, veined like butterflies' wings.

At the bottle bank, a girl hesitated with a blue bottle in her hand, unsure where to deposit it, and as she held it up, blue as butterflies' wings from the Seychelles or the Philippines, Jess made her decision.

'Green!' she called. 'No, brown!'

Too late. The girl had dropped it into the white bin. Blue on white. An arctic landscape. As Jess inserted her card, the cash dispenser's perspex eyelid closed in a slow malevolent wink as if to say, 'I'll give you something to cry for.'

The glass squares in the pavement glowed faintly phosphorescent now. She looked down at one of them: old, adamantine, durable; it would take a pickaxe to break it.

﹗ *A New Poster*

EVELYN SHARP

I

It was the first of Mrs Angelo Milton's original dinner parties. Mrs Angelo Milton had the reputation of being the most original hostess, if not in London, certainly in South Kensington where she lived. Such a reputation, in such a neighbourhood, was not perhaps difficult of acquisition, and Mrs Milton had managed to acquire it by the simple though unusual method of being mildly eccentric within the limits of conventionality. She was thus characteristic neither of Bohemia nor of South Kensington; she amused the one, puzzled the other, and received them both on the third Wednesday in the month. She was daring in her selection of guests, clever in the way she made them entertain one another, and commonplace in her own conversation. The object of her life was to be distinguished, and in a great measure she succeeded in it; the only thing that was wanting was Mrs Angelo Milton herself. Her house, her receptions, her friends all bore the mark of distinction; as a drama, the scenic effect was superb and the company far above the average, but the principal player remained mediocre. She had none of the elements of individuality; her dress was perfect and of the fashionable type, her features were intrinsically good, yet their whole effect was unsatisfactory; her very hair was abundant and ordinary. Yet she was clever – clever enough to know her own defects and to play them off upon other people, clever enough to have begun a fresh career at the age of twenty-six and to have followed it with perseverance and success. She belonged to the few who know how to invest the little capital Nature has given them; and none of the brilliant frequenters of her house who came and talked about themselves to their sympathetic hostess ever suspected that they were really there to establish her personality and not to advertise their own.

A perfectly new dinner party was the luckiest inspiration that ever came to a tired hostess. To see her guests grouped at small tables, to make them all cooperate in the labour of conversation, to enjoy the triumphant consciousness of having combined them in the happiest manner possible, and to have reduced her own responsibility to the entertaining of three people only, was the highest consummation Mrs Angelo Milton had ever attained. She sat in complete satisfaction, bathed in the becoming rose-coloured light shed by numerous shaded candles; and she even allowed herself under the influence of the prevailing ease of manner to become almost natural. She had selected her own party with scrupulous care; a pretty *débutante* for her *vis-à-vis*, who neither eclipsed nor reflected her; a black and white artist, very new, for herself; and an ugly boy to play with the *débutante*, which he was doing very charmingly.

'Such an improvement on the ordinary dinner party,' said little Margaret Cousins, with the experience of a first season in her voice.

'Awfully neat idea, is really; no need to listen to what the other chaps are saying, don't you know,' said the ugly boy, who was still young, though he had left Cambridge a year ago.

'Do you ever listen to what the other chaps are saying, Mr Askew?' asked the *débutante*.

'This is daring of you,' the artist was saying in a lowered tone, not because he had anything confidential to say, but because it suited his style to be impressive.

'Since it proclaims my choice of companions?' asked his hostess, rather clumsily.

'I am more than sensible of the honour. But that was not my meaning; no. I meant because – '

'Because it gives my other guests the opportunity of criticising my new French *chef*?' she interrupted again, but with all the assurance of success.

'Say rather the opportunity of discussing their charming hostess?' rejoined the artist, relieved from the necessity of finding his own reply.

'A new poster? Really?' said Margaret Cousins.

The artist turned round with a scarcely perceptible show of interest.

'What, another?' he asked carelessly.

The ugly boy said it was the same old thing, and then explained that it was one of the new things, a scarlet background with a black lady in one corner and a black tree with large roots in another corner, and some black stars scattered about elsewhere.

'Ah, yes,' said the artist indifferently, 'it is an advertisement for the Shakespeare Fountain Pen, or something to that effect. I saw it this morning.'

'The Milton Fountain Pen,' corrected his hostess with the smile of conversation. 'I have noticed it on the placards sometimes; it bears my name you see.'

The artist said the coincidence had not struck him at the time, but that he should in future use no other pen on that account. The ugly boy, who was occupied with his savoury, said nothing; the *débutante*, who had passed it, asked a simple question as though she wished for information.

'What has a black lady or a black tree got to do with Milton or a fountain pen?'

'Oh, nothing. It has got to advertise it, that's all,' said the artist, smiling indulgently.

The ugly boy, who was now at liberty, said it was howling cheek of the painter chap to stick different things on a scarlet sheet and call it an advertisement for something that wasn't there.

'Perhaps,' said his *vis-à-vis* with his irritating amiability. 'I suppose you would have a penholder and a fountain with no background at all? That would be quite obvious of course.'

'What is a fountain pen?' asked Mrs Milton, who had an idea that the general conversation was not being a success. There were three more or less inaccurate definitions at once; she selected Margaret's, and smiled across at her.

'Margaret always knows these things,' she told the others. 'Margaret is literary, and makes one feel dreadfully frivolous sometimes.'

Dicky Askew looked sad and felt that he could not talk any more about the comic papers. The ugly boy's literature was mainly pink. Margaret blushed and looked pleased, and said, 'Oh, no,' and added something irrelevant about Milton and the Puritan movement which suggested Macaulay.

'Margaret is still so deliciously young,' sighed Mrs Angelo.

'How nice to be at the age of local examinations when one hasn't forgotten all about Milton and those improving people! Really, it is as much as one can do now to get through the books of the people one has to meet in society. By the way,' she added exclusively to the artist, 'Brindley Harrison is here tonight: do you know him? He is over there, just under the Burne-Jones, talking to – yes, that one. Have you read his last?'

After that the conversation remained particular and interesting until the hostess had to give the signal for retreat, upon which conventionality again claimed its victims, and there was no further evidence of innovation either in the music or the conversation that occupied the rest of the evening.

When the last carriage had rolled away, Mrs Angelo Milton rang the bell and ordered something to eat. Then she walked round the room and extinguished all the wax lights herself, and turned the gas low, and sat down in the firelight. She was silent for a long time after the servants had left her, and she was terribly lonely. It was not a loneliness that comes as a natural result of departed company, but the much more subtle solitude of one who is anticipating a new companionship. When she had eaten her sandwiches mechanically, one by one, she stood up and leaned her head on the cold marble of the mantel shelf, and something like an angry sob broke from her lips in the darkness.

'After seven years,' she murmured, 'to lose it all by loving Adrian Marks!'

She turned up the gas again with an impatient movement, then lighted a candle and held it up to a picture on the wall, a portrait of a middle-aged man with a bald head.

'Jim!' she cried involuntarily, 'what would you say if you were to meet him?'

The idea struck her as so incongruous that she gave way to a nervous spasm of laughter and returned hurriedly to her seat by the fire. Her husband had been a successful commercial man, and the source of his wealth had been the invention of the Milton Fountain Pen. When he died in America, seven years ago, his widow came to England with his fortune, assuring herself against detection by prefixing an old family name to his notorious one, and began the career for which she had pined through the whole of her short married life. Those seven years in South Kensington had given her what she wanted, position, association with artistic circles, a certain measure of happiness; she had worked hard for all of these, and yet she was on the point of renouncing them as the price of her attachment to Adrian Marks, the new black and white artist. It seemed very paltry to her as she sat in the empty drawing-room, away from his influence, and she shivered involuntarily, although the fire had responded to her touch and had broken into a cheerful blaze.

'What if I do marry him?' she said, beginning to take down her hair slowly. 'I lose my money – Jim's money; that means that I lose my house, my position, my friends, all the fabric I have built up with the labour of seven whole years. And the gain is the passing love of a man. What fools women are!'

Yet she sat down and wrote to him then, in the great half-lighted drawing-room, with her long brown hair falling round her face – wrote him a pretty playful letter such as women love to write to the men who admire them: a word about Ascot, something about the late spring, and something somebody had told her about him.

At that moment her lover and the ugly boy were having supper at the club. The original dinner party did not seem to have satisfied the hunger of any of its guests.

'I should go for her and chance it,' said the ugly boy.

'No you wouldn't, Dicky, you would come across a pretty girl on the way and never get any further.'

The ugly boy seemed rather proud than otherwise of this tribute to his inconstancy, and ate the rest of his oysters with a pleased smile.

'Margaret Cousins is a seemly maiden, passing fair, and of a goodly wit,' he said reflectively.

'You could say that of any of them. That's the oddest thing about women; the essentials are always the same in the ones we fall in love with,' said Adrian, 'but do keep to the point, little boy. I'll rave about Margaret after, if you'll only talk about Mrs Angelo now.'

'What's her first name? I can't talk about a woman in confidence and call her by her surname, especially when she's a widow.'

'I don't know that she's got one. Heard from her this morning though, let's see what she signs herself; ah, here we are – Cynthia.'

'That's a bit off,' said Dicky in parenthesis, 'never heard of a horse called Cynthia.'

'You see,' continued Adrian with a slightly worried air, 'she doesn't know I twigged all about the Fountain Pen long ago, and she doesn't even know that I did the very poster we were talking about this evening. Shut up, Dicky, any blind idiot could have guessed that! – and she hasn't an idea how hard up I am, nor how many reasons there are for my marrying her.'

'Play lightly,' objected Dicky, 'even for a woman that's an amazing amount of ignorance. And she's in love with you, too.'

'Yes,' sighed Adrian, 'she *is* in love with me. Do you know, Dicky, it makes me almost hate myself sometimes when a sweet unsuspecting woman like that takes me on trust and thinks such an awful lot of me. I should have gone to the dogs long ago if it had not been for my women friends.'

'Do you really think,' asked Dicky, lighting up a cigar, 'they have made any difference?'

Adrian looked across at his plain, shrewd little countenance and shook his head slowly.

'Dicky, you are very young. But if you don't mind we will stick to the subject.'

Dicky said he was quite willing, and that women friends was as far as they had got. Adrian went on rather more gloomily than before: 'So you see it's all right as far as she is concerned. And as for myself – well, I suppose that's settled too. I never meant to get married at all, as you know, but I think it's not a bad thing for a man after all, and I don't see why I shouldn't marry Cynthia – do you? And of course I am extremely lucky to get such a good and sympathetic woman to marry me at all.'

'At your age, and with your tailoring, it is wonderful,' said the irrepressible Dicky. 'By the way, how old is Cynthia?'

'From calculation I make it about thirty-two. She looks less. I am thirty-eight, though of course you wouldn't think it. There is really everything to make our union a happy one. But then, there's the governor.'

'There always is,' assented Dicky sadly.

'And he has sworn to disinherit me if I marry into commerce. He means it too, worse luck.'

'What a played-out idea! Every decent chap marries into dollars nowadays; it's the thing to do. But that needn't matter; she's got fifteen thousand a year – must have – couldn't run that show on less, eh?'

'I haven't seen the will; she may lose it all if she marries again. I'm hanged if that would make any difference though, Dicky. I declare I'm fairly gone on her. I believe,' continued Adrian in a glow of sentiment, 'I really believe I should propose if neither of us had a penny! I should like to know about that will, though.'

'What a set of stale old properties you are inventing, Marks: irate father, inconvenient will, beautiful lady. You might be writing a novel in the last century.'

'You might remember, Dicky,' said Adrian impressively, 'that I have nothing to do with the spirit of any other century than this one. Now, what's your advice? Shall I propose or not?'

Dicky Askew blinked his small eyes at him and considered for a moment.

'You'll never have a better chance of being accepted, I should say. Given a woman who on your own showing adores you so much that she doesn't see your imperfections, and to whom you are so attached that her fortune does not matter a jot – well, there doesn't seem anything else to do.'

'Thanks awfully, little boy, you've helped me no end. I'll propose tomorrow, hanged if I don't. Not sure if I don't go down to Somerset House first, though; think about it in the morning. After all, you must remember Cynthia is not the only woman friend I've got who – I mean, the world is packed with good unselfish women who are ready to give us sympathy and affection and . . .'

'Fifteen thousand a year,' added Dicky maliciously.

Adrian paused before he strolled away.

'If there should be anything wrong about that will, there's always dear little Margaret Cousins,' he said thoughtfully.

'No, there isn't,' shouted Dicky wrathfully. 'You can leave Margaret out of this show anyhow. *She* wouldn't join anybody's army of women friends, so don't you make any mistake about it. You wouldn't catch *her* wanting to save you from the clutches of all the other women, which is what your women friends are mostly engaged in doing for you. Besides, she funks you no end – says she can't make you out, or something.'

'Really?' said Adrian with a gratified smile. 'That's excellent material to go upon. I must cultivate her. See you again soon, little boy.'

Margaret Cousins was lunching with Mrs Angelo Milton the next day when the manservant brought in a visiting card. She had come round to gossip over the dinner party, to eat up the remains, and to find out all there was to know about Dicky Askew; so she had a valid reason to grumble when her hostess said she must go into the drawing-room at once.

'But make yourself at home, child, and have what you want and ring for what you don't,' she said rather absently as she arranged her lace at the glass. 'It is an old friend; I have not seen him for years. You can play with the poodle till I come back, can't you, darling?'

A sunbrowned man, with an expectant smile on his face and rather a nervous consciousness of the hat and stick in his hand, was standing on the rug in the drawing-room when she went in. There was no diffidence in his greeting, however, and no doubt of a welcome in the hard hand he put out to her, though the one she laid in it was cold and passive. They had nothing to say for a minute or two, and when they had settled on two chairs rather far apart, and he had deposited his belongings on the floor, the few remarks they made were necessary and usual.

'So you have come to England after all, Willis? You always said you would.'

'Yes, Cynthia. It is an old promise of eight years' standing, isn't it?'

'When did you arrive?'

'This morning only. I crossed in the night boat from Dieppe. There was a fog in the Channel.'

'Was there? I believe there always is by the night boat. Have you had lunch?'

'I had a chop in the City: chose it myself, and saw it cooked. Not your style, eh? Well, and how long have you lived here?'

'Oh, how did you find out my address?'

'I went to your agents, of course. I saw that new poster of yours at Victoria, though what it means the Lord only knows, and that brought you back to my mind.'

'So it needed a new poster to do that? Oh, Willis, how you must have altered!'

It was the first human note in the conversation, and Willis Ruthven broke into a relieved laugh.

'You haven't altered much, Cynthia, in spite of your dandy house,' he said, and brought his chair closer to hers.

'I don't know. I fancy I must have. Or else it is you,' she replied, meeting the kindly gaze of his keen eye with something like discomfort.

'Why?'

'Well, you look so – so physical,' she said, and laughed.

'In the old days, when Jim was there, you used to tell me I was the intellectual one.'

'Ah yes, when Jim was there. You seemed so by contrast to the commercial element.'

There was distaste, almost contempt, in her voice, and he noticed it.

'Don't be hard on the commercial element; it has treated you well enough,' he said gently, with a swift glance round the room.

'Oh yes, I know all that,' she cried impatiently, 'you have dinned it into my ears so often. It has made England what it is, and so on. I must say that it has not much to be proud of! I *loathe* the commercial spirit.'

'Yet you have so much of it yourself,' said Willis with a smile.

'I? The commercial spirit?'

'Surely. Do you not trade with every bit of resource at your command, and very profitably so? It is your commercial spirit that has made you use up that old Italian ancestor of yours for a second

name. You trade with your beauty, your wits, your position; Jim
traded with the Milton Fountain Pen. Where is the difference?'

'I have always noticed,' said Cynthia, biting her lip, 'that men
who have travelled about alone for eight years become intolerably
prosy.'

Margaret Cousins was very tired of playing with the poodle long
before her friend was at liberty. It was not until tea-time that the
front door banged and Mrs Angelo called down the stairs to her to
come up to the boudoir.

'It is so much cosier to have tea here when we are alone,' she said
cheerfully. 'I hope you have not been dull, dear. Do you mind
bringing the kettle? Such an old friend, I have not seen him for
eight years.'

'He must be rather ancient,' said Margaret candidly. The poodle
had made her cross.

But Mrs Angelo Milton did not hear her remark: she was leaning
back in her chair, smiling at her thoughts.

'Tell me, Margaret,' she said suddenly, 'what do you think women
admire most in men? Is it good looks?'

'No,' said Margaret, thinking of the ugly boy.

'I am not sure,' said Cynthia, thinking of Adrian Marks. 'If not,
what is it?'

'Good tailoring perhaps,' suggested Margaret, still thinking of
Dicky.

'Oh no,' said Mrs Angelo, remembering the cut of Willis's frock
coat, 'I think it is temperament.'

'Conversation I should say,' corrected Margaret.

Cynthia put down her cup with decision.

'We are all wrong, Margaret. I have it. We like them to be
masterful. It doesn't matter what they are if they know how to
master us. Let them do it by their looks, or their brains, or their

qualities; but if they do it, we are theirs. And it isn't a flattering reflection for either sex.'

Margaret pouted, and recalled Dicky Askew, and refused to agree. But Cynthia was convinced. She was thinking only of Willis Ruthven.

II

Cynthia felt very unsettled during the next few days. When a woman has half-unwillingly made up her mind to an action that repels while it enthrals her, she can be easily deterred from it by a very small disturbing element. And the disturbing element in this case was the reappearance of Willis Ruthven. It was not only that the revival of an old friendship had blunted the edge of a new and untried one, nor wholly because the effete and decadent culture of Adrian Marks suffered by contrast with the frank and healthy personality of Willis. For she was affected on the other hand by the dread of being again absorbed in the old atmosphere she had hated, and this dread was kept alive by the knowledge that her early history was no longer her own secret, but was shared by someone else who saw no reason for concealing it. She had a real and strong friendship for Willis Ruthven, one of many years' growth, and she chafed at the influence it still had over her, now that she wanted to turn her back for ever upon all that it recalled to her mind. Willis represented the whole spirit of that time she wished to forget; he knew every detail of the past she had tried to blot out of her life with a persistence that was almost morbid. There was something pathetic in the way this woman, who had lived two different lives, feared lest the first one should claim her again for its own, something pitiful in the unconscious comparison she drew between the two men who competed for her thoughts, between the one who by his presence dragged her down to the old level, and the one who dwelt only in the surroundings she loved.

It is probable that she would not have thought so much about Adrian had not Willis gone out of town directly after his first interview with her, and only testified his existence to her by a refusal of a dinner invitation which annoyed her as much by its brevity and curtness as by the business-like paper on which it was written. Nor would she have bestowed so much notice on this trifling occurrence had not Adrian Marks also piqued her, about the same time, by neither calling upon her nor otherwise seeking her society; and although she made a point of frequenting the houses where there was a possibility of meeting him, all her efforts were attended with failure, as such conscious efforts always are.

She met Dicky Askew one hot day in June at an afternoon reception. It was a great crush, and he was not looking particularly happy on the crowded landing where the stream of people coming upstairs had imprisoned him.

'Let's sit out on the balcony,' he proposed. 'I'm fairly played with this awful crush – aren't you? I had to offend millions of decent people by getting the mother into a chair, and I don't suppose she will be able to move until I go and dig her out again.'

The ugly boy, although he cultivated a pose of selfishness like the others in his set, had a great devotion for his mother, which was so unusual a phenomenon among his friends that they never quite took him seriously about it, and had to suspect him of ulterior motives before they felt in a position to admire him for it. Nobody ever did take the ugly boy seriously about anything, but Cynthia was in the mood this afternoon to be touched by any sign of natural affection, and she followed him outside the window with more graciousness than she usually showed to anyone so unimportant.

'Have you seen your friend Mr Marks lately?' she asked him. She felt that it was not necessary to lead up to the subject with Dicky Askew. He looked steadily across the street at the house opposite, and hesitated.

'Marks? Not for millions of days. Have you?'

'I? Oh no. I don't know why I asked you. I thought you were such friends, that's all. You always suggest Mr Marks, you know.'

Dicky glanced doubtfully at her.

'The fact is,' he said with an impulse of confidence, 'we've had a beastly row; I'm afraid it's really all up this time. I haven't seen him once since Sunday.'

Cynthia murmured something and waited eagerly for more. The ugly boy grew expansive.

'The fact is,' he said again, leaning over the balustrade, 'Adrian is so beastly rotten. And she's an awfully decent little girl, don't you see.'

'Ah,' said Cynthia, also leaning over the balustrade and counting the paving stones feverishly.

'It's all tommy when a man talks about his women friends. It won't wash,' continued the ugly boy in a tone of disgust. 'It only means he likes to ring the changes like all the other boys, and won't own to it. The worst of it is that he does it so well. *She* doesn't care a jot for him, of course.'

'She doesn't?' said Cynthia joyfully.

Dicky looked at her reproachfully.

'What do you think? I never meant she would chuck me over for *him*. A fresh little nipper like that isn't likely to go nuts on a played-out painter chap. That *would* be common. All the same, it isn't fair on a fellow is it?'

'No,' said Cynthia sadly, 'it is not fair on a fellow.'

Something in her tone recalled Dicky for an instant from his own absorbing interests.

'I say, you know,' he said with a smile, 'if you cared to help me I don't know why you shouldn't. You may if you like, you know – really.'

Cynthia failed to express any gratitude, and Dicky wandered on.

'If you weren't playing so poorly with Adrian he wouldn't be fooling around with Margaret, and if you'd only just be decent to him again, don't you know – '

Here he was really obliged to stop, for he found Cynthia staring at him coldly.

'Oh, hang,' he said impetuously, 'I'm fairly gone on Margaret, don't you see?'

'Margaret?'

'Yes, of course. There isn't anybody else, is there?' said Dicky, a little sulkily.

'Oh,' said Cynthia, with a slight curl of her lip, 'I don't think you need be jealous. Margaret is a dear child, but she is not at all the sort of girl Mr Marks would be likely to admire.'

'Wouldn't he, though?' cried Dicky fiercely. 'He couldn't help it – nobody could help it; she's the decentest little brick of a girl – '

'Oh, very well; I thought you didn't want him to admire her.'

'No more I do, confound him! But he can't help admiring her, for all that.'

'Then I don't see how I am to help you. Supposing we change the subject; I am dreadfully tired of discussing other people's love affairs.'

'That sounds like a challenge to discuss your own,' said Dicky, with a shrewd smile. He was an obstinate fellow when he had an object in view.

'Mr Askew!' said Cynthia, rising with great dignity.

'Oh, I say, don't,' he said, anxiously, and placed himself in front of her. 'I'm an awful ass, of course; but I do know that Adrian was right on you a week ago, and – what the dickens has happened to everybody since?'

She nodded to him enigmatically and disappeared in the crowd, and he went to extricate his mother. They met again in the hall as everyone was leaving.

'I shall bring Adrian in to call tomorrow evening, may I?' he said.

'If it will tend to a reconciliation between you, I shall be delighted,' she answered blandly.

So she sent a note round the next day to ask Margaret to drop in to dinner, and assured herself that she was going through the whole tiresome business in order to bring about the child's engagement with the ugly boy. Margaret's chaperon was an aunt who did not look after her much, and the ugly boy was getting on well in his profession and had good connections; so Mrs Angelo felt she was only being virtuous when she put on her most becoming demi-toilette and laid herself out to be amusing the whole of dinner-time.

'By the way, Mr Askew said he might come in to coffee,' she said casually in the drawing-room afterwards. 'That was why I asked you to dinner.'

'I know; so is Mr Marks. I met them both in the park today. That is why I put on my yellow dress. Mr Marks likes me in yellow – I look peculiarly distinguished in it, he says!'

'Mr Marks says a variety of extravagant things to his lady friends.'

'Oh, Cynthia, are there really such a lot of them? Dicky is always dinning Mr Marks' lady friends into my ears till I cease to believe in them at all. There aren't many, are there?'

'Who is Dicky, dear?'

'Dicky Askew, of course,' laughed Margaret. 'Is there another Dicky?'

'Apparently not for you; but it is difficult to believe that you met him for the first time only a fortnight ago.'

'Ah!' said little Margaret wisely, 'but that was at your original dinner party, and that counted for six ordinary meetings with Auntie. Besides, you didn't give me a chance of talking to anyone else that evening; I never spoke to Mr Marks at all except about that hideous new poster. Did you see it noticed in the morning paper, by the way?'

'What poster?' asked Mrs Angelo Milton.

'The Fountain Pen poster, don't you remember? Why we talked ever such a lot about it, and – '

'Oh, I can't recall it, then. Posters don't interest me in the least; they are a vulgar form of art, I never think of looking at them. Are you getting on at the Slade, Margaret?'

'Yes – no – I don't know. But why don't you like posters, Cynthia?' persisted Margaret. 'Mr Marks doesn't call them vulgar; Mr Marks paints them himself.'

'Mr Marks didn't paint that one, anyhow; it is a hideous piece of affectation – '

'Then you do remember it?' cried Margaret triumphantly.

'No, I don't. How you do bother, child,' said Cynthia crossly. 'You've got posters on the brain. Mr Marks has evidently been making you one of his disciples.'

'Mr Marks?' said Margaret proudly. 'Oh yes, he has taught me such a lot about pictures – '

She paused abruptly as the door opened, and the two men were announced.

'Yes, very pretty, isn't it? A present from a friend in America,' said Cynthia, and rose to receive them.

Poor Margaret did not learn any more about posters that evening, for Mr Marks spent it in the boudoir with his hostess. It is true that the door between the two rooms was left half-open, and that Cynthia sometimes raised her voice in the interests of propriety to make a remark to the couple on the drawing-room sofa, but the conversation could not, on the whole, be termed a general one. Nor was it altogether fluent at first. Nobody but Cynthia had really mastered the situation, and she was almost too nervous to play her part. The ugly boy was quite happy at having planned the whole meeting, and felt quite sure it was going to settle the future of everyone present, and he had consequently plenty to say, but he found a curious difficulty in saying it, and Margaret, to whom he said it, was an unwilling listener. She was cross at being supposed to be in love with Dicky, and at having to endure his conversation all the evening; while Adrian Marks, who was far older and more interesting, dismissed her with a handshake and strolled after Cynthia into the other room.

Adrian Marks himself was full of pleasing sensations. A comfortable chair in a softly lighted, pretty room, and a clever woman to talk to, represented his favourite form of diversion; and the gratifying suspicion of having piqued her slightly by his remissness in calling added a zest to the situation.

But he had read the will at Somerset House, and he did not mean it to be more than a pleasant evening.

'Do you mind the window being open? It is hot in here, and besides, I like to see the trees in the square – don't you?' said Cynthia, settling herself in the low window-seat.

'I like anything that affords an excuse for a good pose,' he said, and looked at her and not at the trees.

It was a favourable opening, and Mrs Angelo Milton followed it up well. She had her own game to play this evening, and she was going to stake her happiness to win it. All the thraldom of her American life, all its sordidness and its gilded opulence, lay clearly before her mind and tortured her with its vividness; it only needed a decided action on her part to put it away from her for ever. And the man who could save her from its haunting memories was Adrian, whom she thought she loved sufficiently to marry because she had felt hurt when he neglected her. She knew he loved her too in his narrow, selfish way. And she felt tolerably sure she could win him if she tried; and, ignoble process though it was, she did try.

'You have been out of town?' she asked him when they had touched on various indifferent topics.

'Since I saw you? I hardly remember; I think not – no. Why do you ask?'

She laughed.

'How absurd of me! For the moment I forgot that of course you did not pay conventional calls after dinner parties like everyone else.'

He paused just long enough to give weight to his answer.

'I should not so far dishonour a charmingly unconventional dinner party. When I have made a friendship with a woman I never spoil it by afternoon calls.'

'That sounds rather interesting. But staying away altogether is an odd kind of substitute, don't you think?'

'It is the only substitute for a man who is afraid of what may result from an interview.'

'Afraid? You? After all your experience? I often wonder whether you have the same formula of conversation for all your lady friends, Mr Marks.'

'Well, no. There is the attractive formula for the timid and the reticent for the bold; the intellectual for the young and the playful for the old; the decorous for the matron and the indecorous for the maiden; and so on.'

'And to which class do I belong?'

'To no class, my dear lady. You are unique.'

'You said that so fluently that I shall suspect you of a common formula after all.'

'True fluency is never the result of study, and my remark was a spontaneous one. Won't you acknowledge that you gave me an excuse for spontaneity?'

Cynthia looked into the depths of the plane tree across the road, and yawned lazily.

'We are being dreadfully brilliant, and I am always afraid of you when you are brilliant. Won't you smoke? I have always noticed that when a man has nothing to do with his hands he becomes frankly untruthful.'

'You will join me, I hope?'

'For the same reason?'

'Oh no,' he said, taking a cigarette from the box she handed over to him. 'But I have always noticed that when a woman begins to smoke she becomes dangerously confidential.'

'You are quite safe,' she said drily. 'I never smoke. Mr Askew, will you have a cigarette? Margaret doesn't mind.'

The two from the drawing-room made a diversion by coming in and fetching the cigarettes. There was a search for matches, a few remarks about the beauty of the evening and the size of the plane tree, and then a gravitation towards the former arrangement. This time, Adrian was sitting on the window-ledge, and Mrs Angelo had slipped into a low chair close by.

'Life is very full of stupid arrangements,' said the artist presently. He was thinking of the amazing selfishness of the first husband when he made his will.

'For example?' she murmured. She was thinking of the small flat they would have to take when they were living on his earnings alone, and she had sacrificed her fortune for the artistic atmosphere.

'The distribution of – people,' said the artist. He had almost said – of wealth.

'Yes,' said Cynthia dreamily, 'the wrong ones have to be for ever together, and if we try to sort ourselves differently the old influences go on tugging at us until they prove strongest after all and absorb us again. It is horrible.'

'It is merely the planetary system,' said Adrian, looking up at the stars, 'and it gives the clever people lots of copy.'

'I don't see why we should be sacrificed to the clever people; they have so many compensations. It is the stupid people who can only feel things, who are the really important factors of life, and they have all the suffering,' cried Cynthia bitterly. She was forgetting the part she had planned for herself.

'What are we talking about?' said Adrian suddenly.

'You were being brilliant again,' she said, collecting herself with an effort.

'And my cigarette has gone out,' he laughed, and went across to a candle to light it.

They listened mechanically to the voices through the open door.

'It's no use, it won't draw, I tell you. Nobody could make it draw, it's got stuffed up with something. I am quite sure the strings I have been eating are not tobacco at all. It's the stupidest cigarette I ever smoked.'

'It looks a bit played, doesn't it? You've used all my matches and the spills hang out in the other room. Stick to it a moment while I freeze on to a coal, will you?'

Margaret evidently had no difficulty in sticking to the cigarette, and Dicky must have achieved the extraordinary feat of freezing on to a coal, for there was no more conversation in the drawing-room for the next few moments, and when it began afresh a piano-organ in the street below completely drowned it.

'That's a good effect,' said Adrian, leaning over the window-box, 'the lamps and the background of bushes, and the weird light on that man's face – awfully fine, isn't it?'

She came and looked out with him.

'Very,' she said. 'Have you been painting much lately?'

'No. I've been literally off colour. Weather, I suppose.'

'Or a new lady friend?' she suggested, under cover of the clanging music in the street.

Her eyes had a fascinating light in them when she looked mischievous, and Adrian mentally included his old father and the late Mr Milton in the same big curse. It was hard, and it grew harder as the evening wore on, that everyone should put obstacles in the way of his marrying one of the few women he had ever really liked. He felt quite sorry, too, for her, and wished magnanimously he could do something to lessen her evident infatuation. But he felt most sorry for himself.

'Possibly,' he replied gaily; 'it is generally that. I am a bad lot, you know, Mrs Milton.'

He looked at her narrowly, but she only laughed and ran her fingers through the lobelia in the window-box.

'You don't think I am very bad, do you?' he asked, bending a little towards her.

'I think you would be exceedingly disappointed if I didn't think so,' she retorted, without looking at him. The organ had moved on, and the strains of a popular air came faintly round the corner and mingled with the rustle of the plane trees and the passing footfall of the policeman. The conversation in the drawing-room was no longer distinguishable, and the only distractions came from outside. Adrian drew in his head and stood a little behind her.

'I should like to know what you do think about me,' he said curiously. 'Is it something very bad?'

'It is something quite formless,' she replied indifferently.

'Do you think about me at all?' he asked, putting his hands in his pockets and keeping them there with an effort.

'As much, possibly, as you think about me.'

'And do you know how much that is?'

'Just so much thought as a man is likely to bestow on one woman when there are twenty others.'

She was acting now, not to gain her point, but to hide her real feelings. And unconsciously she won her game, as it must always be won.

'Why do you say that?' he asked, coming nearer to her.

'It is not I who say it. I am merely repeating what you have said to me dozens of times. What nonsense we are talking! Shall we go in to the others?'

Ten o'clock struck slowly from a neighbouring church tower, and they stood and counted the strokes in silence as though the slight mental effort was a sort of relief to their constraint. Then she moved a little and felt his touch on her bare arm.

'Don't go, Cynthia.'

He crushed her hand against his lips and pulled her almost roughly towards him.

'There are not twenty others,' he whispered.

When the two men left the house together half an hour later Adrian uttered an exclamation in an unduly loud tone.

'I say, that's rather strong, isn't it?' said Dicky, whose reflections were of a peculiarly happy nature.

'It's not strong enough for the fools who make wills,' replied Adrian, and drove off alone in a hansom.

III

For a woman who has staked everything and won the game sooner than she expected, Mrs Angelo Milton wore a singularly dissatisfied appearance when she came downstairs the next morning. She wrote letters in her boudoir until the smell of the window flowers became intolerable and she had to take refuge in the drawing-room; and there she had two separate quarrels with the maid over the dusting of the ornaments and the arrangement of the flowers, and ended with the inevitable threat that she would in future do them both herself. This she began at once to carry into effect by walking about the room with a duster and making herself very hot and cross. When she had broken a valuable Venetian glass, and made the startling discovery that all the dust she dissipated settled somewhere else directly afterwards, she hid the duster under a sofa cushion, collected all the flowers out of all the vases and piled them in a heap in the fender. Then she sat down on the hearth-rug and looked at them helplessly, and felt very foolish, when Margaret came in without being announced and laughed at her.

'My dear Cynthia, what *is* the matter, and whatever are you doing on the floor?' cried the girl.

'I'm doing the flowers,' cried Cynthia briskly. 'How jolly you look. Did you trim that hat yourself?'

'Yes, it's my old Louise, don't you remember? But what's the matter?'

'Matter?' cried Mrs Angelo in a tone of amazement, 'what should be the matter? I am particularly happy this morning. Something very nice that I wanted very much indeed has happened to me, and I never felt more pleased about anything in my life.'

'You've got a very funny way of looking pleased,' said Margaret candidly, 'and it's more than I feel myself. I've come round to tell you something, Cynthia, something very important and not at all pleasant to either of us. But hadn't you better get off the floor first?'

'Well, what is it, child?' asked Mrs Angelo when she had limped with two cramped legs to the nearest chair.

'I only wish you to understand quite clearly that I am not in love with Dicky Askew, whatever Dicky Askew may be with me, and that I won't be left alone with Dicky Askew until I have heard all his stories twice over and he is obliged to propose for the sake of more conversation. I never want to speak to Dicky Askew again; I should like him to be – obliterated.'

'My dear,' said Cynthia, 'I don't keep Dicky Askew on the premises. Did you really put on a new hat on purpose to come and tell me something that doesn't concern me at all?'

'Doesn't concern you?' cried Margaret. 'I should like to know whom it does concern then.'

'Dicky Askew, I should say. Really, my dear child, I am very sorry I mistook your feelings; I won't make up a party for you again.'

'It was not,' said Margaret with great dignity, 'the party that I objected to. It was only Dicky Askew.'

'I did it out of kindness,' replied Cynthia, ignoring her insinuation.

'Then I hope you will never ask me to dinner again out of kindness, or if you do, please shut me in here with the man I am *not* in love with,' responded Margaret. 'I should not have minded at all if I had spent the evening with the man I was *not* in love with, last night.'

'I think you are right,' said Cynthia quietly, and she stroked the child's hot cheek soothingly as she spoke. 'Passing the evening with the man you are in love with is very exhausting indeed. We will try the opposite arrangement next time. Will you come out with me this afternoon?'

'Where to?' asked Margaret suspiciously.

'Hurlingham, of course.'

'It's too bad,' cried the girl indignantly, 'you *knew* he was going to be there! One would think there was no one in the world but Dicky Askew.'

'One would, to hear you talk,' said Cynthia.

When she was alone again, she went to the writing-table and tried to write a letter. She made two rough copies and tore them up, began a third and burst into tears in the middle. The anticipation of the artistic atmosphere for the rest of her life did not seem to be exhilarating.

'Mr Ruthven,' announced the manservant.

'Oh, how do you do?' said Cynthia with desperate composure.

'What's the matter?' he asked bluntly, just as Margaret had done. 'And what are all those flowers on the floor for? It looks like a funeral.'

'It isn't – they're not – oh don't,' said Cynthia with an hysterical sob.

Willis had hold of her hand still and drew her on to the sofa beside him.

'Something seems to have disturbed you,' he said, and cleared his throat sympathetically. 'What is it, eh?'

'I can't very well tell you,' she replied with an effort to be calm.

'Then don't,' said Willis, in the tone he might have used in soothing a child. 'We'll talk about something else instead. I was down at Johnson's just now – '

'Johnson's? Whatever did you go to my agent's for?' she asked in a surprised tone.

'To ask him if your affairs were in a satisfactory condition,' he replied frankly.

'Why did you want to know!'

'For reasons I will tell you presently.'

'And pray, what did he say about my affairs?'

'Oh, excellent report, never been selling better, largely owing to that new poster he says; it just wanted that to freshen up the sale a bit. Bless me, what have I said now, Cynthia?'

'Oh, nothing. I am sick of that new poster. Margaret was full of it yesterday. Everybody is full of it. Why did they want a new poster to freshen up the sale just now? I don't want the horrible money.'

She wondered why he looked so pleased.

'Don't you really, Cynthia? Would you give it up willingly if – if you, well, if the terms of the will had to be fulfilled?'

She turned and looked at him with a hunted look in her eyes.

'How did you know? What makes you ask me that?' she burst out.

'Of course I knew, my dear,' he answered with his genial smile. 'Why, I made Jim add that codicil myself.'

'You? *You* made him? Willis, I don't understand. Why did you?'

'For the same reason that I have come here this morning, Cynthia. Is it so difficult to understand, then?'

There was a slight tremble in the bluff tones, but she did not notice it. She was so absorbed in her own engrossing affairs this morning that her faculties had grown incapable of receiving any impression from outside. She continued to look at him questioningly.

'What reason?' she asked.

'Because I knew what you didn't know then, poor child – that Jim was dying. And I meant to come back for you after seven years and take you for my own – if you would come. We were such good friends, Cynthia, and – I thought perhaps you would come. So I made Jim put in that clause about the property. You see, I meant your love for me to stand the test of a sacrifice, and I wanted mine to be free from a suspicion of self-interest. Do you blame me very much, dear?'

She let him finish his speech without interruption. Her first impulse was to laugh hysterically; every nerve and every instinct she possessed seemed alive, it almost hurt her to think, and the main impression she gathered from his words was the humorous aspect of them in the confidence of success that underlay their humility. Why was everyone so sure of being accepted by her?

She did not speak for an instant or two. She sat and stared stupidly in front of her. He came a little closer to her with a smile on his face, and then she broke away from him with a distracted cry. It seemed to his slowly awakening comprehension as though the air he was breathing were shivered by the pain of that cry.

'Oh, Willis, don't! Go away, leave me, hate me, can't you? Oh, don't you see? I can't, I can't. Take your eyes away, they hurt me so. I cannot marry you now. What evil power sent you here this morning? Why couldn't you wait until everybody knew? Don't you understand, I – I have promised someone else? There, go.'

It was his turn now to be silent, and to stare in complete stupefaction. She bore it as long as she could, and then with a bitter sense of the comedy of the situation she stammered out a trembling supplication: 'Oh, Willis, do scold me – or something. Don't be so ridiculously unlike yourself!'

She crouched away from him in the far corner of the sofa, and buried her face in the cushions. There was no sound except the rushing in her ears for several minutes. When he spoke again it seemed as though a wave were receding slowly and unwillingly on the seashore.

'I am very sorry, Cynthia. Of course I am going – to be sure, yes.'

She was conscious that he rose from the sofa and stood a little away from her.

'I suppose you wouldn't mind my knowing his name? Don't tell me if you would sooner not,' said his voice, grown gentler still.

A woman rarely finds it difficult to pronounce the name of her lover, and Cynthia recovered some of her self-possession in the effort.

'I don't suppose you have ever heard of him. His name is Marks – Adrian Marks.

There was one of those rapid transitions from artificial composure to natural display of feeling, and Cynthia, listening dully to his movements, heard the springs of the sofa suddenly creak again as Willis dropped back heavily on to his seat.

'Bless my soul!' he said in his own voice and manner.

Cynthia raised herself and looked coldly at him.

'Adrian Marks?' he repeated, smoothing his hair with a large white handkerchief. 'Adrian Marks?'

'Do you know him?' asked Cynthia curtly.

'Know him? Rather think I do! Little unphysical bit of a man – eh? Hair getting thin on the top, sallow complexion, no hands to speak of – should think I did know him, that's all. Do you really mean Adrian Marks? Impossible!'

'He is an artist. I don't expect you to understand what that means. And I am going to marry him, which I think ought to spare him your jeers. And I really think we had better end this useless discussion.'

'Bless my soul!' exclaimed Willis again, 'but we are only at the beginning of it. My poor Cynthia, you must have wanted to marry very badly.'

Mrs Angelo made a struggle to retain her dignity.

'I don't think you have at all grasped that I am engaged to Mr Marks – '

'Well, it is a bit difficult,' acknowledged Willis. 'Why, I could wipe the floor with him in one – Does he know about the will?'

'He did not know until I told him,' said Cynthia proudly, making the most of her one advantage, 'and then he said my poverty only made me more precious to him: Mr Marks, also, is ready to take me for myself.'

The insinuation in her last words was meant to impress her hearer, but he only thrust his hands into his pockets and nodded at his boots, and made a vulgar exclamation.

'You bet he is, quite ready,' he muttered incredulously. 'That sounds like Mr Adrian Marks, doesn't it? Oh yes, of course.'

Cynthia sat with burning cheeks and said nothing. Willis got up with a sigh and looked down at her searchingly.

'Do you really think you are in love with Adrian Marks, Cynthia? Do you really?'

It was the question she had put to herself doubtingly for many weeks, but to hear it from the lips of another destroyed her last remnant of composure.

'It is easy for you to sneer,' she cried angrily, 'you who never had a thought apart from commerce, and the making of gold, and the heartless game of getting on in the world. What right have you to depreciate a man behind his back because he lives by his intellect and his talent, and because he moves in a world you have no suspicion of? It is mean and unmanly of you.'

Willis by no means showed himself disconcerted at this outburst. She was in the mood that was most familiar to him, the one in which he had seen her most often before, and he brightened considerably at the opportunities it offered him.

'Doesn't he get paid for his pictures then, eh?' he asked with a chuckle.

'I don't mind how much you laugh,' cried Cynthia. 'I have heard all those stale arguments before, and they are quite fruitless, every one. I am glad I never need listen to them any more; I am glad there is someone who can lift me out of my old miserable surroundings, and who can't allude to them either because he never knew anything about them. Adrian will never know any more of my history than I choose to tell him, never! I am glad I am going to throw away my ill-gotten fortune, the price of trade and robbery and everything I loathe. I am glad, glad, glad!'

Willis Ruthven gave a long whistle and strode over to the window before he spoke.

'Who told you that Marks didn't know anything about you?' he asked sharply.

'What do you mean?' she said, with a vague feeling of alarm.

'Well, my dear girl, I suppose that the fool who painted that nonsensical poster of yours must have known what he was painting it for, eh? Not that the poster itself proves it, to be sure.'

Cynthia did not speak. The artistic atmosphere was being slowly dissipated.

'All I know is,' went on Willis from the window, 'that when I was down at Johnson's this morning, this dandy artist you mention happened to descend from a world of his own in order to look in about the payment for that particular poster. Do you mean to tell me he doesn't know who you are? Bless my soul, Cynthia, it's time you had someone to look after you.'

The delusion in which she had been living was shattered at one blow. Cynthia cowered for a moment beneath it, and then collected herself again with an instinct of self-preservation. She rose and walked over to the fireplace and began picking up the flowers. Her face was quite white, but she kept it turned away from him, and when she spoke it was in a tone of exaggerated composure.

'If you have said all you want to say, Willis, we will drop the subject. You have given me a good deal of gratuitous information about my private affairs, and I don't find it very amusing. I am rather busy this morning, too.'

But Willis had no intention of taking the hint to leave. He came away from the window and spoke to her instead.

'You poor little woman, to think that I should have to be the one to tell you what any man would have twigged in a brace of shakes,' he said in a sympathetic tone as he rubbed his hat with his coat sleeve. 'I always did have to look afer you, didn't I, Cynthia?'

Cynthia nearly choked in an attempt to tell him to leave her, but he stood up in the middle of the room and went on speaking, quite unconscious of the storm that was raging in her mind.

'But there, of course it was only a fancy freak on your part. Lord, what inexplicable creatures women are, to be sure. However a fine woman like you, Cynthia, with your taste and your head could have – but there, of course, you didn't care about him really, how could you? Poor child, poor child. I won't bother you any more now; you'll like to think it over a bit – women like to think things over, eh?'

And he really went that time, without the farewell greeting she was dreading and yet longed for; and she sat up and listened to his retreating footstep on the stairs, and felt she would have done anything in her power to make him come back and scold and comfort her all at once for her foolishness. Yet she did not make an effort to recall him, but sat on the floor instead and wept hot tears of shame and disappointment over his stick and gloves. And Willis walked away down the street with his arms swinging and his hat at the back of his head.

How he spent the day never transpired, but to Cynthia it was the longest day of her life. She rang for the maid to clear up the confusion of the drawing-room, and went upstairs to put powder on her face.

Then she gave herself up to the consideration of her misfortunes, and went without her lunch. She countermanded the carriage and issued the mandate of 'Not at home', passed the afternoon in her bedroom where she persuaded herself she was going to be very ill, and took antipyrine, which she had heard was a preventive against something. About five o'clock she changed her dress, and made rather a substantial tea on finding to her disgust that she was healthily hungry, and then she sat on the balcony without a vestige of a headache left, and envied the cheerful people who passed in their carriages, and wished somebody would call.

Somebody did call about an hour before dinner-time, but he sent his card up first with a pencilled message upon it.

'You can show Mr Ruthven up, and tell cook not to make a second entrée tonight,' she said, making herself effective on a couch near the window. She had decided that her attitude was to be smiling indifference, but she never thought of it again when Willis burst into the room in front of the stately footman, seized both her hands in a friendly grasp and straightway burlesqued her studied pose.

'My dear silly little woman,' he said, and looked at her and laughed mirthfully.

'Willis, I'm not, I won't be – '

'You'll have to be,' he said, laughing more than ever, and kissing the tips of her fingers on both hands.

'Let me go,' cried Cynthia fiercely.

'Do you mean that?' he said, loosening his clasp and looking directly at her.

Cynthia turned away from him, and stamped her foot.

'I don't know,' she muttered sulkily.

'Of course you don't,' said Willis jovially, 'women never do. We always have to make up their minds for them. You're as bad as any of them, Cynthia.'

'You talk as though I had nothing to do but to listen to you,' cried Cynthia angrily.

'You don't look to me as though you had done much else since you got up this morning,' replied Willis bluntly.

'Is that my fault?' she exclaimed with burning cheeks. 'Can I help your coming and wasting all my time? When I tell you to go, you don't.'

'Tell me to go? But you don't,' said Willis.

'I – I do,' said Cynthia, looking down.

'When? Now?' he demanded.

'Yes, now,' she said, with her back to him and her hands clenched.

'If I go,' she heard him say slowly and deliberately behind her, 'it will be for always, Cynthia.'

'I don't care,' was her reply.

'For always, Cynthia,' he repeated doggedly.

She shrugged her shoulders and turned a little towards him.

'You know you couldn't keep away,' she said scornfully.

'You know you couldn't do without me,' he rejoined, and began humming a tune.

'I have done without you for eight years.'

'And a pretty mess you've got yourself into at the end of them,' cried Willis.

'I haven't – it's you. It would have been all right if you had not interfered,' she said, facing him again.

'Would it? Then I'm to go, is that it?' he said, and took no notice of her change of expression as he picked up his hat.

'It is for always, Cynthia,' he said, and held out his hand.

Cynthia burst into tears.

'There, I *knew*,' said Willis, coughing violently for no reason whatever.

'What did you know?' sobbed Cynthia, swaying towards him.

'That you would have to give in,' he laughed, coming nearer to her.

'Why?' said she, struggling to free herself as he put his arms round her.

'Because I said so, of course. Bless me, is that going to displease you too?'

'I *hate* you for saying that, but – I'm glad you did,' she whispered. 'I suppose I must ask you to dinner,' she said presently.

'They will be all my dinners in the future,' he said with exultation in his voice. 'How will it please you to come to me for all your pocket-money, eh?'

'As much, possibly, as it will please you to find out how much pocket-money I require,' retorted Cynthia.

'To think,' continued Willis, 'that I owe all my happiness to that ridiculous poster –'

'You don't,' cried Cynthia; 'you owe it all to coming in this morning! I was writing to Adrian when you arrived. I should never have listened to him at all if you had not gone out of town. I am perfectly certain I shouldn't,' she added firmly, in the hope of convincing herself of this comfortable conclusion. Willis had always been convinced of it, and kissed her with a proud sense of victory.

'Do you want me to go and finish him off, or anything?' he asked cheerfully.

Cynthia was alarmed at the vision of her late lover being murdered in his studio by one blow from a heavy walking-stick, and said she thought she would be meeting him herself at Lady Houghton's dance that evening. And she wondered vaguely at the same moment why he had not been to see her all day.

The reason for his absence was quite simple. He had woken up in the morning in a mood that strangely resembled Cynthia's, though it probably showed itself differently in him, and arose from another cause. He stayed in bed and blamed himself until midday; and he tried to paint and blamed his model until sunset. He called himself a fool in no measured terms for having allowed his feelings to run away with him, and he considered carefully every possible way of extricating himself from his predicament. The day wore on, and he arrived at no satisfactory solution of the difficulty. A letter did not commend itself to him because he could not write letters; women always had the best of it, he reflected, when it came to letter-writing. Besides, what had he to say except that he found he had made a mistake on the previous evening? It was not a graceful admission to make in any case, but to say it in his best manner and in carefully chosen surroundings satisfied his sense of the fitness of things more than the idea of seeing it baldly represented in black and white. Besides, he had really persuaded himself that he loved her very deeply, and he had a lingering hope that an interview might present some pathetic though compensating features that could never arise from an exchange of letters. Yet the evening came and he had not fixed a time nor a place for it.

He dined with Dicky Askew at his favourite restaurant; and the dinner was not so good as usual, and Dicky's conversation related entirely to Hurlingham and had a vagueness and an absence of particulars about it which, at any other time, would have aroused his suspicions, but which only succeeded this evening in irritating him more than before. He dressed for Lady Houghton's dance in a dejected frame of mind, and he went forth in a hansom like a victim who knows that his doom is awaiting him.

Margaret, with whom he had his first dance, found him astonishingly dull. She was full of conversation herself, and she rallied him on his mood as he led her into the conservatory after one or two turns round the crowded room.

'Why weren't you at Hurlingham this afternoon?' she said.

'Is it necessary to go to Hurlingham?' he asked with his weary smile. It struck him that she was looking very pretty and well-dressed.

'Of course. Everybody does,' said Margaret conclusively. 'It is bright and amusing, and the best-dressed people go there. There is polo too, I believe.'

'But I am not interested in polo,' objected Adrian.

'Oh, that doesn't matter. Nobody is. I didn't dream of looking at the polo today. But it was perfectly thrilling,' she added with a glow on her face.

'How young and fresh you are,' said the artist involuntarily. 'Is it only Hurlingham that can bring that look on to your face, Margaret?'

'Mr Marks! what have I said? I only meant that I enjoyed myself rather,' said Margaret, looking confused and blushing furiously; 'the drive and the air, you know, and – and the polo of course – '

Adrian was silently rejoicing that she was, to the best of his knowledge, completely untrammelled by any will.

'Don't let me frighten you,' he murmured in his softest tones; 'I was thinking that the man who could make you look like that would be the happiest man in the world.'

Margaret was a little bewildered at first; then her face cleared up and she smiled up at him happily. She remembered that Dicky had been dining with him.

'Do you think so really?' she said. 'Do you think he *is*?'

'Well,' said Adrian, slightly startled, 'that of course depends on whether you will make him so.'

The words escaped his lips without reflection. The intoxicating scent of the hothouse plants, the swing of the music in the next room, his own dissatisfaction – all combined to make him seize the opportunity that she evidently meant to give him.

'Why of course I will!' cried Margaret, turning to him with another blush and smile.

Adrian hardly allowed himself to breathe.

'Do you really mean that, darling?' he said, bending towards her.

'Dicky!' cried the astonished girl, springing up to meet the ugly boy who was coming to claim her. 'Dicky, tell him! I thought you had; he doesn't understand! Where's Auntie?'

And she fled across the tessellated floor and left the two friends face to face.

The ugly boy laughed exultantly.

'Thought you'd guess, old man, after what I said at dinner. Has she been trying to tell you, the little brick? She knows we're pals, you see, that's why.'

'Yes,' said Adrian faintly. 'I expect that's why. Congratulate you, Dicky.'

'Thanks awfully, old chap. I knew you'd be glad,' laughed Dicky, shaking his hand vigorously. 'I am beastly lucky, eh? See you for a drink after this dance.'

Adrian stood irresolute for a moment when the ugly boy had gone. He picked one or two flowers to pieces, ground his heel savagely into them as they lay on the floor, and then strolled aimlessly round the edge of azalea under which he had been sitting with Margaret.

On the opposite side of it he found Mrs Angelo Milton sitting alone. There were only two constructions to be placed on the situation and he desperately assumed the happiest.

'Oh, here you are,' he began, with a wretched attempt at composure. 'I have been looking for you everywhere.'

Cynthia looked at him from head to foot without moving.

'I don't think I have the pleasure,' she said, with a calm smile. 'There seems to be some mistake.'

And Adrian took his dismissal and his departure simultaneously.

'Well, how did your puny little wall-painter take it?' asked Willis Ruthven the next day.

'He seemed surprised,' said Cynthia, and concealed a smile.

❧ *Pass the Parcel*

CANDIA MCWILLIAM

A year younger than the century, I tell the nurses, and watch the expressions form up on their blank young faces. Once, being a year younger than the century meant that I was thirteen, but now it means that I am some age for which I am accounted wonderful and at which no friend remains to me. I have tried to make friends with new people, but their destination is not the same as mine. They will come to rest in another time, when I will have become part of the past, a kind of compost for their own flowering. It doesn't do to look too closely at the components of the compost, but once it has reduced to a fine-textured lumpless loam it will serve its purpose well enough. At the time, of course, we did not know what we were throwing upon the compost heap. Along with the old ways, constricting corsetry and weak emperors, we chucked a multitude of living bones. Those many wars were open-mouthed for food, and liked it fresh. The bodies that did come home had often left their minds behind for good.

We can't seem to pass it on, the awful truth we know. It's a parcel we can't pass, tired and messy now, with out-of-date stamps and string too knotted to be worth saving. It's been redirected so often there's not much room for more words on the wrapping, but it always comes back to the sender. No one wants it. It's not a nice present, the past that is mine.

Here's where the difference is, as I see it, between being me and being the next-door old woman, lying in the bed light and grey as driftwood; it seems to me that her wits have stolen away from her, so she is no longer holding the parcel. She is living, I perceive, in the now, like a baby. Not that I envy her. She is like a baby in other ways, and must be moved and swabbed and powdered in a manner I hope she does not mind. I would mind. I don't like people up close to me; I should hate them near me in that way. Having things done for me is my idea of hell. It is this streak that has kept me going; I've derived my energy from it. It kept up my appearance too, at least fifteen years longer than my poor child's looks lasted. Her softness bloated her and blurred her features, while I have kept myself down to the bone with willpower, discipline, self-restraint. I have not been one to take sugar. You could not show me the occasion on which I have lost command, and so it is here in hospital although I am a year younger than the century, and have hair the colour of old thin polished forks, done like a child's in an Alice band and hanging down my aching back. Here I wear clothes I know are not my own. They come from a room full of uncreasable garments chosen by the dead.

I shall not have a deathbed; it will be a chair. I shall meet death awake and sitting up, though I shall not rise to greet it. It will have come to relieve me of the parcel, which grows heavier in ways I do not care for, while the parts of the parcel that might once have appealed to me, the coloured and scented bows that held my life in shape like good sheets in a linen press, and the folded tissue of memories, seem to have gone to dust.

This had not been my understanding. The old people whom I

knew when I was young remembered not the great impersonal events but the vinegar-and-fruitcake taste of farthing toffee, or the stripes on a spinning top. I have been awaiting these sweet visitations from my early life. But I find that those things I remember are facts, not feelings or sensations. What I recall is old news: wars and bombs, death plural or unnatural, great shiftings of boundaries and skies full of killing rain. The shinier events of the time in which I lived, the sort of events that are recorded in magazines rather than newsprint, have fallen away.

Remembering is accounted an indulgence. Old folk are meant to smile over their memories, turning the pages like a tired mother with her mid-morning coloured paper, in the certainty of small reliable gratifications well earned. If I ever possessed such memories, they have been collected by some operative keen to reduce clutter in the minds of old women. I am left with the dingy impacted weight of a million stored newspapers. As they rot down, they become drier and more acid, the events they record more monumental, arbitrary and heartless. I search my memory for scraps of colour. I enter more rooms stacked with towers of newspaper, great autumnal heaps of events – but bled of the colour of autumn. The rooms frequently display one wall blown off and wallpaper indecently open to the sky. I find no human traces, no boot or bowl or knife. Were I to find such a thing, what would I do? Put it away, certainly, for I have always insisted upon everything in its own place. I am the tidiest person I have ever known; I say it in all modesty. I could reduce the Milky Way to order, given time.

I know I had some moments that must have meant something, that you might expect to have left something of themselves behind; I had a husband and a daughter, after all. Of him I recall his motorcycle sidecar and his hard collars for the office, his household accounting and his succumbing, moribund, to televised boxing, and later to golf. I never loved him as I loved the parquet floor, that made under my houseworking feet a rewarding bony sound of business and direction. But I should never have had that floor without him; perhaps my cool heart has been my salvation.

The daughter was a disappointment. It was fortunate I did not fall for her at once, as I saw other mothers fall for their new babies, or I might have been downcast when things fell out badly. I had the satisfaction of knowing I had tried with her; it was not I but she who failed. Still it is strange that I have no sweet memories of her; children are said to be sweet, after all, and she was once a child, though all I recall of it is the struggling, to get her out of me, and, once she was out, to keep her within the necessary boundaries. She has failed me in that too. She offers no sweet memories, even though she is dead.

It was like her to die, just when the children of our acquaintances were giving them grandchildren. She was too selfish for that. If any man would have had her, to marry that is, which I doubt. There was one she wanted, but we could not have him. My husband had not worked himself to the bone for that, to see his only descendant marry a nobody without prospects and more airs than common sense. He had paint on his twills when he visited, and he encouraged her to cut off her hair. I made her go back and have it made into a switch, naturally. I told her, 'With your face you will find you need all the hair you can get.' She had the features of a horse without the domestic skills. Her hair was her one attribute, and my God how we worked over it, my husband and I. He would skelp her with the brush if ever she mentioned getting it cut, and I would give it a hundred strokes at night with the same brush to keep it shiny from the roots to the bitter end. I had her stand up for this after the hair grew past her sit-upon.

She had dirty gypsy ways and vandalised the frocks I bought her.

There was a mother-of-pearl gown, tight at the waist, with runs of buttons all down the forearm, and pixie detailing. She dyed it. Black, so it shimmered like curtains caught in a house-fire. I said to her, 'What did you think you were doing?' and she said, 'Dyeing.'

She never fitted in with us and the reason is we were too soft. We were generous. I turned out her room for her every day till she died. She would never have had to work, unless she insisted on remaining unmarried. She was not feminine, that was the trouble. She had no idea of how to make the best of herself. It is doubtful that she ever asked herself what it was a man wanted, although I had told her enough times.

I could not have had the progeny of that whore in my house. She took it with her when she went, which was not as stupid as she usually contrived to be. She wasn't far gone, but it would have showed soon and her father would have killed her. She took that off his hands and did the job herself. The boy moved away from here and is no doubt a big noise in the world of paint, up in London. A huge mouth he had, always laughing; he was polite in that way they are when they think they know more than you. His father, unlike my husband, had not made a tidy fortune with his own hands. You could tell that right away.

Of course she had messed it up, but with her gone we returned to the old life. I threw her pyjama-case monkey out, and the shelf of books. I changed the candlewick in her room to a fresh willow green on both the beds. I had told her she could have a friend to stay every year round her birthday, but she said, 'No thank you.' It was as though she didn't think I'd make her precious friend welcome. Now we know what we know, perhaps it's as well we didn't have the birthday visitor. We were not good enough for our daughter, that was it. She wanted messy people, used to bounty, loiterers and loungers taking their blessings for granted. You could tell that boy came from money, he always wore the same old clothes.

No, she was not a feminine creature, my daughter. Her great feet and hands and the way she talked right the way around a thing as though she was eating it, these told against her, and the glasses she needed from the reading she insisted she enjoyed, just to make us feel inferior for having done real work. She had no friends round our home, everyone in the road saw the difficulties we had with her, and the way she took it out of us, smoking cigarettes in the street with no hat on and wearing outfits you would not be seen dead in. I sometimes wondered why we raked the gravel and swept up the leaves when she would be coming home from school to mess them up again. It was worse than a dog, but with none of the gratitude.

It doesn't take genius to see the woman in the next bed has been without the advantages that have made my life what it is. She lies there with only the Complan in the beaker to look forward to. Her nightdresses are shocking, bright robes with no shape and ridiculous pictures on them of bears in space rockets, or dancing carrots in the arms of manly leeks. Her slippers are big furry cows' faces, with a pink curly tongue poking out of the front of each one, and rolling eyes – the scared-soppy eyes of creatures in cartoons. Not feminine. No self-respect. She can't wear the slippers, but she has them. Now, what is the point of that, to have something you do not need? All around her bed is clutter, most of it useless. There are chocolate bars in disorderly piles, and other confectionery including special-occasion boxes with large bows on them, pinned flat like museum moths. There are always flowers, invariably in want of rearrangement. The magazines look no better than they ought, with 'true love' stories printed so large on the pages you could not help reading the words from here where I sit, even if you were not forced to listen while one of the interminable daughters or grandchildren reads to the old object in the bed. They turn her and stroke her and dust off the biscuit crumbs they have made on her as they shout and munch and giggle and coo around the bed. They talk to her all the time. It's pointless, naturally. I could tell them that. They make a great operation of drawing the curtains round her bed – it's a cot really – and changing her nightgown for another unsuitable creation. They hold her hands and kiss them, not on the back as foreign men do in the films, but on the knuckles, sometimes once for each knuckle. Well, it's not my way. The overuse of kissing has not escaped my notice as a general trend. It has at least doubled, and that is among the merely acquainted.

What need has she in the next bed for privacy? She surely has no pride. She knows nothing of her present circumstances. All that old woman can have left to her is her memories, and a soft shapeless little bundle they must compose.

We've open visiting hours here. All day they are at it, the family of the dying old woman, as though they can introduce themselves to death when it comes and make it part of the family.

I shall be alone when we meet, up and dressed, like the bride of the century, than which I am younger by a year. I shall give back the parcel that I have to pass. It is not light at all. How ever I carried it I do not know. And I did so alone. I have never had that much use for other people.

Around the bed of the old woman who does not move sit the members of her family, in dark coats and with bare heads. Some of them have handkerchiefs that are white like letters. The narrow bed is heaped with boxes, wrapped in glowing paper tied with ribbons that seem to shimmer. Light is coming from them in this meanly lit room. There is a warmth like sunlight, not like fire. I cannot tell you where it comes from.

We have open visiting hours here and I see that I have a visitor.

We have not met before, but I feel that I know him at once. So distinguished a person cannot have come for her before me. I am scented and ready. My back is straight. I have something to hand over to him.

With the excellent manners you might expect from him, I see that my visitor is stopping awhile by the bed next to mine. Let him come to me soon. The weight of this parcel is killing me.

Tact comes easily to him, that much is clear. He has seated himself discreetly among those who surround the bed and is taking the hands of the old woman in his. The four hands lie still, in a clasp as loose and strong as a heavy chain, among the heaped parcels, which seem, like the light thrown by coloured glass on pale stone, to be fading as the room grows darker. Can it be that the visitor has forgotten me?

'We have open visiting hours here,' I remind him. But he does not look up.

Here comes the tea woman with her heavy trolley. The large kettle on it is a two-hander, but even with two hands it is hard to control. She pours the tea into the mugs without stopping between each one, like a gardener watering well-rooted bulbs in pots from a watering can without a rose. The upper tray of the trolley is awash with tea. No one has thought to ask me whether in fact I do take milk, so I receive it.

Something appears to be bringing the old woman in the next bed to life.

The tea woman puts the mug of tea upon my table with care. It is considerate of her to avoid slopping it. She is very deaf. Too late, I see her putting sugar in my drink. I look up to remonstrate with her, but she is saying something.

'Sweets for the sweet,' she says.

Martha

MRS MURRAY HICKSON

I

From the first day that she came to Underwood
Terrace Martha interested me. She arrived, I remember, one dull
November afternoon. I saw her pass down the street, peering, in a
short-sighted fashion, at the numbers over the doors. She carried a
large bonnet-box in one hand and a neat brown-paper parcel in the
other. She had no umbrella, and the rain dripped from the limp
brim of her large straw hat. Her skirt, shabby and worn, had slipped
from her overladen fingers and dragged upon the muddy pavement.
I don't know why I noticed her, but, as I glanced up from my book,
my eyes fell upon her forlorn little figure, and I felt that sudden,
curious sensation of pity which sometimes, we don't know why,
takes us by the throat and shakes us out of our egotism and self-
reflection. Very possibly my first interest in her was merely a matter
of mood. Perhaps, had I been happier myself, I should not have
taken much notice of her; but my own concerns appeared, just then,
so dull and grey that it was a relief to turn from them to the
contemplation of somebody else's. For the present, however, the
little figure in the draggled black frock wandered down the street,
and I, returning to my book, lost sight and thought of her.

In the drawing-room, before dinner, Mrs Norris explained to me that, in consideration of the arrival of a new boarder, she had engaged a girl as a sort of 'understudy' for the other servants, and to work between them in the capacity of general help and factotum. The girl was young, she came from Surrey, and her name was Martha. Mrs Norris hoped that she would turn out well, but the training of young girls was always an experiment; she had known few who repaid the trouble expended upon them. This much she told me – the rest I supplied for myself. Help, in our overworked household, was imperatively needed, and a girl from the country (despite the drawbacks of her ignorance and lack of training) would cost little in keep and less in wages. In fact, properly managed, she should prove a good investment.

Late that evening I met a quaint little figure upon the stairs, and instantly recognised the limp, broad-brimmed hat, and the shabby jacket, frayed at collar and at cuffs. Our new maidservant and the girl who had that afternoon attracted my attention in the street represented the same identity. She drew aside to let me pass, shrinking timidly against the wall; but, by a sudden impulse, I stopped and spoke to her. The gaslight fell on the glasses of her spectacles, so that I could not catch the expression of her large, short-sighted eyes; but I saw that the eyelids were red and swollen and I guessed that she had been crying.

'So you found the house after all,' I said. 'You must have got very wet out there in the rain.'

'Yes, m'm,' she answered, and saluted me with a quick, bobbing curtsey. She expressed no curiosity as to how I came to know that she had at first been unable, in the driving mist, to discover number 127. To girls of her class, knowledge on every subject, whether important or trivial, appears, in a lady, as a matter of course. I looked at her again, and it struck me that, in the house, she should wear a cap and apron. But her dress remained unchanged since the afternoon.

'You are not going out now,' I said, 'so late? And it is still raining. Listen, you can hear it on the skylight.'

She listened obediently. The rain, blown by a gusty wind, pattered upon the big skylight in the roof. Martha glanced at me from behind her spectacles.

'Yes, m'm, but the mistress told me to post this letter. After that I may go to bed.'

She held a fat square envelope in her ungloved fingers, and I knew, without looking at it, that it contained the usual daily letter from Amy Norris to her lover. I moved impatiently. Why could not the girl have written earlier in the afternoon? – This going out to catch the late post was an old grievance with the servants, and now I supposed both of them would thrust the distasteful duty upon Martha.

'But do you know the way?' I asked.

'Yes, thank you, m'm,' she answered, and slipped down the stairs away from me.

Before I went to bed that night I ventured on a sketchy remonstrance with Amy Norris upon this subject of the late post.

'The girl is young, and evidently country-bred,' I concluded. 'Don't you think it's a pity to send her out so late into the streets? Could we not all get our letters ready for the last post before dinner?'

Amy looked at me in amazement. She was good-hearted enough, but perfectly stolid and unapproachable when such small matters as this were in question, and consideration for servants was quite beyond her comprehension.

'The pillarbox is only three or four minutes' walk from here,' she said. 'Besides, one can't plan things out like that beforehand – it would be a perfect nuisance. It won't do the girl any harm; Eliza always used to go.'

Eliza was a former servant. She was pretty and feather-brained, and when she left our house some few months earlier, Mrs Norris had refused to give her a character. The reason, no doubt, was unanswerable, but the fault had appeared to me to lie with the mistress as much as with the maid.

I thought of Eliza, looked at Amy's plump, satisfied countenance and laughed a little by way of reply. Long experience had taught me that argument and explanation here – in Mrs Norris's boarding-house – were entirely useless weapons.

As I was preparing for bed, I wondered idly if Martha had found her way safely back, and where she was to sleep. I knew there was only one room available for the servants, and I supposed that she was to share it with the cook and the housemaid. The child interested me; there was about her an unconscious earnestness which appealed to me. Her face was stamped with that expression, at once piteous and irritating, which is the result of a slow but conscientious nature striving its utmost to keep level with the demands made upon it by quicker minds. This first night away from home and in the midst of new surroundings would be very trying for the girl. My thoughts dwelt on her for a brief space and then, turning inevitably towards my own affairs, they dropped her out of their consideration. Presently, I lit a candle and went up to the box-room, where, amongst other things, I had stored away several books, one of which I particularly wanted to read. The box-room was at the top of the house, and was reached by a short staircase, so steep as to be almost a ladder. From the top of this ladder, which was of bare deal, uncarpeted, you stepped directly into the box-room itself, on one side of which was a dark recess holding a large cistern of water. Tonight as I came to the foot of the stairs, I could hear the water gurgling through the pipes into the great tank, and caught an intermittent sound of rain upon the window in the sloping roof. A light shone from the top of the staircase; evidently somebody was there before me, and I blew out my candle ere climbing the ladder. It was late, the house was very still, and I wondered who had thus invaded my territory, for, as my bedroom was small, I kept many things stowed away in my big travelling trunk, and I often came up here to fetch what, at the moment, I required. When my eyes were level with the floor of the box-room I stopped suddenly, and I understood. The room had been turned into a bedchamber. Trunks and portmanteaus were piled along one side of the wall, and a small – very small – truckle bedstead stood underneath the skylight. One chair and a broken-down chest of drawers completed the furniture. A small square of looking-glass, cracked across one corner, hung upon the wall. Martha herself knelt beside the bed, her face hidden in the pillow. Her loosened hair – crisp, and bright chestnut in colour – streamed over her coarse white nightgown; her bare feet, as she knelt, were thrust out from beneath the hem. I stood a moment, and then, for the girl had neither heard nor seen me, crept cautiously down the steep stairs back to the landing below. I would go without my book tonight, for Martha was saying her prayers, and, to judge by the convulsive movement of her shoulders, Martha was also crying.

II

A week later our new lady boarder arrived, and a very fine lady she was. We, the older occupants of the establishment, shrank into insignificance beside her; her gowns were so smart, and her require-ments were so many. Now came the time of Martha's trial, and poor child, a severe ordeal it proved to be. She was called upon, without any previous training, and with no help beyond her own native wits, to wait at the dinner-table. I must say that Martha's wits (being, though tenacious, somewhat slow) at times failed her; but, on the whole, it seemed to me that she did very well indeed, especially as Mrs Norris, during the dinner hour, confiscated her spectacles, so that she was obliged to find her way about the room in that semi-mist which blurs the vision of very short-sighted people. Her appearance, however, as her mistress justly observed, was enormously improved thereby; and her eyes, albeit often red and swollen with much weeping, were so well-shaped and charmingly fringed with long lashes that one could hardly regret the absence of the ugly, though useful, glasses. Poor little Martha! She used to hand the dishes, I remember, with awkward haste and alacrity, born of an earnest desire to give satisfaction and to succeed. Her cheeks were flushed, her small hands a trifle tremulous; her hair – usually dragged back from her forehead and twisted into a tight knot behind – had become, by this time in the evening, slightly loosened: here and there a stray curl crept above her brow. She was still very shabby; and in consequence of much hard work and little leisure, her hands, I noticed, had lost their first appearance of cleanliness, and become permanently roughened and begrimed. But, in spite of this, I began to look upon Martha as quite a pretty girl.

She did not have a particularly good time of it, I am afraid; she was far too sweet-tempered and anxious to conciliate everybody. Most of the hard words of the household, and a good deal of its concentrated ill-temper, fell to her share, and was borne by her with uncomplaining patience. Now and again – for Martha was occasionally both slow and uncomprehending – I myself felt tempted to speak sharply to her; but something in the expression of her earnest little face, some unconscious pathos in her personality, restrained me. Gradually, as the weeks passed, I found myself more and more interested in her – once or twice almost painfully so.

One day in particular, I remember, things had gone awry with Martha from morning until night. She let fall, and smashed to atoms, a vegetable dish which she was handing to her mistress at luncheon. Mrs Norris was, naturally, much annoyed, and the poor girl went through the rest of her duties with burning cheeks, and an increased clumsiness of manner. Afterwards I heard one of the other servants scolding her about a fire which had been allowed to die out, and, later in the evening, I found her in the hall, undergoing a severe reprimand from Amy Norris, whose nightly letter she had dropped into the mud on her way to the post.

'It isn't only that,' said Amy, with concentrated scorn and annoyance. 'Though such stupidity is bad enough, goodness knows. But she must needs bring the letter back again, to show to me – as if that would do any good! And now she's missed the post from the pillarbox. Isn't it inconceivable?'

As the last few words were addressed to me, I nodded in reply. It certainly did appear inconceivable – I should have posted the letter and said nothing about it.

Amy rubbed the envelope vigorously with her handkerchief.

'I thought, Miss, I'd better tell you about it; I thought perhaps you'd like to write it over again,' said Martha, submissively.

'You thought – you thought – you've no business to think,' snapped Amy. She turned into the dining-room to rewrite the address. The front door was open, and the gaslight from the hall streamed out into the night. The steps were shining with wet; because of the fog, one could hardly see beyond them. The street, at this time, was almost deserted, but the throb and roar of a big London thoroughfare close at hand came to us through the darkness.

I looked at Martha, who stood waiting beside me. She was pale, and I noticed that she shifted wearily from one foot to the other as though too tired to rest her weight upon either. Before, however, I had time to say more than a hasty word to her, Amy came back with the letter.

'You must go to the post office now,' she said. 'Be quick, Martha, don't lose a moment.'

The girl ran hastily down the steps, and Amy shut the door behind her.

'Stupid little thing,' she said vexedly. 'She seems always to be doing something idiotic. I really don't see how we are to keep her.'

I should like to have represented the matter from my point of view, but upon other people's affairs, silence is presumably golden; therefore I held my peace.

Martha's cup had been so full all day that, when she came to my room with hot water at bedtime, a kindly word or two overcame her completely. She set down the hot-water can, and mopped her streaming eyes with a crumpled pocket-handkerchief. I waited till her sobs became less suffocating. Presently she stammered an excuse and an explanation. The mistress, it appeared, had called her into her room half an hour earlier, and, complaining that her only black gown was too shabby for daily wear, had commanded her to buy another with the least possible delay. Also the broken vegetable dish must be made good out of her next month's wages.

'I can't do it, m'm, indeed I can't,' she said, breathlessly; 'I don't have but seven pound a year; and I've got to help Mother all I can. Father died just before I came here, and Mother has four children besides me to look after; she's not strong either, isn't Mother.'

'Your frock *is* shabby, Martha,' I said severely; 'it's shiny at the seams and frayed at the hem. As for the vegetable dish – well, you break a lot of things, you know, and Mrs Norris is not rich enough to replace them.'

Martha sniffed sadly.

'But white caps and aprons do run into money,' she remarked, with apparent irrelevance, and turned towards the door to depart. Her head drooped disconsolately, her tired feet dragged as she walked.

'Martha,' said I, 'stop a minute, and come here.'

She came back at once, standing before me with tear-stained cheeks; her breath, like that of a grieving child, caught now and again in a vagrant, shivering sob.

I meant to give myself the luxury of a kindness, and Martha the pleasure of a new gown.

'The vegetable dish,' said I, 'you must replace yourself; but the frock I will give to you. I will buy the stuff, and we must find somebody who can make it up for you nicely. But, if I do this, you must promise me to be very careful in future, and to break no more dishes.'

For a minute the girl made no reply, then the ready tears brimmed again into her eyes.

'Oh! m'm, you are good – you are good,' she said eagerly. 'And I will try; that I will. But I'm that stupid, I never seem able to do right.'

'Well, don't cry – you've cried enough today. Go to bed, now, and have a good night; it's long past eleven. By the way, don't I hear you up very early in the morning?'

Martha's room was over mine.

'Yes m'm. Now it's so cold I get up at a quarter to six to make tea for the other servants. They like a cup in bed in the mornings.'

She said it in all simplicity, and I made no comment upon the communication. If it had been my own house . . . But it wasn't, and I had no excuse for interference.

*

I bought Martha a thick stuff gown – and she needed it. Winter, which set in late that year, made up for its loitering by an intense severity. I could barely keep myself warm, even with the help of a big fire in my bedroom; Martha's little chamber next to the great water-cistern must have been bitterly cold. It contained no fireplace, and Mrs Norris, whose fear of fire amounted to a craze, would not allow the use of a gas-stove. In all weathers, at all hours, Martha ran the errands of the household. She was up early, she went to bed late; how, when she got there, she contrived to sleep at all, is a mystery to me, save that youth and hopefulness are potent to achieve miracles. The bitter cold froze our tempers below zero; we were fractious and difficult to please, and Martha, as usual bore the brunt of everybody's dissatisfaction; yet, in spite of her difficult lot, the girl seemed to expand and flourish. She looked very neat in her new frock, and I noticed that her hair was arranged more loosely, so that the fluffy little curls about her forehead showed to advantage. This was the result of a chance remark of mine – whether wise or not I am now uncertain. When, at last, winter left us, and the streets of London broke into an epidemic of violets and of primroses, Martha had grown into a positively pretty girl.

I had a chat with her one morning in April, and I learnt the reason of her altered looks. Martha had got a 'young man' – a young man who, she believed, really cared for her, and wished to marry her. Meantime they intended 'to keep company' together. All this she confided to me shyly, with many blushes, and I – whom love and youth seemed alike to have deserted – I sighed a little as I listened to her.

Perhaps because I envied her somewhat, perhaps because (now that the girl was comparatively happy) she no longer appealed to my warmest sympathies, I did not, from this time, take so keen an interest in her. And for this I have many times, especially since my own life warmed under a new sunshine, reproached myself.

Martha was much happier than she had been, but Martha would have been glad of a little sympathy from me all the same. She had grown accustomed to my interest in her; but now, I fear, she looked for it in vain. She used sometimes to linger beside the door when she came into my bedroom, and once, looking up quickly, I caught a wistful expression on her face which it hurts me now to remember. But there was much to occupy me just then, and Martha had her lover; I did not consider that she needed me.

I wonder how far, and how often, we are responsible for the misfortunes of those who live under the same roof, and yet are not upon the same level, with ourselves. I wonder how often a frank word of warning, of sympathy, or of advice would save our servant-girls from the miserable marriages, or the still more cruel abandon-ments, which so frequently become their portion. I don't know. Perhaps no one of us can stand between another and her fate; perhaps a hundred impalpable differences of thought, custom, and education build a wall between us and our servants, which only a very rare love and sympathy can overclimb. I can't be sure; but – be that as it may – I never think of Martha, and of Martha's patient service and uncomplaining diligence, without a pang of self-reproach. I was old enough to be her mother, and, since her mistress would not dream of doing so, I ought to have kept an eye upon her. But I grew accustomed to her coming and going; to her anxious, flushed little face as she handed the dishes at meal-times; to the sound of her heavy feet as, when everyone else had gone to bed, she climbed the carpetless ladder to her attic under the roof, and I forgot how eagerly, in so dreary a life, she must welcome a litle freedom and a little love.

*

I was away for some time in the early summer, and, on my return, I found that Martha's place was filled by a stranger. I made instant inquiries. Mrs Norris answered, with full information. Amy drew herself up in prim and conscious rectitude. She was to be married in the autumn, and could afford to look with severity upon the frailty of a servant-maid.

Martha, it appeared, had got herself into trouble. Martha, like Eliza, had been dismissed at once, without a character. She and her meagre baggage – the same bonnet-box with which she had arrived, and a rather larger brown-paper parcel – had been turned out of the house at an hour's notice. She had begged for my address, but that, in order to save me from annoyance, had been withheld from her.

I said very little – what was the use? – but I found out the name of the Surrey village from which she had come to us, and I went down there in the course of the week. My memory of the girl, as so often happens, was more pathetic than her actual presence had been. I felt uneasy until I could get news of her.

It was June weather in the heart of Surrey – that still June weather which is the essence of an English summer. The lanes were sweet with dog-roses; the vines on Martha's cottage home were already covered with many small bunches of quaint green fruit. The air was soft and full of perfume; the tiny garden was ablaze with old-fashioned flowers.

Martha's mother was at home – a tall, frail woman, aged prematurely by poverty and the stress of early motherhood. She received me, wondering; but, when I explained my errand, she burst into sudden tears. I do not know whether grief or anger held the uppermost place in her heart; certainly it never occurred to her that she was to blame for sending her girl, unprepared, into a world of danger and temptation.

She could give me no news of her daughter – there was no news to give. Martha had never come home; her mother evidently did not expect her to do so. She had stepped over the threshold of 127 Underwood Terrace, and had disappeared into that outside world which, to such as she, shows little of mercy, and even less of sympathy and comprehension.

Her mother hardly desires to see her again; and I – though I do not forget her – I recall her only as a pathetic memory which, each year, grows less and less distinct.

❧ *The Actress*

ALICE THOMAS ELLIS

At Christmas time Kay thought of spring, of the celandines that grew beside the streams running to join the river, the flood-swept grasses, the shards of ice creaking as they broke. Of the catkins on the hazels growing with the blackthorn in the hedges that marched at right angles to the river, and the remembered surprise at finding green life amidst desolation.

Now she bought daffodils and narcissi that had flowered in other countries – anachronisms, promises – and put them with the holly and the trailing ivy on her sitting-room table; grew hyacinths in bowls and dreamed even beyond spring. In some ways age was greedier than youth: eager for what might remain of small experience.

'How can you bear the smell of those hyacinths?' demanded her daughter-in-law when she came on the annual visit to collect her. 'They make the place smell like a funeral parlour.' She was a nice, outspoken woman of extreme conventionality and Kay, who was really quite fond of her, thought it a pity that her reactions were so circumscribed that she must connect the scent of flowers with death. And yet, thought Kay, as well as being the occasion of a birth,

Christmas was the beginning of a death. Perhaps her daughter-in-law in her ebullient simplicity stood quite close to truth. It was confusing and few things grew less so as you grew older. At least she was beginning to learn humility, she reflected, watering her hyacinths for the last time before leaving. At one time she would have despised her daughter-in-law so strongly that she would have been unable even to see her clearly. She asked herself if she had spent a lifetime following tortuous and circuitous routes on a quest for truth only to find herself standing beside her daughter-in-law who had been there all the time.

'What are you smiling about?' asked her granddaughter. 'Shall I lock this window now?'

'Yes,' said Kay. 'Lock all the windows. And we'd better throw away the daffodils. They won't last until I come back.'

'Pity,' said the girl. 'They're not dead yet. Shall I wrap them in paper and take them with us? The holly and the ivy will be all right. Tough old winter things.'

Like me, thought Kay. Or am I more akin to a dying daffodil?

'What *are* you smiling at?' asked the girl again. 'You nearly laughed out loud that time. I could nearly hear you.'

'Old jokes,' said Kay. 'I was just remembering old jokes.'

'You should tell them to me,' said her granddaughter; and she sounded both envious and nervous, as though she suspected that old jokes could not be any good or of any relevance to her, but then perhaps they *might* be and if they were then she had missed something.

'I'll tell you some of the better ones,' said Kay. 'When I've put them all back into words.'

'Aren't they in words now?' asked the girl.

'No,' said Kay. 'Only pictures and memories and impressions, and they only mean anything to me. For you I should have to put them all back into words.'

'Perhaps not,' said the girl, assuming an intense expression. 'I am of your blood after all. Perhaps you could give them to my dreams. Perhaps I have them already.'

'Perhaps . . .' said Kay, and her daughter-in-law said to her own daughter, 'I do hope you're not going to talk like that all over Christmas or everyone will think you're soft in the head.'

Or else they will recognise affectation for what it is, thought Kay, and she thought again that it was unfortunate for one's descendants if one had oneself been famous and much in the public eye, and then she wondered whether her granddaughter's posturings disguised a true imagination and ability. She had known several people who had used this method of protecting themselves from intrusion, from that final horror of the minor artist – the prospect of being understood.

'Only the great can tolerate understanding,' she said, putting on her fur coat. She spoke to herself, speaking as she would have done had she been alone, regretting that words, which she had thought soon to dispense with, would be necessary for the next few days; thinking that possibly she had been mistaken and precipitate and that words would continue to be necessary even in solitude.

Her daughter-in-law laughed; a little bark like a dog's. 'Can *you?*' she asked. She might have sounded hostile but did not, for she was not much interested in the theatre and found her mother-in-law's fame incomprehensible and amusing. She could not see how someone as ordinary as the mother of her husband could be regarded by the world with respect.

Kay said, 'No.'

Her granddaughter looked at her with eyes like her grandmother's

– wide, blue – and remarked uncertainly, 'They said you were very great.'

'Oh, yes,' said Kay. 'Very great.' How sad it was, she thought, grinning into the collar of her coat, where once there would always have been pinned a bunch of violets, that humility in the old was incompatible with the expectations of one's grandchildren. How disappointed the child would be if her acclaimed grandmother should announce that she was not great at all. Something of a failure really.

She picked up the daffodils. 'I have always loved flowers,' she said. 'Flowers and water, flowing water, and water when it turns into ice. And ice when it forms and when it breaks. I love the sound of breaking ice.' There, she thought. That should satisfy the child. That was surely sufficiently pretentious to be worthy of a woman the world considered great.

'Come on,' said her daughter-in-law impatiently. 'It's a long drive and we'll need a rest before Midnight Mass. Come on.'

At Mass Kay still thought of flowers. Of the one who blossomed as a child in winter and died, a man, in spring. Banked candle-flames bloomed around the altar and the incense scented the air like potpourri. Art is a substitute – doing instead of being – she thought; and while once she would have thought it a substitute for life, now she saw it as a substitute for God and wished that she had herself been a better instrument, tuned to the images of spring that winter evoked.

At dinner the next day naturally she said nothing of this. At no celebratory meals do you speak of what has gone before. Of the hopes of christening, the vows of marriage, or the dead you have buried. She recited lines that her son had forgotten and her grandchild had never known and reflected that for such an old woman she was quite entertaining; yet she knew that it was not what she said but what she was that gave the occasion its self-congratulatory glitter; that the animation of the faces of her son's friends arose not from her conversation but from the pleasure they intended to derive from divulging to other friends the fact that they had dined on Christmas Day with a truly famous person. They would say, 'She is quite amazing for her age.'

'More goose, Mother,' asked her son, 'and some apple sauce? Or would you prefer the pork?'

'Leave some space for the pudding,' urged her daughter-in-law, glancing over the laden table and the sideboard, where piled fruit gleamed and bowls of trifle flanked glistening cakes. Kay felt tired. The meal would go on for a long time and already she had eaten more than enough.

'You must have had some wonderful Christmases,' said the guest on her right as she fell silent.

'All the crowned heads in Europe,' cried her granddaughter leaning forward and laughing excitedly. 'Rome, Milan, New York . . . Tell us, Grandmother.'

Kay made a little pattern with her fork on the sage stuffing that lay in a pool of gravy on her plate.

'Come on,' said her granddaughter, her eyes filled with visions of silk and topaz, the skins of animals and the heat of spotlights.

'The Christmas I remember best,' said Kay, 'was so long ago . . .'

'Yes,' said her granddaughter eagerly, clasping her hands together and turning her head, leaning forward, so that the candlelight shone on her cheekbone.

'My father was in the army,' said Kay, 'garrisoned in a provincial town, and my mother and I went on a train to join him. It was dark because no lights were permitted for fear of bombs. He was waiting for us at the station and he took us to a house where he had rented a room, and when my mother saw the room she wept because it was dirty. She turned back the covers of the beds and saw that they had been slept in and the sheets not changed. Then she took all her petticoats and her camiknickers and spread them over the dirty sheets for me to lie on, and I lay down because it was very late and I was so tired, and for a while I heard my mother and father talking and I went to sleep.' Kay took a sip of champagne.

'But Grandmother . . .' began her granddaughter, slightly petulant.

'Ssh,' said several people. The girl stopped and sat back, unsmiling.

'Then I heard my mother shriek and I woke up. She had pulled back the covers to make sure I was all right and discovered bedbugs. My mother was a patient woman but she would not put up with bedbugs. It was snowing quite heavily and it must have been the early hours of Christmas Day, but she dressed me and packed all the things back in our suitcase and banged on the bedroom door of the woman who owned the house. She told her her house was a very great disgrace and not fit for decent people to live in, and the woman followed us into the street, screaming. She was a horrible woman with fat arms . . .'

'She sounds disgusting,' said her granddaughter sulkily.

'Ssh,' said everyone.

'Then,' said Kay, 'we started walking in the snow, and I thought I should be feeling frightened but I wasn't because the town was so silent and so still in the snow. Then my father remembered that a sergeant he knew had taken a house nearby in a terrace leading to the river; we went there and knocked on the door and the sergeant's wife opened it in her nightgown. It was a tiny house, two up and two down, and she had lots of children, but she took us in and moved all the children into one bed and we had theirs, and although the beds had been slept in, they had only been slept in by clean children and my mother didn't mind that so much. The sergeant's wife had fat arms too, but she was kind. Christmas dinner must have been a terrible problem because my father hadn't thought about food, and rationing was very strict, and all the sergeant's wife had in the house was sausages and potatoes and a tin of fruit salad, and I cannot imagine how it all went round, but I don't remember not having enough to eat. And after dinner my father and I went down to the river and walked until we came to the blackthorn hedges. The ditches were frozen and the mud on the river bank, and it was cold, but I kept thinking how beautiful the blackthorn would be in spring and how the celandines would grow along the ditches, and the willows bend over the river and I don't remember ever being so happy in my life.'

'My grandfather was killed in the war,' said her son after a while.

The party broke up soon after that and the next day Kay's granddaughter said that she was going to make lunch. She was an equable girl and had regained her temper quickly.

'It's a surprise,' she told them when they asked what she was cooking. Kay wasn't altogether surprised because, after all, the child was of her blood.

She had cooked sausages and potatoes and had made the shopkeeper sell her a tin of fruit salad at his back door. The gesture could have been made out of spite but was not. It was, thought Kay, at once an affectation and an affirmation, and what else was Art? And what more could the children of Eve, the dispossessed heirs of the flowering garden, expect of each other?

A Pen-and-Ink Effect

FRANCES E. HUNTLEY

He was writing a letter, and, as his pen jerked over the paper, he smiled with a fatuous softness. She had betrayed herself so helplessly – had cared so much. And he? Well, yes, he had cared too, a little; who could have been quite unresponsive to that impetuous inquiring tenderness, that ardent generous admiration? He remembered it all with amused regretful vanity – the summer evenings by the window, the gay give-and-take of their talk, the graver moments when their eyes met, and hers spoke more eloquently than words. 'Eager telltales of her mind' – how often he had quoted Matthew Arnold's line when he thought of her eyes! It might have been written for her; and when he had told her so, she had not been angry. Little goose! She ought to have been, of course – but he might say anything, he knew.

Well! they had been pretty days, those; 'a fragrant memory' – she had taught him some of her phrases – and now they were over. Quite over! The involuntariness of his sigh pleased him, and the reluctance with which he took up his pen again seemed to complete the romance of the moment.

She knew already. That was certain; he had sent a telegram on his wedding day, thinking it might not be quite so bad if she knew he had thought of her even then. And now he was writing. Not to her – dear, no! he had too much tact, knowledge of the world, for *that*, he hoped – but to her father. They had been 'pals'; he was so much older than she, 'quite fatherly', he used to say, delighting in her conscious look . . . So it was natural, quite natural, for him to write and tell him how it had happened.

For in some ways it was a queer business, not quite what had been expected of him, and yet – what everyone had expected. *That* he knew, and it galled him sorely. It was hardly a *mésalliance*, but – a mistake? He felt that it might be called one; a horrid saying jingled in his ears, 'There's no fool like an old fool' – and yet he had chosen it so, always guessed that it would end so. Romantic? No! There was the sting – not even romantic.

But she? Would she look at it in that way? Would she smile and think that he had made a mess of it, compare herself mentally – her fastidious high-bred self – with his bride and – pity him? He moved restlessly. No, she wouldn't; he knew her better. She would mind – mind horribly. Her mouth would set itself, her eyes would look bright and pained – oh! she was brave enough; but she would be silent, sadder than her wont, and – envious? His smile grew broader. Poor little dear!

Well, his letter would be some comfort. He had finished it; now to read it over . . . Yes! all was admirably conveyed, the regret, the remembrance, the veiled messages to her, the (he rather liked this part) – the hinted depreciation of his choice, the insinuated unhappiness and foreboding – and then the allusion to 'his wife' . . . in fancy he heard the sharp quick breath, saw the darkening of the blue eyes, the pain of the firm little mouth. . . . But perhaps she might not read it at all; men didn't hand letters round. He must provide for that. It was written for her, she must see it. How should he manage? Ah! that was it! 'Your daughter will help you to make out my scrawl,' in a prominent postscript; that was clear enough. Now to post it.

The end of the little episode, so delicate, so transient! Men were rather brutal, weren't they? Well, when girls fell in love and were so charming! It *was* a shame, though, he thought, complacently. Poor little dear! The letter slid into the box.

Everything was going on just the same – and he was married. But then she had always known it must end so – everyone had known it. There were two sorts of knowing, though, she thought, drearily.

It all seemed quite natural; even having no letter to expect when the post came in seemed so natural, and it *had* been the roseate moment of the day. Did everything happen so? It was odd. Browning's poignant question came into her head: 'Does truth sound bitter as one at first believes?' She used to imagine he had been wrong for once ('that omniscient Browning of yours'), but now that she knew . . .

How *was* it? She could laugh quite naturally, read and be interested in her book. Stay, though! Yesterday she had been reading a story in which the heroine had reminded her of herself, and had, of course, loved and been beloved. She had shut that book hastily and taken up a volume of essays, but soon she had reopened and devoured it with envious, aching eyes.

That was the day after the telegram had come. It had stung her a little, though it had pleased her too. So even at that moment he had thought of her; but how sure he had been! . . . It galled her; and, besides, it seemed to proclaim it all to the curious eyes around her. They were her own people, and she loved them and they her; but their eyes were curious. She caught stolen glances, interchange of looks, imagined them talking of her, 'Does she mind?' 'Not so much as I expected'; oh, the torturing *espionage* of family life. If she could only be quite alone! She recalled the scene. From her bedroom window she had seen the telegraph boy, had thought nothing of it, telegrams were so frequent. 'Effie! Effie!' First her youngest brother, wide-eyed, observant, when the room-door burst open; then her father, half-understanding, but innately unsympathetic for 'love-affairs', gratified, too, at the remembrance of him, careless or unconscious of the intolerable under-meaning of the message. Something had told her what it was, what the pink scrawl contained; she had felt a burning rebellion, a hard hatred of somebody or something.

'A telegram? from whom?' Her voice was sharp and cold. 'From Luttrell?' This was one of the things she loathed – that she called him 'Luttrell', *tout court*; her morbid sense of humour saw the painful absurdity of it – to speak so of a man you cared for! Incredible! Yet she did it. Was anything in life what you had once fancied it?

'From Luttrell?' Bravado had forced the name from her – and if it should not be from him? Even now she could recall the lash of the stinging thought.

'Yes – from Luttrell. Funny fellow! Fancy his thinking of sending it! Like to see it!'

She had taken it with a laugh at the 'funny fellow', had read it . . .

'So he's really married. Well, she's a pretty girl, and a clever girl; I daresay he'll be very happy. A very clever girl.'

How often, in her wayward moments, she had laughed with Luttrell over the 'canonisation' of the newest *fiancé* or bride! 'She had fulfilled the whole duty of woman!' she used to declare with ironic grandiosity, and he used to smile admiringly at her spirited nonsense – and now it was he himself! But she must say something.

'Yes, she's pretty. Clever? Well, I never had the pleasure of her acquaintance.' The tiny thrust had relieved her a little. 'And where do they go for their honeymoon, I wonder?'

It was said: 'they', 'their honeymoon'. Had her voice really sounded so thin and cold? She had felt just like it, 'thin and cold', a meagre, desolate sort of creature. 'Meagre!' How descriptive! Her lips curled into a small morbid smile. She remembered the odd sensation.

Well, that was over; the telegram-scene was two days ago now, and she was going down to lunch in that odd, dreamy sort of way, as if she was walking on air – everything was so natural, yet so unreal! . . . 'The post just in? What letters?' she said, carelessly, passing through the hall.

'One from Luttrell.'

'Why, Effie, Luttrell doesn't seem absorbed in his bride,' her eldest brother said, reading his own letters. 'Strikes me he'd rather – '

She could have struck him – but this must be answered in its own vein. Would it never end? 'Bored on the honeymoon, I suppose; they say everyone is.'

'He wouldn't be, though of course he'd pretend he was – ' her father laughed, opening the envelope. 'Dear, dear! what a scrawl! I can't read it . . . Effie, you read it out.'

'No, indeed. I can't bear reading things aloud.'

'Well, I can't. Take it, and read it to yourself, then?'

'You'd better both read it.'

'Over his shoulder,' one of the brothers said, mockingly.

Well, it if had to be done.

She stood and read it over her father's shoulder.

It was long, illegible; she spelt it out slowly to her wondering, faltering heart. This was what he had written – this?

'A nice letter, very friendly. Eh, Effie?'

'Yes, very – nice. Very – friendly.'

She escaped.

In her room at last. 'He wrote that? *That*?'

Her eyes met the wide dark ones in the mirror.

'Poor girl! Oh, the poor, poor girl!' The mirror looked clouded, vanished quite, grew clear again.

'To think I could ever have loved him!'

For a moment she hid her shamed, white face.

'Feel up for a game of tennis, Ronald, Sydney, Edith!' her voice pealed out. One must do something to work off this mad joyous thrill of freedom, liberty . . . looking forward!

She dashed down the stairs with a wild whirl of frills and lace-edges.

❧ *The Woodcutter's Upright Son*

BRIGID BROPHY

Having grown up among them, the woodcutter's son was not sentimental about the deer. When accidents befell them in the forest, he rescued if he could, and if not, wasted no time in regret. He did not disguise from himself that they were, on the whole, sensitive animals rather than intelligent ones. But neither did he disguise from himself that each was an individual personality. The terms on which he mixed with them were those of personal acquaintance and, with a few, personal friendship.

His only attempt to be hypocritical with himself was made in his early childhood, and even so it was not the deer but humans he was attempting to prettify. For at first he declined to believe that the hunters who once a year came in hosts to the forest actually killed the deer. He watched his father, the taciturn old woodcutter, help the deer hunters drag the corpses into their shooting brakes. But until he was about eight the woodcutter's son managed to believe that the arrival of the hunters and the high casualty rate among the deer were merely coincidental facts, and that the townsmen who temporarily invaded the forest came merely to collect accidental corpses in the same way that he himself, ever since he could remember, had collected sets of antlers and sometimes even skulls which he came upon in the forest.

When he was eight, however, he was already handy enough and sturdy enough to be bidden help his father during the hunting season. At dawn he had to stand in the clearing around the woodcutter's cabin, greet the drivers of the first vans to arrive, and beckon them into parking places. At sunset he had to help his father haul the heavy bodies along the forest paths and hump them up into the appropriate van. The boy could no longer avoid noticing that the wounds were gunshot wounds and admitting to himself that shot does not fly in forests by accident.

As he grew stronger and his father feebler, he had to undertake more and more of the work. When he was thirteen he found himself dragging the corpse of a deer which had been his particular friend. Bright red, watery blood stood like raindrops in the nostrils of a nose which had often nuzzled his hand.

About the same time the boy realised that his father took – though the son never witnessed the act of taking – large tips from the hunters in return for his son's labour and the use of the cabin as a hunting lodge. Without being told, he understood that his father's earnings from cutting wood were tiny and that the hunting season was his only big chance.

The boy came to spend quite half the year in acute but unex-pressed dread of the approaching season. When the season was over, he would run for relief and bitter solace into the deepest thickets, where he would find such deer as survived huddled in terror. He would try to comfort himself by resolutely considering only the fortunate fact that this or that individual had been spared. The deer, having always known him, let him move among them like one of themselves. They even seemed to take a certain calm from his sad caresses. He supposed that they must smell the blood of their species on his hands. Yet as a result of their stupidity or innocence they never, for all their timid startings at every noise on the breeze, flinched from him, even when he had to kill deer whom the hunters had left mortally wounded.

He grew up, becoming twice as tall and heavy as his father. Even so, he never discussed the hunting season with his father. The old man's grumpiness held a forbidding authority, which, his son noticed, even the hunters respected. They hated the old man but paid him largely. They found the son, with his more willing manners and more educated, fluent speech, charming – and gave him nothing but orders.

Sometimes the son wondered if the old man had retreated into grumpiness because he was fleeing a bad conscience.

Suddenly the old man was seized with a pain around the heart and died. It happened just after the close of the hunting season, which made the son wonder whether his father's heart had in fact been finally broken by the massacre. He found himself mourning more deeply than he had expected.

When he came back from the funeral in the town, he changed out of his smart suit and made at once for the depths of the forest, unthinkingly wanting to be among the deer. They seemed to respond in the same unthinking way to his grief, rubbing up against him like snowdrifts or, in brushing past, delivering him a velour slap from their sides. Taking comfort from them, he remembered an accident he had read about in a newspaper years earlier and perhaps stored in his head for this moment. Weaving thoughts around it, he began to elaborate his plans, which he would have a whole year to bring to perfection, for the next hunting season.

The season opened to an exhilarating frosty morning. While the sky was still the colour of a duck's egg, the woodcutter's son was up and out, stamping his feet and blowing vaporously into his hands in the clearing, his head as alert as a deer's to the first sound of a car engine.

When it came, he ran out along the path, papery ice on thin puddles crackling beneath his boots, to accost the first hunter.

The driving-seat window was rolled down and puffs of congealed breath exchanged as the woodcutter's son delivered uncharacteristically hearty greetings and gave the news of his father's death with inappropriate cheerfulness, explaining that he had taken over the business. After last year's record bag, he told the hunter, there would be a run of hunters on the forest and competition for the quarry would be strong. Moreover, he said, the deer, warned by experience, had grown cunning. They would not be shot without the help of a ruse, which he would disclose exclusively to a favoured hunter. Then he waited winningly beside the car door. A banknote was passed to him through the window. Hastily, he bade the hunter drive his car into the undergrowth and conceal it, while he himself fetched the necessary apparatus from the cabin.

He came running back carrying a set of antlers, one of those it had been his childhood's work to collect. Explaining rapidly that the deer were now so suspicious that the only way to come within shooting range of them was to pass oneself off as one of them, he bound the antlers to the hunter's head with strings it had been his last year's work to devise and construct. Warning the hunter that he could not expect to get a full view of the now alerted deer but must shoot – low, of course – the instant he saw a pair of antlers moving among the bushes, and promising him, as the only possessor of this subterfuge, a splendid day's sport, the woodcutter's son bundled the first comer off into the depths of the forest and hurried up the path to meet the next comer, to whom he gave exactly the same explanation and promise and a further set of antlers.

The morning rose high. Hunters poured into the forest. The

woodcutter's son, waylaying each into secret colloquy, issued his entire collection of antlers. Each of the hunters tipped him. Yet he suspected they did not give him such large amounts as they had been in the habit of giving his father.

The forest began to be noisy with shots. Soon the bangs were joined by cries of pain, shouts of anger, altercations, and groans. A walking casualty limped furiously up to the cabin door and began to abuse the woodcutter's son. Compassionately helping him up the steps and into a rocking chair, the woodcutter's son explained that the hunter had misunderstood his instructions and had better, unless he wanted to be laughed at for his stupidity and ignorance of forestcraft, make no mention of them. He unstrapped the antlers which the hunter was still wearing and hooked them back into their place on his cabin's wall. Then, after doing his best for the man's wound, he walked the three miles to the nearest phone and summoned an ambulance.

Parties of wounded hunters were already, when he got back to the cabin, carrying in the bodies of dead hunters. Four or five corpses were stretched, under what blankets the woodcutter's cabin could provide, in the clearing. The clanging of relays of ambulances was added to the groaning that filled the forest.

The woodcutter's son worked untiringly all day. Not only did he help the ambulance parties at loading and comforting. He made forays alone in search of the dead and wounded, hurrying along the tracks only he thoroughly knew and usually contriving to arrive first at the place of a fatality, where he would unstrap the antlers from the hunter's head and discard them in the undergrowth, so as to make the corpse lighter for the stretcher-bearers to bring in.

By sunset the size of the disaster was patent. Even of the wounded, many had died in the cabin or in the ambulances. And great numbers of the hunters had been killed outright where they stood. Their fellow marksmen, calculating downward from the glimpsed tip of an antler, had often put a bullet accurately through the centre of the forehead.

The woodcutter's son wore his smart suit again to go into the town for the inquest. He comported himself modestly and winningly in the witness box and was commended for the help he had given the casualties.

In the lobby of the court, and again at the inn where he stopped on his way home, he made sure of the result. The carnage had already given the forest a superstitiously ill-repute. No hunter would set foot in it again. The innkeeper regretted the takings he would lose.

Returned to the cabin, the woodcutter's son changed his clothes and hurried out, in the dusk, to the deer. From a distance he could discern the shadowed forms; there were no gaps, no deer had been killed.

As he approached, a sentinel deer at the edge of the group threw up its nose, sniffed, and wheeled away. The whole group took nervous alarm. Breaking into a silly trot, they all hurried deep into the forest, where they were hidden by the night.

The next day the woodcutter's son went into the town again. He bought himself an entirely new set of clothing – which used up nearly all the money he had taken in tips on the day of the carnage – and then bought large quantities of soap, disinfectant, deodorant, and aerosol sprays of every type and scent.

He went home and thoroughly cleansed both himself and the cabin.

Yet when he approached the deer again, they ran away. He tried all year. He tried three years later, when he expected a new generation to have forgotten the smell of human blood on him. But the signal of caution had been transmitted throughout the group.

He missed his friendship with the deer, but unsentimentally. He stayed on in the forest, living on the small wages of woodcutting. For sheer lack of anyone to talk to, he grew as taciturn, but not as grumpy, as his father had been. He never for a moment repented. On summer evenings it gave him deep content to watch the deer from the distance and rejoice in their safety.

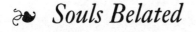 *Souls Belated*

EDITH WHARTON

I

Their railway-carriage had been full when the train left Bologna; but at the first station beyond Milan their only remaining companion – a courtly person who ate garlic out of a carpetbag – had left his crumb-strewn seat with a bow.

Lydia's eye regretfully followed the shiny broadcloth of his retreating back till it lost itself in the cloud of touts and cab drivers hanging about the station; then she glanced across at Gannett and caught the same regret in his look. They were both sorry to be alone.

'*Par-ten-za!*' shouted the guard. The train vibrated to a sudden slamming of doors; a waiter ran along the platform with a tray of fossilised sandwiches; a belated porter flung a bundle of shawls and bandboxes into a third-class carriage; the guard snapped out a brief '*Partenza!*' which indicated the purely ornamental nature of his first shout; and the train swung out of the station.

The direction of the road had changed, and a shaft of sunlight struck across the dusty red velvet seats into Lydia's corner. Gannett did not notice it. He had returned to his *Revue de Paris*, and she had to rise and lower the shade of the farther window. Against the vast horizon of their leisure such incidents stood out sharply.

Having lowered the shade, Lydia sat down, leaving the length of the carriage between herself and Gannett. At length he missed her and looked up.

'I moved out of the sun,' she hastily explained.

He looked at her curiously: the sun was beating on her through the shade.

'Very well,' he said pleasantly; adding, 'You don't mind?' as he drew a cigarette-case from his pocket.

It was a refreshing touch, relieving the tension of her spirit with the suggestion that, after all, he could *smoke* – ! The relief was only momentary. Her experience of smokers was limited (her husband had disapproved of the use of tobacco), but she knew from hearsay that men sometimes smoked to get away from things; that a cigar might be the masculine equivalent of darkened windows and a headache. Gannett, after a puff or two, returned to his review.

It was just as she had foreseen; he feared to speak as much as she did. It was one of the misfortunes of their situation that they were never busy enough to necessitate, or even to justify, the postponement of unpleasant discussions. If they avoided a question it was obviously, unconcealably because the question was disagreeable. They had unlimited leisure and an accumulation of mental energy to devote to any subject that presented itself; new topics were in fact at a premium. Lydia sometimes had premonitions of a famine-stricken period when there would be nothing left to talk about, and she had already caught herself doling out piecemeal what, in the first prodigality of their confidences, she would have flung to him in a breath. Their silence therefore might simply mean that they had nothing to say; but it was another disadvantage of their position that it allowed infinite opportunity for the classification of minute differences. Lydia had learned to distinguish between real and

factitious silences; and under Gannett's she now detected a hum of
speech to which her own thoughts made breathless answer.

How could it be otherwise, with that thing between them? She
glanced up at the rack overhead. The *thing* was there, in her
dressing-bag, symbolically suspended over her head and his. He
was thinking of it now, just as she was; they had been thinking of it
in unison ever since they had entered the train. While the carriage
had held other travellers they had screened her from his thoughts,
but now that he and she were alone she knew exactly what was
passing through his mind; she could almost hear him asking himself
what he should say to her . . .

The thing had come that morning, brought up to her in an innocent-
looking envelope with the rest of their letters, as they were leaving
the hotel at Bologna. As she tore it open, she and Gannett were
laughing over some ineptitude of the local guidebook – they had
been driven, of late, to make the most of such incidental humours of
travel. Even when she had unfolded the document she took it for
some unimportant business paper sent abroad for her signature, and
her eye travelled inattentively over the curly *Whereases* of the
preamble until a word arrested her: 'Divorce'. There it stood, an
impassable barrier, between her husband's name and hers.

She had been prepared for it, of course, as healthy people are said
to be prepared for death, in the sense of knowing it must come
without in the least expecting that it will. She had known from the
first that Tillotson meant to divorce her – but what did it matter?
Nothing mattered, in those first days of supreme deliverance, but
the fact that she was free; and not so much (she had begun to be
aware) that freedom had released her from Tillotson as that it had
given her to Gannett. This discovery had not been agreeable to her
self-esteem. She had preferred to think that Tillotson had himself

embodied all her reasons for leaving him; and those he represented had seemed cogent enough to stand in no need of reinforcement. Yet she had not left him till she met Gannett. It was her love for Gannett that had made life with Tillotson so poor and incomplete a business. If she had never, from the first, regarded her marriage as a full cancelling of her claims upon life, she had at least, for a number of years, accepted it as a provisional compensation, – she had made it 'do'. Existence in the commodious Tillotson mansion in Fifth Avenue – with Mrs Tillotson senior commanding the approaches from the second-storey front windows – had been reduced to a series of purely automatic acts. The moral atmosphere of the Tillotson interior was as carefully screened and curtained as the house itself: Mrs Tillotson senior dreaded ideas as much as a draught on her back. Prudent people liked an even temperature; and to do anything unexpected was as foolish as going out in the rain. One of the chief advantages of being rich was that one need not be exposed to unforeseen contingencies: by the use of ordinary firmness and common sense one could make sure of doing exactly the same thing every day at the same hour. These doctrines, reverentially imbibed with his mother's milk, Tillotson (a model son who had never given his parents an hour's anxiety) complacently expounded to his wife, testifying to his sense of their importance by the regularity with which he wore goloshes on damp days, his punctuality at meals, and his elaborate precautions against burglars and contagious diseases. Lydia, coming from a smaller town, and entering New York life through the portals of the Tillotson mansion, had mechanically accepted this point of view as inseparable from having a front pew in church and a parterre box at the opera. All the people who came to the house revolved in the same small circle of prejudices. It was the kind of society in which, after dinner, the ladies compared the exorbitant charges of their children's teachers, and agreed that, even with the new duties on French clothes, it was cheaper in the end to get everything from Worth; while the husbands, over their cigars, lamented municipal corruption, and decided that the men to start a reform were those who had no private interests at stake.

To Lydia this view of life had become a matter of course, just as lumbering about in her mother-in-law's landau had come to seem the only possible means of locomotion, and listening every Sunday to a fashionable Presbyterian divine the inevitable atonement for having thought oneself bored on the other six days of the week. Before she met Gannett her life had seemed merely dull: his coming made it appear like one of those dismal Cruikshank prints in which the people are all ugly and all engaged in occupations that are either vulgar or stupid.

It was natural that Tillotson should be the chief sufferer from this readjustment of focus. Gannett's nearness had made her husband ridiculous, and a part of the ridicule had been reflected on herself. Her tolerance laid her open to a suspicion of obtuseness from which she must, at all costs, clear herself in Gannett's eyes.

She did not understand this until afterwards. At the time she fancied that she had merely reached the limits of endurance. In so large a charter of liberties as the mere act of leaving Tillotson seemed to confer, the small question of divorce or no divorce did not count. It was when she saw that she had left her husband only to be with Gannett that she perceived the significance of anything affecting their relations. Her husband, in casting her off, had virtually flung her at Gannett: it was thus that the world viewed it. The measure of alacrity with which Gannett would receive her would be the subject of curious speculation over afternoon-tea tables and in club corners. She knew what would be said – she had heard it so often of others! The recollection bathed her in misery. The men would probably back Gannett to 'do the decent thing'; but the ladies' eyebrows would emphasise the worthlessness of such enforced fidelity; and after all, they would be right. She had put herself in a position where Gannett 'owed' her something; where, as a gentleman, he was bound to 'stand the damage'. The idea of accepting such compensation had never crossed her mind; the so-called rehabilitation of such a marriage had always seemed to her the only real disgrace. What she dreaded was the necessity of having to explain herself; of having to combat his arguments; of calculating, in spite of herself, the exact measure of insistence with which he pressed them. She knew not whether she most shrank from his insisting too much or too little. In such a case the nicest sense of proportion might be at fault; and how easy to fall into the error of taking her resistance for a test of his sincerity! Whichever way she turned, an ironical implication confronted her: she had the exasperated sense of having walked into the trap of some stupid practical joke.

Beneath all these preoccupations lurked the dread of what he was thinking. Sooner or later, of course, he would have to speak; but that, in the meantime, he should think, even for a moment, that there was any use in speaking, seemed to her simply unendurable. Her sensitiveness on this point was aggravated by another fear, as yet barely on the level of consciousness; the fear of unwillingly involving Gannett in the trammels of her dependence. To look upon him as the instrument of her liberation; to resist in herself the least tendency to a wifely taking possession of his future; had seemed to Lydia the one way of maintaining the dignity of their relation. Her view had not changed, but she was aware of a growing inability to keep her thoughts fixed on the essential point – the point of parting with Gannett. It was easy to face as long as she kept it sufficiently far off, but what was this act of mental postponement but a gradual encroachment on his future? What was needful was the courage to recognise the moment when, by some word or look, their voluntary fellowship should be transformed into a bondage the more wearing that it was based on none of those common obligations which make the most imperfect marriage in some sort a centre of gravity.

When the porter, at the next station, threw the door open, Lydia drew back, making way for the hoped-for intruder, but none came, and the train took up its leisurely progress through the spring wheat-fields and budding copses. She now began to hope that Gannett would speak before the next station. She watched him furtively, half-disposed to return to the seat opposite his, but there was an artificiality about his absorption that restrained her. She had never before seen him read with so conspicuous an air of warding off interruption. What could he be thinking of? Why should he be afraid to speak? Or was it her answer that he dreaded?

The train paused for the passing of an express, and he put down his book and leaned out of the window. Presently he turned to her with a smile.

'There's a jolly old villa out here,' he said.

His easy tone relieved her, and she smiled back at him as she crossed over to his corner.

Beyond the embankment, through the opening in a mossy wall, she caught sight of the villa, with its broken balustrades, its stagnant fountains, and the stone satyr closing the perspective of a dusky grass-walk.

'How should you like to live there?' he asked as the train moved on.

'There?'

'In some such place, I mean. One might do worse, don't you think so? There must be at least two centuries of solitude under those yew trees. Shouldn't you like it?'

'I – I don't know,' she faltered. She knew now that he meant to speak.

He lit another cigarette. 'We shall have to live somewhere, you know,' he said as he bent above the match.

Lydia tried to speak carelessly. *Je n'en vois pas la nécessité!* Why not live everywhere, as we have been doing?'

'But we can't travel forever, can we?'

'Oh, forever's a long word,' she objected, picking up the review he had thrown aside.

'For the rest of our lives then,' he said, moving nearer.

She made a slight gesture which caused his hand to slip from hers.

'Why should we make plans? I thought you agreed with me that it's pleasanter to drift?'

He looked at her hesitatingly. 'It's been pleasant, certainly; but I suppose I shall have to get at my work again some day. You know I haven't written a line since – all this time,' he hastily emended.

She flamed with sympathy and self-reproach. 'Oh, if you mean *that* – if you want to write – of course we must settle down. How stupid of me not to have thought of it sooner! We oughtn't to lose any more time.'

He hesitated again. 'I had thought of a villa in these parts. It's quiet; we shouldn't be bothered. Should you like it?'

'Of course I should like it.' She paused and looked away. 'But I thought – I remember your telling me once that your best work had been done in a crowd – in big cities. Why should you shut yourself up in a desert?'

Gannett, for a moment, made no reply. At length he said, avoiding her eye as carefully as she avoided his: 'It might be different now; I can't tell, of course, till I try. A writer ought not to be dependent on his *milieu*, it's a mistake to humour oneself in that way; and I thought that just at first you might prefer to be – '

She faced him. 'To be what?'

'Well – quiet. I mean – '

'What do you mean by "at first"?' she interrupted.

He paused again. 'I mean after we are married.'

She thrust up her chin and turned toward the window. 'Thank you!' she tossed back at him.

'Lydia!' he exclaimed blankly; and she felt in every fibre of her averted person that he had made the inconceivable, the unpardonable mistake of anticipating her acquiescence.

The train rattled on and he groped for a third cigarette. Lydia remained silent.

'I haven't offended you?' he ventured at length, in the tone of a man who feels his way.

She shook her head with a sigh. 'I thought you understood,' she moaned. Their eyes met and she moved back to his side.

'Do you want to know how not to offend me? By taking it for granted, once for all, that you've said your say on this odious question and that I've said mine, and that we stand just where we did this morning before that – that hateful paper came to spoil everything between us!'

'To spoil everything between us? What on earth do you mean? Aren't you glad to be free?'

'I was free before.'

'Not to marry me,' he suggested.

'But I don't *want* to marry you!' she cried.

She saw that he turned pale. 'I'm obtuse, I suppose,' he said slowly. 'I confess I don't see what you're driving at. Are you tired of the whole business? Or was I simply a – an excuse for getting away? Perhaps you didn't care to travel alone? Was that it? And now you want to chuck me?' His voice had grown harsh. 'You owe me a straight answer, you know; don't be tenderhearted!'

Her eyes swam as she leaned to him. 'Don't you see it's because I care – because I care so much? Oh, Ralph! Can't you see how it would humiliate me? Try to feel it as a woman would! Don't you see the misery of being made your wife in this way? If I'd known you as a girl – that would have been a real marriage! But now – this vulgar fraud upon society – and upon a society we despised and laughed at – this sneaking back into a position that we've voluntarily forfeited: don't you see what a cheap compromise it is? We neither of us believe in the abstract "sacredness" of marriage; we both know that no ceremony is needed to consecrate our love for each other; what object can we have in marrying, except the secret fear of each that the other may escape, or the secret longing to work our way back gradually – oh, very gradually – into the esteem of the people whose conventional morality we have always ridiculed and hated? And the very fact that, after a decent interval, these same people would come and dine with us – the women who talk about the indissolubility of marriage, and who would let me die in a gutter today because I am "leading a life of sin" – doesn't that disgust you more than their turning their backs on us now? I can stand being cut by them, but I couldn't stand their coming to call and asking what I meant to do about visiting that unfortunate Mrs So-and-so!'

She paused, and Gannett maintained a perplexed silence.

'You judge things too theoretically,' he said at length, slowly. 'Life is made up of compromises.'

'The life we ran away from – yes! If we had been willing to accept them' – she flushed – 'we might have gone on meeting each other at Mrs Tillotson's dinners.'

He smiled slightly. 'I didn't know that we ran away to found a new system of ethics. I supposed it was because we loved each other.'

'Life is complex, of course; isn't it the very recognition of that fact that separates us from the people who see it *tout d'une pièce*? If *they* are right – if marriage is sacred in itself and the individual must always be sacrificed to the family – then there can be no real marriage between us, since our – our being together is a protest against the sacrifice of the individual to the family.' She interrupted herself with a laugh. 'You'll say now that I'm giving you a lecture on sociology! Of course one acts as one can – as one must, perhaps – pulled by all sorts of invisible threads; but at least one needn't pretend, for social advantages, to subscribe to a creed that ignores the complexity of human motives – that classifies people by arbitrary signs, and puts it in everybody's reach to be on Mrs Tillotson's visiting-list. It may be necessary that the world should be ruled by conventions – but if we believed in them, why did we break through them? And if we don't believe in them, is it honest to take advantage of the protection they afford?'

Gannett hesitated. 'One may believe in them or not; but as long as they do rule the world it is only by taking advantage of their protection that one can find a *modus vivendi*.'

'Do outlaws need a *modus vivendi*?'

He looked at her hopelessly. Nothing is more perplexing to man than the mental process of a woman who reasons her emotions.

She thought she had scored a point and followed it up passionately. 'You do understand, don't you? You see how the very thought of the thing humiliates me! We are together today because we choose to be – don't let us look any farther than that!' She caught his hands. '*Promise* me you'll never speak of it again; promise me you'll never *think* of it even,' she implored, with a tearful prodigality of italics.

Through what followed – his protests, his arguments, his final unconvinced submission to her wishes – she had a sense of his but half-discerning all that, for her, had made the moment so tumultuous. They had reached that memorable point in every heart-history when, for the first time, the man seems obtuse and the woman irrational. It was the abundance of his intentions that consoled her, on reflection, for what they lacked in quality. After all, it would have been worse, incalculably worse, to have detected any overreadiness to understand her.

II

When the train at nightfall brought them to their journey's end at the edge of one of the lakes, Lydia was glad that they were not, as usual, to pass from one solitude to another. Their wanderings during the year had indeed been like the flight of outlaws: through Sicily, Dalmatia, Transylvania and Southern Italy they had persisted in their tacit avoidance of their kind. Isolation, at first, had deepened the flavour of their happiness, as night intensifies the scent of certain flowers; but in the new phase on which they were entering, Lydia's chief wish was that they should be less abnormally exposed to the action of each other's thoughts.

She shrank, nevertheless, as the brightly looming bulk of the fashionable Anglo-American hotel on the water's brink began to radiate toward their advancing boat its vivid suggestion of social order, visitors' lists, Church services, and the bland inquisition of the *table-d'hôte*. The mere fact that in a moment or two she must take her place on the hotel register as Mrs Gannett seemed to weaken the springs of her resistance.

They had meant to stay for a night only, on their way to a lofty village among the glaciers of Monte Rosa; but after the first plunge into publicity, when they entered the dining-room, Lydia felt the relief of being lost in a crowd, of ceasing for a moment to be the centre of Gannett's scrutiny; and in his face she caught the reflection of her feeling. After dinner, when she went upstairs, he strolled into the smoking-room, and an hour or two later, sitting in the darkness of her window, she heard his voice below and saw him walking up and down the terrace with a companion cigar at his side. When he came up he told her he had been talking to the hotel chaplain – a very good sort of fellow.

'Queer little microcosms, these hotels! Most of these people live here all summer and then migrate to Italy or the Riviera. The English are the only people who can lead that kind of life with dignity – those soft-voiced old ladies in Shetland shawls somehow carry the British Empire under their caps. *Civis Romanus sum*. It's a curious study – there might be some good things to work up here.'

He stood before her with the vivid preoccupied stare of the novelist on the trail of a 'subject'. With a relief that was half painful she noticed that, for the first time since they had been together, he was hardly aware of her presence.

'Do you think you could write here?'

'Here? I don't know.' His stare dropped. 'After being out of things so long one's first impressions are bound to be tremendously vivid, you know. I see a dozen threads already that one might follow – '

He broke off with a touch of embarrassment.

'Then follow them. We'll stay,' she said with sudden decision.

'Stay here?' He glanced at her in surprise, and then, walking to the window, looked out upon the dusky slumber of the garden.

'Why not?' she said at length, in a tone of veiled irritation.

'The place is full of old cats in caps who gossip with the chaplain. Shall you like – I mean, it would be different if – '

She flamed up.

'Do you suppose I care? It's none of their business.'

'Of course not; but you won't get them to think so.'

'They may think what they please.'

He looked at her doubtfully.

'It's for you to decide.'

'We'll stay,' she repeated.

Gannett, before they met, had made himself known as a successful writer of short stories and of a novel which had achieved the distinction of being widely discussed. The reviewers called him 'promising', and Lydia now accused herself of having too long interfered with the fulfilment of his promise. There was a special irony in the fact, since his passionate assurances that only the stimulus of her companionship could bring out his latent faculty had almost given the dignity of a 'vocation' to her course: there had been moments when she had felt unable to assume, before posterity, the responsibility of thwarting his career. And, after all, he had not written a line since they had been together: his first desire to write had come from renewed contact with the world! Was it all a mistake then? Must the most intelligent choice work more disastrously than the blundering combinations of chance? Or was there a still more humiliating answer to her perplexities? His sudden impulse of activity so exactly coincided with her own wish to withdraw, for a time, from the range of his observation, that she wondered if he too were not seeking sanctuary from intolerable problems.

'You must begin tomorrow!' she cried, hiding a tremor under the laugh with which she added, 'I wonder if there's any ink in the inkstand?'

Whatever else they had at the Hotel Bellosguardo, they had, as Miss Pinsent said, 'a certain tone'. It was to Lady Susan Condit that they owed this inestimable benefit; an advantage ranking in Miss Pinsent's

opinion above even the lawn tennis courts and the resident chaplain.
It was the fact of Lady Susan's annual visit that made the hotel what
it was. Miss Pinsent was certainly the last to underrate such a
privilege: 'It's so important, my dear, forming as we do a little
family, that there should be someone to give *the tone*; and no one
could do it better than Lady Susan – an earl's daughter and a person
of such determination. Dear Mrs Ainger now – who really *ought*,
you know, when Lady Susan's away – absolutely refuses to assert
herself.' Miss Pinsent sniffed derisively. 'A bishop's niece! – my
dear, I saw her once actually give in to some South Americans – and
before us all. She gave up her seat at table to oblige them – such a
lack of dignity! Lady Susan spoke to her very plainly about it
afterwards.'

Miss Pinsent glanced across the lake and adjusted her auburn
front.

'But of course I don't deny that the stand Lady Susan takes is not
always easy to live up to – for the rest of us, I mean. Monsieur
Grossart, our good proprietor, finds it trying at times, I know – he
has said as much, privately, to Mrs Ainger and me. After all, the
poor man is not to blame for wanting to fill his hotel, is he? And
Lady Susan is so difficult – so very difficult – about new people.
One might almost say that she disapproves of them beforehand, on
principle. And yet she's had warnings – she very nearly made a
dreadful mistake once with the Duchess of Levens, who dyed her
hair and – well, swore and smoked. One would have thought that
might have been a lesson to Lady Susan.' Miss Pinsent resumed her
knitting with a sigh. 'There are exceptions, of course. She took at
once to you and Mr Gannett – it was quite remarkable, really. Oh,
I don't mean that either – of course not! It was perfectly natural –
we *all* thought you so charming and interesting from the first day –
we knew at once that Mr Gannett was intellectual, by the magazines

you took in; but you know what I mean. Lady Susan is so very –
well, I won't say prejudiced, as Mrs Ainger does – but so prepared
not to like new people, that her taking to you in that way was a
surprise to us all, I confess.'

Miss Pinsent sent a significant glance down the long laurustinus
alley from the other end of which two people – a lady and gentleman
– were strolling toward them through the smiling neglect of the
garden.

'In this case, of course, it's very different; that I'm willing to
admit. Their looks are against them; but, as Mrs Ainger says, one
can't exactly tell them so.'

'She's very handsome,' Lydia ventured, with her eyes on the lady,
who showed, under the dome of a vivid sunshade, the hourglass
figure and superlative colouring of a Christmas chromo.

'That's the worst of it. She's too handsome.'

'Well, after all, she can't help that.'

'Other people manage to,' said Miss Pinsent sceptically.

'But isn't it rather unfair of Lady Susan – considering that nothing
is known about them?'

'But, my dear, that's the very thing that's against them. It's
infinitely worse than any actual knowledge.'

Lydia mentally agreed that, in the case of Mrs Linton, it possibly
might be.

'I wonder why they came here?' she mused.

'That's against them too. It's always a bad sign when loud people
come to a quiet place. And they've brought van-loads of boxes – her
maid told Mrs Ainger's that they meant to stop indefinitely.'

'And Lady Susan actually turned her back on her in the *salon*?'

'My dear, she said it was for our sakes; that makes it so
unanswerable! But poor Grossart *is* in a way! The Lintons have
taken his most expensive *suite*, you know – the yellow damask

drawing-room above the portico – and they have chan.
every meal!'

They were silent as Mr and Mrs Linton sauntered by; ι
with tempestuous brows and challenging chin; the gentlem.
blond stripling, trailing after her, head downward, like a relucι
child dragged by his nurse.

'What does your husband think of them, my dear?' Miss Pinsent
whispered as they passed out of earshot.

Lydia stooped to pick a violet in the border.

'He hasn't told me.'

'Of your speaking to them, I mean. Would he approve of that? I
know how very particular nice Americans are. I think your action
might make a difference; it would certainly carry weight with Lady
Susan.'

'Dear Miss Pinsent, you flatter me!'

Lydia rose and gathered up her book and sunshade.

'Well, if you're asked for an opinion – if Lady Susan asks you for
one – I think you ought to be prepared,' Miss Pinsent admonished
her as she moved away.

III

Lady Susan held her own. She ignored the Lintons, and her little
family, as Miss Pinsent phrased it, followed suit. Even Mrs Ainger
agreed that it was obligatory. If Lady Susan owed it to the others
not to speak to the Lintons, the others clearly owed it to Lady Susan
to back her up. It was generally found expedient, at the Hotel
Bellosguardo, to adopt this form of reasoning.

Whatever effect this combined action may have had upon the
Lintons, it did not at least have that of driving them away. Monsieur
Grossart, after a few days of suspense, had the satisfaction of seeing

them settle down in his yellow damask *premier* with what looked like a permanent installation of palm trees and silk sofa-cushions, and a gratifying continuance in the consumption of champagne. Mrs Linton trailed her Doucet draperies up and down the garden with the same challenging air, while her husband, smoking innumerable cigarettes, dragged himself dejectedly in her wake; but neither of them, after the first encounter with Lady Susan, made any attempt to extend their acquaintance. They simply ignored their ignorers. As Miss Pinsent resentfully observed, they behaved exactly as though the hotel were empty.

It was therefore a matter of surprise, as well as of displeasure, to Lydia to find, on glancing up one day from her seat in the garden, that the shadow which had fallen across her book was that of the enigmatic Mrs Linton.

'I want to speak to you,' that lady said, in a rich hard voice that seemed the audible expression of her gown and her complexion.

Lydia started. She certainly did not want to speak to Mrs Linton.

'Shall I sit down here,' the latter continued, fixing her intensely shaded eyes on Lydia's face, 'or are you afraid of being seen with me?'

'Afraid?' Lydia coloured. 'Sit down, please. What is it that you wish to say?'

Mrs Linton, with a smile, drew up a garden chair and crossed one openwork ankle above the other.

'I want you to tell me what my husband said to your husband last night.'

Lydia turned pale.

'My husband – to yours?' she faltered, staring at the other.

'Didn't you know they were closeted together for hours in the smoking-room after you went upstairs? My man didn't get to bed until nearly two o'clock and when he did I couldn't get a word out of him. When he wants to be aggravating I'll back him against anybody living!' Her teeth and eyes flashed persuasively upon Lydia. 'But you'll tell me what they were talking about, won't you? I know I can trust you – you look so awfully kind. And it's for his own good. He's such a precious donkey and I'm so afraid he's got into some beastly scrape or other. If he'd only trust his own old woman! But they're always writing to him and setting him against me. And I've got nobody to turn to.' She laid her hand on Lydia's with a rattle of bracelets. 'You'll help me, won't you?'

Lydia drew back from the smiling fierceness of her brows.

'I'm sorry – but I don't think I understand. My husband has said nothing to me of – of yours.'

The great black crescents above Mrs Linton's eyes met angrily.

'I say – is that true?' she demanded.

Lydia rose from her seat.

'Oh, look here, I didn't meant that, you know – you mustn't take one up so! Can't you see how rattled I am?'

Lydia saw that, in fact, her beautiful mouth was quivering beneath softened eyes.

'I'm beside myself!' the splendid creature wailed, dropping into her seat.

'I'm sorry,' Lydia repeated, forcing herself to speak kindly; 'but how can I help you?'

Mrs Linton raised her head sharply.

'By finding out – there's a darling!'

'Finding what out?'

'What Trevenna told him.'

'Trevenna – ?' Lydia echoed in bewilderment.

Mrs Linton clapped her hand to her mouth.

'Oh, Lord – there, it's out! What a fool I am! But I supposed of course you knew; I supposed everyone knew.' She dried her eyes and bridled. 'Didn't you know that he's Lord Trevenna? I'm Mrs Cope.'

Lydia recognised the names. They had figured in a flamboyant elopement which had thrilled fashionable London some six months earlier.

'Now you see how it is – you understand, don't you?' Mrs Cope continued on a note of appeal. 'I knew you would – that's the reason I came to see you. I suppose *he* felt the same thing about your husband; he's not spoken to another soul in the place.' Her face grew anxious again. 'He's awfully sensitive, generally – he feels our position, he says – as if it wasn't *my* place to feel that! But when he does get talking there's no knowing what he'll say. I know he's been brooding over something lately, and I *must* find out what it is – it's to his interest I should. I always tell him that I think only of his interest; if he'd only trust me! But he's been so odd lately – I can't think what he's plotting. You will help me, dear?'

Lydia, who had remained standing, looked away uncomfortably.

'If you mean by finding out what Lord Trevenna has told my husband, I'm afraid it's impossible.'

'Why impossible?'

'Because I infer that it was told in confidence.'

Mrs Cope stared incredulously.

'Well, what of that? Your husband looks such a dear – anyone can see he's awfully gone on you. What's to prevent your getting it out of him?'

Lydia flushed.

'I'm not a spy!' she exclaimed.

'A spy – a spy? How dare you?' Mrs Cope flamed out. 'Oh, I don't meant that either! Don't be angry with me – I'm so miserable.' She essayed a softer note. 'Do you call that spying – for one woman to help out another? I do need help so dreadfully! I'm at my wits' end with Trevenna, I am indeed. He's such a boy – a mere baby, you know; he's only two-and-twenty.' She dropped her orbed lids. 'He's younger than me – only fancy! a few months younger. I tell him he ought to listen to me as if I was his mother; oughtn't he now? But he won't, he won't! All his people are at him, you see – oh, I know *their* little game! Trying to get him away from me before I can get my divorce – that's what they're up to. At first he wouldn't listen to them, he used to toss their letters over to me to read; but now he reads them himself, and answers 'em too, I fancy; he's always shut up in his room, writing. If I only knew what his plan is I could stop him fast enough – he's such a simpleton. But he's dreadfully deep too – at times I can't make him out. But I know he's told your husband everything – I knew that last night the minute I laid eyes on him. And I *must* find out – you must help me – I've got no one else to turn to!'

She caught Lydia's fingers in a stormy pressure.

'Say you'll help me – you and your husband.'

Lydia tried to free herself.

'What you ask is impossible; you must see that it is. No one could interfere in – in the way you ask.'

Mrs Cope's clutch tightened.

'You won't, then? You won't?'

'Certainly not. Let me go, please.'

Mrs Cope released her with a laugh.

'Oh, go by all means – pray don't let me detain you! Shall you go and tell Lady Susan Condit that there's a pair of us – or shall I save you the trouble of enlightening her?'

Lydia stood still in the middle of the path, seeing her antagonist through a mist of terror. Mrs Cope was still laughing.

'Oh, I'm not spiteful by nature, my dear; but you're a little more than flesh and blood can stand! It's impossible, is it? Let you go, indeed! You're too good to be mixed up in my affairs, are you? Why, you little fool, the first day I laid eyes on you I saw that you and I were both in the same box – that's the reason I spoke to you.'

She stepped nearer, her smile dilating on Lydia's like a lamp through a fog.

'You can take your choice, you know; I always play fair. If you'll tell I'll promise not to. Now then, which is it to be?'

Lydia, involuntarily, had begun to move away from the pelting storm of words; but at this she turned and sat down again.

'You may go,' she said simply. 'I shall stay here.'

IV

She stayed there for a long time, in the hypnotised contemplation, not of Mrs Cope's present, but of her own past. Gannett, early that morning, had gone off on a long walk – he had fallen into the habit of taking these mountain tramps with various fellow-lodgers; but even had he been within reach she could not have gone to him just then. She had to deal with herself first. She was surprised to find how in the last months, she had lost the habit of introspection. Since their coming to the Hotel Bellosguardo she and Gannett had tacitly avoided themselves and each other.

She was aroused by the whistle of the three o'clock steamboat as it neared the landing just beyond the hotel gates. Three o'clock! Then Gannett would soon be back – he had told her to expect him before four. She rose hurriedly, her face averted from the inquisitorial façade of the hotel. She could not see him just yet; she could not go indoors. She slipped through one of the overgrown garden-alleys and climbed a steep path to the hills.

It was dark when she opened their sitting-room door. Gannett was sitting on the window-ledge smoking a cigarette. Cigarettes were now his chief resource: he had not written a line during the two months they had spent at the Hotel Bellosguardo. In that respect, it had turned out not to be the right *milieu* after all.

He started up at Lydia's entrance.

'Where have you been? I was getting anxious.'

She sat down in a chair near the door.

'Up the mountain,' she said wearily.

'Alone?'

'Yes.'

Gannett threw away his cigarette: the sound of her voice made him want to see her face.

'Shall we have a little light?' he suggested.

She made no answer and he lifted the globe from the lamp and put a match to the wick. Then he looked at her.

'Anything wrong? You look done up.'

She sat glancing vaguely about the little sitting-room, dimly lit by the pallid-globed lamp, which left in twilight the outlines of the furniture, of his writing-table heaped with books and papers, of the tea roses and jasmine drooping on the mantelpiece. How like home it had all grown – how like home!

'Lydia, what is wrong?' he repeated.

She moved away from him, feeling for her hatpins and turning to lay her hat and sunshade on the table.

Suddenly she said: 'That woman has been talking to me.'

Gannett stared.

'That woman? What woman?'

'Mrs Linton – Mrs Cope.'

He gave a start of annoyance, still, as she perceived, not grasping the full import of her words.

'The deuce! She told you – ?'

'She told me everything.'

Gannett looked at her anxiously.

'What impudence! I'm so sorry that you should have been exposed to this, dear.'

'Exposed!' Lydia laughed.

Gannett's brow clouded and they looked away from each other.

'Do you know *why* she told me? She had the best of reasons. The first time she laid eyes on me she saw that we were both in the same box.'

'Lydia!'

'So it was natural, of course, that she should turn to me in a difficulty.'

'What difficulty?'

'It seems she has reason to think that Lord Trevenna's people are trying to get him away from her before she gets her divorce – '

'Well?'

'And she fancied he had been consulting with you last night as to – as to the best way of escaping from her.'

Gannett stood up with an angry forehead.

'Well – what concern of yours was all this dirty business? Why should she go to you?'

'Don't you see? It's so simple. I was to wheedle this secret out of you.'

'To oblige that woman?'

'Yes; or, if I was unwilling to oblige her, then to protect myself.'

'To protect yourself? Against whom?'

'Against her telling everyone in the hotel that she and I are in the same box.'

'She threatened that?'

'She left me the choice of telling it myself or of doing it for me.'

'The beast!'

There was a long silence. Lydia had seated herself on the sofa, beyond the radius of the lamp, and he leaned against the window. His next question surprised her.

'When did this happen? At what time, I mean?'

She looked at him vaguely.

'I don't know – after luncheon, I think. Yes, I remember; it must have been at about three o'clock.'

He stepped into the middle of the room and as he approached the light she saw that his brow had cleared.

'Why do you ask?' she said.

'Because when I came in, at about half-past three, the mail was just being distributed, and Mrs Cope was waiting as usual to pounce on her letters; you know she was always watching for the postman. She was standing so close to me that I couldn't help seeing a big official-looking envelope that was handed to her. She tore it open, gave one look at the inside, and rushed off upstairs like a whirlwind, with the director shouting after her that she had left all her other letters behind. I don't believe she ever thought of you again after that paper was put into her hand.'

'Why?'

'Because she was too busy. I was sitting in the window, watching for you, when the five o'clock boat left, and who should go on board, bag and baggage, valet and maid, dressing-bags and poodle, but Mrs Cope and Trevenna. Just an hour and a half to pack up in! And you should have seen her when they started. She was radiant – shaking hands with everybody – waving her handkerchief from the deck – distributing bows and smiles like an empress. If ever a woman got what she wanted just in the nick of time that woman did. She'll be Lady Trevenna within a week, I'll wager.'

'You think she has her divorce?'

'I'm sure of it. And she must have got it just after her talk with you.'

Lydia was silent.

At length she said, with a kind of reluctance, 'She was horribly angry when she left me. It wouldn't have taken long to tell Lady Susan Condit.'

'Lady Susan Condit has not been told.'

'How do you know?'

'Because when I went downstairs half an hour ago I met Lady Susan on the way – '

He stopped, half smiling.

'Well?'

'And she stopped to ask if I thought you would act as patroness to a charity concert she is getting up.'

In spite of themselves they both broke into a laugh. Lydia's ended in sobs and she sank down with her face hidden. Gannett bent over her, seeking her hands.

'That vile woman – I ought to have warned you to keep away from her; I can't forgive myself! But he spoke to me in confidence; and I never dreamed – well, it's over now.'

Lydia lifted her head.

'Not for me. It's only just beginning.'

'What do you mean?'

She put him gently aside and moved in her turn to the window. Then she went on, with her face turned toward the shimmering blackness of the lake, 'You see of course that it might happen again at any moment.'

'What?'

'This – this risk of being found out. And we could hardly count again on such a lucky combination of chances, could we?'

He sat down with a groan.

Still keeping her face toward the darkness, she said, 'I want you to go and tell Lady Susan – and the others.'

Gannett, who had moved towards her, paused a few feet off.

'Why do you wish me to do this?' he said at length, with less surprise in his voice than she had been prepared for.

'Because I've behaved basely, abominably, since we came here: letting those people believe we were married – lying with every breath I drew – '

'Yes, I've felt that too,' Gannett exclaimed with sudden energy.

The words shook her like a tempest: all her thoughts seemed to fall about her in ruins.

'You – you've felt so?'

'Of course I have.' He spoke with low-voiced vehemence. 'Do you suppose I like playing the sneak any better than you do? It's damnable.'

He had dropped on the arm of a chair, and they stared at each other like blind people who suddenly see.

'But you have liked it here,' she faltered.

'Oh, I've liked it – I've liked it.' He moved impatiently. 'Haven't you?'

'Yes,' she burst out; 'that's the worst of it – that's what I can't bear. I fancied it was for your sake that I insisted on staying – because you thought you could write here; and perhaps just at first that really was the reason. But afterwards I wanted to stay myself – I loved it.' She broke into a laugh. 'Oh, do you see the full derision of it? These people – the very prototypes of the bores you took me away from, with the same fenced-in view of life, the same keep-off-the-grass morality, the same little cautious virtues and the same little frightened vices – well, I've clung to them, I've delighted in them, I've done my best to please them. I've toadied Lady Susan, I've gossiped with Miss Pinsent, I've pretended to be shocked with Mrs Ainger. Respectability! It was the one thing in life that I was sure I didn't care about, and it's grown so precious to me that I've stolen it because I couldn't get it in any other way.'

She moved across the room and returned to his side with another laugh.

'I who used to fancy myself unconventional! I must have been born with a card-case in my hand. You should have seen me with that poor woman in the garden. She came to me for help, poor creature, because she fancied that, having "sinned", as they call it, I might feel some pity for others who had been tempted in the same way. Not I! She didn't know me. Lady Susan would have been kinder, because Lady Susan wouldn't have been afraid. I hated the woman – my one thought was not to be seen with her – I could have killed her for guessing my secret. The one thing that mattered to me at that moment was my standing with Lady Susan!'

Gannett did not speak.

'And you – you've felt it too!' she broke out accusingly. 'You've enjoyed being with these people as much as I have; you've let the chaplain talk to you by the hour about "The Reign of Law" and Professor Drummond. When they asked you to hand the plate in church I was watching you – *you wanted to accept.*'

She stepped close, laying her hand on his arm.

'Do you know, I begin to see what marriage is for. It's to keep people away from each other. Sometimes I think that two people who love each other can be saved from madness only by the things that come between them – children, duties, visits, bores, relations – the things that protect married people from each other. We've been too close together – that has been our sin. We've seen the nakedness of each other's souls.'

She sank again on the sofa, hiding her face in her hands.

Gannett stood above her perplexedly: he felt as though she were being swept away by some implacable current while he stood helpless on its bank.

At length he said, 'Lydia, don't think me a brute – but don't you see yourself that it won't do?'

'Yes, I see it won't do,' she said without raising her head.

His face cleared.

'Then we'll go tomorrow.'

'Go – where?'

'To Paris; to be married.'

For a long time she made no answer; then she asked slowly, 'Would they have us here if we were married?'

'Have us here?'

'I mean Lady Susan – and the others.'

'Have us here? Of course they would.'

'Not if they knew – at least, not unless they could pretend not to know.'

He made an impatient gesture.

'We shouldn't come back here, of course; and other people needn't know – no one need know.'

She sighed. 'Then it's only another form of deception and a meaner one. Don't you see that?'

'I see that we're not accountable to any Lady Susans on earth!'

'Then why are you ashamed of what we are doing here?'

'Because I'm sick of pretending that you're my wife when you're not – when you won't be.'

She looked at him sadly.

'If I were your wife you'd have to go on pretending. You'd have to pretend that I'd never been – anything else. And our friends would have to pretend that they believed what you pretended.'

Gannett pulled off the sofa-tassel and flung it away.

'You're impossible,' he groaned.

'It's not I – it's our being together that's impossible. I only want you to see that marriage won't help it.'

'What will help it then?'

She raised her head.

'My leaving you.'

'Your leaving me?' He sat motionless, staring at the tassel which lay at the other end of the room. At length some impulse of retaliation for the pain she was inflicting made him say deliberately: 'And where would you go if you left me?'

'Oh!' she cried, wincing.

He was at her side in an instant.

'Lydia – Lydia – you know I didn't mean it; I couldn't mean it! But you've driven me out of my senses; I don't know what I'm saying. Can't you get out of this labyrinth of self-torture? It's destroying us both.'

'That's why I must leave you.'

'How easily you say it!' He drew her hands down and made her face him. 'You're very scrupulous about yourself – and others. But have you thought of me? You have no right to leave me unless you've ceased to care – '

'It's because I care – '

'Then I have a right to be heard. If you love me you can't leave me.'

Her eyes defied him.

'Why not?'

He dropped her hands and rose from her side.

'Can you?' he said sadly.

The hour was late and the lamp flickered and sank. She stood up with a shiver and turned toward the door of her room.

V

At daylight a sound in Lydia's room woke Gannett from a troubled sleep. He sat up and listened. She was moving about softly, as though fearful of disturbing him. He heard her push back one of the creaking shutters; then there was a moment's silence, which seemed to indicate that she was waiting to see if the noise had roused him.

Presently she began to move again. She had spent a sleepless night, probably, and was dressing to go down to the garden for a breath of air. Gannett rose also; but some undefinable instinct made his movements as cautious as hers. He stole to his window and looked out through the slats of the shutter.

It had rained in the night and the dawn was grey and lifeless. The cloud-muffled hills across the lake were reflected in its surface as in a tarnished mirror. In the garden, the birds were beginning to shake the drops from the motionless laurustinus boughs.

An immense pity for Lydia filled Gannett's soul. Her seeming intellectual independence had blinded him for a time to the feminine cast of her mind. He had never thought of her as a woman who wept and clung: there was a lucidity in her intuitions that made them appear to be the result of reasoning. Now he saw the cruelty he had committed in detaching her from the normal conditions of life; he felt, too, the insight with which she had hit upon the real cause of their suffering. Their life was 'impossible', as she had said – and its worst penalty was that it had made any other life impossible for them. Even had his love lessened, he was bound to her now by a hundred ties of pity and self-reproach; and she, poor child! must turn back to him as Latude returned to his cell . . .

A new sound startled him: it was the stealthy closing of Lydia's door. He crept to his own and heard her footsteps passing down the corridor. Then he went back to the window and looked out.

A minute or two later he saw her go down the steps of the porch and enter the garden. From his post of observation her face was invisible, but something about her appearance struck him. She wore a long travelling cloak and under its folds he detected the outline of a bag or bundle. He drew a deep breath and stood watching her.

She walked quickly down the laurustinus alley toward the gate; there she paused a moment, glancing about the little shady square. The stone benches under the trees were empty, and she seemed to gather resolution from the solitude about her, for she crossed the square to the steamboat landing, and he saw her pause before the ticket-office at the head of the wharf. Now she was buying her ticket. Gannett turned his head a moment to look at the clock: the boat was due in five minutes. He had time to jump into his clothes and overtake her –

He made no attempt to move; an obscure reluctance restrained him. If any thought emerged from the tumult of his sensations, it was that he must let her go if she wished it. He had spoken last night of his rights: what were they? At the last issue, he and she were two separate beings, not made one by the miracle of common forbearances, duties, abnegations, but bound together in a *noyade* of passion that left them resisting yet clinging as they went down.

After buying her ticket, Lydia had stood for a moment looking out across the lake; then he saw her seat herself on one of the benches near the landing. He and she, at that moment, were both listening for the same sound: the whistle of the boat as it rounded the nearest promontory. Gannett turned again to glance at the clock: the boat was due now.

Where would she go? What would her life be when she had left him? She had no near relations and few friends. There was money enough . . . but she asked so much of life, in ways so complex and immaterial. He thought of her as walking barefooted through a stony waste. No one would understand her – no one would pity her – and he, who did both, was powerless to come to her aid . . .

He saw that she had risen from the bench and walked toward the edge of the lake. She stood looking in the direction from which the steamboat was to come; then she turned to the ticket-office, doubtless to ask the cause of the delay. After that she went back to the bench and sat down with bent head. What was she thinking of?

The whistle sounded; she started up, and Gannett involuntarily made a movement toward the door. But he turned back and continued to watch her. She stood motionless, her eyes on the trail of smoke that preceded the appearance of the boat. Then the little craft rounded the point, a dead-white object on the leaden water: a minute later it was puffing and backing at the wharf.

The few passengers who were waiting – two or three peasants and a snuffy priest – were clustered near the ticket-office. Lydia stood apart under the trees.

The boat lay alongside now; the gangplank was run out and the peasants went on board with their baskets of vegetables, followed by the priest. Still Lydia did not move. A bell began to ring querulously; there was a shriek of steam, and someone must have called to her that she would be late, for she started forward, as though in answer to a summons. She moved waveringly, and at the edge of the wharf she paused. Gannett saw a sailor beckon to her; the bell rang again and she stepped upon the gangplank.

Halfway down the short incline to the deck she stopped again; then she turned and ran back to the land. The gangplank was drawn in, the bell ceased to ring, and the boat backed out into the lake. Lydia, with slow steps, was walking toward the garden . . .

As she approached the hotel she looked up furtively and Gannett drew back into the room. He sat down beside a table; a Bradshaw lay at his elbow, and mechanically, without knowing what he did, he began looking out the trains to Paris . . .

Motel Marriage

ELIZABETH JOLLEY

She calls it having sex. She says men have to have sex. She knows this. Don't ask her she says she just knows it. Mr F. she says Mr F. did you know? Mr F. she keeps on Mr F. listen to this Mr F. Mr F. I must tell you Mr F. just you listen to this. Listen! She starts everything she says with 'listen'. And if it isn't Mr F. it's Mrs Porter. Mrs Porter says Mrs Porter believes Mrs Porter . . .

Dalton Foster, driving the hired car with the special care of one who, at a late age, has recently obtained a licence but has not had much practice, allows himself the consolation of being quietly, in his thoughts, irritated.

'Some men Mr F.,' his companion in the passenger seat reiterates, returning as if to previous thoughts of her own, or worse as if reading his mind, 'some men have to have sex. It's part of their body they have to have it no matter what. I do know this. But I do know too,' she makes as if snuggling closer to the uncompromising space between them, 'that sex isn't everything. I've always been broad-minded, but. Mrs Porter's always telling me, "The trouble with you E.V." Mrs Porter says if she's said it once she's said it a dozen times, "The trouble with you E.V. is that you're too broadminded." Oops! There! I've snagged me. There on the four in the floor. What a giggle . . .'

The sharp scent, previously unfamiliar but now all too well known to Dalton, of nail varnish, fills the confined space between the front seats and the dashboard as the new Mrs Dalton Foster sets about a hungry-fingered, nimble dabbing at the tiny ruptures in her new nylons. 'Mrs Porter, you know,' the new Mrs Dalton Foster says, 'Mrs Porter always said that Mr Right would turn up for me eventually. "E.V.," she would say, "sure as I'm sitting here with this teapot Mr Right is waiting just out there around the corner. He's here as large as life in these tea leaves. I see him plain. He's closer than you think." And, did you know, I never ever reelly ever thought Mr Right would be you. It's a laugh, it reelly is. You and me. Well we're not a bit alike are we. Attractions of the opposites that's what Mrs Porter said.'

Heraclitus said that all things flow, it is not possible to step in the same river twice. Dalton Foster is accustomed to the swift and silent movement of his mind. As the car travels through the summer-brown countryside the cows in the paddocks, on both sides of the road, do not raise their heads. They are occupied with their own short-sighted view of the bleached grass. Heraclitus, Dalton seeks further consolation in thought, Heraclitus did not add that images of things are even more fleeting. Images, he warms privately to his theme, images change with the maker of them – whether he is in good health, whether he is tired or hungry or disappointed. Images, he allows himself one final internal pronouncement, are essentially personal. Dalton is both tired and hungry and, he supposes, he is not disappointed so much as profoundly depressed. Surrounded, as he feels he is, by acres of unendurable boredom, he envies the cows their acres of poor feed. Being unable to get away from the source of the boredom is similar to being in prison. During the journey while his companion is talking, hopping endlessly with a happiness that is frightening, about Saddam Hussein – we never see his wife do we I mean we see Mrs Bush quite a lot on TV funny she's white-haired you can't help wondering what Mrs Hussein is like – about President Bush, about oil – that poor little baby bird drowned in the oil slick really makes your heart ache – about bathrooms – I reelly like matching towels and pillowcases, you know embroidered HIS and HERS – and on to bedroom suites, designer wardrobes, fashion silk jackets and scarves, Trax and Reeboks with blow-ups . . . he watches the passing scenes of unknown townships, all with ramshackle buildings and verandah posts crazy enough to have been put there recently for a shoot-out in a Western. He notices that each place has its own hotel and its own petrol station. A storage tank, a silo, a railway siding and what looks like obsolete farm machinery alongside the main road give an impression of scattered toys left by children too tired to go on playing. He cannot help noticing too the frightening lack of evidence of attempts to ameliorate the heat which could be even worse than it is at present.

'I mean,' the new Mrs Foster remarks, following his troubled gaze with her own eyes and changing the subject, trying to be a part of his unspoken thoughts, coming upon them yet again with unexpected insight, 'all those tin roofs out there and not a bit of shade.'

Mr Foster, though he has never wanted to be married himself, has often thought that it would be comfortable to have someone to come back to, perhaps to talk things over with and to exchange anecdotes, or to notice and mention things like darker patches on ceilings, or wallpaper which is perfectly hideous, or to be able to say things like, 'Isn't Mrs Porter absolutely dreadful,' and then to laugh with that other person. But he knows that he did not want a wife. The word 'wife' suggests all kinds of unmentionable things.

'I do so like a nice bathroom,' the new Mrs Foster is insisting. 'I know Mrs Porter says people put all their money into their bathrooms and you don't live in a bathroom and having more than one makes more to clean but I have seen some lovely bathrooms you know black and gold and marble all mirrors too and telephones at the places where I go babysitting and some places have ducky little bathrooms specially for their children and then there's bathrooms for visitors. All the same I've always felt comfortable in the bathroom at Mrs Porter's. I've always liked the green painted floor-wood you know and in the mornings the sun comes right in there makes it seem somehow cosy and freshens you up if you've been at someone's place all night – babysitting . . .'

It is certainly not possible to laugh about Mrs Porter with the new Mrs Foster. Mr Foster tries instead to think of books, of the pleasure of dying surrounded by books, the window-sills piled high with books, 'arranged three by three' with books. He tries to remember something he read once, years ago when he was a student, about books 'keeping watch like angels with outspread wings' and being like an image or a sign of resurrection.

'There was a man crushed to death it was in the paper crushed to death he was by books. A bookcase fell on him while he was choosing a book to take to bed. Imagine!' the new Mrs Foster said, the evening before, when she saw the little pile of reading material he had prepared for their journey.

'Imagine what it would be like to have all books falling on you you'd suffocate. Didn't you read about the man crushed to death? It said in the paper he'd written some of them himself. Just goes to show Mrs Porter said it was a judgement.'

*

The motel, for the first night of their honeymoon, is hard to find, being set back from the main road and dark, hidden in trees. An immediate inspection, while Mr Foster is still clutching the key on its little painted board, reveals heavy dust-laden curtains hanging without any possibility of being drawn back. The curtains cover the full length of the windows which resemble shop windows in size and thickness, but having nothing displayed, he discovers, except the ugly side wall of the next unit. The fixed furniture bothers him. It is not possible to move the table or the chairs, and there is no door between the living space and the bedroom. This worries him too, as does the unforgettable and inescapable smell of frying, of sausages burst and burned and stuck in the pan, a legacy from the previous occupants. He feels himself responsible for a certain amount of chivalry.

'Miss Vales,' he says at the end of their industrious and uneasy examination, 'I noticed upon arrival that there is a restaurant attached to this motel.' The new Mrs Foster, accustomed to being called Miss Vales for a great many years of her life, does not seem to see any reason for correction. She settles, with delight, in front of the dingy mirror, patting and teasing her new perm, turning her head first to one side and then the other. With some extra pullings and twistings she manages, Mr Foster thinks, with great skill to aid the extraordinary pile of hair to maintain its erection. Women's hair, he comes to the conclusion, seems to be either a gleaming metallic tower of smooth impenetrable brilliance, or it is a mass of ropes and coils indescribably tangled, sometimes drawn back from the face, but mainly, like deadly poisonous creepers in pictures of rainforests, hanging over and obliterating features and expression completely. Both are equally impervious. Miss Vales' edifice, he notices, is inclined to lean.

The motel is cool but depressing. The path which leads to the beach turns out to be long, and its dreary curves are well supplied with tins and bottles and litter of a more personal sort. Flies and mosquitoes are in abundance. The idea of a walk before dinner is abandoned quickly.

They are the only guests in the darkened dining-room. Seeing their self-conscious reflections in the cave of gold-edged mirrors, Dalton thinks, during the meal, that he is the more pathetic in appearance. He feels sorry for Miss Vales, all the more so at the beginning of the meal when she managed to be excited and quite noisily frivolous about a decision over the menu. 'Oh Mr F. you choose and order.' He feels he will never forget the desperation behind the apparently light-hearted request. Gulping, he had glanced up at the waitress, a red-cheeked country girl who settled the problem by saying, 'There's only the tuna and sweetcorn mornay tonight. Everything's off excepting that.'

'Well Mr F. tomorrow's motel might be quite different and there might be a moon, you can never tell, it takes all sorts,' the new bride chatters mercilessly, back once more, perched before the mirror, patting and teasing all over again her hair, turning her head from side to side as she studies her own reflection. Keeping her knees together, she slides, in her new nightgown, from the fixed stool to the edge of the fixed bed and finally, with her knees still neatly pressed together, she slides under the covers lying down near the edge of the bed as gingerly as Mr Foster, buttoned in his new pyjamas, does on his side. She begins to explain about her headache almost at the moment when he is wondering how best to announce his.

Mr Dalton Foster wishes now during the night that he had taken Miss Vales back into the town for dinner. Though he was unfamiliar and nervous then, he is sure now that there would have been a better restaurant there. He wishes too that he could open the heavy curtains or loop them over a chair, and then he remembers all the furniture is immovable. Even the padded stool, his new wife's favourite perch, in front of the dressing table is a fixture. A fat woman could easily become wedged in the small space. Mrs Porter for example. The constant chatter about Mrs Porter during the day has made him feel that he has only to stretch out his hand to open his door at Mrs Porter's place. Or that he could meet Perce and Winch if he walked outside, or Miss Mallow, in the way he is used to meeting them on the stairs or in the hall. Sometimes lying in bed in his room at Mrs Porter's he hears Miss Mallow playing, with over use of the soft pedal, the piano parts of the Saint-Saëns piano concerto.

'It's Saint-Saëns,' she told him once without being asked, at the foot of the stairs. 'It's Saint-Saëns Piano Concerto Number Two.' She told him then that she seemed to hear the orchestra in her head and then was able to come down with emphasis on the piano. She told him too that she often tried to sing the orchestral melody and harmony aloud, but the sound which came out was never the same as it was in her head. He knew from what he was able to hear that on some days she did not even raise the shabby blistered lid. He knew, without seeing the piano, just how the veneer had come off in places. Until recently, she told him once, she had not noticed how old it looked. The sound, she explained then, did not matter. It had never mattered even when the older girls at the school practised their sonatas, their études, their sarabands and their marches. It had seemed to her then, she said, as if the ancient instrument had a certain charm reminiscent of some authentic masterpiece made by a craftsman in musical contrivances. 'The vibration of the strings,' Miss Mallow lowered her voice as if in reverence, 'produced sound then almost similar to that of the harpischord. Clementi,' she continued, her voice lower still, 'Clementi was said to be the father of modern pianoforte playing. *And*,' Mr Foster remembers her smile as she went on, '*and*, I like to think that my piano could be said to resemble an instrument made and played by this great man.'

Mr Foster, moving his stiff legs with caution on his side of the bed, tries not to breathe. It is not possible for him to know if his bride, the word does not come easily to him, is asleep. As she is not chattering he presumes that she is.

Once at Mrs Porter's Miss Mallow, peering from her door as if waiting for him, waylaid him in the hall.

'It's the small things I take,' she said. 'Only the small things. Small things which will slide from my pocket into the lining of my coat, a bread roll, a teabag in its envelope, a tiny three-cornered cheese wrapped in foil, an egg lifted carefully from a carton of eggs, a small chocolate bar, a tomato and perhaps an onion. Not all at once,' she assured him, 'because, you know, there are special people who watch for thieves. I never thought, you know, that I would be a thief. You understand don't you, you see I have to find a little supper somewhere. I have never told anyone about all this. I never thought I would sit, without money, waiting on the benches in the arcade where the supermarket is. When I'm back in my room at Mrs Porter's I tell Mr Afton everything. Mr Afton was my old headmaster. He it was gave me the piano. I tell him things all the time, in my head, you understand . . .

Thinking about Miss Mallow during this long uncomfortable night Dalton Foster can see clearly that there is really not much difference between her future and his except that he has more money, not much more, than she has. And, of course, he is married and she is not. The marriage, as it is, he feels does not make all that much difference. The difference, if there is one, is chiefly that though he is ignorant, naïve perhaps, he is not innocent as she is. He tries not to think of his time in prison and in hospital. Trying not to turn over and so disturb the silent Miss Vales he reminds himself of something he read years ago in a literary paper. Unable to remember the exact words he recalls the essence, which was, that life has stipulations from which certain requirements spring. Life, he thinks, in its bleakness does not hold much for Miss Mallow or Miss Vales or himself.

The honeymoon, like the wedding, had been Mrs Porter's idea. He supposes that she meant well, but the thought of spending the money he is really unable to afford, the thought of the future, even a second night in a motel is appalling apart from everything else. Mrs Porter made it clear that three nights were the minimum acceptable for a honeymoon.

'Three nights E. V. he owes you three.' Mrs Porter held up three large fingers; even in his presence she did this and he remained silent. Silence during the prison and the hospital had become his way and there did not seem any possibility of changing this.

'I mean,' Mrs Porter said, 'you can't go away for less, where in Gawd's name can you get to in less? And then you've to get back haven't you. You can't get anywhere in one day.' Mr Foster's silence was, he understands, regarded as an acquiescence. He is deeply sorry now. Sorry for Miss Vales because he is silently irritated with her the whole time. He is sorry that he has no qualities fitting for a bridegroom. His dealings with women have always been mainly by accident.

'I've been talking to a lady on the telephone,' he told his aunt when she asked him what he had been doing.

'Who could our precious child have been talking to?' Aunt Dalton and his mother pondered. They really wanted to know.

'He is *excited*,' Aunt Dalton said. 'See how flushed his little face is. And look at his eyes, they're bright. Perhaps he's feverish.' His aunt and his mother, deciding that he was, put him to bed immediately in his mother's room.

'You know,' his aunt said, 'it must have been the operator. He must have called the operator simply by accident.' The two women enjoyed reasoning. 'Perhaps he'll do other things by accident.' They seemed then to be cautiously considering an uncertain future while at the same time brushing and arranging each other's hair, bunching the curls, holding them up and back exposing on each neck the soft white nape.

'Bone or grosgrain?' Aunt Dalton questioned while selecting the ornamental hairbands. 'This corded silk, this greeny-black silk, like the arched tail feathers of a young cock, my dear, is striking and very strong, but see, the bone is irresistible, smooth and simple, absolutely aesthetic, very dependable, a certain generator of clear penetrating thought. Which will you . . .?' The laughter, starting as a soft breathless whispering and a catching of breath, began to change as Dalton lay encircled by the two women, their arms reaching across caressing each other so that immediately above him their breasts, escaping the soft folds of clothing, naked and scented, caught him lightly as they moved, touching and nudging his face and his lips till he too was caught up in the long low sigh, the forerunner of the magic of exquisite sensation.

Mr Foster, hardly breathing, raises himself. The smallish mound on the other edge of the bed makes no movement. Miss Vales could be dead for all that she is so still. He feels his way, with all the stealth of a thief, to the tiny bathroom. It occurs to him that Miss Vales might be lying there under the covers awake and prepared to endure with absolute silence the whole long night. There were people who would do this sort of thing. They would sit something out. It is not his sort of phrase, but then this night, this whole journey and the reason for it, is not his sort of thing . . .

❧ *Three Dreams in a Desert*

Under a Mimosa Tree

OLIVE SCHREINER

As I travelled across an African plain the sun shone down hotly. Then I drew my horse up under a mimosa tree, and I took the saddle from him and left him to feed among the parched bushes. And all to right and to left stretched the brown earth. And I sat down under the tree, because the heat beat fiercely, and all along the horizon the air throbbed. And after a while a heavy drowsiness came over me, and I laid my head down against my saddle, and I fell asleep there. And, in my sleep, I had a curious dream.

I thought I stood on the border of a great desert, and the sand blew about everywhere. And I thought I saw two great figures like beasts of burden of the desert, and one lay upon the sand with its neck stretched out, and one stood by it. And I looked curiously at the one that lay upon the ground, for it had a great burden on its back, and the sand was thick about it, so that it seemed to have piled over it for centuries.

And I looked very curiously at it. And there stood one beside me watching. And I said to him, 'What is this huge creature who lies here on the sand?'

And he said, 'This is woman; she that bears men in her body.'

And I said, 'Why does she lie here motionless with the sand piled round her?'

And he answered, 'Listen, I will tell you! Ages and ages long she has lain here, and the wind has blown over her. The oldest, oldest, oldest man living has never seen her move; the oldest, oldest book records that she lay here then, as she lies here now, with the sand about her. But listen! Older than the oldest book, older than the oldest recorded memory of man, on the Rocks of Language, on the hard-baked clay of Ancient Customs, now crumbling to decay, are found the marks of her footsteps! Side by side with his who stands beside her you may trace them; and you know that she who now lies there once wandered free over the rocks with him.'

And I said, 'Why does she lie there now?'

And he said, 'I take it, ages ago the Age-of-dominion-of-muscular-force found her, and when she stooped low to give suck to her young, and her back was broad, he put his burden of subjection on to it, and tied it on with the broad band of Inevitable Necessity. Then she looked at the earth and the sky, and knew there was no hope for her; and she lay down on the sand with the burden she could not loosen. Ever since she has lain here. And the ages have come, and the ages have gone, but the band of Inevitable Necessity has not been cut.'

And I looked and saw in her eyes the terrible patience of the centuries; the ground was wet with her tears, and her nostrils blew up the sand.

And I said, 'Has she ever tried to move?'

And he said, 'Sometimes a limb has quivered. But she is wise; she knows she cannot rise with the burden on her.'

And I said, 'Why does not he who stands by her leave her and go on?'

And he said, 'He cannot. Look – '

And I saw a broad band passing along the ground from one to the other, and it bound them together.

He said, 'While she lies there he must stand and look across the desert.'

And I said, 'Does he know why he cannot move?'

And he said, 'No.'

And I heard a sound of something cracking, and I looked, and I saw the band that bound the burden on to her back broken asunder; and the burden rolled on to the ground.

And I said, 'What is this?'

And he said, 'The Age-of-muscular-force is dead. The Age-of-nervous-force has killed him with the knife he holds in his hand; and silently and invisibly he has crept up to the woman, and with that knife of Mechanical Invention he has cut the band that bound the burden to her back. The Inevitable Necessity is broken. She might rise now.'

And I saw that she still lay motionless on the sand, with her eyes open and her neck stretched out. And she seemed to look for something on the far-off border of the desert that never came. And I wondered if she were awake or asleep, And as I looked her body quivered and a light came into her eyes, like when a sunbeam breaks into a dark room.

I said, 'What is it?'

He whispered, 'Hush! the thought has come to her, "Might I not rise?"'

And I looked. And she raised her head from the sand, and I saw the dent where her neck had lain so long. And she looked at the earth, and she looked at the sky, and she looked at him who stood by her; but he looked out across the desert.

And I saw her body quiver; and she pressed her front knees to the earth, and veins stood out; and I cried, 'She is going to rise!'

But only her sides heaved, and she lay still where she was.

But her head she held up; she did not lay it down again. And he beside me said, 'She is very weak. See, her legs have been crushed under her so long.'

And I saw the creature struggle; and the drops stood out on her.

And I said, 'Surely he who stands beside her will help her?'

And he beside me answered, 'He cannot help her: *she must help herself*. Let her struggle till she is strong.'

And I cried, 'At least he will not hinder her! See, he moves farther from her, and tightens the cord between them, and he drags her down.'

And he answered, 'He does not understand. When she moves she draws the band that binds them, and hurts him, and he moves farther from her. The day will come when he will understand, and will know what she is doing. Let her once stagger on to her knees. In that day he will stand close to her, and look into her eyes with sympathy.'

And she stretched her neck, and the drops fell from her. And the creature rose an inch from the earth and sank back.

And I cried, 'Oh, she is too weak! She cannot walk! The long years have taken all her strength from her. Can she never move?'

And he answered me, 'See the light in her eyes!'

And slowly the creature staggered on to its knees.

And I awoke: and all to the east and to the west stretched the barren earth, with the dry bushes on it. The ants ran up and down in the red sand, and the heat beat fiercely. I looked up through the thin branches of the tree at the blue sky overhead. I stretched myself, and I mused over the dream I had had. And I fell asleep again, with my head on my saddle. And in the fierce heat I had another dream.

I saw a desert and I saw a woman coming out of it. And she came to the bank of a dark river; and the bank was steep and high.[1] And on it an old man met her, who had a long white beard; and a stick that curled was in his hand, and on it was written Reason. And he asked her what she wanted; and she said, 'I am woman; and I am seeking for the land of Freedom.'

And he said, 'It is before you.'

And she said, 'I see nothing before me but a dark flowing river, and a bank steep and high, and cuttings here and there with heavy sand in them.'

And he said, 'And beyond that?'

She said, 'I see nothing, but sometimes, when I shade my eyes with my hand, I think I see on the further bank trees and hills, and the sun shining on them!'

He said, 'That is the Land of Freedom.'

She said, 'How am I to get there?'

He said, 'There is one way, and one only. Down the banks of Labour, through the water of Suffering. There is no other.'

She said, 'Is there no bridge?'

He answered, 'None.'

She said, 'Is the water deep?'

He said, 'Deep.'

She said, 'Is the floor worn?'

He said, 'It is. Your foot may slip at any time, and you may be lost.'

She said, 'Have any crossed already?'

[1] The banks of an African river are sometimes a hundred feet high, and consist of deep shifting sands, through which in the course of ages the river has worn its gigantic bed.

He said, 'Some have *tried*!'

She said, 'Is there a track to show where the best fording is?'

He said, 'It has to be made.'

She shaded her eyes with her hand; and she said, 'I will go.'

And he said, 'You must take off the clothes you wore in the desert: they are dragged down by them who go into the water so clothed.'

And she threw from her gladly the mantle of Ancient-received-opinions she wore, for it was worn full of holes. And she took the girdle from her waist that she had treasured so long, and the moths flew out of it in a cloud. And he said, 'Take the shoes of dependence off your feet.'

And she stood there naked, but for one white garment that clung close to her.

And he said, 'That you may keep. So they wear clothes in the Land of Freedom. In the water it buoys; it always swims.'

And I saw on its breast was written Truth, and it was white; the sun had not often shone on it, the other clothes had covered it up. And he said, 'Take this stick; hold it fast. In that day when it slips from your hand you are lost. Put it down before you, feel your way: where it cannot find a bottom do not set your foot.'

And she said, 'I am ready; let me go.'

And he said, 'No – but stay; what is that – in your breast?'

She was silent.

He said, 'Open it, and let me see.'

And she opened it. And against her breast was a tiny thing, who drank from it, and the yellow curls above his forehead pressed against it; and his knees were drawn up to her, and he held her breast fast with his hands.

And Reason said, 'Who is he, and what is he doing here?'

And she said, 'See his little wings – '

And Reason said, 'Put him down.'

And she said, 'He is asleep, and he is drinking! I will carry him to the Land of Freedom. He has been a child so long, so long I have carried him. In the Land of Freedom he will be a man. We will walk together there, and his great white wings will overshadow me. He has lisped one word only to me in the desert – "Passion!" I have dreamed he might learn to say "Friendship" in that land.'

And Reason said, 'Put him down!'

And she said, 'I will carry him so – with one arm, and with the other I will fight the water.'

He said, 'Lay him down on the ground. When you are in the water you will forget to fight, you will think only of him. Lay him down.' He said, 'He will not die. When he finds you have left him alone he will open his wings and fly. He will be in the Land of Freedom before you. Those who reach the Land of Freedom, the first hand they see stretching down the bank to help them shall be Love's. He will be a man then, not a child. In your breast he cannot thrive; put him down that he may grow.'

And she took her bosom from his mouth, and he bit her, so that the blood ran down on to the ground. And she laid him down on the earth; and she covered her wound. And she bent and stroked his wings. And I saw the hair on her forehead turned white as snow, and she had changed from youth to age.

And she stood far off on the bank of the river. And she said, 'For what do I go to this far land which no one has ever reached? *Oh, I am alone! I am utterly alone!*'

And Reason, that old man, said to her, 'Silence! what do you hear?'

And she listened intently, and she said, 'I hear a sound of feet, a thousand times ten thousand and thousands of thousands, and they beat this way!'

He said, 'They are the feet of those that shall follow you. Lead on! Make a track to the water's edge! Where you stand now, the ground will be beaten flat by ten thousand times ten thousand feet.' And he said, 'Have you seen the locusts how they cross a stream? First one comes down to the water-edge, and it is swept away, and then another comes and then another, and then another, and at last with their bodies piled up a bridge is built and the rest pass over.'

She said, 'And, of those that come first, some are swept away, and are heard of no more; their bodies do not even build the bridge?'

'And are swept away, and are heard of no more – and what of that?' he said.

'And what of that – ' she said.

'They make a track to the water's edge.'

'They make a track to the water's edge – ' And she said, 'Over that bridge which shall be built with our bodies, who will pass?'

He said, *'The entire human race.'*

And the woman grasped her staff.

And I saw her turn down that dark path to the river.

And I awoke: and all about me was the yellow afternoon light, the sinking sun lit up the fingers of the milk bushes; and my horse stood by me quietly feeding. And I turned on my side, and I watched the ants run by thousands in the red sand. I thought I would go on my way now – the afternoon was cooler. Then a drowsiness crept over me again, and I laid back my head and fell asleep.

And I dreamed a dream.

I dreamed I saw a land. And on the hills walked brave women and brave men, hand in hand. And they looked into each other's eyes, and they were not afraid.

And I saw the women also hold each other's hands.

And I said to him beside me, 'What place is this?'

And he said, 'This is heaven.'
And I said, 'Where is it?'
And he answered, 'On earth.'
And I said, 'When shall these things be?'
And he answered, 'IN THE FUTURE.'

And I awoke, and all about me was the sunset light; and on the low hills the sun lay, and a delicious coolness had crept over everything; and the ants were going slowly home. And I walked towards my horse, who stood quietly feeding. Then the sun passed down behind the hills; but I knew that the next day he would rise again.

Moon Walk

EMILY PRAGER

I remember the first day I seen her, she was crying. It must have been spring because the outdoor tables were set up. Yeah, it was definitely outside, in front of the restaurant, a while ago because I was still waiting tables, not in the lofty position of manager as I am now, looking toward the future with a wing and a prayer. Yeah, I have this memory of this cat-like, really pretty woman, sitting down in a chair in these big black Jackie O. sunglasses. Mascara-ed tears were rolling down her cheeks like oil drips on desert sand.

I don't know how old she was, anywhere from thirty-three to forty. Her atmosphere was young though, you know, and helpless, her shape, the feel around her, the fuzzy part, the part you notice from afar. But later when I saw her eyes, some fucking explosive intelligence was there, and purpose, so I knew she wasn't just a kid. I'm twenty-seven. I'm a jerk and an asshole. I know what one looks like.

But the first time I seen her, even before I talked to her or anything, I fell in love. There she was, crying her eyes out like a fucking betrayed ballerina, and, of course I knew right away – some jerk did this, some low slimeball on a mission to kill. Her despair was so big, it was billowing toward me like smoke. I just kept refilling her coffee cup. The way I did it let her know I'd protect her.

She was class this woman. I know class. I'm from Bensonhurst, Brooklyn, where in my opinion, there is very little. I can say this because I'm from there, you know? I'm not some little spook bastard film-maker out to prove every Italian from Brooklyn is a vulgar bone-crunching wop animal who can't feel love.

No. I'm lower-middle-class Italian, and I know class when I see it because I know I don't have any. It's very simple. And she had it. Very slender. Very little makeup. Very polite. After two refills, she noticed me, took me in, and smiled at me gratefully through the tears. Classy people include other people, no matter what's going on. Death, destruction, they still know there's other people in the world besides them. They don't have to be told.

I kept watching her while I waited on the other tables. Sobbing, just sobbing her little heart out. Once, she caught me looking and blushed, a condition I had not seen in quite a while, let me tell you. She was waving around with grief like a flower in a windstorm, and it just confirmed to me what a goddam fucked-up world I'm living in where women like that only got me to comfort them.

Finally, I couldn't take it no more. I walked over to her, refilled her cup, and I said, 'Excuse me, Miss, I know this is none of my business, but that's never stopped me before so I'm just going to say it: the guy ain't worth it. No, let me rephrase that: no guy is worth it. Trust me, I know what I'm talking about.'

She laughed, choking on some tears in the process. I patted her on her little bony back, and handed her an extra napkin. She blew her nose and then looked up at me. I could see her eyes were kind right through those black lenses.

'I'm trying to help you, I almost killed you,' I joked.

'Thank you,' she managed and started bawling again.

'I mean what I'm talking about,' I said seriously. 'Do you mind if I sit down?'

She waved toward a chair with her hand.

'Look,' I began, 'we're living in a goddam pit, excuse me talking like this but I have to. It's violent. It's ugly. And it's mean and men are the perpetrators. Men cannot be trusted. No men. No way. Not even me and I'm a nice guy.'

'Things have changed,' she said. Her voice was low and slinky but sure. An older voice.

'Changed how?' I asked.

She glanced away from me out into traffic.

'It used to be so simple,' she replied. 'Now everything's so fraught.'

'Fraught,' I repeated. 'What's that mean exactly?'

She looked at me curiously. 'Surrounded by fear, I think.'

'Oh that. Oh, yeah. So, what are we talking about here, AIDS?'

'Everything,' she said. 'I hate the present. I want to go home to the past.'

'Me too,' I replied. 'I agree with you on the one thing: I too hate the present, but I also hate the past. I'm looking to the future. My money's on the future. It's got to be up from here.'

Tears drooled down her cheeks again. She grabbed a napkin and hung her head. On her slender fingers were a ton of copper rings. Her fingernails were all different lengths. It was clear she bit them.

'I have no future,' she said sadly.

'What?' I yelled this. 'What?!' I was going to go on but the boss came out then.

'Phone for you, Sal,' he said, and I could tell it was my bookie. I had a three-point spread on the play-off game and the man had to be dealt with.

'I'll be back to you,' I told her. 'Do not leave.' And I went in and took the call.

'She's lovely,' my boss said as I walked with him to the phone. He's fucking from the Bronx and wants to be someone else. Lace-curtain Irish on the way up, dresses like a fucking preppie. I hate him.

While I was getting Rocco to give me time on the pay-off, I watched her through the window. I hadn't had sex for months. Naw, that wasn't true. I had sex once with a well-known floosie from the neighbourhood who threw herself at me after a night of drinking. I couldn't even remember the act, but I like to think I used condoms 'cause there were ripped packets all over the floor. The next morning she was gone and I wanted to die. I don't get it. I thought it was supposed to be the other way around.

Since then, I didn't want to touch anybody. I didn't want to get involved. When I thought about sex a black mist settled around me and I went ice-cold. The idea of exchanging bodily fluids made me puke. And as for love – fuck, man, who the fuck had it? What the fuck was it? The sight of the back of the catwoman's neck was warming me up, though. This is it, I told myself. This is as good as it gets.

Rocco was giving me a hard time. I was on the phone longer than I expected, pleading my guts out, which really pissed me off 'cause I was just trying to live like a human being here in America which was my birthright. I had to have my own place, and a TV, and a stereo, and a telephone. I wasn't asking for the Taj Mahal, but things were getting like Calcutta out there. So I bet. And sometimes I lost and sometimes I won, and Rocco knew that, but he was having a bad day. The cops were putting the screws on, stopping his walk-in trade, and I was his whipping boy. Now, ordinarily, I would not take the shit, but he knew my father and my brothers and – you get the picture? I wanted my business to remain my own.

'Things are not always going to be this way,' I told Rocco. 'In the future, things are going to be very different.' And then I saw Francis, my rat Mick boss, strolling outside and hanging by her table, pretending to overlook the place like it was the goddam Tara or something. I could see he was glancing down at her, getting ready to spew some lines down to her which he got out of books which I recommended to him off my sister's college reading list. Short, fat scum had some confidence. He was the kind you could beat with a stick and he still wouldn't take it personal.

'I'm coming over,' Rocco said and he hung up on me.

'What the fuck good's that going to do, I don't know,' I said into the receiver and I set the phone down on its cradle. Linda, a waitress who, one of these days, I'm going to kill, passed by and said, 'You need to go to Gamblers Anonymous. Why don't you just face it?!'

'Mind your own fucking business,' I snapped.

'I love that woman out there, don't you?' she added as she sped into the kitchen. 'I always wanted to look like that.'

Maybe my luck was turning. Francis had not yet spoken to her. The fat crap was standing out there, whistling, for fuck's sake, like bad acting in a bad movie. He was blown away by her class. The fact that a woman like her was even sitting at one of his tables meant he had made it up one claw higher. He was so happy, he was rocking back and forth on the tips of his toes. It was sad. I hadn't seen him this intimidated since the day Cardinal O'Connor came in to use the phone.

Francis was in AA which was maybe how he got religion. But, anyway, at the age of thirty-five, a young Turk, he was always throwing on his camel's-hair coat and, in his pussy tasseled shoes, rushing off to Mass. He had scoured the city for churches that did Mass in Latin. It burned me that someone who was such a shit in life did so much time in church. And then it just burned me, period. When the Cardinal came in, I thought Francis was going to die. I hoped he was going to die. Like I said, I hate him. But, because he's my boss, I have to like him.

I got outside just as Francis was bending down about to say something really sleazy. She was facing away from him, not paying attention.

'*Veni, vidi, vici*,' he said.

She looked up at him, astonished.

'You know Latin, am I right?' he went on.

'Yes,' she replied, perplexed. Who wouldn't be?

'Phone for you, Francis,' I interrupted. 'Your mother. I think she's calling from the Bronx.'

He glanced at me stonefaced and then smiled down at her.

'We'll continue this in a moment,' he said and rushed back into the restaurant.

Her eyes followed him and then flicked back at me whereupon her face broke into a sun-coming-out type of smile that broke my heart. I saw us in a little house in Park Slope, her lighting candles on the fireplace mantel so everything would be sweet for me when I came home at night from, from where? The restaurant? The betting parlour? Sure, that's exactly the way it would be. Like some Hollywood fucking thing that has no business being on this planet in this time, that cheats people of every realistic hope they might have and leaves them begging on their knees for something that don't exist.

'What's the matter?' she asked, softly, full of concern. Evidently, she saw my hopes dashed.

'You want to marry me?' I asked, just in case.

Instantly, she started crying again.

'I was only kidding,' I said quickly. 'You don't have to. Don't worry.'

'No, I – ' she began and stopped.

'Forget about it,' I said and dropped down into the chair opposite her. 'Now, what's this about having no future?'

She blushed again and looked away.

'It's all downhill from here,' she murmured.

'You mean since I asked you to marry me?'

She laughed while a tear escaped down her cheek.

'Nooo,' she said, purring. Her voice was licking me, like a rough little cat's tongue, smoothing out my ragged edges, softening my ugliness. 'It has nothing to do with you.'

'Now there's the sad part,' I said.

'It's just that I can't stand not being free,' she said.

'Free?'

'I'm surrounded by limitation. Everywhere I turn. I can't stand it. For the first time in my life, I don't feel free. I can't stand it.'

'Are you married?' I asked.

She smiled at me.

'You don't understand,' she said. 'No. That isn't it.'

'No, I know. I know that isn't it. What is it?'

I took in the ring finger on her left hand. A brass ring with a name carved in it which I couldn't read.

I was looking as deeply into her eyes as I could through the Jackie O. lenses. There was real pain there. I felt fucking terrible. After a moment or two, she gave out with a sigh. She was looking me over, trying to find a language in which to explain the thing to the idiot child. Not that she was mocking me or anything. Oh no. She wanted me to get it. She was right with me on the thing. She looked dizzy from thinking. Nobody had ever expended this much energy on me unless it was Rocco and there was something in it for him.

'Did you ever see the movie *2001 Space Odyssey*?' she asked finally.

'Sure. Oh, sure. In high school. The part where the ape kills the other ape with the rock, the tool? Beautiful. Genius.'

I saw her relax as I said this and I relaxed. Okay, I was back on the track.

'Have you seen it recently?'

'No.'

'Watch it again,' she said. 'That was to be nine years from now. That was what, twenty-two years ago, we thought it would be like nine years from now.'

She made a disgusted little sound with her perfect rosebud lips, which I don't think I've mentioned before because I'm not an animal who divides women up into body parts. The dismemberment that goes on in mens' heads when it comes to women is fucking frightening. It's out of the fucking tabloids. A lot of guys I know go to bed with a pair of tits, and an ass and some ankles and a pair of perfect rosebud lips like they're in an autopsy lab. This is romance? If I can't handle a woman, I want to not be able to handle her as a whole person. So call me feminist. I don't give a shit.

'Do you understand?' she asked.

I decided to be honest. I was so tired of being dishonest, I couldn't even get it up any more.

'I'm trying to do the math,' I said.

'The future,' she said passionately, 'it didn't pan out. The power, the glory, the boundlessness of space, the technological advance, the human as superhuman, none of it. It was just a fantasy.'

'And you believed it? You counted on it?'

'Oh, yes.'

She said this with such love it hurt my heart. I felt that way about winning in the beginning, when I first went into the betting parlour and started up with Rocco. But she was talking about nothing tangible here. She was not talking about money.

'I remember the night I watched the Moon walk,' she went on, 'July of 1969. The most beautiful, the most powerful thing I've ever seen. The triumph I felt about who I was and where I lived and whither I was going remain unequalled in my lifetime. I felt joy, you know? Pure, limitless joy.'

'I was five,' I said, feeling like crap. 'I don't remember it.'

She looked at me curiously. Now she was doing the math.

'Sal, table 5.' It was Francis. He was outside again, steamed from the Bronx reference. He was gesturing toward some patrons with his thumb.

'So, you're older, so what? We'll have children right away. Think it over.'

I got up and did my job. Fucking Francis bounded toward her like an unleashed pitbull, but Linda, my favourite waitress in the western hemisphere, caught him on the fly.

'Phone for you. The meat man.'

'All right. All right,' he said, putting off Linda like she was some worthless speck. Then he said to my catwoman, 'When you're an owner of a place, you never sit down. When you're just a waiter – '

He almost pointed to me with his fat paws, but she didn't look my way. She stopped crying instantly. That warmed my heart. She didn't trust him with her feelings. Smart woman.

'*Arma virumque cano*,' he said then.

'*Troiae qui primus ab oris Italiam, fato profugus, Lavinaque venit litora,*' she replied.

'Bravo!' Francis shouted. 'Bravo!' He was leaping up and down like someone gave him the hot foot I had planned for him for later.

She laughed. Of course she laughed. He looked like a goddam fool. You'd have to be goddam dead not to laugh.

'I'll be right back,' he said, his beady little eyes twinkling like a rat who's found a burger in the trash. I knew I'd have to kill him to stop him, that's all there was to it. There were plenty of knives around, or I could just fucking beat him to death which might be more fun.

He rushed past me into the restaurant and I saw Linda hand him the phone and give him the high sign. Maybe my luck was changing. The sign meant the meat man was pissed. He wanted his money, and Francis to calm him would have to pay him a visit.

I went back in the kitchen and put in the orders. Francis was putting his coat on and swearing like he could read my thoughts.

'Where'd you learn that talk – church?' I asked him.

'Very funny,' he said. 'I'll be right back. You don't know where I am. Got it?'

I watched him as he ran out of the restaurant and prayed he'd get run over at the crosswalk. He stopped short at her table and said something to her and waved to her as he galumphed down the block.

I felt sick, you know? I'm fucking nothing, I know that, but I don't like everyone knowing it. It's my little secret.

She was hanging her head now, sad again from the look of it, which, in a fucked-up way, made my heart leap. She was just posing for him, being polite, is what it was. That was her way.

I tried to think what she was talking about. The Moon Walk. I'd seen it on TV, once maybe, maybe not. When I thought about rockets, I thought about the one that was blown up with all the teachers on it. I saw that piece of film about a million times, them coming out of the hangar, waving, smiling, then everybody watching them about to land and everybody's faces changing from hope to horror. Another fucking tragedy. Another fucking instance of how you shouldn't count on one damn thing. Some asshole didn't check the O-ring, that's what it was. They didn't make it right or they didn't check it. Un-fucking-believable except it's all I fucking know and it didn't surprise me.

I grabbed the coffee pot and went out to her table.

'You're trying to tell me that you've lost hope,' I said.

'Yes,' she replied, looking up at me.

'Take off your glasses,' I said.

She looked down, took off her glasses, and looked back up again. Tears welled up in her big blue eyes.

'You're drop dead beautiful.' It just popped out of my mouth. It was the truth. Even with her eyes kind of swollen and red, streaks of mascara down her cheeks, she looked like a French movie star. Like that Simone Signoret before she became a boozer. Womanly but so feminine, with the childlike thing outside and this powerful inner life.

'Jesus,' I gasped. She could change everything for me, she could change my miserable life.

'Thank you.' She smiled modestly.

'Look,' I had to get to the bottom of it. 'This is about a guy, isn't it? Tell me the truth. I know about these things. I can smell 'em.'

She didn't reply.

'I know you're from the Sixties and you believed in love, am I right? "Love is all you need", Beatles, the whole number. How old are you, thirty-seven, thirty-eight? You're having a little mid-life crisis, maybe? But darlin', darlin', look with me – the twenty-first century is coming. Things are gonna change. It's going to be beautiful. I know this. They cannot get any worse.'

She laughed. She looked like Myrna Loy now. I wanted to hug her.

'This guy, whoever he is,' I began. 'This guy is one major scum – '

I didn't finish 'cause something weird was going on in her face. She was looking past me suddenly like she'd seen a ghost. I turned around and looked where she was looking and there was Rocco whipping up the street like packs of dogs were at his heels. He looked fucking splendiferous as always. Handmade suit and the Italian shoes, the greying temples on a head of hair as full as when he was fifteen years old and I first saw him playing craps with my brothers. The crisp white shirt with the cufflinked cuffs sparkled in the sunlight, and his eyes were flashing that flash that the girls in the neighbourhood called 'the drop-your-pants gleam'. He walked right up to the table, stopped short and stared down at her. My luck. My son-of-a-bitch luck again. She was looking at him like he was God.

'Introduce me,' Rocco snapped without looking at me.

'Rocco, I don't know her. She's a customer. Come back in the restaurant with me.' I tried to take his arm, but he shook me off. He was in a mean fucking mood. The tone of his voice had an edge that could cut throats.

'Get the money,' he said menacingly. 'Get it now.'

'Rocco, I told you,' I began, and now he did look at me and I had to back away from the force of it.

He stuck out his hand toward the catwoman and said harshly, 'Rocco Fanelli.'

Never taking her eyes off his face,' she clasped his hand in hers and said, 'Stella Ames.'

The air around them was crackling like river ice on a warming day. They were fixated on each other, their hands hanging there, hugging each other in the spring air.

'Get the money, Sal. Go.'

It was a final command.

'Rocco, please,' I couldn't go on. I couldn't believe what was happening. I didn't have a fucking dime. I didn't have a fucking prayer. He was practically family. What was he doing? I thought of running in the restaurant and calling my brother, Richie, but if he called my father and he found out I was gambling again and losing – and as for her, she was fucking stuck in the man's gaze like it was flypaper.

'You're right, Sal,' she said suddenly. She was looking at him but she was talking to me. 'Things can't get any worse, but they're not going to get much better. Not for me. They're just going to be the same, only different.'

'No. Listen,' I began, but what? I was going to have a conversation now? I was going to convince her what a great guy I was while Rocco was slicing off my eyelids which, I know, is his fucking speciality?

I was staring at their hands now wondering what the fuck to do. Rocco made a move. He put his left hand on their clasped hands and released his right. He stuck it in his pocket and pulled out his knife. He popped it open. She lowered her eyes and looked at it and then looked back at him.

'He owes you money?' she asked.

My balls were around my ankles and I was stepping on my dick. I was going to the cash drawer. Francis would understand. I'd beg for his fucking Christian mercy. As I turned to go, I put my hand to my face. I was crying now. I was standing in the fucking street, crying.

'Yes,' Rocco said.

'How much?' she said.

Tears were dripping off my chin. Linda, who was not going to live much longer, was standing in the door of the restaurant shaking her head like the ghost of my mother.

'Three thousand bucks,' Rocco said.

'Have me instead,' she said.

I turned around and looked at her. She was smiling at him, that sun-coming-out type of smile tinged with some kind of wickedness you'd never guess she had in her. I looked at him. He was grinning now. Holding that evil fucking death weapon and grinning like he used to when he was fifteen and full of fun.

'What?' he asked. He was laughing, really laughing, squeezing her hand tight and laughing.

'Three thousand dollars for an afternoon with me,' she said again.

Now she was laughing with him. They were hysterical together in their own little world. I glanced over at Linda. Her mouth was open. She couldn't believe it. She saw me looking at her and rolled her eyes in her head.

'Done,' Rocco said, and with the one hand flipped the knife closed and put it in his pocket. With his other hand, still holdings hers, he pulled her up out of her seat.

She released herself, put on her Jackie O. sunglasses and looked over at me.

'May I have the check, please?' she asked, so fucking demure I thought I was at a fucking tea party.

'Allow me,' Rocco said. A fucking gent. And he threw down a ten-dollar bill.

'Keep the change,' he said, and without looking at me, they went off together down the street.

I dropped into a chair and Linda came over and Francis appeared. He'd been hanging back, the little fuck, in case something ugly transpired, like the man killing me.

'She went off with him? What's the world coming to? When the upper classes mix with the lower classes like this – the woman knew Latin. She went to private school, an Ivy League college. What is the world coming to?'

He was genuinely upset. I would have killed him right then but I couldn't move, I was so drained.

'Gamblers Anonymous,' Linda said. She wasn't a woman. She was a fucking parrot.

That black mist was setting over me and I didn't want anyone near me or around me. I got up and moved toward the door of the restaurant. I had to get to the john. I had to be by myself.

'What, Sal? What?' Francis was blocking my way.

'It isn't always going to be this way, Francis,' I said. 'In the future, things are going to be very different.'

৵ BIOGRAPHIES

BRIGID BROPHY was born in London in 1929 and is the daughter of the novelist John Brophy. She was educated at St Paul's Girls' School and St Hugh's College, Oxford.

She is the author of several novels, including *Flesh* and *The King of a Rainy Country*, two collections of short stories and several works of non-fiction; among the latter is her famous study *Mozart the Dramatist*. A vice-president of the National Anti-Vivisection Society, she has consistently championed animal rights. In 1984 she developed multiple sclerosis, a progressive disease of the central nervous system.

'The Woodcutter's Upright Son' first appeared in *The Adventures of God in His Search for the Black Girl* (1973).

ELLA D'ARCY (1851–1939) was born in London of Irish parents and educated in Germany and France. She was assistant literary editor of *The Yellow Book*, and her stories also appeared in other literary magazines in the 1890s. They were collected in two volumes, *Monochromes* (1895) and *Modern Instances* (1898), and she also published a novel, *The Bishop's Dilemma* (1898). After the turn of the century she wrote no more fiction, although she translated André Maurois's fictional biography of Shelley, *Ariel*, into English. Most of her later life was spent in Paris. According to her friend

Netta Syrett, Ella D'Arcy was 'clever and amusing', but also 'the laziest woman I ever met'.

GEORGE EGERTON was the pseudonym of Mary Chavelita Dunne (1859–1945). She was born in Melbourne, Australia, and travelled the world before working in London and New York as a nurse. In 1887 she eloped to Norway with her father's friend, Henry Higginson; he died two years later, and in 1890 she returned to London where she translated the novel *Hunger* by Knut Hamsun. A year later she married George Egerton Clairmonte and moved to Ireland. In 1893 her first volume of short stories, *Keynotes*, was published and caused an immediate sensation, and a year later a second volume, *Discords*, appeared. The couple had a son in 1895, but the marriage ended and in 1901 she married the drama critic Reginald Golding Bright.

At the height of her fame Egerton's romantic feminism aroused considerable hostility; she was mocked in *Punch* as Borgia Smudgiton, and accused of being an 'erotomaniac'. Her fame was short-lived, and she published nothing after *Flies in Amber* (1905). 'A Nocturne' was first published in *Symphonies* (1897).

ALICE THOMAS ELLIS is the pseudonym of Anna Haycraft, who was born in Liverpool in 1932. She lives in London and is the author of numerous novels including *The 27th Kingdom*, which was short-listed for the Booker Prize. *The Inn at the Edge of the World* won the 1991 Writer's Guild Award for fiction; her most recent novel is *Pillars of Gold*.

CLAIRE HARMAN was born in Surrey in 1957 and now lives in South Manchester with her three children. She read English at university and worked as coordinating editor on *PN Review* in the early 1980s. Her first book, a biography of the writer Sylvia Townsend Warner, was awarded the John Llewellyn Rhys prize in 1990, and she is also the editor of the poems and diaries of Sylvia Townsend Warner.

Mrs Murray Hickson was the pseudonym of the novelist and poet Mabel Kitcat (d. 1922). She was the daughter of a prominent judge, and a great-niece on her mother's side of Harriet Martineau. She was born and died in Esher, Surrey, and married Sidney A. P. Kitcat, a member of the London Stock Exchange. She shared her husband's interest in cricket and wrote many articles and stories about it. She was also co-author, with Keighley Snowden, of *The Whip Hand*, a play about the 'smart set'. On her death *The Times* recorded that 'she had not only a brilliant mind, fertile and lucid, but, more exceptionally, a character of rare sweetness and strength, that made her the centre of a great circle of friends'.

'Martha' first appeared in Vol. VII of *The Yellow Book*, in October 1895.

Frances E. Huntley was the pseudonym used for her early work by the novelist, biographer and translator Ethel Colburn Mayne (d. 1941). She was educated privately in Ireland and began contributing stories to magazines in London in the mid-1890s. Her best-known works are her two-volume biography of Byron and her life of his wife, Annabella, which was published in 1929.

'A Pen-and-Ink Effect' appeared in Vol. VI of *The Yellow Book*, in July 1895.

Elizabeth Jolley was born in England in 1923. She trained as an SRN and worked as a nurse during the second world war, emigrating to Western Australia with her husband and children in 1959.

She is the author of three collections of short stories and several novels, including *Miss Peabody's Inheritance*, *Milk and Honey* and *Palomino*.

Ada Leverson (1862–1933) was born in London and educated privately at the home of her father, a property investor. She endured an unhappy marriage to Ernest Leverson, a gambler and speculator, for almost twenty years until he went to Canada alone in 1900. A notable hostess, Leverson became friends with Oscar Wilde after parodying *The Picture of Dorian Gray* in 'An Afternoon Party'. She is best known by his affectionate nickname for her, 'the Sphinx'. She remained loyal to him after his trial, and visited him as soon as he left prison.

Her early works were short stories, parodies and sketches which appeared in various magazines; she published six novels between 1907 and 1916. In 1926 'The Last First Night', her account of the first night of *The Importance of Being Earnest*, was published in *The Criterion* by T. S. Eliot.

SHENA MACKAY was born in Edinburgh in 1944 and now lives in London. She has written plays, novels and short stories, including *Redhill Rococo*, *A Bowl of Cherries* and *Dreams of Dead Women's Handbags*. Her most recent novel is *Dunedin* and she is currently at work on a collection of short stories.

MOY MCCRORY has published three volumes of short stories, *The Water's Edge*, *Bleeding Sinners* and *Those Sailing Ships of his Boyhood Dreams*, which appeared in 1991. She is the author of one novel, *The Fading Shrine*, and has written for television and radio.

She has been a Writer in Residence for the Salisbury Festival and is the tutor for London University's creative writing course. She is a reader for the regional arts scheme, and a member of the Southern Arts Literature panel. She is now working on a second novel.

CANDIA MCWILLIAM was born in Edinburgh in 1955. She has written two novels, *A Case of Knives* (1988) and *A Little Stranger* (1989). She lives in Oxford.

CHARLOTTE MEW (1869–1928) was born in Bloomsbury, the daughter of an architect. She was educated at a school in Gower Street and later attended lectures at University College, London. Two of her siblings became insane and spent their adult lives in lunatic asylums, a development which led Charlotte and her sister Anne to give up any thoughts of marriage and children. She published a number of stories after her first, 'Passed', appeared in Vol. II of *The Yellow Book* in July 1894. Her first collection of poetry, *The Farmer's Bride*, was published in 1916, and praised by Thomas Hardy, Virginia Woolf and the novelist May Sinclair. Nevertheless it sold badly, and Mew published little more in her lifetime (the *Collected Poems* appeared in 1953).

In 1927 Anne Mew died of cancer and Charlotte was devastated. In 1928 she entered a nursing home where, on 24 March, she killed herself by drinking Lysol.

EMILY PRAGER is the author of *A Visit from the Footbinder*, *Clea and Zeus Divorce* and *Eve's Tattoo*. She writes a regular column for *Penthouse* and lives in New York.

OLIVE SCHREINER (1855–1920) was born in a remote part of South Africa, the daughter of a German Methodist minister and his English wife. In 1880 she came to London and in 1883 her first novel, *The Story of an African Farm*, was published to a mixed reception. In London she met and became friends with a number of feminists, including Eleanor Marx; she also fell unrequitedly in love with Karl Pearson. She returned to South Africa in 1889, marrying an ostrich farmer, Samuel Cronwright, five years later. In 1895 she gave birth to her only child, a daughter who died shortly afterwards.

Her massive study, *Women and Labor*, appeared in 1911. Olive Schreiner died in 1920 and is buried in South Africa.

'Three Dreams in a Desert' first appeared in *Dreams*, published in Britain in 1891.

EVELYN SHARP (1869–1955) was born in London, the youngest of nine children. One of her brothers was Cecil Sharp, who later became famous for his efforts to revive English folk dance and song. She was educated privately and left school at sixteen, leading a 'purposeless existence' until 1894, when one of her stories was accepted by *The Yellow Book* and a novel, *At the Relton Arms*, by the publisher John Lane.

Her interests were diverse; an ardent suffragette, she turned to relief work in Germany and Russia once women got the vote. The organisations she actively supported in later life included the Labour Party, the National Council for Civil Liberties, the Council for the Abolition of the Death Penalty and the English Folk Dance and Song Society. In 1933 she published a partial autobiography, *An Unfinished Adventure: Selected Reminiscences*, and she wrote the libretto for Ralph Vaughan Williams's opera,

The Poisoned Kiss, which was produced in 1936. She married an old friend and fellow *Yellow Book* contributor, Henry Nevinson, in 1933, and they lived happily together until his death in 1941.

HELEN SIMPSON was born in Bristol. She was a staff writer on *Vogue* for five years and her collection of short stories, *Four Bare Legs in a Bed*, won the *Sunday Times* Young Writer of the Year Award. She lives in South London.

NETTA SYRETT was the pseudonym of Christina Middleton (1865–1943). She wrote thirty novels and several plays for children. Her obituary in *The Times* recorded that 'her work always bore the stamp of a woman of education and intelligence'. Her autobiography, *The Sheltering Tree*, appeared in 1939.

'Thy Heart's Desire' was published in Vol. II of *The Yellow Book*, in July 1894.

LYNNE TRUSS was born in 1955. She has been a journalist since graduating from University College, London in 1977. For three years she edited the books section of *The Listener*. Now a full-time writer, she stays indoors a good deal and writes a column about 'Single Life' for *The Times*, as well as a weekly television review.

EDITH WHARTON (1862–1937) was born in New York City and travelled widely as a child in Italy, Spain and France. In 1885 she married a Boston socialite, Teddy Wharton, but the marriage was unhappy. Her most famous novel, *The House of Mirth*, was published to critical acclaim in 1905, and she is the author of twenty novels, ten collections of short stories and several works of non-fiction. In 1907 Teddy Wharton's mental troubles were diagnosed as 'neurasthenia' and a year later he embezzled fifty thousand dollars from Edith's trust fund to set up his mistress in a flat in Boston. He confessed to the theft the following year, and they divorced in 1913. A close friend of Henry James, Edith Wharton is considered by some the superior writer. She won the Pulitzer Prize in 1921 and 1935, and was the first woman to receive an honorary LittD. from Yale. She died in France, where she spent much of her later life.

'Souls Belated' first appeared in *The Greater Inclination* in 1899.